# ANGEL'S SIN
## Debra Falcon

**PINNACLE BOOKS**
**WINDSOR PUBLISHING CORP.**

PINNACLE BOOKS are published by

Windsor Publishing Corp.
850 Third Avenue
New York, NY 10022

First Printing: November, 1994

Printed in the United States of America

*This book is dedicated to my husband Ed and our children Kurt, Jill and Christie, with much love.*

A very special thank-you to my agent, Robin Kaigh and to Bob Feltoon for their help and assistance. Your efforts are greatly appreciated.

# One

Streaks of lightning clawed at the clouds that churned above Natchez bluff. Thunder boomed in answer. A gust of wind swept through the trees and died into eerie silence. Below the towering bluff, the Mississippi River lay beneath a hovering gray fog, reminiscent of the River Styx. On the western shore, cypress trees, moss and vines formed a tangled gnarl—like the bony fingers of the damned rising from stagnant swamps. Barely visible in the incongruous shadows, a steamboat that had long been mired in sawyers and sandbars silently cried for mercy—and received none.

It was the kind of night when one might expect the devil himself to make an appearance—if he hadn't already.

Nick Sinclair reined his steed to a halt at the peak of the bluff and surveyed his surroundings. He glanced down Silver Street, the main thoroughfare that led to Natchez Under-the-Hill. The community—said to be the toughest district on the Mississippi—was tucked beneath the cliff. Every vice known to man could be found in the muddy slums beside the river. As he motioned his mount forward, Sin saw the lanterns glowing in the fog as river vessels jockeyed for position along the wharf, and he heard the muffled voices that closed in as he descended into the hodgepodge of humanity and hotbed of crime.

When mingling with the denizens Under-the-Hill, folks were advised to forget what they saw and heard. This was a place where men kept to their own concerns—if they knew what was good for them.

Under-the-Hill had come to be known as Hell's Fringe, but of course, most folks only thought they knew what hell was like. Sin had been there—plenty of times. Hell was the place where you checked your heart and soul at the door. It was where you faced your darkest secrets and tested the limits of your strengths. It was the place where the only reality you understood was survival and you were just too damned scared of dying to give way to paralyzing fear. And when you endured a few hundred torments you scratched and clawed your way out. *That,* Sin reminded himself, was what hell was like and that was why it was hard to rattle a man who had stared death in the face so often that he had forgotten how to flinch.

Drunken keelboatmen lurched past, hurling foul curses and stumbling away from the darkly clad rider who appeared from the soupy fog. Amid the sounds of tinny pianos and loud guffaws, Sin heard a sailor raging that he had been rolled and robbed by the shrieking woman who dashed away from him. On the upper gallery of one of the shanties that was built into a hill of mud, an agonized screech caught Sin's attention. He glanced up to see two men wrestling for possession of a knife.

One man lost.

Sin hadn't ridden far when a dagger's blade glistened in the lamplight and a shadow leaped at him. He jerked his mount sideways, ramming his steed into his would-be assailant. The burly cutthroat who entertained thoughts of raiding Sin's pockets and stealing his muscular stallion didn't entertain those thoughts overly long. The thief received a taste of Sinclair's boot for his efforts.

Before the man could gather his wits the carved end of a pearl-handled cane settled around his neck. With one hard fierce yank on the cane the would-be thief was gasping for breath. The toe of Sin's polished black boot connected with the man's fist, sending the dagger cartwheeling into the mud. With the speed of a striking snake, Sin swung the cane in an arc, landing a punishing blow to the man's midsection and cheek. Wailing in pain, the assailant staggered back against the wall of the brothel where several scantily-dressed women watched the scuffle through the window.

When the cane struck, like a sword, the mugger careened sideways, tripped and sprawled in the mud. He panted for breath as the rider pulled his snorting steed to a halt, scant inches from the man's skull. The thief stared up into eyes as black as coal pits that were embedded in a hard, expressionless face framed with midnight hair. There was something terrifying about the way the rider held himself, the skillful ease with which he had thwarted the attempted robbery.

A breath of wind stirred the fog and a flash of lightning illuminated the looming figure. The mugger's eyes widened in alarm when he saw the blood-red sash and whipping cape above him, noted the white scar on that square jaw and the glow in those black eyes that bore down in silent threat.

The thief shivered, as an icy chill settled in his bones. He swore he had taken a fall that had landed him in hell to face the devil. "Dear God . . ." he choked out.

The deadly hooves stamped closer and the cloaked rider leaned down to press the tip of his cane into the downed man's heaving chest, robbing him of precious breath. "No, the name is Sin. Remember it . . ."

With a nudge of his bootheels, Sin walked his stallion over the thief and continued on his way along the shelf of mud and endless row of gambling halls, barrooms and bordellos. Sin halted his horse beside a narrow flight of steps and swung to the ground. Bracing his stiff leg against the pearl-handled cane, Sin ascended the flagstone steps and opened the wrought-iron gate that led into Mealy's Tavern.

The tavern reflected French, Spanish and English tradition in a city that had been the mistress of several nations before America had taken possession of her. Like Natchez herself, the tavern had a dual personality. The lower floor of stone and timber catered to the rougher elements of society. Above, amidst the decorations of airy French windows, ornamental molding, slender white colonettes and marble mantels, the gentry could saunter along the wide piazza and look down their aristocratic noses at the social outcasts who swarmed like pesky mosquitoes.

Sinclair tapped his cane against the door of the end room and then braced himself on the crutch to take the pressure off his mending leg. He had spent too many hours on his feet these past two weeks, overseeing and assisting in the renovations of his new home on Raven's Hill. Tired though he was, he was well-pleased with the progress he and his men had made. And if Hiram Brodie had done his job well, Sin could fall asleep tonight knowing he would soon satisfy his personal vendetta against his sworn enemies.

The door creaked open to reveal the tall, lean frame of Hiram Brodie. Nodding a silent greeting, Hiram stepped aside and watched Sin limp toward the vacant chair at the table.

From the tavern room below, Sin heard the squawk and chatter of parrots. It was a shame he hadn't brought Fiddler along to socialize with birds of his own feather. But the oversized parrot that now resided on Raven's Hill was still trying to adjust to having solid ground beneath him instead of swaying planked decks. Sin and his entourage of beached mariners seemed to be having the same difficulty in adapting to life on land.

Hiram Brodie appeared to be adjusting nicely though, Sin noted. The man who was two years Sin's junior had been sent on an assignment that required a good deal of legwork. Knowing Hiram's penchant for perfection, Sin expected grand results.

"Would you like a drink, Captain?" Hiram Brodie inquired as he pushed his wire-rimmed spectacles back up the bridge of his nose.

Sin held up an empty glass. The lip of the bottle clanked against the rim of the goblet. Bubbling liquid splashed into the glass and Sin took a welcome sip. It had been another long, tedious day.

Three swallows of wine later, Sin set the goblet aside

and motioned for his associate and financial adviser to sit at the table.

"You certainly have been the subject of great speculation and rumor," Hiram remarked, dropping into his chair. He glanced at the flowing cape, bright red sash and trim-fitting breeches that had become Sin's trademark during his years at sea. "Folks are whispering that the mysterious newcomer they have seen pacing Raven's Hill of late is in league with the devil, if he's not the very devil himself. It seems the gentry Above-the-Hill are trying to decide what nefarious means you employed to purchase old man Fifkin's dilapidated plantation."

Sin shrugged nonchalantly and let the subject drop. "Your note indicated you had much to report." He stretched his long legs out in front of him and stared at Hiram. "You have been busy yourself, I take it."

"Aye, Captain—"

"Sin," he corrected. "From now on, it is only Sin."

Hiram nodded his brown head, mentally adjusting to a less formal title than the one he had used the past ten years. Sinclair had rescued Hiram from a mob of thieves on Charleston wharf and welcomed him aboard the *Siren*. Hiram had nothing but admiration and respect for this dark and sometimes mysterious skipper who had provided his crew with thrilling adventures in every exotic port along the Seven Seas.

Hiram and the other men who sailed with Sin had become exceptionally skilled and experienced over the years. Sin always drove close to the edge of danger, but he had never lost a man or a spar on his voyages. He was just cautious enough to take advantage of danger by shortening a sail in a strong wind, so as to make good time without blowing out the topmast. He could make a voyage to China in seventy-eight days and return home with two or three hundred percent profit, as if they had not battled storms, pirates or treacherous coral reefs along the way.

Sin was a tough, sturdy skipper who had what mariners called "Dead Reckoning"—the rare, unerring combination of calculated logic, precise navigational charting and nautical instinct. His skills bordered on phenomenal. Time and again, the crew relied on Sin to save them from dire straits, and they had all enjoyed a share of the fortune he had amassed. But something very strange and unexplained had overcome the captain of the *Siren* two years earlier, something that now drove him like the savage typhoons that pounded the China Seas.

Nick Sinclair had drawn even deeper into himself and no one seemed to know why. Not one member of the crew understood Sin's fanatic determination to triple the fortune at his disposal. No one questioned his driving need, they merely observed it.

Since that day the *Siren* had slipped her moorings at New Orleans and cruised around Cape Horn to the South Pacific and on to Calcutta and the bustling hongs in Canton, Sin had focused on a single-minded purpose that he alone understood. It was as if some demon were whipping at his sails like a strong gale, urging him to drive harder bargains when he sold his expensive cargo. It was as if Sin were preparing himself for a crusade that required tremendous financial backing . . .

"Well, Hiram, don't keep me in suspense," Sin said in a carefully controlled voice. "I've waited a long time for this news."

Hiram didn't have the faintest notion why he had been placed on this assignment. He had very nearly had his sea legs run off him over the past two weeks. His expertise leaned more toward ledgers and numerical columns in accounting books. Years earlier, when Sin had discovered Hiram's talent and interest in tallies, he had dropped the ledgers in Hiram's lap. That was the day Hiram realized how much wealth Sin had acquired during his years in the Far East trade.

At age thirty, Nick Sinclair could not only have purchased the run-down plantation home on Raven's Hill, he could have bought the whole damned town that sat on the looming bluff that overlooked the sinful squalor of Under-the-Hill . . .

"Brodie?"

Hiram jerked up his head to meet those alert obsidian eyes that were surrounded by half-shuttered black lashes.

"My leg is paining me somewhat, and the spars lashed to my temper are strained. You, on the other hand, look as if you're adrift in the doldrums. Could we get on with this?"

"Sorry, Captain—"

"Sin," he cut in, his bland voice concealing the hint of impatience that nagged at him. "What information do you have for me?"

Hiram reached inside his jacket to retrieve several pages of notes and spread them out beside the lantern. He readjusted his droopy glasses and sighed, befuddled. "I still don't understand why you had me gadding all over town to track down these men. What possible interest could you have in the life histories of—?"

"Just tell me what you have learned."

Hiram inwardly flinched when Sin's baritone voice dropped to a near whisper. Hiram and the other men knew that the softer Sin's voice the more anger simmered beneath that incredibly calm surface. And when Sin's voice dropped to an icy whisper that rivaled temperatures in the Arctic Sea, most men had the sense to scurry away, giving Sin all the space he needed—and some to spare. A man could never tell by the well-schooled expression on Sin's craggy features what he was thinking or feeling. However, that soft, frigid voice was a dead giveaway. Hiram reminded himself that he had already been warned that Sin was not in the best of moods.

That was another thing a man could depend on, Hiram mused. Sin gave one warning—and one warning only. Not a mariner in any port in the world dared to cross him twice unless he suffered suicidal tendencies. Hiram could relate accounts of pirates and scalawags who refused to heed warnings. Although there was an aura of cool reserve surrounding Sin, there was also a shadow within his shadow—some strange presence that separated him from the average man.

Sin was definitely not a man to cross—unless you wanted your legs taken out from under you or your teeth rammed down your throat. Sin was a powerhouse of finely-tuned muscle and lightning-quick reflexes, even if he was presently nursing an injured leg. The shark that tried to take a bite out of Sin during a dive off the coast of a remote tropical island had been skinned alive and its teeth had become a trophy in the form of a necklace. As for the men who challenged Sin, they were either floating in Fiddler's Green or buried several feet underground.

Hiram caught himself dawdling and cleared his throat. "I did some thorough checking on Jerome Kimball, sir . . . Sin."

Black diamond eyes focused in an unnerving stare. Sin said not one word, he simply waited for Hiram to proceed.

"From what I could glean, Jerome arrived in Natchez about eighteen years ago to establish his hotel at the corner of Main and Commerce Street. No one seems to know where Jerome came from or what he did before opening the hotel and restaurant."

Sinclair knew exactly what Jerome Kimball had been doing with himself before he fled inland to Natchez. Flashbacks of a night that could haunt the sanest of men flooded through him. With vivid clarity, he recalled the sights, sounds and scents of the nightmarish scene. Deeply buried emotion struggled to surface, but Sin tapped it down, determined to digest every word of Hiram's report. This was not the time to feel, it was the time to listen, to plan, to calculate every move.

"Jerome also manages a plush bordello on the top floor of his hotel," Hiram went on to say as he shoved his glasses back in place. "He caters to the socially elite of Natchez and other dignitaries who visit the city. Jerome is one of the wealthiest pillars of society. The other hotel owners have had difficulty competing with him. He also owns an estate on the outskirts of town near King's Tavern. From there, Jerome lords over his property like the town baron." Hiram glanced at Sin over the rim of his spectacles. "He is also said to consort with rougher elements Under-the-Hill when he feels threatened by upstart competitors."

"In other words, Lord Kimball has henchmen to prevent him from dirtying his own hands with questionable deeds," Sin paraphrased before sipping his wine. "He relies on land pirates, highwaymen and thieves who are loyal to the coin."

Hiram nodded bleakly.

"It seems our friend Kimball has a dual personality, just like Natchez. And what of Jerome's family? Will they inherit the wealth he has acquired?"

"No, sir. Jerome isn't married, but he apparently keeps himself busy with his female employees on the top floor." Hiram grinned wryly. "He is said to be intimately acquainted with each paramour who entertains his affluent guests."

Even though Sin hadn't seen Jerome Kimball in almost two decades, the news came as no surprise. As Sin recalled, Jerome had been lusty and self-indulgent in his prime. Jerome hadn't changed; he'd only grown older and wealthier—on blood-money . . .

The bitter thought condensed in Sin's mind and he silently cursed all memories associated with Jerome Kimball. Sin could not allow resentment to influence his dealings with that bastard. Jerome would pay the devil his due, even if it had taken Sin an eternity to locate the man. And that, Sin thought, had been by a stroke of luck, or fate. But very soon, Jerome and his three conspirators were going to wish they had never heard of Sin.

Easing back in his chair, Sin focused ebony eyes on his long-time friend and financial consultant. "Considering what you have learned about the esteemed Jerome Kimball, what would you say is the greatest love of his life?"

The casually posed question caught Hiram off guard. "His greatest love?" he repeated stupidly.

Sin nodded his raven head. "To a pirate it is his treasure. To a pearler it is that one flawless marble-size gem worth its own fortune. What is Kimball's obsession?"

Hiram studied his notes for a thoughtful moment. "The hotel," he decided. "It is the foundation of his vast fortune. Kimball Hotel has become a landmark, the epitome of the finest physical luxury money can buy."

"You are very astute, Hiram. That's why I chose you for this assignment and why you will be rewarded for your trouble." Although Sin didn't change expression, there was a hint of a smile in his voice.

Hiram, however, was more transparent than Sin. His face lit up in a pleased grin. "Thank you, Capt- . . . Sin."

"No need to thank me. I had naught to do with your gift of intelligence. Now what about Owen Porter? How has he fared these last eighteen years?"

Hiram blinked, wondering how Sin knew the length of time Owen Porter had been in Natchez. "As you say, Owen Porter arrived about the same time Jerome Kimball did." He glanced up. "A coincidence?"

"Hardly." There was no inflection of voice, not even the blink of an eye or curl of lip that suggested Sin was affected by the mention of the name.

But he was. Hatred vibrated through every fiber of his being.

"Owen Porter bought a plantation northeast of Natchez and acquired enough slaves to cultivate cotton. He doubled his wealth very quickly. According to reports, Owen has also developed a fascination with breeding and racing horses. He and his elite circle of aristocrats have established the race track of Pharsalia along St. Catherine's Creek. Thousands of dollars have been won and lost at bettors' tables. Occasionally tempers have flared and duels have been fought because of it. Owen has been involved once or twice himself, but I'm told he is a fair shot. His penchant for horses has prompted him to pay fine salaries to stable boys and jockeys who exercise the prize steeds that have become the envy of Natchez."

"Family?" Sin inquired.

"No longer." Hiram glanced up from his detailed notes. "Owen married a frail young heiress a year after his arrival in town. The lass survived only ten months of wedlock before she and her newborn son were stricken with cholera."

"And Owen's priceless treasure?" Sin questioned.

This time Hiram didn't hesitate. "His horses. Owen has his valuable steeds delivered to Natchez in padded stalls of sailing vessels. When traveling artists come to town Owen contracts them to immortalize his steeds on canvas."

Hiram chuckled in amusement. "It is said that the water troughs at Porter stables are made of marble. Each superb specimen of racer, brood mare and colt has a mahogany-paneled stall, a silver hitching post and chains holding silver name plates above the stall. Owen has decorated his home with pink and black marble mantels to hold his racing trophies.

"His brood stock's ancestry can be traced to the sires of thoroughbreds—the Darley Arabian, Godolphin Arabian and French-Anglo Arab." Hiram grinned conspiratorially at Sin. "And of course, you already know Owen is waiting for the descendant of the Byerley Turk to arrive from the Orient."

Sin nodded mutely. It was the Byerley Turk that had led Sin to Owen Porter and the other men after years of futile searching. When Sin dropped anchor in New Orleans two years earlier to deliver his cargo from the Far East, he had been approached by an agent who requested that he ship the grand Turkish stud to America.

The legendary breed of dark bay horses was descended from the seven original ancestors that had been selected by King Solomon from his fifty thousand royal chariot and saddle horses. The steeds had been bred for their intelligence, power and impressive speed, and the Byerley Turk was hailed to be the spitting image of its legendary ancestor.

That famed stallion—which Owen Porter had spared no expense to obtain—was presently standing outside Mealy's Tavern, champing at the bit. Sin had brought the horse from the East and purchased it from Owen's agent. Very soon, that well-proportioned mass of horseflesh would be dangled under Owen's nose like a carrot. Sin relished seeing the look on Owen's face when he realized the Turk had been bought right out from under him.

"What of Frederick Limestall?" Sin questioned as he poured himself another drink.

"I'm afraid Frederick Limestall Sr. was killed in a duel five years ago, due to an obsessive affection for a married woman," Hiram reported.

Sin's expression didn't register disappointment, but he silently cursed. He had been deprived of one facet of his revenge. The devil had obviously gotten his hands on Frederick before Sin could.

"Frederick left behind one son," Hiram went on, anticipating the next question. "Fritz, as he is called, inherited his father's dry goods shop, which outfits frontiersmen with weapons, ammunition, bedding and food supplies. Frederick's wife and son accompanied him to Natchez within a few weeks after Kimball and Porter arrived. Fritz's mother passed on shortly after Frederick was killed in the duel. Some say she died of a broken heart. Others insist it was shame and humiliation that sent her to her grave."

Sin couldn't fathom why anyone would grieve Limestall's passing.

"Fritz is a scatterbrained man of twenty-three," Hiram continued, adjusting his sagging spectacles. "He has mismanaged his father's fortune. At his present rate he is going to be bankrupt in three years."

"He obviously lacks a competent financial advisor," Sin inserted blandly. "If he had hired a man of your talents, he would have doubled his profits rather than depleted them."

"Thank you—" Hiram closed his mouth when Sin's thick brow lifted in silent reminder that no appreciation was needed or expected. Sin was stating what he considered to be a foregone conclusion.

"Do you wish to know Fritz's greatest love as well, Sin?"

Before Sin could respond, a female shriek erupted from the room next door. A thunking sound seeped through the paper-thin wall, followed by a masculine growl and the pelting of footsteps. The door banged against the outer wall. Sin went to investigate. From the sound of things the squealing female was in need of as-

sistance and she wasn't likely to get it from the pack of
wolves that prowled the darkness Under-the-Hill, waiting
their turn to attack.

# Two

"Don't tease me with that delicious body of yours and then think you can flit off, wench," Reginald Foster snapped as he grabbed his female companion by the hair of her head. "I paid good money for a tumble in bed."

A raft of French curses spewed from the harlot's mouth when Reginald pawed at her, refusing to let her escape him. She bit into the fist that gripped the shoulder of her gown.

Muttering obscenities, Reginald recoiled, reflexively raising his arm to backhand the vicious chit. Before he could land a retaliatory blow, a pearl-handled cane came out of nowhere, fastened around his neck and wrenched him backward.

Sin was discovering that his cane had several practical purposes. Before the besotted aristocrat could strike the girl's cheek, Sin had yanked him off balance. The dandy fell on his backside, skidding across the fog-slick planks of the piazza.

Sin wondered how the cocky rakehell could even see who had intervened, what with all those red streaks in his blue eyes. Sin surveyed Reginald's elegant attire, noting the gaping buttons on the placket of his skin-tight breeches and his frustrated state of arousal. A pretty boy,

Sin thought with a silent smirk, a blond-haired, blue-eyed Adonis with the manners of a guttersnipe. A pity the man had turned so nasty when deprived of having his way. The dandy obviously hadn't learned the art of gentle persuasion.

"I do believe the lady has had more than enough of you," Sin observed glibly. His dark eyes dropped to the gaping placket of Reginald's breeches. "Or is it that there is not enough of you to interest the female?"

The insult was spoken so conversationally that it took a moment for it to register in Reginald's pickled brain. When it did, Reginald braced himself up on his elbows, intent on surging to his feet in lethal challenge.

A booted foot smashed into Reginald's belly before he could stand up. He was pinned to the floor. His breath surged out in a pained grunt and he stared up at the cloaked figure who resembled a swashbuckling pirate. The noticeable white scar that slashed across that bronzed cheek accentuated those piratelike features and riveting midnight eyes that bore down on Reginald. From where Reginald lay, his challenger appeared to be at least ten feet tall if he was an inch.

When pride provoked Reginald to make a second attempt to gain his feet, the cutlass that hung menacingly at Sin's waist miraculously leaped into his hand. Once again, Reginald made it no farther than his elbows. The blade of the cutlass swung like the pendulum of a clock, coming to rest above the private parts of Reginald's anatomy.

"I wouldn't advise getting up just yet, not if you are the least bit concerned about retaining your manhood."

Hiram, who stood behind Sin, recognized that quiet

tone of voice, even if the drunken Reginald Foster didn't. *Deadly* didn't do that particular tone justice. The besotted dandy had received his first and last warning, whether he realized it or not.

Reginald blinked past the blur in his eyes to meet a gaze as cold as a headstone. Something in the way the dark stranger stared at him, the confident way he held himself, advised Reginald not to press the issue while he was at such a disadvantage. Reginald swallowed with a nervous gulp and stared at the cutlass.

"I suggest you close and lock your door, mademoiselle," Sin said, without releasing his downed prey from his piercing stare. "Your friend is on his way back to the rock he crawled out from under."

Another casually delivered insult stung Reginald's aristocratic pride, but he continued to stay down on the floor for fear of being castrated where he lay. Now was not the time to avenge his wounded dignity, not when eyes like pinpoints of black steel were drilling into him, making silent promises Reginald did not wish to see kept.

Offering a quiet murmur of appreciation, the buxom brunette clutched together her gaping gown and scuttled back into her room to secure the door. Sin said nothing, nor did he cast the chit so much as a glance. His gaze was fixed on Reginald. Very slowly and deliberately Sin sheathed the cutlass.

When Sin stepped away, Reginald scraped himself and his bruised pride off the floor. He tilted his chin to look down his patrician nose at the swarthy buccaneer who had humiliated him in front of witnesses. "I will have your name, *sir,*" he demanded.

One black brow lifted, though the expression on Sin's

rugged face never altered. "Why is that? Don't you have one of your own?"

Hiram's throttled laughter dried up as quickly as it erupted when Reginald clenched his fists at his sides and threw back his blond head to meet Sin's impassive gaze. "I intend to call you out for interfering in an affair that was none of your damned business!"

Sin looked around nonchalantly. "I believe I am already *out,*" he noted. "It was the fiasco in the next room that brought me here. And you have only your clumsy techniques with women to thank for it."

"Clumsy tech—" Reginald was so furious he could barely speak! "How dare—" His gaze caught on the man who stood a few inches shorter than the demon swathed in black.

Hiram laid his index finger to his lips and gave his brown head a discreet shake. It seemed to him that young Reginald was either too drunk or too stupid to know he should quit while he still had a head.

It must have been the sobering effect of coming dangerously close to being castrated at the height of his sexual prime that prompted Reginald to slam his mouth shut. Either that or the cold glitter in the pirate's eyes had stolen the words from his tongue. But Reginald realized he was not physically capable of meeting the challenge he had issued. He was staggering drunk at the moment. Hopefully he would meet this scoundrel again, and next time Reginald would have his wits about him.

With a wordless sneer, Reginald executed a wobbly about-face and weaved off, bracing his hand against the wall to ensure his balance. It annoyed him to no end that this night had ended in such disaster, and it was that fiery little heiress's fault that he had sought out the haughty French doxy to appease him.

Reginald had made a daring play for the wealthy beauty he had set his sights on, in hopes of relieving his financial woes. But the much-sought-after heiress was too clever be trapped. She had spirited off into the night, and Reginald had been left to find a release for the hunger that gnawed at him.

Several drinks later, Reginald had propositioned the French doxy and had come on too strong too quickly. Things had gone downhill from there. The next thing he knew, the devil himself had threatened to turn him into a eunuch.

Muttering to himself, Reginald stamped down the steps and disappeared into the fog, vowing he would soothe his stinging pride and seek out that interfering scoundrel at a more convenient time.

With the calm detachment of a man who had engaged in hundreds of battles, Sin watched the drunken aristocrat stagger away. Emotion had never interceded in confrontations, nor did it now. Sin had learned to react with cool, deliberate precision. Anger, he had learned, made a man reckless.

When Reginald spoiled his regal retreat by tripping down the last few steps that led to the tavern below, Sin turned away and walked back into the hotel room. The incident was quickly forgotten. He had more important matters on his mind.

"You were telling me about young Fritz," Sin prompted Hiram. "Does he have a noticeable obsession?"

"Wine," Hiram replied as he followed Sin back to the room to resettle in his chair.

"Much like our most recent acquaintance," Sin commented.

Thunder rumbled again, rattling the window panes. Hiram flinched, as if he had taken a bolt in the back. Sin didn't even bat an eyelash. His thoughts were focused on the last name on the list.

"And how has Charles Sheridan fared over the years?" Sin questioned.

Hiram inhaled a deep breath and rattled off what he had learned about Sheridan. "Charles showed up in Natchez with his family more than six months after the other three men arrived. He purchased a cotton plantation, reinvested part of his profits and expanded his land holdings. At present Charles Sheridan has two plantations, more than three thousand acres of cultivated land to his credit, a stable full of prize steeds that he purchased from Owen Porter and enough pasture to graze all his livestock."

"I presume brood mares and race horses have also become his obsession."

"No," Hiram replied. "Although Charles takes great pride in his plantation and livestock, his daughter is his greatest treasure."

Sin frowned slightly and Hiram hurried to explain. "It is said that Charles's wife was once the driving force in his life, that his admiration and respect for her were well known and even joked about by men less enamored of their wives. Ten years ago Emily Sheridan died while giving birth to an infant son who only survived for a few hours. Charles was beside himself with grief. All the af-

fection he had bestowed on his wife was then directed
to his daughter. He dotes upon her and gives in to her
with little more than token objection."

"Her name?"

"Angelene . . ."

Hiram was unaware that he smiled whimsically as he
uttered the melodic name, but Sin duly noted the expression and he inwardly chuckled.

"You have met her then?"

Hiram snapped out of his trance and fiddled with his
notes. "No, sir, I haven't. I simply find her name captivating."

Hiram adjusted his glasses and continued in a more
businesslike manner. "According to my information, Angelene displayed such keen intelligence as a child that
her private tutor suggested she be sent to Madame Green-
land's Institute in Philadelphia to further her studies. She
has been drilled in literature, mathematics, history and
arts and she is fluent in four languages. Because she is
said to have a fine mind for business, her father put her
in charge of all his financial accounts when she returned
from her last school session. Angelene has been quite
busy revamping the accounting ledgers and commuting
between Sheridan Hall and Oak Gables. She has come
to be known as the Jewel of Natchez by the wife hunters
who congregate in town during social season."

Sin sipped his wine and listened intently.

"Natchez is referred to as a paradise for men seeking
to secure the staggering incomes of eligible planters'
daughters. I also heard that the Sheridans received so
many requests for audiences from would-be suitors since
Angelene returned from her last school term that the path

leading to Sheridan Hall has sunk another two feet into the soft soil due to all the traffic. The road to the plantation is said to be paved with the broken hearts of men who failed to draw Angelene's interest."

"And did this celestial creature finally agree to wed one of the fortune seekers who fell all over themselves to court her?" Sin inquired.

"No, that is the most fascinating part," Hiram continued, missing Sin's faint sarcasm. "The lady appears to be exceptionally particular and balks at being rushed into marriage by any of her fawning beaus."

Sin checked his timepiece when another clap of thunder grumbled overhead. His leg was throbbing in rhythm with his pulse and Sin was not anticipating a swift ride home in the brewing storm. He had heard enough of Hiram's report to formulate his plans for the men who had arrived in Natchez to build their fortunes with their ill-gotten gains.

It made no difference to him if Charles Sheridan's little "Angel" was as ugly as Original Sin or as dense as a coral reef in the South Seas. All that mattered was that Angel was what Charles Sheridan loved best. That tidbit of information, along with the noted obsessions of Porter and Kimball, were the reasons for this fact-finding mission. Now that Sin had all the vital information, he could analyze the situation and proceed accordingly.

"First thing in the morning, I want you to inquire about buying a hotel in town, preferably one that is situated near Kimball Hotel."

Hiram blinked like an awakened owl. "You're going into the hotel business? But why—?"

"Please do as I request," Sin interrupted as he surged

to his feet. "We will spare no expense in refurbishing the building to my specifications. As you well know, there are ample funds for the project."

Hiram sat there with his jaw scraping his chest. "I can understand why you wanted that plantation that overlooked the two clear-water coves, but what do you want with a hotel? The crew and I are all mariners. What do any of us know about managing a hotel?"

The faintest hint of a smile tugged at the corners of Sin's lips as he pivoted, bracing himself on his pearl-handled cane. "We have only to hire dependable employees who are experienced in the hotel business," he said reasonably.

"But where are we going to find competent help when we have only just arrived in town, Capt—Sin?"

Sin tossed Hiram a look of indulgent amusement. "I don't believe you were paying close attention to the information you supplied, my friend. Kimball Hotel obviously employs the most qualified staff in town. They will ensure our success."

Dumbfounded, Hiram gaped at the darkly cloaked figure who did indeed fit the persona of a pirate rather than that of a gentleman. "You want me to steal Kimball's help out from under his nose?"

"No, we shall *buy* their loyalty for higher wages," Sin replied. "Everyone has his price. Money is no object; it is the means to a desired end."

Hiram had no time to ponder the comment, for Sin pivoted toward the door. Hurriedly, Hiram scooped up the papers that held more notes. "I haven't finished telling you about Angelene."

"I know all I need to know about her," Sin said without a backward glance.

"But there's more—"

Hiram hadn't even gotten to the part about what a fiercely independent and wary female Angelene Sheridan had become after being so zealously pursued by flocks of bachelors who sought to gain control of her fabulous fortune. And Hiram had been looking forward to relating some of the wild antics that had been conveyed to him. Indeed, from all accounts, Angelene Sheridan was not the typical genteel heiress who spent her time lounging in drag rooms and thriving only on the gay parties that were so much a part of baronial society.

Her travels and extensive education had made her somewhat of a free spirit, a vibrant unconventional woman who insisted on living by her own rules. From what Hiram had heard, Angelene was immune to all the usual lines of flattery that were cast out like seines by her fortune-seeking admirers. She was not going to be an easy woman to deal with, no matter what Sin had in mind.

Hiram's arm dropped limply to his side when the door creaked shut and thunder crackled overhead. "I wonder what the devil Sin has up his sleeve?" Hiram asked the room at large.

The only answer was the click of bootheels on the gallery and another rumble of thunder.

# Three

Sin swung onto the Byerley Turk and reined toward the chalk-white bluffs that overlooked the shanties of Under-the-Hill. Cutting a swath through the drunken hordes and ignoring the come-hither calls from the harlots who were draped over the rails of the brothels, Sin trotted up Silver Street.

The wind had picked up, blowing the gray fog across the river and revealing the silt-laden delta known as Vidalia. The Louisiana town on the opposite bank of the Mississippi was said to be the place where duels were often fought. Why Mississippi men were inclined to row across the river to Louisiana soil to settle their grievances Sin didn't know. It must have been the insect-ridden atmosphere of vice, and the steamy climate, that made the citizens of Natchez such a reckless and irritable lot, he decided.

The sound of feminine laughter drifted up from the shacks and Sin twisted in the saddle. He had bypassed the opportunity to ease his male needs, but he had been determined to establish himself in Natchez. The plantation renovations had monopolized most of his time and left him exhausted by day's end. Answering the willing calls from the courtesans below the hill was not nearly as important as sitting himself down to gather his thoughts and plot his course of action. Sin had waited eighteen years to attain the position he was now in. Nothing was going to deter him.

Every curse Sin had screamed into the night while he and his brother were left adrift at sea—every vow he had made—would be fulfilled. After years of futile searching, the time of reckoning had finally come. It was essential that he become even more calculating than he had ever been. He had promises to keep and a death to avenge.

A stiff breeze sent Sin's cloak billowing around him like a black sail, and stirred up the chalky soil of the bluff. There were very few places on earth where loess soil could be found, Sin reminded himself as he dusted himself off. Natchez was one of them. China was another. Sin should know. He had visited every major port along the Seven Seas, as well as dozens of nameless islands in the tropics. He had acquired the kind of education that spoiled little Angel Sheridan could only visit in her schoolbooks.

Angelene . . . Sin recalled the way Hiram had murmured the name, as if the chit were an immortal goddess. All Angelene Sheridan represented to Sin was a device that would allow him to torment Charles Sheridan. A prize horse and a refurbished hotel would also provide the means to strike Owen Porter and Jerome Kimball where they could be hurt the most.

Each of the three surviving men would find himself on his knees, begging for mercy before Nick Sinclair revealed his true identity. And then each man would understand why he had been singled out and why he would lose what had become most precious to him in his new life in Natchez.

Perhaps no one else knew where those three bastards hailed from, what they had done in a previous life, but Sin knew. He could never forget the pact he had made that fateful night . . .

Sin's bitter thoughts trailed off when he heard the rapid pelting of hooves and saw a horse and rider illuminated by streaks of lightning that leaped from cloud to cloud. Sin had been so immersed in thought that he couldn't remember trotting all the way through town to reach the open meadow southeast of Raven's Hill.

From the look of things a runaway horse—apparently startled by the thunder and lightning—was galloping hell-for-leather. Sin reined toward his plantation, but he paused when the hooded cloak whipped off the rider's head, revealing a mass of long hair. Sin had been prepared to let a man regain control of his flighty mount, but a woman was another matter entirely. This seemed to be his night to aid damsels in distress.

Sin took time to appraise the situation before charging off in pursuit. He was not a man who leaped before he looked. His best chance to halt the alarmed steed was to chart a perpendicular course that led to a point where the horse was headed, not where it was now.

Ignoring the nagging pain in his leg, Sin nudged his stallion forward. The Turk gathered himself behind and moved forward, eating up the ground at amazing speed. Sin was beginning to understand why Owen Porter was anxious to acquire this particular stallion. Turk had been born to run and the racehorse exploded with the force of a discharging cannon.

Forked lightning speared the sky. The glorious mane of red-gold hair lit up like a flame. Long, curly tendrils undulated in the wind, framing a face that immediately captured Sin's attention. It would be a shame to see such exquisite beauty destroyed by a fall.

Throughout his extensive travels, Sin had met and shared the company of women who were highly praised for their exotic beauty. He could not, however, conjure up a face to match the pearlescent glow radiating from this particular face.

Sin was sorry to say that he had one weakness—pearls. Some of them had nearly cost him a leg in the not too distant past. This hapless female, who had ventured out on such a stormy night, reminded Sin of the lustrous white rosé pearls found in a remote corner of the Indian Ocean.

This living pearl looked as rare and unblemished as the gems Sin had acquired, but she was headed for a traumatic tumble if he didn't reach her in time.

The horse the woman rode was entirely too spirited and too powerful a creature for her to control, even without the threat of the descending storm. She was too petite and she obviously lacked the strength to bring the runaway to a halt. On a collision course with a clump of tangled grapevines and magnolia trees, she would be scraped off the saddle before she knew what hit her.

Sin prodded the Turk and used the tip of his cane to demand all the thoroughbred had to give. Anchoring his legs to the horse's ribs, Sin raced toward the runaway and leaned out to snatch the woman off her mount, momentarily leaving her dangling in midair before he could maneuver her onto his horse.

Angelene Sheridan shrieked when she was unseated and deposited on Sin's lap. When he tried to settle her in place and slow down Turk at the same time, his arm accidentally bumped against her breasts.

"What the devil do you think you're doing?" Angelene railed as she raked the wild tangle of red-blond hair from her face.

"Saving your lovely neck. You're welcome, by the way."

Seeing the woman at close range quickly confirmed that she possessed the kind of face and body that could have launched several thousand ships. Perfection, living perfection, Sin thought admiringly.

Lightning danced through the clouds, reflecting off eyes as green as the Emerald Isle, as sparkling clear as a spring-fed stream. Sin caught his breath, mesmerized. No exotic island native or Oriental beauty could match the exquisite texture of this woman's oval face or the lively intelligence glinting in her eyes. Every time the lightning flashed, it spotlighted her enthralling attributes and left Sin marveling at her.

Sin had the crazed desire to brush his thumb over her flawless cheek, just as he took excessive pleasure in rubbing his fingers over a lustrous pearl, lost to its powerful mystique. He hadn't realized that his forefinger had lifted to limn the delicate line of her jaw until she jerked away from his touch and placed a respectable distance between them.

The feel of her rounded bottom gliding against his thighs lessened the pain in his leg and sensitized the most private part of his anatomy. Sin decided he had definitely overlooked his basic needs too long.

Angelene slapped Sin's hand away as if he were a pesky gnat. She glared at him indignantly. "Put me down this instant!" she huffed. "Eluding one pawing male was enough for one night. Just what is it with you men anyway? Where do you get the crazed notion that women were placed on the planet to cater to your pleasures? I swear, a woman cannot even turn around without bumping into one or another of you."

Outspoken and spirited was a good way to describe this female, Sin decided. There were no demure smiles, no coy batting of those long eyelashes, no breathless whisper of gratitude. There was only an offended outburst of temper in response to what she had erroneously assumed to be another zealous pursuit.

While Sin sat there analyzing the vivacious beauty's reactions, she attempted to launch herself off his lap. The crook of his cane looped around her waist, was holding her in place.

An indispensable tool, Sin mused. With a few alterations, this crutch could prove valuable in any situation. Sin made a mental note to set Pearly Graham to work on modifying the cane for other practical purposes. The crusty old sailor was a whiz at that sort of thing.

"Sit still." Sin requested when the woman continued to wriggle for release.

"I most certainly will not! Let me go!"

After writhing for a full minute to gain her freedom—and to no avail—she blurted out, "Men! Curse the whole lot of you!"

Sin almost smiled when she hissed at him like a disturbed cobra. The incident that had turned his life upside down eighteen years ago had taken most of the smile out of Sin.

"Although you consider all of us males a tiresome lot—"

"Positively boorish and underhanded," Angelene cut in, her head swiveling to glower at him again. "The most recent example of male obtuseness came from a fop who tried to take uninvited privileges, forcing me into a compromising situation that would have worked to his advantage if he had been successful."

"Which he was not, I gather," Sin said blandly.

Angelene answered with another glare.

"You are convinced we men are totally immersed in ourselves, I take it," Sin added indulgently. "We are driven by our selfish wants, needs and desires. Does that about cover it?"

Angelene tilted her head back to scrutinize Sin's craggy features and his tousled crop of raven hair. Her eyes narrowed disapprovingly. "Do I detect mocking amusement beneath that implacable expression you wear so well?"

"Perhaps. I have been told that I have a rather peculiar sense of humor."

"Then you have obviously been lied to," she sniffed. "You have no sense of humor at all. You are simply amusing yourself at my expense. Men have an annoying tendency toward being patronizing. I strongly resent it."

Sin watched her assess him, as if he were a sculpture on display. The young lady's astute gaze missed nothing, not the darkness of his eyes and hair, nor the smooth white scar that cut across his cheek and disappeared under his jaw.

Angelene eyed Sin warily after taking inventory of his swarthy physique, black cape, shirt and red sash. "Are you by chance a misplaced pirate?"

Sin was instantly aware of the moment when she arrived at the notion that she had traded one dangerous situation for another. He could feel her body tense, ready to leap off his lap if he posed the slightest threat.

"I asked you to sit still."

When Sin's voice dropped to a quiet pitch, Angelene recoiled, misinterpreting his intent. She fought in frantic desperation, despite his attempt to hold her in place without alarming her further.

"Hold still," he demanded more brusquely than he intended.

"Go to hell and meet the devil!" she sneered as she lurched sideways.

"I've already met the devil, witch," Sin assured her. "He sends his regards."

It was growing increasingly apparent that the feisty female had been restrained one too many times during the course of the evening. Her flammable temper exploded, accompanied by a clap of thunder. To Sin's disbelief, her fist connected with the scar on his cheek. Lightning reflected off her wild eyes and Sin blinked in astonishment when another blow lanced off the side of his head. He released one end of the cane he had clamped around her and attempted to deflect the third blow aimed at his nose.

When Sin shifted in the saddle Angelene was flung off balance. Squawking in surprise, she somersaulted to-

ward the ground. Her curses were muffled by a crack of
thunder. She did have the presence of mind to brace her
arms before she swan-dived into the grass, and Sin hurriedly clamped his hand around her ankle to prevent her
from swallowing a mouthful of grass and dirt.

When skirts and petticoats cascaded over Angelene's
head Sin barked an uncharacteristic laugh. Several more
unladylike curses erupted from beneath the pile of petticoats. Perhaps the fiery female was not having a good
night, but Sin had no complaints.

A smile twitched his lips while he stared down at
the woman's pantaloon-clad bottom. He tried to recall
when he had spent a more unusual evening in a
woman's presence. Most of his encounters leaned more
toward early-to-bed and quick-to-rise before he and his
crew cast off and set sail. Now, Sin sat here holding
onto this temperamental chit, as if she were an anchor
dragging the ocean floor. He rather enjoyed peeking beneath her sails to appraise frilly petticoats and shapely
legs.

"Let me go, you . . . you despicable pirate!" she spluttered furiously.

"I did let you go once and look what happened." Sin
said calmly. "You were turned on your beam's end. And
you do have a nice beam, by the way."

"I demand that you unhand me before I am forced to
resort to drastic measures," she threatened.

Sin assessed the situation, trying to decide whether to
haul her back into his lap or simply drop her on the
ground. No doubt, the hot-tempered little shrew would
object, no matter what he did. This female had a short
fuse on her temper.

When Sin didn't immediately obey her command, Angelene rammed the heel of her shoe into Turk's underbelly.

"Whoa!" Sin jerked on the reins when the startled horse reared up and twisted around to avoid another discomforting blow.

Another outraged shriek burst from Angelene's lips when the horse's upward motion, and the viselike grip on her ankle, hoisted her even higher off the ground. Sin jerked his arm above his head before the horse came down on all fours. He released his grasp on her ankle and hooked his arm around her waist. Satin skirts and petticoats floated over his head and her chin landed on the muscled flesh of his thigh.

A most interesting position, Sin thought. A few more inches and . . .

"Ouch, damn it!" Sin grimaced in pain when the she-cat sank her teeth into his thigh. The woman simply didn't know the meaning of gratitude. Sin had saved her from rubbing her nose in the grass and this was the thanks he got.

Sin accidentally rammed his heels into the Turk's flanks in his attempt to remove his leg from range of her teeth. The horse bolted off and Sin couldn't tell where the hell he was going, what with all those lacy petticoats draped over his head.

It was bad enough that Sin was unfamiliar with the terrain, but now he had this female-turned-wildcat scratching and clawing to upright herself in his lap. The cool detachment Sin had faithfully practiced for almost two decades abandoned him when he found himself engaged in a brawl on the back of his horse. "Dead Reckoning" nautical skills were no use to him now. He didn't know where the reins had gotten off to during the scuffle, but he was no longer in control—of horse or woman. Turk had taken the bit between his teeth and charged off, as if launched from the starting blocks on a racetrack.

When the horse cut sideways to avoid whatever obstacle was in its path, Sin felt himself clawing air in an attempt to anchor himself to Turk's mane. He tried to twist in midair to brace himself for the inevitable fall, but he made a pancake landing atop the woman responsible for this fiasco.

Served her right, Sin thought. This was proof positive that responding to temper rather than logic complicated problems instead of resolving them.

There was no doubt that the woman who cushioned his fall had no breath left when mashed beneath six feet two inches and two hundred and twenty pounds of masculine weight. Sin heard the air leave her lungs in a *whoosh*. She was pinned beneath him, his legs wedged between hers, his chest pressed against her cheek. The last thing she wanted turned out to be exactly what she got and she had herself to thank for it.

Now this was more like it, Sin mused wickedly. Too bad the ill-tempered female beneath him wasn't the type who appreciated the intimate position they were in. Knowing her—and he now had a fair measure of her temperament to go by—she was going to be furious once she gathered her wits and recovered her breath.

Sin took his own sweet time in removing himself from the soft curves and swells beneath him. The man in him wanted something other than a battle, though he was sure that was all he was likely to get from the woman who was presently dragging air into her collapsed lungs and girding herself up to blast away at him.

As Sin had anticipated, she let him have it with both barrels.

# *Four*

"You clumsy dolt! In all my twenty years, and in all my dealings with you conniving males, I have never found myself in such a frustrating predicament. Blast it, this is worse than fending off—" Angelene clamped her mouth shut and struggled to free herself. "Get off me this instant, you bastard!"

Sin rocked back to his knees, leaving the furious female's skirts pinned beneath him, making it impossible for her to escape. "Technically, I am not a bastard," he informed her. "My parents were very married when I was born."

"I swear you have the sensitivity of a rock, and feel like one too! As for your imperturbability, it's almost as infuriating as finding myself in this position . . ."

Sin not only saw but felt the woman's immediate transformation. She had stopped being furious long enough to realize how potentially dangerous the situation had become. She knew he had the strength and the opportunity to do whatever he wanted to her while she was flat on her back. When her eyes narrowed on him, Sin knew she expected him to press his advantage. She was mentally scrambling to save herself before he could do his worst.

"I implore you to let me up," Angelene said carefully.

"Implore?" His brow quirked as his gaze dropped to her heaving breasts, noting the creamy texture of her skin. He wished he wasn't quite so aware of the tantalizing swells exposed by her scoop-necked gown, but a man would have to be dead not to have noticed. "I could have sworn you only knew how to issue commands rather than make requests."

"I will pay you handsomely if you will let me go."

"I presume you are speaking in terms of coins. Or are you suggesting a more intimate medium of exchange?"

Angelene gritted her teeth. "Don't bait me, sir. I am having enough difficulty controlling my temper. It is one of my worst flaws."

Her only flaw, Sin silently corrected. Sin couldn't remember the last time he had been amused enough to grin.

Very few people surprised or distracted Sin, but this fascinating female did. She was brimming with fiery spirit and lively intelligence. She knew she was vulnerable and she was casting about for a way to extricate herself before her feminine virtue became as soiled as her gown. Sin was waiting for her to bring out the most common weapon in the feminine arsenal—tears. But it was becoming apparent that this particular woman only turned on the tears as a last resort.

Angelene cocked her head to one side to regard Sin from a different angle when he made no move to ravish her. He knew he looked like the very devil in his black cape that whipped in the wind, with his cutlass strapped around his hips, and a blood-red sash tied around his waist. He had already been mistaken for a landlocked pirate or prowling highwayman. It was only natural for the woman to assume by his attire that he also had the decadent morals of a criminal. His appearance gave him an air of dangerous intrigue that held people at bay. Unfortunately, it did nothing to reassure this willful woman. She didn't trust his motives, and the way she was staring at him said as much.

"If you release me," she bargained, "I promise there will be no charges brought against you because of this attack."

Sin swallowed a chuckle, amazed at this woman's ability to amuse him. He hadn't met anyone—especially a female—who practically demanded his surrender in the face of her defeat.

"How kind and generous of you," he replied. "But the truth is I was hoping for more than your silence in the matter."

She regarded him warily. "What do you want in exchange for my silence and my freedom?"

Nothing could work to Sin's advantage more than being accepted into baronial society, allowing him entrance into the circles Kimball, Porter and Sheridan traveled. And one by one, Sin would destroy the men who had turned his life upside down and left him for dead.

The vengeful thought wiped all expression from Sin's craggy features. He had allowed himself to be distracted from his purpose. Encountering this rambunctious female had proved entertaining, but he had objectives to accomplish.

"What I want most is a letter of introduction into every respectable home in Natchez," he requested.

"Why? So you can rob your hosts blind?"

"No, I have my own funds," he assured her.

"I'm sure you do, but I wonder who the funds belonged to before you got your hands on them." She stared inquisitively at him. "And how do you know I am in a position to secure these letters of introduction, Mister—?" She paused, waiting for him to fill in the blank.

Sin rose to his feet and grasped the woman's hand, hauling her up beside him. "The name is Sinclair," he introduced himself. "Nick Sinclair."

If the name registered with her, she didn't let on. She simply studied Sin in the flash of lightning that speared through the clouds.

"As for your ability to procure introductions for me, your eloquent manner of speaking and your expensive gown assure me that you are well received among the gentry," he explained reasonably, his gaze sweeping over the elegant ball gown she wore. "If you agree to open aristocratic doors for me, I will forget that this encounter took place."

"Thank you, Mr. Sinclair. I appreciate your silence about this . . . er . . . incident."

Angelene scooped up the pearl-handled cane that had fallen by the wayside and handed it to him. "You will have your letter of introduction. Just don't abuse the privilege." She glanced pointedly at his cloak and sash. "And if you are the least bit sensitive to gossip, I suggest you change your style of dress. You could easily be mistaken for a salt-water bandit."

"And you, my lady, could be mistaken for a witch," he replied, surveying the wild tumble of hair. "You and I look like a matched pair."

She jerked up her head at the casually uttered observation and reassessed him with her keen gaze. An impish smile spread across her lips. Even the darkness couldn't disguise the twinkle in her eyes.

"Perhaps you're right, Mr. Sinclair. A pity that there isn't a costume ball scheduled for this social season. You and I could simply go as we are."

Sin stared down at the five-foot-three-inch bundle of irrepressible spirit. This was indeed a very intriguing female. Although she had the poise and manners of an aristocrat, she had entirely too much spunk to be contained within the normal confines of womanhood.

"We witches are warned not to get wet, for fear of melting into a cloud of steam. If you will excuse me, I think it best if I chase down my *broom* before the sky opens." With that, she spun on her heels and walked off to retrieve her mount.

Sin leaned against his cane and watched the woman swing onto the saddle and race off at the same breakneck speed she had employed earlier. Sin had the unshakable feeling that the lady's steed had not been out of control at all. It was the woman herself who was out of control, Sin decided as he chased down Turk. The woman was a far better rider than he was. No wonder she had objected so strongly when he had *rescued* her . . .

Sin stopped short when he realized he had failed to ask the lively elf's name. But he quickly reminded himself that he had not come to Natchez to join the fortune seekers in their quest for wealthy wives to support them. Sin had all the money he needed, money enough to turn Porter, Kimball and Sheridan every which way before he enjoyed the final phase of his revenge against the men who had established themselves as impeccable gentlemen—at his expense.

Respectable aristocrats? Sin silently scoffed at the thought. Hardly. And before long, all of Natchez would know the truth. Sin was about to expose the bastards for what they were.

The following day Hiram Brodie swung down from his horse, serenaded by the pounding of hammers that echoed around Raven's Hill. Pushing back his spectacles to the bridge of his nose, he stared approvingly at the changes in the run-down mansion Sinclair had purchased.

After more than two weeks of industrious labor performed by the men who had once served as the *Siren*'s crew, the plantation looked brand new. No more warped and sagging trim boards dangled from the eaves. The broken railings on the upper gallery had been replaced. The marble steps that led to the second level of the palatial home had been polished, buffed and decorated with familiar designs the mariners had come to appreciate.

Hiram smiled in satisfaction. This was to be his new home while he served as Sinclair's financial adviser. He would soon be enjoying the life of luxury promised to him.

"Hello, mate!"

Hiram glanced up to the third floor gallery to see Cyrus Duncan waving at him. Cyrus, four years his senior, had been second in command on board the *Siren*. The brawny sailor had a delightful sense of humor and was notorious for pranks. When the ship bogged down in the blistering heat of the doldrums, Cyrus always devised ways to liven things up. The jovial Australian whom Sinclair had picked up at Sydney eight years earlier had proved to be an asset, whether the *Siren* was sailing across smooth waters or storm-tossed seas.

Of course, Hiram reminded himself, Nick Sinclair had an uncanny knack of collecting sailors from ports around the world who were experts at specific duties.

Most of the men who now labored to refurbish the house on Raven's Hill had been eager to give up the sea when Sinclair announced he was going to become a land-lubber. Sin had offered all of his men new jobs and a home that didn't sway with the wind.

The unexpected declaration had nearly knocked the entire crew overboard. But when tempted by an increase in salary and a promise of a grand home, the mariners had waded ashore. Only two of the young sailors had declined the offer. One of them had become the *Siren*'s new captain, the other the first mate. The arrangement had worked superbly for the two men and Sinclair for he kept his contact with overseas agents and his long-standing connections with the hongs—waterfront factories in Canton that were leased by Americans who delivered merchandise to the Orient.

Sinclair was respected by the powerful group of mandarins who had been appointed by the ruling emperor in China. He had established good relations with Houqua and Paunkeiqua, two of the richest dignitaries who controlled the hongs. The last trip from the Far East had found the *Siren* laden with gifts of hand-painted porcelain vases, urns, Chinaware, bronzes and silks that could have been sold for a fortune in the States. Sinclair, however, had added them to his collection of rare and beautiful souvenirs from around the world.

Ah yes, Hiram thought, Sinclair may now be dry-docked, but he had brought part of the sea with him when he settled in Natchez. Not one member of the crew yearned for long voyages and dangers. Sinclair had given them a home and new purpose.

"How goes it, Cyrus?" Hiram called to the ex-first mate.

Cyrus Duncan hammered another section of railing in place and smiled broadly. "Fine, mate. From this crow's-nest, I can almost see all the way to the Falkland Islands." He cupped his hand over twinkling golden eyes. "I do believe I see a herd of seals in the distance. The hong merchants will be bobbin' their queues in excitement, ready to pay three dollars for every hide we unload."

Hiram chuckled, remembering the stir caused by the heaping stacks of seal skins they had delivered to Canton. The cargo had vanished as quickly as it had been unloaded from the *Siren*. The Chinese buyers were always anxious to acquire hides and furs from the Pacific Coast and tortoise shells from Galapagos. Another favorite was the root of a weed that farmers in New England considered undesirable. The Chinese were anxious to acquire ginseng for its medicinal powers. They readily paid three hundred to four hundred dollars an ounce for it.

Cyrus stared down at Hiram, frowning curiously. "Where have you been so long, mate? Trippin' the fantastic with the ladies, eh?"

Hiram gave his brown head a shake and fished the

newly acquired deed from his vest pocket. "I just purchased a hotel and restaurant for Capt—Sin."

"What the blazes are we gonna do with a bloody hotel?" Cyrus croaked.

The other men who were within earshot paused from their carpentry tasks to peer at the man who was Sinclair's financial genius.

"We don't know nothin' 'bout managin' a hotel," one of the men spoke up.

Hiram shrugged noncommittally. "According to Sin, we don't have to. As usual, he's worked all that out."

The answer satisfied the ex-sailors. They went back to work, assured that the captain had considered every detail, just as he always did. Years of experience taught them that Nick Sinclair knew what he was doing, even if he did make a frustrating habit of keeping his own counsel.

"Can you tell me where to find Sinclair?" Hiram requested.

All arms pointed southward toward the coves where Sin spent every spare minute.

"Might have guessed," Hiram murmured as he slung his jacket over his shoulder and hiked off across the lawn.

Jerome Kimball halted his carriage on Main Street and frowned. The abandoned hotel that he had forced out of business a year earlier now boasted a fresh coat of paint and a new sign—South Sea Paradise.

Carpenters were trailing in and out of the establishment like ants in a colony. Jerome didn't know who had purchased the place, but the hired men appeared to have been working around the clock on renovation. Their manner of dress suggested they were suited to a pirate ship instead of a carpenter's labor force.

A muddled frown creased Jerome's brows as he watched two men hang a second sign below the first: *NICK SINCLAIR, proprietor.*

Jerome smirked as he popped the reins over the horse's rump, sending the buggy lurching toward his hotel. Whoever Nick Sinclair was, he wouldn't be in the inn and restaurant business long. No one outsmarted or outlasted Jerome Kimball. He provided the best accommodations, the finest meals and all the intimate pleasures any traveler desired.

Patrons flocked to Kimball's doors in droves—wealthy local barons and traveling dignitaries alike. The Kimball name was synonymous with luxury, and Kimball Hotel had become a landmark on the red-brown bluffs. Only the elite hotels three hundred miles downriver in New Orleans could compete. Nick Sinclair wouldn't last long with Jerome as competition.

Yet a feeling of foreboding rattled Jerome's confidence when he entered the lobby of his hotel. One of the guests at the register's desk was fussing about the lack of room service and the poor quality of food at breakfast. The clerk—one of the men who usually took inventory in the storerooms—was manning the desk.

Jerome strode forward to take command of the situation. After assuring the guest that his every need would be met, including a visit with one of the young ladies on the upper level—at no charge, of course—the grumbling guest went on his way.

"What is the meaning of this?" Jerome growled at the clerk. "Where is Dobson? He's supposed to be on duty, just as he is every day."

"Dobson resigned yesterday," the young clerk reported. "And so did the five best maids on staff. And the lady you mentioned to that disgruntled customer is no longer in residence on the top floor, either."

Jerome blinked in disbelief. "What? I take a few days off for rest and relaxation and the place falls down around my ears! What possessed my staff to abandon me without giving notice?"

"They were offered other employment."

"By whom, for God's sake?" Jerome snapped in question.

"By Nick Sinclair, or *Sin* as he insists on being called."

Fury thrummed through Jerome's veins. He whirled around to glower at the troops that filed in and out of the refurbished establishment that sat catty-corner from Kimball Hotel. That devil called Sin had another think coming if he thought he could undermine Jerome's flourishing business by stealing his employees!

Jerome knew all the tricks of the trade. He also had his ways of handling pesky competition and he wouldn't bat an eyelash at resorting to drastic measures.

Muttering, Jerome swiped a hand across the bald spot on the crown of his head and crammed his hat low on his forehead. Like a charging bull, Jerome stamped across the street to South Sea Paradise Hotel to give the new proprietor a good piece of his mind.

\* \* \*

Sin stepped back to survey the elegant chandelier—
decorated with polished seashells, tortoise shells and
chunks of coral—that had been hung in the hotel lobby.
The newly installed white marble mantels and delicate
blue netting, draped with colorful coral and starfish, were
reminiscent of the sandy beaches of the remote islands
Sin and his crew had visited. Seascapes, painted in oils
by one of his talented crew members, added to the tropical atmosphere. Oriental objects had been strategically
placed around the wide vestibule, and graced the shelves
in the adjoining restaurant. Teak and sandalwood totems,
acquired from South Sea islanders, dangled like good
luck charms on the freshly polished banisters that led
upstairs.

The seagoing atmosphere lent a unique touch to the
previously plain decor. A treasure chest, with its shiny
brass handles and hinges, sat in the far corner, filled with
Chinese silk, ivory figurines and tins of Oriental tea.
Oyster shells, lined with Mother-of-Pearl, were displayed
in another corner of the lobby.

"I've got to hand it to you, Cap'n," Cyrus Duncan
spoke up as he swaggered down the steps. "I wasn't
too sure about this idea at first, but I bloody well approve." He glanced from port to starboard and nodded
admiringly. "This place is enchantin'. Makes me feel
right at home, it does, but without the threat of Malayan pirates, Chinese sea robbers and destructive typhoons."

"The best of all worlds," Sin agreed as he and Cyrus
ambled into the restaurant where tables were being
draped with Oriental linens, depicting scenes from the
Far East.

"I wondered why you'd been collectin' all this para-
phernalia without sellin' it in the States the past two
years," Cyrus remarked, watching the new chef direct
traffic and spout orders as fast as he could flap his jaws.
"Did you have visions of establishin' a restaurant and
hotel way back then?"

"Actually, no," Sin admitted. "But I intended to be
prepared for anything."

And indeed he had. The moment Sin discovered Owen
Porter's whereabouts and learned the man had a penchant
for horses, Sin decided to cover every conceivable base—
just in case. Although he hadn't anticipated opening a
hotel to drive Jerome Kimball out of business, the collection of South Sea treasures had provided the inn with
decor that would intrigue guests.

Most Americans were intensely curious about life in
the Far East. Sin offered Natchezians a glimpse of island paradise and Oriental mystique. The decorative
lanterns that served as centerpieces on the tables, the
bronze dragons that bookended the counter and guarded
the door, and the bamboo awning that covered the doorway added touches of majesty to what had been an
ordinary room.

"Brilliant idea, Cap'n—"

"Sin," he automatically corrected his ex-first mate.

"You'll lure in clientele like schools of fish," Cyrus
predicted. "These landlubbers are brimmin' with curiosity about this place already. Folk have been smashin' their
noses against the bamboo curtains at the windows, tryin'
to sneak a peek from outside. When's the grand
openin'?"

Sin surveyed the restaurant and then pivoted toward

the lobby. "It's all a matter of timing, Cyrus. I'll know very soon when to open for business, I expect."

"What kind of timin'?" Cyrus questioned curiously.

"It depends on our social invitations and formal introductions," Sin replied.

He wondered if the spirited young beauty he had chanced to meet that dark stormy night had kept her promise. He also wondered when the unappeased craving that had hounded him each time the woman's vision rose before him—most especially while he lay alone in bed—would go away. He didn't need distraction while he was laying the groundwork for his revenge.

Not that Sin could have sought the spirited young lady out, even if he wanted to. He didn't have a name to attach to the enchanting face. He had only the memory of an animated voice, stunning features and unusual amusement she had provided. Mostly, Sin harbored a gnawing craving, wishing he had tasted that cupid's-bow mouth when he'd had the chance.

For a week he had envisioned himself sprawled atop that lively beauty, discovering whether she really tasted as good as she looked.

The thought stirred Sin's blood and he shifted uncomfortably. Perhaps he would happen across the woman at one of the social functions. He could mix business with pleasure. But next time, Sin faithfully promised himself, he would at least discover the pleasure those lush pink lips hinted at. And when he had settled his score with Kimball, Porter and Sheridan, he might try his hand at courtship. Unfortunately, his schedule didn't allow for tantalizing pastimes. Right now Sin had traps to bait . . .

"I wish to speak with Nick Sinclair and I wish to speak with him NOW!"

The booming voice stripped all other thought from Sin's mind. A cold knot coiled in the cavity that had once been his heart. He remembered that voice as if he had heard it only yesterday. Sin had been expecting a visit from Jerome Kimball. He wondered if the bastard would recognize him after all these years.

For certain, Jerome would not recall his name because Sin had assumed a new identity after that hellish night. The young lad who had damn near lost his sanity after the horrifying ordeal at sea had—for all practical purposes—perished.

Jacob Montague had died with his brother that night, he just hadn't sunk to the bottom of the sea when the dinghy capsized.

When rescued by privateers, Sin had taken his father's given name and his mother's maiden name. Nick Sinclair had been born at the bitter age of twelve and found himself engaged in war against the British. He had grown up overnight on board the ship whose captain and crew didn't think twice about resorting to piracy when the situation presented itself.

The all-too broad education Sin had received had made him wise beyond his years. But thanks to Pearly Graham, Sin had survived several unpleasant ordeals and pocketed away the money he had made.

Now Sin had gathered more than enough funds to repay the men who had put him through hell. And Jerome Kimball was about to endure the first phase of his long-deserved punishment.

With extreme satisfaction, Sin pivoted around and

strolled into the lobby to renew his acquaintance with Jerome Kimball. Before long he, Owen and Sheridan would be wishing Sin had indeed perished at sea. Sin would make certain of it.

# *Five*

Jerome Kimball ground to a halt when he found himself staring at the fascinating likeness of an island paradise. Jerome already resented Nick Sinclair, sight unseen. He cursed the fact that he hadn't dreamed up such an intriguing decor.

"Sinclair at your service."

Jerome lurched around at the sound of the voice that came from behind him. He sized up his tall, powerfully built rival who leisurely leaned against his pearl-handled cane. Onyx eyes bore down on Jerome. The white scar that marred the ruggedly handsome face twitched slightly. Other than that Jerome could tell nothing about the man's mood.

"I have been told that my best employees have defected to your hotel," Jerome snapped.

"Did they?" Sin questioned blandly. "How unfortunate for you."

"I wish to speak with each and every one of them," Jerome demanded huffily.

Cyrus Duncan stood aside, smiling in amusement. He had seen Sin handle the most irascible agents and merchants around the world. While other men fell victim to their own tempers, Sin always remained calm and unflappable. It was impossible to get a rise out of this self-restrained bloke, Cyrus reminded himself.

"I'm sorry," Sin said in a voice that was neither taunting or apologetic. "But my employees are extremely busy at the moment. I will, of course, pass along any information you feel compelled to convey."

Jerome exploded. "I want my hired help back this instant! You seem unaware of who I am and the power I wield in Natchez."

"The question is not whether I know who you are, it is: Do I care who you are," Sin countered impassively. "And the answer is: No, I do not."

Jerome gnashed his teeth, growing madder by the minute. He was accustomed to receiving deferential treatment and he wasn't getting it.

"I could make or break you, Sinclair," Jerome seethed.

Sin inclined his raven head and propped both hands on the curve of his cane. "I advise you not to make an attempt to break me. As for making me, I hardly need your assistance. I am quite capable of creating my own success."

Cyrus's amber gaze narrowed. He had noted the first—and last—warning Sin issued. It had become the man's trademark, the world round. Sin never voiced idle threats. Once provoked, he followed through in a manner that promised no mercy and provided none.

Jerome expelled a disrespectful snort. "You young upstart, do you think that by stealing my competent staff you can run me out of business? Ha! Eager employees will line up to apply for positions at my hotel, because they know I own the best accommodations to be found between St. Louis and New Orleans."

"At present perhaps," Sin casually conceded. "But of course, I have yet to open for business."

"You'll be closed down shortly thereafter, for *lack* of business," Jerome scoffed. "And you can tell my previous employees that they will have to agree to work extra hours at reduced wages when they come slinking back to me with their tails tucked between their legs."

"I will be sure to relay your message," Sin said in an infuriatingly phlegmatic tone.

Hazel eyes narrowed on the vaguely familiar face that was capped with jet black hair. There was something about this man that triggered a distant memory, but damned if Jerome could figure how, when or where they might have met. Sin's steady calm incensed Jerome. Jerome would find a way to run Sinclair out of business if it was the last thing he did.

"Sin? The tailor is here and he wants to know if these garments meet with your approval—"

Dobson's voice evaporated when his previous employer wheeled around to glower at him. Dobson grimaced and nodded an awkward greeting.

"Traitor," Jerome snarled before he looked his ex-clerk up and down. "And what the hell are you doing in that ridiculous get-up? You look like a damned pirate."

"The costume is exactly as I requested," Sin said as he veered around Jerome. He stretched out his hand to tug at the fabric on Dobson's shoulder. "Tell the tailor to take a tuck on this seam." Sin pulled the patch over Dobson's left eye, giving the mild-mannered clerk a rakish appearance. "This is precisely the effect I hoped for, Dobson. Tell the tailor he will be generously rewarded for a job well done."

Dobson turned around, braced the heel of his hand on the wooden cutlass that hung from the red sash at his waist and swaggered off as if he'd come from the Barbary Coast.

"What do you expect to accomplish by dressing the man in such outlandish garb?" Jerome smirked.

Sin pivoted, his impassive expression intact—as usual. "I am providing my guests with a taste of the adventurous romance they have come to associate with the sea, of course. These accommodations will provide a fantasy for landlubbers, without the hazards and discomforts of sailing halfway around the world."

"The aristocracy will laugh you out of business when they clap eyes on those ludicrous costumes of uncivilized buccaneers," Jerome assured him. "I won't have to drive you out of business. You'll cut your own throat, *Pirate Captain.*"

When Jerome flung his nose in the air and spun around to make his dramatic exit, Sin's all-too quiet words halted him in his tracks.

"You have no appreciation or taste for the salty sea, Jerome? I would have guessed differently. But then, I suppose we all must come aground eventually, mustn't we?"

Jerome could think of no reason why the casually uttered questions should unsettle him, but they did. It was as if Sinclair were subtly hinting at something that he could not possibly have known.

"G'day to you, mate." Cyrus called to Jerome.

Jerome swiveled his head around to see the tall, wavy-haired Aussie flashing him a jaunty salute.

"Go to hell, *mate,*" Jerome sneered at him.

"Been there," Cyrus replied good-naturedly.

"Disrespectful as a salt-water bandit," Jerome muttered as he tramped off.

Sin watched Jerome Kimball disappear from sight and battled down his smoldering hatred. Resolutely, Sin locked the wasted emotion into its berth deep inside the hull that had once been his soul. He vowed that Jerome Kimball would pay the devil's full due—one day at a time. And finally Sin would divulge his true identity and watch Jerome sweat blood. When Jerome had lost what he held dearest he would understand a measure of the suffering Sin had endured.

"A rather unsociable swab, our competitor," Cyrus observed. "Our new chef claims Kimball has friends in low places who don't bat an eyelash at buryin' a dagger in a man's back."

"So I have already heard."

"Do you think that blusterin' old whale will put up as good a fight as Malayan freebooters and Caribbean sea dogs?"

"No," Sin replied. "But I imagine the blustering old whale will be breaching and snorting when his business starts to sag like limp sails. Just keep your eyes open and watch your own back, Cyrus. There's no telling when Kimball's henchmen will be ordered to dispose of the competition . . . and his closest friends."

"Aye, mate, I'll do that. And you guard your own spine. Can't have the cap'n of South Sea Paradise Hotel walkin' 'round with a stiletto stickin' out his back. It would be too realistic for your uppity guests."

Cyrus's engaging smile eased the lingering tension that hounded Sin. He would have time enough to watch

Jerome's downfall in the weeks to come. There were other arrangements to make, Sin reminded himself. He couldn't show favoritism by directing all his vengeance toward Kimball. Porter and Sheridan deserved their own private niches in hell, too.

"Sin, I have the information you requested."

Sin was jostled from his pensive musings when Hiram Brodie strode inside, wearing a bemused frown and glancing over his shoulder.

"I just received a sound cursing from a stranger on the street, for absolutely no reason I can think of," Hiram announced.

"That was Kimball," Cyrus informed him. "He left here with his sails poppin' and his spars strained to the limit."

Hiram nodded in understanding. "I assume Kimball just got wind of his employees' resignation."

"Yes, and an ill wind blew him to our doorstep," Sin reported. "Anyone seen entering this hotel automatically invites Kimball's wrath. If he has as much difficulty controlling his temper while in the presence of his peers at upcoming social gatherings, he will lose the respectability he gloats upon."

"He'll be cuttin' his own throat," Cyrus predicted. "You'll have him goin' and comin'." His brows gathered over his tawny eyes. "Just what have you got against that hot-aired bloke anyway? You never said."

Hiram waited, anxious to hear the answer to the question he had posed the previous week. But it looked as if he were doomed to wait even longer before discovering what this affair was about. Sin simply shrugged a broad shoulder and reached for the paper in Hiram's hand.

"Ah yes, the social calendar for the gentry of Natchez. Good work, Hiram." Sin scanned the names, dates and locations of the homes that would be entertaining guests during the height of social season. "It looks as if the three of us will be attending a ball held at Brantley's Plantation this weekend."

"We will?" Cyrus chirped. "Come now, Cap'n, you know I've got the social graces of a bloody walrus. I'm more at home in the barrooms Under-the-Hill and in the bamboo huts of Hog Lane in Canton."

"*Were,* past tense," Sin corrected. "As the esteemed manager of the cotton plantation and stables, earning a fine salary, you will soon be one of the most eligible bachelors in Natchez. Can't have you slogging through the mud Under-the-Hill now that genteel ladies will be clamoring to make your acquaintance."

"Cotton plantation and stables?" Cyrus choked on his breath. "I don't know a blessed thing about raisin' cotton and all I know about a horse is which end bites and which end kicks."

"Not a problem," Sin replied, unconcerned.

"Not a problem?" Cyrus parroted. "I'd say there's a major problem, mate."

Hiram smiled wryly, for he knew exactly what was coming when Sin glanced in his direction. Hiram explained, "We'll simply hire the best help in the area to run the plantation and stables you will be overseeing."

"You're catching on, Hiram," Sin complimented.

Cyrus glanced at the hotel employees who scurried off to attend their chores. "Just like here at South Sea Paradise?"

"Exactly," Sin confirmed.

Cyrus flicked an imaginary piece of lint off the sleeve of his linen shirt and struck a sophisticated pose, mimicking Jerome Kimball's air of self-importance. "Then I s'pose I should be off to see the tailor. I plan to be a bloomin' Cind'rella when I make my social debut." He sashayed off and then halted, turning inquisitive amber eyes to Sin. "Plantation and livestock manager, ya say, Cap'n?"

Sin nodded his dark head.

"Just when will my employees be showin' up at Raven's Hill?"

Sin glanced questioningly at Hiram Brodie.

"I suppose you want me to hire Porter's stable manager and best grooms, and Sheridan's plantation overseer," Hiram speculated.

"You do catch on quickly, Hiram."

"Who are Porter and Sheridan?" Cyrus queried.

Sin's reply was an evasive shrug.

"Are Porter and Sheridan gonna be as peeved as Kimball was?" Cyrus wanted to know.

"One can only hope," Sin answered placidly.

Cyrus's keen gaze narrowed on Sin's well-disciplined expression. "One day soon, I hope you'll tell me exactly what's goin' on around here. I always did enjoy a good prank, ya know, mate."

After Cyrus strode off to order a new ensemble for the social engagements, Sin focused his full attention on Hiram. "When you have hired the most skilled employees Porter has to offer, check on purchasing Sheridan's slaves."

"Slaves?" Hiram echoed. "We're going to buy slaves?"

"Purchase them under your own name. I want no connection to me just yet."

"But—"

"And inform the slaves that as soon as they have worked off the initial amount of payment, they will be granted their freedom. They can continue to work for us at a fair salary if they choose."

Hiram's eyes bulged. "By the time news gets around that you free slaves after they have earned their original cost, folks will be begging for employment at Raven's Hill. Sheridan and Porter won't be able to keep good help."

"I sincerely hope I don't lose any sleep over that," Sin replied blandly.

Hiram grinned. "Will there be anything else?"

"Yes, see what you can do about hiring the cook from Sheridan Hall. I have heard Agnes Ralston is one of the best in the area," Sin added. "I would also enjoy having Porter's most trusted valet and Sheridan's butler on staff at Raven's Hill. I intend for us to go first class, Hiram. Nothing but the best my neighbors have to offer."

Hiram chuckled. "I hope you are aware that you are cutting deep enough to draw blood—or vicious temper."

"I assure you, my friend, I know exactly what I'm doing."

Hiram jotted down Sin's requests, pushed his spectacles back in place and glanced up. "You'll be making enemies aplenty within the upper echelon of Natchez society. And like Cyrus, I'm very interested to know what untold offenses Kimball, Porter and Sheridan and Limestall committed against you that have earned them the biting edge of your cutlass."

Sin retrieved his timepiece from his pocket. "If you are as efficient as usual, you can set my plans in motion and still have time to take your fitting with the tailor. I expect all of us to make our debut in grand fashion, Hiram."

Hiram heaved an exasperated sigh. "As you wish, Sin, but I would ask a favor."

"Anything," Sin generously offered.

"If I offend you at some future date, I would appreciate knowing about it so that I might apologize immediately." Hiram smiled dryly. "I'm not anxious to have my legs chopped out from under me one slice at a time like Kimball, Porter and Sheridan. Whatever they did, they have a formidable adversary in you."

Something dark and brooding flashed in Sin's black diamond eyes. "Believe me, my friend, you could never do what those men have done. And also believe me when I tell you that they deserve everything they will receive."

"Was it a betrayal of sorts?" Hiram ventured.

"Of sorts," Sin's voice hit a cold, quiet pitch, warning Hiram that he had posed too many questions already.

Hiram cleared his throat and avoided Sin's glittering stare. "I'll start with Porter's jockeys and grooms. Can't have our good man Cyrus strutting off to his first social function in Cind'rella's pumpkin. He'll need a coach and a team of strapping horses to fill the stables he now oversees."

"And don't forget the experienced cotton laborers," Sin called after Hiram. "It is your duty to make Cyrus Duncan look good, no matter what his endeavor."

"Aye, sir," Hiram promised before he shoved off like a schooner scudding before the wind with a set of full sails.

# Six

Sin was feeling oddly restless. Something vital was missing, not from his life, but within himself. It wasn't that running aground after eighteen years left him yearning for the sea. And it wasn't that he hadn't settled comfortably in the spacious mansion on Raven's hill, surrounded by his trusted and dependable crew. It certainly had nothing whatsoever to do with his plans for Porter, Kimball and Sheridan, for things had fallen neatly into place. Thus far, Sin had everything he desired. Who could want more?

Sin paced across the rise of ground that overlooked the clear-water coves, watching the sun make its final descent. Although he had a great deal on his mind, he kept getting caught up on the memory of a stormy night and the intriguing young woman he had met.

Heaving an unsettled sigh, Sin stared down the hill at the stables where the new grooms were accomplishing the last of their daily chores. His gaze drifted to the dark bay stallion that grazed in the pasture. Although Sin told himself it was a foolish whim, he found himself moving down the hill to have Turk saddled. He had the overwhelming urge to take a late-afternoon ride.

Sin soon found himself practicing his riding skills in

the open meadow on the edge of town where he had happened across the lively female who constantly preyed on his mind. Of late, Sin "happened by" this stretch of road nearly every evening. He was annoyed with himself for being preoccupied with that little elf when he had so many details to arrange. But here he was again, just like clockwork.

The sound of pounding hooves drifted in with the breeze and Sin glanced north to see the familiar tangle of red-gold hair catching flame in the sunset. The restlessness that had plagued him quickly subsided. He watched in fascination as the young woman blazed across the meadow as if she were riding a runaway steed. The breathtaking creature was born to run wild—and so was her horse.

Sin had made several feminine acquaintances at social functions the past week, but other women hadn't intrigued him the way this uninhibited beauty had. He had been disappointed that she had not attended the party at the Brantley Plantation.

Considering the time of evening the young lady chose to race at breakneck speed, Sin wondered if her family knew of her penchant for reckless adventure. He wondered how many of the gentry this closet misfit had deceived into thinking she was the epitome of gentle propriety.

When the rider turned around to race back in the direction she had come from, Sin dug in his heels giving Turk his head. The stallion's muscles bunched as he flattened his ears and shot off. Sin had the feeling his horse detested being outrun. Some horses were born to lead the pack. Turk was obviously one of them.

It didn't take long for Sin to realize that the roan horse the woman was riding had the same temperament as Turk. The roan gelding caught a glimpse of Turk closing in, and its nostrils flared.

Sin didn't have time to nod a greeting when Turk exploded in a burst of speed. He simply held on for dear life to prevent breaking his neck.

Damnation. Maneuvering a schooner through the eye of the wind during a storm was as difficult as remaining on Turk. The horse tried zigzagging in front of the roan and kept breaking stride, throwing Sin off balance. Turk suddenly leaped forward to avoid collision and Sin swore he'd suffered whiplash when Turk thundered off with the roan nipping at his rump.

Enchanting laughter erupted behind Sin, but he didn't dare glance back while Turk was bounding sideways every other second to avoid another painful bite. Male pride demanded that Sin at least finish this foolish race, rather than landing in a tangled heap and being trampled.

It galled him to realize that the young lady was a far better rider than he was. But then, he reminded himself, she would be out of her element on a quarterdeck with a cross-stall, compass and chronometer to guide her.

When the roan was running nose to nose with Turk, Sin decided to end the challenge in a tie, even if Turk didn't approve. Horse and rider battled momentarily before Sin regained full control. His leg was throbbing after being held so tightly in an effort to retain his seat. He noticed that his bewitching companion didn't look the least bit fatigued after the wild race. Whoever this woman was, she had spent almost as many years straddling a saddle as he had spent manning a ship.

"I assume you make a habit of this sort of thing," Sin said as he swung to the ground and braced himself on his cane.

Angelene lifted an elegant brow and smiled challengingly. "And you do not approve, Mr. Sinclair?"

"My friends call me Sin," he told her as he watched her hop to the ground.

Green eyes twinkled at him. "And what, I wonder, do your enemies call you?"

"You don't want to know. The descriptive names aren't fit for a lady's ears."

"And I suppose you, like most men, believe a woman must always have a lady's ears."

Sin had the odd feeling he was being tested. For what reason he had no idea. "That depends."

She looked up at him and frowned. "On what?"

"On whether a woman expects a man always to portray the gentleman in her presence, even when she prides herself in not always portraying the proper lady."

Angelene stared deliberately at his dark cape and red sash. "Since you persist in dressing in such an unusual fashion, I presume you and I both have alternate personalities. You seem to be part gentleman and part bandit, Mr. Sinclair."

"I believe I mentioned that my friends call me Sin."

"We are new acquaintances and you are avoiding the question."

Sin admired her lively wit and challenging smile. He was also exceptionally partial to that emerald green riding habit that displayed her figure to its best advantage. Sin imagined he wasn't the only man who became distracted by this spirited female.

After tethering Turk, Sin ambled down the slope. "I don't believe I caught your name when we first met."

Angelene secured her horse and followed a safe distance behind him. "I don't believe I mentioned my name, and you still have not answered my question."

Sin pivoted to find the saucy woman measuring the width of his chest and shoulders with her scrutinizing gaze. He wondered if she found him half as appealing as he found her. If the look he had intercepted was anything to go by, this was not a one-sided attraction.

"The fact is, I have no complaints about women who enjoy themselves. As for me, I have no aspirations of being a gentleman. They're too stuffy and pompous for my tastes."

"A gambler then?" she pried as they strolled along the skirting of trees that lined the creek.

"Yes, in the sense that life itself is a gamble."

Bright ringing laughter hovered over the meadow. "You have the gift of evasion. Some people might find that very exasperating."

"Certainly not you," he parried. "You have been artfully dodging my questions. Perhaps we both have secrets to hide. You have no name and I have no occupation. A fair trade, I should think."

"As I recall, we made a bargain last time we met. I returned home unscathed and you were given proper introductions to every social event the aristocracy has to offer. As you said: A fair trade."

"And you were good to your word. But when I attended the Brantleys' party you were nowhere to be seen."

She grinned saucily. "Disappointed, Mr. Sinclair?"

Sin felt the makings of a smile tugging at his lips, but he managed to stifle it. "But of course, I was curious to see if witches dance as skillfully as they ride."

Angelene half turned, inhaling a breath of fresh air. She stared appreciatively at the sunset. "I pick and choose the parties I attend. Dealing with men at such affairs can be very tiresome."

"Men, like the one who irritated you immediately before we first met," he guessed. "The one who has given all of the male persuasion a bad name?"

"Exactly. Natchez is not only known for the size and abundance of mosquitoes and alligators, but also for its aggressive wife-hunters who can be as much of a nuisance as reptiles and insects. Why should I waste my time tolerating men who wish to wed an inheritance or endear themselves to married women who can support them in the manner to which they aspire? In my experience, most men usually turn out to be disappointments."

Sin regarded her for a long, pensive moment. "Just who is it that you judge all mankind by? The suitor who jilted you?"

"My father, of course," came her breezy reply.

"Ah, the paragon of gentlemanly behavior. How touching."

"I detect a hint of sarcasm. You really must do something about that immovable expression of yours," she playfully chided him. "Your other acquaintances who haven't learned to listen closely might miss the flippant tone of your voice."

"I'll work on that, elf. Now back to the subject at hand. What is the name of this perfect man who sets the unattainable standards for my gender?"

Laughter filled the air and Sin was amazed at his pleasurable response to the sound. There were times when he wished he could display emotion as easily.

"You may mistake me for a witch, but do not mistake me for a fool."

"Does your father bear the same last name as you?" he questioned nonchalantly.

"Perhaps. And then again, perhaps not. It would depend on whether I am married or single."

Sin scrutinized her impish smile for a moment, trying to see beneath her beguiling expression. "You are the one who is being exasperating," he said, stepping closer. "Who are you, elf?"

She instinctively retreated into her own space. "Does it matter so much what name I go by? Will you be more or less impressed?"

"No, but I would like to have a name to attach to this vision who appears at twilight and during thunderstorms. I'm beginning to think you are a figment of my imagination." Before Sin could stop himself, his hand lifted to trace the delicate curve of her jaw. She dodged his fingertips and arched beautifully sculpted brows.

"What do you want from me, Sin?"

He stared into those thick-lashed eyes that sparkled like priceless jewels, noting there was no demure lowering of her gaze, only sharp, intelligent curiosity that demanded to know his intentions.

"Are you sure you really want to know the answer to that, elf?"

"Would I have asked if I didn't?"

His thumb trailed over the lush curve of her mouth, marveling at the soft texture that reminded him of a lily petal. "Having these lips under mine would do for starters," he murmured.

"And if I permit your kiss, then what?" Her voice wavered in response to the gentle caress of his fingertip.

"And then, of course, you will be obliged to marry me," he teased without the slightest change of expression.

That was obviously the wrong thing for him to say, even in jest. Green eyes snapped and her chin tilted a notch.

"Marriage? Perhaps the fact is that I find myself married to a man who refuses to treat me with the consideration and respect I want. Or perhaps the truth is that I am virtually penniless and have set my cap for a wealthy planter's son. Or maybe I was deflowered and then jilted by the insensitive suitor you speculated on earlier."

"Were you?"

Sin noticed the abrupt alteration in her mood. *Volatile* and *kaleidoscopic* described this stunning woman. Indeed, the seven bands of weather that Sin navigated through to reach the Far East were equally unpredictable. She grew stormy in the blink of an eye and yet she could roll as blue as a peaceful sea. Sin was beginning to think he had met tamer typhoons off the China coast. So why was he so relentless in pressing her for answers she obviously didn't wish to give? Damned if he knew.

"Was I what?" she asked.

"Jilted," he prompted.

"Once . . . perhaps," Angelene replied, a hint of mischief returning to her eyes.

Sin couldn't drag his gaze away from her sensuous

mouth. "Very long ago?" he questioned, his voice hitting
a husky pitch.

"A week ago."

He nodded perceptively. "Right before we met. Just
as I thought."

*"When* we met," she teased him. "I was left oddly
dissatisfied when you turned out to be very much the
gentleman you assure me you have no wish to be."

"Imp," Sin chuckled as his arm slid around her waist,
drawing her full-length against him. "I have the feeling
you have been pulling my leg, even when you know it's
injured—"

Her hand flattened against his chest to steady herself,
her palm resting against the hair-roughened flesh revealed by his gaping shirt. The feel of her hand against
his sensitive skin was like a brand. Air clogged his throat
when long-denied need coiled inside him.

Sin had no time for this kind of playful distraction,
but he was sorely tempted to make time. However, judging by the defensive comments this female made, she
had no intention of succumbing to a man's desires. All
he was doing was tormenting himself. He hadn't realized
he had become such a glutton for torment. Obviously he
had his embittered past to thank for it.

While Sin was weighing the pros and cons of letting
himself become intrigued by this enchanting beauty, his
body was ignoring the good advice sent down by his
brain. Her tantalizing scent was fogging his senses, lur-
ing him ever closer. The instant his lips slanted over
hers, Sin felt her tremble in his arms. He deepened the
kiss—one that was becoming more overpowering by the
second.

It had been too long since he had indulged in the pleasures a woman could provide. The hesitant yet answering flame he felt burning beneath her cautious reserve fed his hungry craving. Damn, wasn't it amazing how a man could become addicted in the space of a kiss . . . ?

Angelene pulled back and stepped out of his arms, refusing to meet his intense gaze. "I better go. It's getting late," she whispered shakily.

"Yes, you probably should," he agreed.

"I won't be back."

"I think that's for the best."

Sin caught himself before he reached out to draw her luscious body back against him. He was a man with a mission and no time for distractions.

Angelene stared up into Sin's bronzed features and limned the scar that curved over his jaw. "Sin, I—" Her hand dropped to her side and she glanced toward her grazing mount.

Whatever it was she wanted to say, she decided against it. Sin held his ground, watching the nameless vision of beauty and spirit vanish into the gathering darkness. He cursed himself soundly for sampling the sweet nectar of her kiss. Instead of satisfying his curiosity and craving, he had intensified it.

Heaving a frustrated sigh, Sin ambled down to the creek and stared into the distance to gather his thoughts. He had scores of arrangements to make, none of which included involvement with a woman who seemed to have her own mysterious secrets and troubles to resolve.

Striding off to fetch his horse, he vowed to keep his mind on the business at hand. He was *not* returning to this meadow again, either. All he was doing was tormenting himself. *That* he didn't need. It was Porter, Kimball and Sheridan who deserved to be frustrated to the limits. And Sin was the man who was going to see that they were!

# Seven

Angelene Sheridan sank down at the far end of the dining table and smiled at her father. She was quick to note his stiff table manners and the taut lines bracketing his mouth. Charles snapped out his napkin and spread it over his lap. He picked up his knife and fork, ready to carve into whatever was irritating him.

Angelene had seen the gesture and expression several times—immediately before a lecture was directed at her. She knew her father was a mite put out with her, but she was confident of her ability to tease him back into good humor.

Manufacturing a cheery smile, Angelene shook out her napkin and smoothed it in place. "Did you have a good day, Papa?" she asked.

"Not particularly."

He was miffed. She'd suspected as much. Having given Charles the opening needed to vent his frustration, Angelene waited for Charles to air whatever was grieving him.

"I have always tried to be a fair and understanding father—"

"And you have been. The best father, in fact, that any

daughter could hope for," she hurriedly assured him, her brightest smile intact.

One graying brow elevated. Charles stared at his daughter from the opposite end of the mahogany table. "Do not think that buttering me up like a slice of bread is going to work this time, Angel. I am very perturbed about last week's incident and today's escapade."

Angelene squirmed uncomfortably when her father's disapproving gaze pinned her to her seat. Honestly, she didn't know what was the matter with her lately. She had returned from her classes in Philadelphia, thinking she was prepared to settle into the plantation routine of working beside her father and sharing the responsibilities. But there had been an insatiable restlessness gnawing at her for more than two weeks. She continued to think about the cloaked stranger with eyes as black as sin and hair as dark as midnight. She kept remembering the feel of his powerful body dwarfing hers as he lay sprawled above her on that rainy night. She remembered the appealing scent of him as he leaned close, kissing her so gently she felt her knees melt, tempting her in ways she had never before been tempted.

This was ridiculous. The man looked like the kind who spent most of his time cavorting with the denizens from Under-the-Hill. Damn, for all she knew, he could be a thief who preyed on aristocrats and then vanished into the first rays of sunlight, like the warlocks and werewolves she had read about.

A restless streak in her personality must have drawn her to that dashing rake. She recognized that he was potentially dangerous and yet she was attracted to him. Of course, she had always been plagued with a craving for adventure. It was one of her worst faults, or so her father claimed. Those hoyden tendencies of her youth had been another reason Charles had decided to pack her off to the elite school in Pennsylvania, and afterwards to an institute of higher learning. He had tried to make a dignified lady of her, but Angelene's temperament always got in the way of her father's aspirations for her.

"Why did you feel the impulsive urge to go thundering off from Kimball's party during the storm. You have yet to explain yourself to me," Charles continued as he sawed at the dry chunk of ham on his plate. "And tearing off yesterday evening, leaving Reginald Foster choking in your dust, proved a bit embarrassing while I was lounging on the gallery with Congressman Phelps."

Charles set his knife aside, braced his forearms on the edge of the table and flashed his daughter a disgruntled frown. "Honestly, Angel, it is proving quite tedious that you cannot choose one man from the scores of suitors who pursue you. The most eligible bachelors of the decade are being snatched up by ladies who do not begin to compare to your beauty and intelligence."

Charles had hit a raw nerve and Angelene was unable to retain her breezy smile. "I don't want a husband who intends to wed me for your money. You have allowed me to speak freely and act as I see fit—"

"Something I have begun to regret, believe me," Charles said with a grimace.

"Nonetheless, I have come to enjoy my independence and free thinking. I have no desire to enter a marriage where a man expects subservience from his wife. You have seen to it that I have been challenged intellectually, that I developed my mind and talents."

"Am I being blamed because you can't find a man who pleases you?" Charles asked, startled.

Angelene smiled impishly. "No, Papa. It is hardly your fault that eligible suitors have so many irritating flaws. You would not believe the hypocritical fops who indulge me with a smile and then announce that such foolishness as differences of opinion will have to come to a halt at the threshold of matrimony. Gad!" she mimicked caustically. "One can't have a woman who actually entertains an innovating thought before a man has time to reach the conclusion all by himself!"

Charles, despite his exasperation, felt a smile tugging at his lips. He adored Angelene's flair for the dramatic, that vital lilt in her voice, the irrepressible sparkle in her eyes. She had her mother's striking beauty and an inordinate supply of spirit—and then some.

"Then I suggest you select a weak, compliant man who doesn't mind letting his wife supply all of the brains in the union, a man you can walk all over and lead around by the nose."

Angelene sniffed disdainfully at the jest. "I cannot tolerate milktoast suitors who scrape and bow over me, Papa. There is no challenge in outwitting an imbecile."

"I do not consider Reginald Foster and the other suitors who keep showing up around here complete idiots, though how they keep their dignity when you outride them, loudly refute their political views and abandon them the way you did Reggie at Kimball's ball I have no earthly idea. It seems to me that Reggie and the others are exceptionally good sports."

"Reggie and the rest of his kind are professional wife-hunters who will tolerate almost anything I say and do if it will get them what they want—access to your money," Angelene insisted. "Gossip says that Reggie is spending a great deal of his spare time gambling. He is also known to develop a nasty disposition when he sinks too far into his cups."

"Then why do you keep accepting his invitations?" Charles questioned, baffled.

"Because Reggie is an adequate buffer against all the others who are just like him," Angelene explained between bites of tough ham.

Charles blinked in stunned astonishment. "You are seeing Reggie for no other reason than to keep other men at bay? Really, Angel, I'm beginning to think you will never find a man who meets your high expectations."

She grinned. "When I find a man who possesses all your admirable qualities I'll snatch him up in a second." Angelene bit down onto another piece of ham. Try as she might, she couldn't sink her teeth into the meat. It was as tough as shoe leather. "Dear Lord, Agnes is really slipping, isn't she?"

Charles made a stab at the half-cooked potato that was swimming in only God knew what kind of sauce. "I'm afraid Agnes departed."

"She died?" Green eyes widened in alarm.

Charles gave his curly red head a shake. "No, I mean Agnes up and quit."

"But why? I thought she was happy here."

"All I know is that she resigned to take a job else-where. And then Brownley announced he had found other employment."

"Our overseer?" Angelene slumped back in her chair,

stupefied. "Brownley is one of the most competent men in the area. Replacing him will be next to impossible."

"I know." Charles chewed on the raw potato. "I considered it a stroke of luck when a young man arrived, offering to purchase some of our slaves from the fields. He was willing to pay one-and-a-half times the going rate. I planned to use the extra cash to hire another overseer and replace the slaves."

Angelene's gaze narrowed warily. She had a bad feeling about this. Sarah Wilhelm, one of the worst gossips east of the Mississippi, had mentioned something about Jerome Kimball's employees taking jobs at the refurbished hotel in Natchez, leaving him shorthanded and in an atrocious fit of temper. What was going on around here?

"I don't suppose the slaves you sold happened to be the most dependable and competent ones?" she questioned.

"I don't know," Charles admitted. "Brownley always managed the field hands."

Angelene had the uneasy feeling that her father had unknowingly sold off the best hands on the plantation, immediately after he lost his competent overseer and cook.

"I plan to travel to New Orleans this week to seek replacements. You're welcome to come along. Perhaps you'll find a suitor more to your liking there."

Angelene doubted that, but a trip to New Orleans might cure this odd restlessness that had plagued her since she'd happened upon Nick Sinclair.

Thus far, they had not crossed paths at social gatherings and Angelene hadn't spent much time in town. Poring over the financial ledgers and tending managerial duties at Oak Gables was more challenging than gadding about town where professional gossips bent her ear and men flocked like feeding herons.

Of course, when Angelene and Sin finally did cross paths in public, she would no longer be able to keep her identity a secret. In a way, Angelene preferred that. And yet, she was curious to see if Sin would change his attitude toward her once he realized that she was an heiress.

Most men changed their attitude quickly when they discovered who she was. For now, Sin provided an intriguing challenge of wits and wiles. Angelene enjoyed his company, and her mischievous nature constantly had her striving to alter his impassive expression. She had come to the conclusion that Nick Sinclair was a man who had learned to conceal his feelings. She couldn't help wondering why that was. It was part of the attraction she felt toward him, she supposed.

It was a shame Angelene couldn't be more like Sin though—when it came to curbing temper. Maybe that was one of the many reasons Sin intrigued her so. He seemed to be her exact opposite in temperament. He conducted himself with such restraint that she felt the wicked desire to crack his iron-willed composure.

Nick Sinclair seemed to be a walking contradiction with the dashingly rugged looks of an adventurer and the manners of a gentleman . . . Angelene frowned ponderously. He was nothing like the men who stumbled all over themselves to court her fortune. But then, Sin could prove to be just as shallow and mercenary as all the others when he realized who she was.

Not even once, while she artfully eluded marriage traps, had she felt she had been wanted and appreciated for who she was. Except when she was with Sin, she amended. He treated her as his equal and he seemed to respect her intelligence. He alone intrigued her, lured her against her will, wary and mistrusting though she had become of men in general.

But oddly enough, Sin hadn't offered to escort her to a single social function. He simply showed up at the meadow, as if the time they shared was a space out of reality. It was odd. And maybe that was why Angelene had declared she wouldn't be back, that and the fact that there was something rather unsettling about the kiss they had shared. When Angelene was in Sin's arms, she had felt as if she were coming apart at the seams, as if someone had ignited a fire in her blood. It had been totally unexpected. She was leery of sensations she didn't understand and wary of a man she wasn't sure she should trust.

Yes, Angelene convinced herself. She had been wise to announce that they should stop what had gone too far. Sin could be a charading thief for all she knew . . .

"Now about this business of flitting around on unchaperoned evening rides on your way back from Oak Gables and leaving escorts wandering around trying to locate you," Charles said, jarring Angelene from her pensive reverie.

Angelene glanced up at his serious expression. "Papa?"

"Yes, Angel?"

"Do you think I'm asking too much to postpone plans of marriage until I find a man who actually wants me for who I am rather than for the luxury your money can provide?"

The solemn question caused Charles's hand to stall in midair. He stared into those vibrant green eyes and felt the frustration flood out of him. "So that is the crux of the problem, the reason for these impulsive escapades and the sidestepping of offered betrothals."

"I'm afraid so, Papa," she admitted. "I'm being cautious. Is that so hard to understand?"

"No, daughter," he said quietly. "I don't think it's too much for a man to appreciate you for what you are, and for you to look deeper than winsome smiles and shallow charm."

"Thank you." Her sparkling smile would have melted Charles's knees if he had been standing up. "Then you will overlook the . . . er . . . escapades resulting from dealings with one too many devious suitors during the course of parties? I am only trying to outrun the possibility of a marriage arranged for all the wrong reasons."

"And what do you perceive as the right reason?" Charles questioned.

Angelene's smile faded and she was very serious when she said, "All I want is to have someone love me the way you loved Mother. Even after all these years you have never betrayed her memory, have you, Papa?"

Charles lowered his brown eyes and stared at his plate, as if something there had drawn his undivided attention. Memories came leaping back at him. A lovely face and an enchanting smile materialized before him. He remembered those adoring gazes that indicated he was Emily's greatest treasure, despite his weaknesses and failings.

"No, Angel, I have not betrayed Emily's memory. Your

mother was the only woman I ever wanted so badly that I was willing to do anything to make her happy. You have always meant that much to me, too. When you were a sick, frail little child I even—"

Charles swallowed the remainder of the comment and fiddled with his silverware.

"You and Mother defied her parents to marry, didn't you?" Angelene questioned, vaguely recalling the tale her mother had told of those embittered years.

He nodded and smiled sadly. "Your maternal grandparents didn't think I was quality stock. It was of no concern to them that your mother and I were deeply devoted to each other. They disowned Emily and refused to accept our messages for the first four years we were married. Your grandfather thought Emily should have married for money, certainly not something as frivolous as affection. The very fact that your grandparents left a trust for you when you wed, bypassing me completely, indicates they never wanted anything to do with me."

"But you prospered and proved that you were every bit the good provider that Grandpapa was," Angelene insisted.

Charles inwardly winced. "Yes well, that was a lifetime ago and best forgotten. The point is, Angel, that while you search for a man who can truly make you happy, try to employ ladylike reserve," he requested. "I don't want to see your reputation ruined by impulsive antics that have the gossipmongers' tongues wagging from both ends."

"I will try to behave myself." Angelene smiled elfishly. "But I cannot be held accountable when men refuse to behave themselves. They are well and truly asking for trouble when they do."

"Meaning?"

Angelene tossed her father a sententious glance. "I think you know what I imply."

"Do I need to take some young dandy to task for offending you? Young Reggie perhaps?"

Angelene shook her head. "Thank you, Papa, but I have devised my own ways of dealing with offenders. It comes as a relief to know that you are not thinking of throwing up your hands and dumping me in the lap of the next man who shows up at the door."

"Never that, Angel." Charles focused intently on his daughter. "You are my most precious treasure, the living symbol of what Emily and I meant to each other. I would do anything within my power to see you well and happy . . ."

His voice trailed off when an unpleasant memory leaped from a shadowed corner of his mind. Charles sincerely wished he could forget that time in his life when the desperate desire to please and protect had led into disaster.

# *Eight*

"Sin?" Cyrus chuckled at his distracted companion who sat at the gaming table in the men's club, staring off into space, ignoring the cards in his hand. "Are you admittin' defeat, mate?"

Sin glanced down at the winning hand clenched in his fist and expelled a sigh. He tossed the cards on the table and levered out of his chair. The moment he stood up, several heads turned toward him and confidential whispers circulated the room, echoes of Jerome Kimball's snide insults, no doubt.

If Sin wasn't drawing attention with his customary attire that had served him well enough at sea, Jerome's ridicule about South Sea Paradise Hotel had Natchezians murmuring behind his back. Sin had become the subject of excessive speculation. Not that he cared. It only added to the mystique of who and what he was. That would inevitably play to his advantage in his dealings with Kimball, Porter and Sheridan.

"You and Hiram can play without me. I feel like taking a ride."

Cyrus grinned outrageously. "On anyone I know?"

Hiram choked on his ale and sputtered to catch his

breath. "That is not the kind of remark a gentleman is supposed to make," he wheezed.

"The hell ya say, mate," Cyrus replied, undaunted. When Sin lifted a challenging brow, Cyrus shrugged off the silent rebuke. "I'll bow and scrape and strut like the rest of these dandies when I have to, just as I did at the first ball we attended. But I have my pride, ya know. A seaman only puts on snobbish airs for the duration of parties."

While Hiram tried to smooth the rough edges off the incorrigible Cyrus Duncan, Sin left the club. The dark bay stallion he had ridden into town had drawn considerable attention outside the men's club. The news about Turk had spread—and in just the right circles. Most of Natchez knew about the valuable horse Sin owned. If news hadn't reached Owen Porter yet, it would soon.

"I've heard this horse is a descendant of Byerley Turk," said the young dandy who was admiring the steed when Sin stepped outside.

Sin patted the steed's sleek neck. "Yes, he is."

"Owen Porter has been expecting the arrival of a horse like this one."

"Has he?"

"From all Owen's lengthy description, the animal could be your horse's blood brother."

"Then perhaps Porter and I will have to race the two of them." Sin swung onto Turk's back and reined away. "It should be an interesting challenge if his horse is equal to mine."

Sin trotted off, confident that Porter would get wind of the information Sin wanted him to have. He predicted his enemy would turn up one day soon to accuse him of stealing the horse that had been shipped from the Orient.

That should prove to be an interesting encounter.

Despite his vow to avoid the meadow where a green-eyed spirit appeared at dusk to tempt a man, Sin found himself on that very spot, hoping . . . he muttered at his ridiculous preoccupation. His plans did not include the complications and distractions of romantic encounters, especially because of the arrangements Sin had in mind for Charles Sheridan's daughter. But still . . .

Sin glanced sideways when he heard the familiar sound of pounding hooves and saw a mane of red-gold hair catching flame in the sunset. It was as if some invisible attraction kept pulling them together like a magnet to metal.

Entranced, Sin watched the long-legged gelding race the wind, responding to its rider's skillful commands. He knew the instant she noticed him beside the clump of pines. Their gazes locked from across the meadow and anticipation rippled through Sin as she trotted toward him.

Sin swung to the ground to tether Turk. "I thought you weren't coming back."

"I thought you weren't, either," Angelene replied.

Sin made no move to assist her from the saddle. If he touched her, no matter how innocent the gesture, he wasn't sure he could stop.

"Did you come to escape unwanted confinement again?" he asked, watching her fiddle with the roan's bridle.

Angelene flicked him a quick glance. "No."

Sin came as close as he dared—just beyond arm's

reach. "Then it must be my sparkling sense of humor and engaging charm that brought you back when you vowed not to come."

Angelene smiled airily. "And, of course, it was my even-tempered disposition that brought you back."

Despite better judgment, Sin moved a step closer and found himself trapped in the alluring aura that surrounded this mysterious beauty. Before he realized it, he was sketching her features with his forefinger, marveling at the texture of her skin.

"I'm beginning to think we are both grand liars. I have no sense of humor, and your disposition is anything but even . . ."

Sin felt her shiver beneath his caressing touch, saw her lips part on a sigh. He inwardly groaned when answering heat surged through his body.

"Sin?" Her voice quavered.

"What, elf?" So did his.

Angelene retreated a step and turned away. "Have you ever felt as if you were held prisoner inside your own body, as if the world's perception of you was anything but what you really were? Deep down inside, have you ever wondered why you felt the driving need to be free?"

The question provoked the glimmer of a smile. "Quite often, about this time of night," he admitted. "It's rather like your skin doesn't fit, and squirming out of it seems the natural thing to do."

Angelene spun around to peer into his craggy features. "That's how I feel when I'm with you. Does that shock you?"

No, Sin thought. Shocked wasn't what he was feeling. Aroused was a more accurate description of the throbbing warmth that coiled in essential parts of his male anatomy. There was a strong biological attraction at work here, one he would be a fool to ignore . . . and wise to avoid.

Sin peered down into that enchanting face and shimmering green eyes. He was starving to death for another taste of these dewy lips. Instinctively, he bent to take her mouth under his, and drink his fill of heaven's sweetest nectar. And when he satisfied this impossible craving he would do the sensible thing and back away, reminding himself why he had put down roots in Natchez.

Perhaps in a few months, when the furor he ignited died down, he could properly court this beguiling beauty, but not now. She could become the innocent victim, just as Sin had once been. And he of all people knew how bitterness could poison the mind. He didn't want to suffer the brunt of this particular woman's anger; he would much prefer to experience a more satisfying pleasure . . .

Sin muffled an unholy groan when her slender arms glided over his shoulders and he felt her tongue fence experimentally with his. Whether on purpose or by feminine instinct, she moved against him, and Sin instantly responded to the combustible spark that flared between them. His hands drifted down her ribcage, settling on her hips. He pressed her into the hard cradle of his thighs, leaving no doubt about how ardently she affected him.

His exploring fingertips glided to the small indentation of her waist and then lifted to swirl over the full swell of her breasts. His thumbs brushed the fabric that concealed the taut peaks and she arched into his hands in a sensuous gesture that nearly brought him to his knees.

Sin knew he was making a mistake, even as he made it, but nothing short of a bullet between his eyes could have restrained him from savoring her, memorizing each luscious curve and swell. He wanted to feed the fire that could easily rage out of control.

Angelene broke the kiss long before Sin felt the need to come up for air. He had learned to hold his breath for extended periods while diving for pearls. He could have lasted another minute without air—maybe two, if kissing her became as vital as breathing, and it felt as if it already had.

"I'll probably live to regret this," Angelene whispered shakily.

"Sin?"

"Hum?" It was the best he could do. His vocal apparatus was tied in a knot to match the tormenting coil below his belt—or sash.

"Do you care who I am at the moment?"

The abrupt question threw him mentally off balance. When she tilted her head up to compensate for the differences in their height, he inwardly groaned at the sight of kiss-swollen lips and eyes shining with passion.

"What I need to know is would any woman do—?"

The crackling of twigs caused Sin to spin about. His foot hooked on the curve of his discarded cane. He quickly jerked up the crutch to clamp it in his hand. Although deepening shadows had settled into the cedar trees, Sin detected lurking figures.

He stepped behind a tree and protectively tucked Angelene behind him, but the shadows leaped out from different directions at once. Sin found himself staring down the barrels of two pistols, both of which were aimed at his chest.

"Out enjoyin' yerself with a bit o' fluff, are ya?" Chester Wiffle taunted. "Well, friend, hate to be the one to spoil yer fun, but you've got a date with the devil. I s'pect the lass will appreciate that, by the by."

Jonathan Stanley gestured with his weapon. "Send the lady on her way, gent. Our bus'ness be with you."

Sin cursed up one masthead and down the other for being so totally distracted. He knew Jerome Kimball had his ways of disposing of rivals who cut into hotel profits. Sin had the inescapable feeling Jerome had arranged for him to have a nasty accident before the grand opening of South Sea Paradise.

Sin gave Angelene a nudge. "I think you better leave."

"I'm not going anywhere," she insisted, stepping up beside him.

Sin admired her spunk—but not now. "Go back to your horse."

Angelene heard that frosty pitch in a voice that was barely more than a whisper, but she didn't budge from her spot.

Damn, daring female, Sin scowled to himself. She wouldn't be feeling so courageous when she got that lovely head of hers blown off by a stray bullet.

Sin forced himself to think rationally, to ignore the daredevil female beside him and concentrate on his would-be assassins. "I'm sure your employer has paid you handsomely to take a few inches off my hide, but I will pay you twice the fee to walk away without looking back."

Chester Wiffle chuckled beneath his mask that concealed his identity. "Sounds like a fair trade to me, Sinclair. But we was told to bring back that fancy walkin' stick of yers as proof. Our boss might come lookin' for us a mite too soon if we don't give it to him. A bit impatient and temperamental he is. Me and my friend got to have time to pack before we leave town if we double-cross the boss. Don't want him breathin' down our necks before we're good and gone, ya know."

Sin expected these two scavengers intended to collect their fees coming and going. He seriously doubted he would be allowed to survive, even after he handed over the cash he promised.

"Now is the time for you to make yourself scarce, elf," Sin insisted a second time.

"If I turn away, I expect it will be the last time I see you alive. The odds aren't in your favor," she told him. "Therefore, I will not leave and that is that."

Sin cursed silently and kept his gaze pinned on the two men, who inched closer.

"Ye'r makin' this difficult, lass," Chester grumbled. "We've got no fight with you. Our business is with Sinclair. You run along now. We ain't gonna lay a hand on him."

And alligators fly, she thought to herself. Angelene wasn't entirely stupid. These scalawags wanted Sin's money and that of their employers. Sin would be lucky if he only wound up with a couple of bullet holes in his chest.

Sin slowly lifted his hands, allowing the cane to dangle from his fingertips, indicating that he was unarmed. "If you have no objection, I'll retrieve my money pouch and our business will be concluded."

With deliberate care, Sin fished into the pocket of his breeches, purposely jingling the poke of coins. "It's all yours, friends. There is far more here than what your tight-fisted boss would have paid you."

He tossed the pouch to Chester and kept his eyes trained on both men, waiting for the opportunity to pounce.

"And now the cane," Chester demanded. "Hand it over nice and easy, Sinclair."

Sin extended the blunt end of the cane toward Chester and darted a discreet glance at Jonathan. "Have a care with that cane. I've grown partial to it—"

Chester heard the click, but what was happening didn't register until he felt the prick and thrust of the retractable dagger stabbing into his belly—twice. Before he could squeeze the trigger of his pistol, the fist that was knotted around the curved end of the crutch slammed into his jaw. A furious curse tumbled from Chester's lips as he reeled and fired.

Angelene sprang into action when she saw Sin level the punishing blow to Chester's chin. She picked up a fallen branch and swung wildly, knocking Chester's pistol aside, misdirecting the bullet intended for Sin's chest. Angelene shrieked and instinctively ducked when she heard the bullet whizz past her head.

Jonathan Stanley panicked when his companion's knees buckled and blood soaked the front of his shirt. Wild-eyed, Jonathan leveled his pistol at Sinclair. But before Jonathan could get off a shot, the crook of the cane hooked around his elbow, spinning him sideways. A jarring hatchet blow, delivered with the side of Sin's hand, landed on the vulnerable spot between Jonathan's neck and shoulder, numbing his arm. The pistol dropped from his useless fingers. His terrified gaze focused on that penetrating stare that promised death—and delivered it.

The retractable dagger Pearly Graham had installed in the end of Sin's cane slashed an X across Jonathan's chest and then plunged deeply. Jonathan pitched forward on the grass, lifeless.

When Jonathan keeled over and Chester gurgled a curse to Sin's name, Angelene staggered back, inhaling panting breaths. The fallen branch she had snatched up to club Chester dropped from her trembling hand. The scent of death nearly gagged her and she wheeled away while Sin retrieved his money pouch with a nonchalance that indicated he had dealt with similar situations— plenty of times.

Sin reached down to retrieve Chester's flintlock. His hand was shaking, for God's sake! He inhaled a steadying breath, battling the frustration, fury and . . . fright . . .

Sin couldn't remember being frightened in the last eighteen years. He had known complete terror then, and nothing had scared him since . . . until tonight. It was all because of this daring female who had nearly gotten her head blown off trying to fight a battle that was none of her concern. She had made him feel vulnerable, knowing he had to be twice as competent as usual to protect both of them.

In all the years Sin had sailed the seas, battling blood-thirsty buccaneers and devastating storms, he had been assisted by competent sailors. When he issued a command the crew knew it was imperative to obey without question. This foolhardy blonde had defied him . . . and that was why he was so furious!

Damn it. She had almost gotten herself killed trying to protect him. Didn't he have enough bitterness simmering inside him without facing the prospect of having her death on his conscience?

The thought provoked Sin to wheel around. His glittering gaze landed on Angelene, who had sagged against a tree for support. Sin felt the cables attached to his temper snap like riggings in a stiff gale.

"Do not ever disobey me again!" Sin yelled at her. He was stunned by his inability to keep his voice down. That hadn't happened since he couldn't remember when. He was mad as hell and he didn't care who knew it.

Angelene gulped for breath and jerked up her head, only to catch a glimpse of the bandits' lifeless forms. "I was only trying to help—" She swallowed the foul tasting lump that gathered in her throat.

"You were trying to get yourself killed for no purpose other than the fact that you don't have the sense to get out while the getting's good!" Sin snarled at her. "Where I come from, two to one odds is considered a fair fight and self-defense is a way of life. I didn't need your help, and when I give you an order I expect it to be carried out immediately!"

When Sin's blistering remark hit sensitive nerves, Angelene pushed way from the tree to confront him. "Leave it to a man to be all soft whispers when he wants something from a woman," she hissed at him. "I should have known infuriating male domination would eventually rise to the surface."

She inhaled a deep breath and glared at him. "Obey without question? I have no sense?" she repeated bitterly. "I thought you were different from other men, but you're the same. You believe women shouldn't think or act for themselves, that we should follow your orders. Like hell!

"And furthermore, you've answered the question I asked before we were interrupted. I am nothing more to you than just a body you considered using for your selfish pleasures. You only wanted me to appease your lusty appetite. The minute you closed those pit-black eyes I became a faceless figure who could have been anyone. Isn't that right?"

Green eyes clashed with smoldering black. Sin was still mad as the devil for succumbing to the physical needs that had distracted him so he had been unaware of danger until it closed in on him.

"Isn't that right?" Angelene spewed at him.

"That's right," he lashed out at her. "Now get on your horse and don't look back. I'll deal with this matter without dragging your name into it."

Her chin elevated a notch higher. "You don't even know my name, but then what does it matter to you or any other man? I should consider myself fortunate that we were interrupted before I found myself on my back. I should have known better than to put faith in anyone wearing breeches. You men are all alike!"

After she wheeled around and stormed off, Sin dragged in a purifying breath of air and slowly exhaled. He made no attempt to chase her down or call her back. Better that he and that green-eyed elf part on a sour note. She was becoming an influence that he could ill afford.

Jerome Kimball had already reacted to the threat of fierce competition. Sin wasn't surprised; he was simply put out that he had handled the situation—and the young woman who thundered off—so poorly.

No doubt, Owen Porter would soon be gunning for him. And Charles Sheridan would revert to his old ways when his most precious treasure was threatened. Another distraction like this one and Sin might not live long enough to satisfy his long-held vendetta.

Forcing himself to concentrate on the mental and emotional discipline that had become his trademark, Sin ignored the inner turmoil gnawing at him. He strode off to retrieve Turk and dispose of the would-be killers who had found themselves at the sharp end of Sin's retractable dagger.

Sin had heard it said that the bogs and swamps around Natchez were thick with uncounted hundreds of highwaymen and innocent victims who had met bad ends. Skeletons were washed up from shallow graves. Travelers who spotted the nameless corpses looked the other way. No one bothered with floating bodies. Natchezians chose to shrug them off, assuming that someone had caused too much trouble once too often and had been quieted—permanently. There was little curiosity about murder in these parts.

No doubt Sin would have been dragged off to the soupy bogs if Kimball's henchmen had accomplished their dastardly deed. Jerome Kimball was going to be furious to learn his scheme had foundered.

The more furious Jerome became, the better Sin was going to like it. It would compensate for the frustration that was eating Sin alive. Every time he remembered how close that daring female had come to getting her head separated from her shoulders he felt like cursing!

# *Nine*

Owen Porter swore under his breath and stamped to the stables to mount one of his prize steeds. His gray-blond hair whipped in the wind as he raced off to Raven's Hill. Or rather to *Devil's Landing,* as he had been referring to it after hearing the gossip about the cloaked stranger who prowled the hillside at dusk.

When Owen heard Sinclair had been giving Jerome Kimball fits with the new hotel and restaurant, he had shrugged off Jerome's grumbling and turned his attention to training his horses for the races at Pharsalia. But Owen was beginning to understand why Jerome was outraged with Sinclair. Not even a week after Jerome began complaining about losing his best employees and several of his most sought-after courtesans, Owen had received the resignation of his best horse trainers and jockeys. Sinclair's assistant had hired Owen's valued grooms right off his prize horses. The nerve of the man!

But to make matters infuriatingly worse, Owen had heard from reputable sources that Sinclair had been seen gadding about town on the prize stallion Owen had arranged to have delivered to his estate. He had waited two years for that horse and Sinclair had obviously bought Owen's horse out from under him. He vowed to have his agent's head for this. And Sinclair's, too, while he was at it. Curse the man, how dare he swipe that priceless stallion!

Steel blue eyes flashed as he trotted down Main Street. Owen had no need to travel farther. The descendant of the Byerley Turk was tethered in front of South Sea Paradise Hotel, left standing in the sweltering sun like a plodding nag!

Infuriated, Owen swung from the saddle and appraised the dark bay. The magnificent creature possessed all the qualities of breeding that Owen admired—long, powerful legs, broad chest, sloping croup and proud, straight shoulders. The animal was said to have the same color and exact markings of the original bloodline. Now, this valuable steed had been purchased by the bastard named Sinclair. The man had arrived in town, flaunting a fortune from a questionable source, and attempting to establish himself as not only a hotel entrepreneur but a horse breeder.

Owen swore foully. This priceless package of horseflesh should have been pampered and enclosed in a padded stall, sipping water from a marble trough and munching on hay and grain rations. Instead, the Turk was baking in the sun like a damned clam. It was outrageous!

Turning around, Owen stalked inside the hotel lobby. He flagrantly ignored the posted sign that declared only hotel staff was allowed. Nobody told Owen Porter where he could go and where he couldn't.

Owen pulled up short, his blue eyes wide in disbelief. He studied the exotic decor that provided an intriguing South Seas atmosphere. No wonder Jerome Kimball was fit to be roped and tied. Walking into this hotel was like washing ashore on a paradise island. Seashells, polished treasure chests, starfish and colorful nets, displaying effigies of fish molded in brass and copper, were everywhere. The damned place even smelled like the sea. Owen should know. He had been there once upon a time . . .

Owen stifled the thought and glanced around. Jerome was in serious trouble, Owen decided. This unique hotel would draw patrons like swarms of mosquitoes. The gentry of Natchez would become the victims of their own curiosity and their craving for romantic adventure. They would come, Owen grimly predicted, if only to say they had been to South Sea Paradise.

As for Owen, he was in danger of losing his position as the reigning king of Pharsalia Race Track. His best stablemen were now in Sinclair's employ. It would take weeks to acquire other trainers and jockeys to replace the ones he had lost.

"Someone had better point me in Nick Sinclair's direction and they had best do it now!" Owen bellowed.


Sin stared down at his nemesis from the flight of stairs. Bottled resentment knotted inside him as he studied the wiry, blustering aristocrat who was in his mid-forties. The blond hair Sin remembered was now flecked with gray. The weather-beaten face had been pampered over the years. The blue eyes were the same though—a little older but every bit as cold as Sin remembered.

Owen Porter had made his melodramatic entrance, looking mad enough to spit horseshoe nails. The riding quirt clamped in his whitened fist slapped against the tiled floor like a striking snake. The employees who had been buzzing around tending to their tasks halted in their tracks when Owen snarled at them.

All eyes lifted toward the staircase when the click of Sin's boots announced his arrival. Sin cast a discreet glance toward the doorway of the restaurant, where Cyrus Duncan and Hiram Brodie had propped themselves to observe the encounter. There was an ever-present smile of mischief upon Cyrus's tanned face and a look of wry anticipation stamped on Hiram's angular features. Both men knew about Jerome Kimball's visit. Now both men were anxious to see how Sin would handle this newest visitor.

"What did Sin buy out from under this chap?" Cyrus questioned quietly.

"That remarkable specimen of horseflesh called Turk, plus several trainers and jockeys," Hiram whispered back as he shoved his drooping spectacles in place. "This should be interesting."

Cyrus nodded his sandy blond head and grinned. "Sin appears to enjoy collectin' enemies. Certainly has made sport of it of late, hasn't he? I'd love to know who will be next to come stormin' in here like a hurricane."

Hiram had a pretty good idea who would be arriving on their doorsteps. Sheridan was the last name on the mysterious list of men he had investigated. Hiram hated to speculate on what Sin had in mind for Sheridan's most precious possession.

Owen Porter frowned as he watched the swarthy rogue descend the steps, leaning lightly on his pearl-handled cane. There was something faintly familiar about that face, and yet Owen was certain he had never met this muscular giant who towered over him with casual menace.

"You wish to see me?" Sin's tone of voice was so carelessly indifferent that it made Owen's blustering demand sound foolish.

"I hear you own that prize specimen that is standing outside the door," Owen growled.

"You heard correctly."

Owen erupted like a spouting whale. "That stallion is supposed to belong to me! I have waited two years for that horse to be shipped from the Orient."

Sin crossed his arms over his chest and watched Owen paw the tiles like a mad bull. His riding quirt popped and crackled in barely restrained anger.

"And furthermore," Owen fumed when Sin made no comment, "I want my trainers and jockeys back."

Sin rocked back on his heels, pretending to ponder the demand. "I'm afraid my new trainers and jockeys are content where they are. As a matter of fact, my plantation overseer and stable manager said so this morning." His gaze darted to Cyrus. "Am I not correct, Mr. Duncan?"

"Aye, the blokes are as happy as pearls in their oysters," Cyrus confirmed with an ornery grin.

Owen looked down his nose at the tall, lanky blond whose Australian accent rattled with amusement. Owen was not the least bit amused. His flashing blue eyes narrowed on Sin.

"And what did you promise my hired help to lure them away from me?"

Sin's broad shoulders lifted in a lackadaisical shrug. "Nothing earth-shaking, only what every competent and loyal employee deserves. My plantation and stable manager gave them shorter hours and better wages. Men need to pursue pleasurable pastimes, after all. Can't have them working their fingers to the bone, 'round the clock."

Owen jerked up his head and glowered. "Is that what they claim? That I worked them day and night?"

"Did you?" Sin raised a dark brow. "No wonder they were so anxious to change employment."

"I did not—" Owen slammed his mouth shut when he realized his voice was crashing off the walls and booming in his own ears. "I . . . want . . . my . . . horse," he growled, slowly and succinctly.

"I'm sure we can come to a satisfactory arrangement," Sin said reasonably.

Owen's rigid shoulders relaxed. "Glad to hear you plan to do the honorable thing, Sinclair."

Honorable? Sin silently scoffed. Owen Porter didn't have an honorable bone in his body.

When Owen pulled the money belt from beneath his riding jacket, Sin stared at the bank notes extended to him. "I'm afraid I have become immensely fond of Turk. I couldn't think of selling him for less than three times what I paid for him."

"Three—" Owen's breath clogged in his gullet and he crowed like a plucked rooster. "Why, that's highway robbery!"

"You're right. Much too cheap for such a fine specimen. Four times the original cost will suffice."

"You sneaky son of a bitch—" Owen was in such a fit of rage that he hadn't realized he had lashed out with his quirt until the whip snapped against the scar on Sin's cheek.

A leaf could have dropped to the floor and it would

have sounded like a crashing anchor. Nobody moved. No one dared to breathe.

Sin watched apprehension claim Owen's doughy face. He wondered if this hotheaded bastard remembered delivering a similar blow eighteen years ago with the sharp side of his cutlass. Sin remembered all too well.

"If you ever lay a hand on me again, you'll find yourself buried on your favorite mount, outfitted for a ride to hell."

Hiram grimaced at the deadly soft tone. Owen had received his first and last warning.

"I will have my horse at a fair price," Owen snarled threateningly.

"I think not. Your behavior indicates you have an uncontrollable temper. I have decided not to sell Turk, especially not to an abusive man who probably takes a quirt to a horse as quickly as he takes it to a man."

"That horse belongs in a stall, not hitched outside alongside those nags!" Owen blustered.

"Turk didn't mind standing out in the rain last week. I doubt he minds today's sunshine."

"You left that priceless creature out in the rain?" Owen howled in disbelief. "You are mad."

"No," Sin calmly countered. "I believe you are the one who is mad, Mr. Porter—striking mad, in fact. I hope word of your tantrum doesn't reach the ears of your peers. Why, they might begin to wonder if you are really the blueblooded gentleman you have passed yourself off as being."

Owen recoiled as if he had been slapped across the cheek. His quirt shot upward in reflexive retaliation, but he regained control of his temper before he made the mistake of striking Sin twice.

Obsidian eyes glittered down on Owen, though his expression gave nothing away. Owen felt an unnerving chill slither down his spine. There was a ruthlessness about Sinclair that went bone-deep. It was not so much the way Sin looked that could thoroughly intimidate; it was that almost tangible aura about him, a coldness resembling a blast of polar air. Owen was beginning to think this rascal wouldn't cower from the devil himself. Sinclair had dared to take on two of the most influential men in Natchez and now Owen Porter and Jerome Kimball were left looking like irate fools.

"Fascinating, isn't it, Mr. Porter, what a man will do when his most valued possessions are threatened and stripped away from him?"

Owen watched Sin walk off, dismissing him as if he were no more important than the lowliest of servants. Scowling, Owen turned on his heel and stalked out. His horses and his stables were being threatened by this rapscallion, and Owen fully intended to put a stop to Sinclair, one way or another. No doubt, Jerome Kimball shared Owen's need for retaliation. Between the two of them, they would find a way to deal with unwanted competition.


Hiram stared bleakly at Cyrus after Owen stormed off like a misdirected cyclone. "Two down and one to go."

"There'll be more fireworks?" Cyrus questioned. "Sure would like to know what this is all about. Never seen Cap'n on such a relentless campaign to collect enemies."

"These men made a powerful enemy in Sinclair. Whatever they did must have been unforgivable."

"Aye." Cyrus nodded pensively. "Owen Porter is damned lucky his head didn't roll when he popped his whip."

When Sin ambled outside, Hiram followed in his wake. Cyrus joined both men at the door to watch Owen trot his mount toward Kimball Hotel.

"Kimball and Porter are likely to join forces," Hiram predicted.

"They're good at that," Sin murmured, lost to anguishing memories. "I expect more riffraff will be lying in wait for all of us after Owen and Jerome put their heads together."

*"More riffraff?"* Cyrus repeated. "You mean you've already encountered trouble?"

Sin nodded gravely. "Jerome lost both of his henchmen after our encounter a few nights ago."

"What the bloody blazes is this all about?" Cyrus demanded to know.

"It's about paying dearly and losing what you love most," Sin said cryptically before he mounted Turk and rode away.

Puzzled, Hiram and Cyrus stared at each other, wondering exactly what Sin meant.

# *Ten*

Pearly Graham glanced up from the table inside his cottage that was buried deep in a clump of oaks below Raven's Hill. The sparkling jewel he held between his fingertips escaped him, dancing across the marble table-top like the pattering of miniature feet.

"Blow me down," Pearly murmured. His aging eyes focused on the red welt that slashed across Sin's scarred cheek. "Don't seem right to take a beatin' on the same spot twice. Who's the cur who did that?"

Sin strode into the cottage that had been decorated like a cabin on a schooner. He plopped down at the table to study the necklace Pearly was stringing. Picking up the loose gem that had escaped Pearly's grasp, he handed it back to him.

"Well, boy?" Pearly demanded impatiently. "Who left another mark on ya?"

"The same man who left the first."

Pearly eased back in his chair and stretched his pegleg out in front of him, tapping it against the floor. The sound caused the colorful parrot called Fiddler to chirp and jabber while he sat on his perch.

"Makes it hard for a man to forget the thing he'd least like to remember, don't it? Ain't likely I'll ever forget the bastard who took the best dancin' leg I had, either—may he burn in hell."

Sin glanced down from the chattering parrot to the wooden appendage that was fastened around Pearly's kneecap. As Sin recalled, that pegleg hadn't slowed this salty sea dog down much. Persistence was something Sin had learned from this gray-haired old man who had pulled him from the sea when others on board would have just as soon left Sin to sink to Fiddler's Green.

It was Pearly who had taken that young, disillusioned boy under his wing to protect him from the scalawags on board the privateer. Pearly had encouraged Sin to fight to survive after swallowing half the water in the gulf, so he could repay the men who had left him to die. And it was Pearly who knew the terrifying ordeal Sin had endured, knew the reason Sin had come to Natchez.

This wise, worldly old sailor, who had reached his sixty-fifth year, was the one man alive who understood Sin's obsession for revenge. Pearly had soothed a young boy from his haunting nightmares and he was the closest thing to family Sin had left. What Sin knew of the sea, of life and of men—Pearly had taught him.

Pearly picked up a perfectly shaped black pearl and held it up to the light. With deft fingers he pushed the string through the hole he had drilled in the center of the gem. "I bet you've got those two young friends of yers skimmin' waves, wonderin' what ye'r up to," he mused aloud.

Sin made a muted sound that could have meant anything or nothing.

"Oughta tell Brodie and Duncan," Pearly advised. "You'll have 'em thinkin' ya walked off yer plank and dropped in the deep end if ya don't." When Sin responded with nothing but a shrug, Pearly studied him through pale green eyes. "Duncan and Brodie have followed in yer wake all 'round the world and back. Loyal as two pups, they are. Tell 'em the truth."

Pearly heaved an audible sigh when Sin simply stared at the wall, locked in his own thoughts. The old sailor went back to stringing the necklace and changed the subject. "You got those sons-a-bitches running scared yet?"

"Running mad," Sin corrected. "Except for Sheridan. I intend to deal with him very soon."

Pearly nodded his fuzzy gray head and scooped up another pearl. "Eye for an eye, I always said, especially when a man makes his fortune off another man's tragedy. Blood money, it was, every red cent of it. Those rascals got it comin', even if ye'r lettin' Duncan and Brodie think the tar is peelin' off yer hull." His gaze darted to Sin. "Still think ya oughta tell 'em. Or maybe you'd prefer I do it—"

"No," Sin cut in. "I don't want their pity. I only want revenge."

"Hell, Duncan and Brodie won't offer pity when they learn those mutineers killed yer brother and left ya for dead in the middle of the sea. They'll be fightin' mad, ready to lend a hand.

"You had yer inheritance stripped away by those greedy bastards. Now they're livin' off money that's rightfully yers, pretendin' to be upstandin' citizens. Don't ya think Duncan and Brodie would want to help ya get even for that?"

Sin grimaced when Pearly put words to the thoughts and memories that Sin preferred not to discuss.

"I'd be out there helpin' ya myself if I could get around as well as I used to in my prime, even with this stump leg. You lost the one person ya loved most. And for what? So four men could take the booty and make new starts? They sure as hell deserve what they've got comin'. They deserve to know how it feels to lose what they value most and not be able to do a damned thing about it."

When Pearly scooped up another pearl and slid it on the string, Sin renewed his vow of revenge. He had allowed himself to become distracted by a woman. She had intrigued him and tempted him to pursue the fantasy that had begun to monopolize his dreams. Unfortunately, that spirited beauty had crossed his path at the worst of all possible times. If Sin had met her six months from now, a year . . .

Pearly eyed Sin perceptively. "Somethin's botherin' ya, lad, what is it?"

Sin handed the old sailor another black pearl. "Nothing. I'm merely impatient to see Kimball, Porter and Sheridan stewing in their own juice. As of yet, they don't remember who I am, nor can they fathom why I've targeted them."

"They'll puzzle it out eventually. If they don't, you can toss a grenade in their laps and startle the hell out of 'em." He grinned broadly, exposing the gap between his front teeth. "You might try droppin' a few subtle hints to jar their memories and rattle their consciences—if they've got 'em."

When Sin stared straight through the parrot that was jabbering and prancing on his perch, Pearly frowned. "You've got somethin' on yer mind. I can tell by lookin' at ya, so don't bother denyin' it. What's troublin' ya?" he persisted.

Sin heaved a sigh. Pearly knew him too well. "I met someone," he reluctantly admitted, watching Fiddler fluff his feathers and crane his neck around to his back.

"Did ya now? A lass? Who is she?"

"I don't know. She wouldn't say."

Pearly chuckled in amusement. "Don't tell me ya introduced yerselves without exchangin' names."

Sin flicked the smirking mariner a quick glance. "It isn't what you're thinking, Pearly."

"No?"

"No," Sin confirmed. "She's different from most women, but the timing is all wrong since I have specific plans for Charles Sheridan's daughter."

Pearly nodded in understanding. "Ya can't pursue promisin' possibilities at the moment. A real shame that, lad. You could use a little spark in yer life. But maybe after ya settle yer old scores with—"

The quiet rap at the door had Pearly scrambling to collect the scattered pearls. He stuffed them in a leather poke and dropped them in the cabinet drawer. A smile of anticipation settled on his wrinkled features when Agnes Ralston appeared with a tray of food. Pearly licked his lips as the appetizing aroma wafted across the room.

"I don't know where ya found this culinary angel, but she cooks divinely. Best food I ever ate. Every time I sink my teeth into her fluffy biscuits I swear I died and took a chariot ride to heaven."

The cook, whose plump body testified to her culinary talents, beamed with delight. She set the heaping tray in front of Pearly, who showered her with effusive flattery.

"Sneaky ole sea dog. You sing my praises, just to ensure heaping plates."

Pearly eyed the steaming food and flashed the cook a mischievous grin. "Appears to be workin', I'd say, Agnes. If you keep feedin' me like royalty, I'll have to carve out a wider stump to hold this broad body up."

Sin listened in quiet amusement while Agnes and Pearly exchanged playful banter. If he didn't know better he would swear the confirmed bachelor was weakening a bit. Pearly perked up like a watered plant each time Agnes trooped out of the kitchen to personally deliver his meals. Sin suspected Pearly had declined to eat with the rest of the men, just to receive Agnes's private attention. The cook was always late retiring to the house, he recalled. A friendship—or something—was blossoming between them.

Taking his cue, Sin exited, leaving Pearly to spin another fascinating yarn about his adventures on the high seas. For Agnes, who apparently had spent most of her fifty-odd years behind the handle of a skillet, the tales Pearly could tell were intriguing. Of course, Sin didn't need to hear them. He had lived them.

But those days were behind him now, Sin reminded himself as he strode down to the cove to check on his pet project. But Pearly's insistent words came back to him and Sin frowned meditatively. He supposed the old man was right. Perhaps it was time for Cyrus and Hiram to hear the bleak account, Sin mused as he tugged on the rope attached to the cage that held freshwater mollusks. He checked the shells for moss and then lowered the cages back into the cove.

Sin had developed a fascination with transplanting

small pearls into mollusks after seeing the procedure practiced in the Far East. The pearlers of South China had invented the art of seeding oysters and mollusks to help Mother Nature produce a larger supply of priceless gems.

Since Sin could no longer make dives in the tropics to pluck up the oysters' treasures, he had set up his own seed bed in the coves. Tending the shells had a calming effect on him, allowed him time alone to plot his next move.

His next target was Charles Sheridan, if the man and his daughter would ever show up at the parties Sin attended. Another week had gone by and he had yet to meet the supposed Jewel of Natchez.

Sin smiled wistfully. He imagined Angelene Sheridan was appreciated more for the staggering fortune she would inherit than for her good looks. Angelene was undoubtedly a spoiled, pampered, fickle little chit who expected men to bow and scrape over her and come running when she crooked her finger. Sin doubted anyone could match the captivating beauty and spirit of the green-eyed elf he had met at the meadow near Raven's Hill . . .

Forcefully, Sin tucked those memories in the corner of his mind. He had sent that daring female away with harsh words and he didn't expect to see her again anytime soon. There was no future in it, he reminded himself sensibly. Sin needed to focus his attention on Angelene Sheridan. The "Jewel's" reputation was about to be tarnished, provoking her doting father to come storming after Sin. That was only the first phase of the man's personal torment, Sin vowed as he peeled off his clothes to take a swim. Porter, Sheridan and Kimball were going to be treated to several phases of torture before Sin launched them into hell where they belonged.

Owen Porter was still fuming when he tracked Jerome Kimball down. Jerome had been on the upper floor of his hotel, indisposed, and Owen had been forced to wait in the lobby until Jerome made his appearance an hour later. When Jerome closed the door to his office to grant them privacy, Owen dropped into a chair and expelled a frustrated breath.

"We have got to do something about Sinclair."

Jerome frowned warily. "Is that nuisance still among us? I had heard that he had an unfortunate accident." Or at least Sinclair was supposed to have had. Jerome had made his instructions glaringly clear and he was expecting a visit from Wiffle and Stanley shortly after dark.

"Accident?" Owen snorted. "You were fed erroneous gossip. I clashed with Sinclair an hour ago. He was in perfectly good health, damn the luck."

Jerome gnashed his teeth. His hazel eyes flashed angrily. Those muttonheads he had hired must have taken his money and run off to parts unknown. He had agreed to pay his henchmen half the amount he had promised before the deed was done and the remaining balance when they returned with that pearl-handled cane. Next time he dealt with undependable cutthroats there would be no cash exchanged until there was a body as proof!

"I take it you are at cross purposes with Sinclair, too. What's he done to rile you, Owen?"

Owen was out of his chair in a flash, pacing the imported Aubusson carpet. "He somehow managed to persuade my agent in New Orleans to sell him the stallion I ordered from the Orient. To add insult to injury, Sinclair hired away my best trainers and jockeys!"

Jerome's gaze narrowed pensively. "That sounds suspiciously like the tactic he used on me."

"Exactly like it," Owen grumbled. "It's as if he's singled us out and decided to hit us where we hurt the most." He turned around and paced in the opposite direction. "I swear there is something vaguely familiar about that man, but damned if I can recall where we've met. How could he have known my penchant for horse breeding and racing?"

Jerome had been struck by the same nagging sensation when he'd confronted Sinclair. Like Owen, he had racked his brain to make some logical connection and had come up empty-handed. "Why would a mysterious stranger who came from out of nowhere target me as his competition?" he mused aloud for the hundredth time. "It's almost as if Sinclair is taunting me, daring me to retaliate."

"The same with me," Owen muttered. "Unfortunately, I gave in to temptation in front of Sinclair's employees at the hotel. I struck him with my quirt in a burst of temper after he announced he would sell my horse to me for four times the price I had agreed to pay. And how he knew what I had planned to pay I have no idea."

"There is definitely something disturbing about Sinclair," Jerome declared. "I have had to increase the salary of my hotel employees to prevent losing the rest of them. He's cutting into my profit and he hasn't even had his grand opening yet."

Owen stopped pacing and braced his hands on the oak desk. "We've got to act, Jerome."

Jerome eased back in his chair, studying Owen speculatively. "Are you suggesting something drastic?"

Owen's blue eyes glittered and his lips curled. "I will not have my name wagging on gossiping tongues and I refuse to become the laughingstock at Pharsalia Track. If word gets out that I lost my prize horse and my grooms, the competition on the tracks might decide to use the same tactics to steal the trainers I hire next. The going rates I charge to sell my halter-broke colts will drop. Sinclair's effect on me could become wide-flung. He could conceivably ruin my name in the horse-breeding and the racing world. I won't have it, I tell you!"

Jerome nodded grimly. "I can see that you and I are of the same sentiment. Sinclair has got to go."

"The sooner the better," Owen gruffly affirmed.

"I will make the necessary arrangements and contact you soon."

Owen stared at Jerome. "And I will be willing to pay handsomely to stop that man before he ruins both of us. I got a look at his new hotel today and I don't need to tell you that Sinclair is fierce competition. Curiosity alone will draw clientele and the atmosphere will lure the gentry back again and again."

Jerome winced. "I am aware of the situation. When I have located ample manpower to alleviate our problem, we will discuss the details of when and where."

Owen nodded curtly, spun on his heels and stalked out. Jerome glanced at the window to see darkness settling around him. It looked as if he was going to have to venture Under-the-Hill to gather a strike force. And this time there would be no mistakes, because he and Owen would be lurking in the distance to ensure that the situation was handled—fatally.

# Eleven

Cyrus Duncan poked his head out the carriage window to survey the evergreen arch that led to a driveway illuminated with torches. Wilhelm's palatial home was a blaze of lights, like a welcoming beacon for arriving guests.

"Bloody hell, Sin, this place looks like a gov'nor's mansion. A bit too stuffy for my tastes," he added as he sank back beside Hiram on the seat. "Raven's Hill is more to my likin'. Reminds me of our sailin' days. These pettifoggers probably won't be singin' any sea chants, either, I reckon."

"You reckon right," Hiram insisted. "And don't start spinning some of your raunchy tales about the places we've been and the things we've done, like you did at the Brantleys'. I had to drag you off before you stuck your foot in your mouth."

Cyrus smirked at Hiram, who was fussing with his cravat and straightening the red cummerbund that encircled his waist. "You're turnin' into a regular landlubber, mate."

Hiram jerked up his head, poked his glasses in place with his forefinger and pinned Cyrus to his seat with a hard glare. "When in Rome, *mate* . . ."

"This ain't Rome," Cyrus said playfully. "Been there,

too. And direct from the halls of Montezuma to the shores of Tripoli, so don't go talkin' down to me."

While Hiram and Cyrus badgered each other in their customary manner, Sin sat on his side of the coach, mentally preparing himself for the upcoming ball. He had learned that Kimball and Porter would be in attendance and he had several objectives in mind for tonight. The first order of business was to make Jerome Kimball's assassination attempt public knowledge. The second was to rile Owen Porter's hair-trigger temper every chance he got. Thirdly, if the Sheridans were in attendance, he was going to re-introduce himself to Charles Sheridan and initiate the man's personal form of torment.

Sin intended to do more than make Angelene Sheridan's acquaintance tonight. The Jewel of Natchez would have a blemish on her sterling reputation very soon—the first of many blemishes. Charles Sheridan would rush to defend his precious daughter and Sin would have the man exactly where he wanted him—under his thumb.

Sin had finally heeded Pearly Graham's advice and taken Cyrus and Hiram into his confidence about the incident that had changed his life. Both men had sat on the sofa in the parlor, drinking and listening attentively to the grim tale. Just as Pearly had predicted, Hiram and Cyrus had not plied Sin with unwanted pity. They had declared their loyalty and offered to assist him in spoiling the "good names" and destroying the fortunes the three mutineers had amassed with blood money.

And since that night, Cyrus had begun to take his managerial duties at Raven's Hill more seriously. He vowed to see Owen Porter's colors trampled in the dirt at Pharsalia Race Track. And to link his name to the abusive incident at the hotel, Cyrus had spread the story at the men's club and at every business establishment in town.

Hiram had been busy hiring away even more staff members from Kimball Hotel and promoting the grand opening of South Sea Paradise. Advertising announcements had been ordered and Hiram declared that the posted signs would be hanging in every shop in Natchez and distributed up and down the Mississippi by the end of the week.

Sin's devoted friends had left the matter of Angelene Sheridan to him. Sin fully intended to use the spoiled little chit as a gambit to torment her mutineering father. Angel was going to become Charles's private set of Chinese thumbscrews.

The faintest semblance of a smile touched Sin's lips when a spiteful thought popped to mind. He really should compromise that chit and force her into wedlock. Nothing would infuriate a doting father more than to know his fortune would one day be dropped in the lap of the man who had tarnished his most prized possession, the same man who was hell-bent on having his revenge . . .

A vision of expressive green eyes and animated features flashed across Sin's mind. If he chose that method of torment for Charles, he would spoil any chance of enjoying the company of the saucy young woman he had chanced to meet. Despite his attempt to discard her memory and focus solely on his objective, The Elf kept coming uninvited to his thoughts.

The taste of those petal-soft lips and the feel of her body continued to assail Sin. He was still craving what he had told himself a thousand times he could not have. There could be no reconciliation with the elusive elf if Sin chose to coerce Angelene Sheridan into marriage to spite her father.

No, Sin decided. He was going to stick to his original plan. The ruination of Angelene's reputation would serve as the first phase of his revenge. No sense torturing himself by tying himself to a wife he didn't want, a cold fish who couldn't respond to him.

When the coach rolled to a stop behind the carriages that lined the circle drive, Sin speculated on whether the daring beauty who had come dangerously close to getting her head blown off—on his account—might also be in attendance. He really would like to have a name to attach to that bewitching face, even if she refused to speak to him after he had sent her sailing off in a huff.

Sin stepped down from the landau to survey the throng of elegantly attired guests who filed up the steps. Although Sin and his friends were dressed in the best money could buy, Sin had taken great care to make a distinction between them and the conventional barons of Natchez society. Red cummerbunds, reminiscent of sashes, and long flog black cloaks provided an air of mystery and intrigue. Sin had every intention of being conspicuous. The mystique would lure patrons to his hotel and restaurant, undermining Kimball's profit.

"I still think you should let me rake Owen Porter fore and aft, just for sport," Cyrus declared as he strode beside Sin. "I could provoke that hot-tempered old kangaroo into an argument and deck him, right smack dab in the middle of Wilhelm's ballroom."

"No," Sin declined. "We can't fight our battles the

same way we did at sea. Natchezians are more civilized. But there are ways to go for your enemies' throats without actually cutting the jugular. I intend to leave my mark without drawing a weapon. See that you follow the same procedure.

"My main target tonight is Charles Sheridan," Sin continued. "I do not need fisticuffs. When I allow Kimball, Porter and Sheridan to see the connection, we will be prepared for a joint attack and you can do your worst."

"Good," Cyrus grunted. "I haven't had a good fight since we keelhauled those Caribbean picaroons who tried to sneak aboard the *Siren* while we were docked in Barbados."

"Put away your blunderbuss and mind your manners, Cyrus," Hiram advised. "You'll be mingling with the upper crust of society again. Try to keep that in mind and don't make a fool of yourself."

Cyrus grinned wryly. "I'll bet these bloody blokes put their breeches on the same way I do, aristocracy or not."

"Just guard your tongue, Cyrus," Sin requested as they ambled up the steps to greet their hosts. "I have great expectations for the evening. Scrape the rust off your charm and dazzle the ladies. That was always your forte when you hit port."

Cyrus broke into that devilishly handsome smile that had led him to many a berth behind feminine doorways.

"That's better. And if anything happens tonight, make certain we appear the victims not the culprits of injustice," Sin added. "I prefer to turn society against Kimball, Porter and Sheridan and elevate my standing—at their expense."

"What are you going to do if Sheridan and his daughter aren't in attendance again tonight?" Hiram asked as he adjusted his spectacles.

Sin's eyes glittered as he stared back through time. "I've waited eighteen years. I suppose I can wait a little longer if that proves to be the case."

Hiram and Cyrus pasted on their best smiles and extended their hands to greet their plump host.

"Sinclair and company," Sin announced. "I believe you were given our letters of introduction."

"Sinclair—"

Aubrey Wilhelm's eyes widened in recognition. His daughter Sarah had been spreading the most interesting gossip about this swarthy stranger. Something about Sinclair getting off on the wrong foot with Kimball and Porter, as Aubrey recalled. There were also rumors circulating about the source of Sinclair's fortune, about the silhouette often seen prowling Raven's Hill. The man had proved himself to be a bit mysterious and intriguing.

Aubrey smiled to himself, thinking his social gathering would be the talk of the season. There were almost a hundred guests in attendance, including the newest member of baronial society. It should prove to be a memorable evening.

"You honor us with your presence," Aubrey said, pumping Sinclair's hand. "We have been hearing intriguing news about the grand opening of South Sea Paradise. My wife and daughter had been hounding me to make reservations at your restaurant the minute it opens."

"Consider yourself an honored guest," Sin confirmed. "Your table will be waiting next Saturday evening. We will look forward to your arrival, sir."

Aubrey beamed in delight. Despite Sinclair's, and his

associates', rather unusual attire, the man possessed dip-
lomatic charm. And despite the scar that marred Sinclair's cheek, Aubrey predicted this sinewy giant would
receive considerable feminine attention. Indeed, Sarah
had been aglow with anticipation when she had added
his name to the guest list. Sinclair would make a fine
catch for Aubrey's nineteen-year-old daughter.

Sin found himself staring down at a brunette with daring decolleté. He also noted that Hiram and Cyrus had
perked up immediately when introduced to the eligible
and attractive Sarah Wilhelm.

"Mr. Sinclair," Sarah purred in her most sultry voice.
"I have been hearing a great deal about you. I'm glad
we finally have the chance to meet."

"Call me Sin," he insisted.

Sarah obviously had been groomed to portray the perfect lady. She lowered her sooty lashes and smiled de-
murely. "What a provocative nickname, sir. It sounds
devilishly intriguing." Her violet eyes caught and held
his momentarily, before darting away. "I'm sure our female guests will approve of you, though I doubt their
envious escorts will . . ."

Sarah's voice trailed off when Cyrus Duncan bent at
the waist and pressed a kiss to her wrist. "A pleasure,
m'lady," he murmured charmingly. "Cyrus Duncan at
your service."

Sarah's lashes fluttered like rioting butterflies when
she met Cyrus's winsome smile. "I—"

"So do I," Cyrus whispered rakishly. "In fact—" He
swallowed a pained grunt when Hiram discreetly gouged
him in the ribs.

"Don't proposition the hostess in front of her parents,"

Hiram murmured aside. "You've already got the lady drooling."

Sin finished his last round of how-do-you-dos in the receiving line and strolled into the spacious room to the left of the vestibule. Several muckamucks were playing cards and billiards while others partook freely of Aubrey's stock of wine and liquor. He introduced himself and his associates around the room, keeping a constant lookout for new arrivals. Sin was anxious to see Charles Sheridan and to meet the so-called Jewel of Natchez. He hoped the Sheridans wouldn't disappoint him again by not showing up at this social function.

According to Hiram's information, Angelene Sheridan was a woman of beauty. But then, Sin cynically reminded himself, fortune hunters who frequented the men's clubs and gaming halls—in between their quests for wealthy wives—were blinded by the sparkle of gold coins. Sin wondered if the nickname of "Jewel" had been heaped on Angelene because of her vast wealth, rather than her stunning appearance and endearing personality.

Hiram had learned that Angelene's mother had been from old money in the East and that her parents had willed the fortune to their granddaughter when she wed. Angelene's dowry, plus her grandparents' inheritance, were reason enough to refer to the chit as the jewel of opportunity . . .

Sin's wandering thoughts evaporated when he recognized an older version of the man he had met eighteen years earlier. Burning sensations seared Sin when he saw the last of the three surviving men who had turned a young boy's life into living hell and cast him out on uncertain seas.

Here was the last of the men who had left Sin sailing from port to port with a crew of privateers until he could afford to establish his own trade business in the Far East. Had it not been for Pearly Graham's protection, Sin cringed to think how much worse those first few years might have turned out for him, how bad they were in spite of Pearly running interference between him and the more ruthless members of that crew.

Aye, whatever torment Sheridan, Porter and Kimball suffered at Sin's hands, it couldn't begin to compare to that of an impressionable boy whose older brother had been tossed into the sea and who found himself tumbling after. And nothing, Sin reminded himself with a silent snarl, could compensate for being adrift in a lifeboat with his dead brother until high winds and rising waves threw the craft on beam's end and sent Joshua Montague's remains into inky depths . . .

A cold chill skittered down Sin's spine. He took a large swallow of wine to warm the icy cavern in his chest. For the two days of untold torment he endured, those murdering mutineers would pay dearly!

Sin glanced past Charles Sheridan's red head to see the back of a pudgy female who was poured into a pink satin gown. Sin cringed as he surveyed the pile of carrot-colored hair that was piled up on her narrow head. This was the jewel? If she looked as unappealing from the front as she did from the back, it would require considerable acting ability to pretend enough interest in the twit to charm her.

Hell and damnation, Sin thought as he chugged another drink, Angelene Sheridan was obviously a diamond in the rough . . .

His shoulders sank like a shipwrecked schooner when

the woman half-turned. Sin had seen water kegs on deck with better shapes. Pale brown eyes, surrounded by nearly invisible amber-colored lashes, set in the woman's chalky face. She had narrow shoulders, a flat chest and wide hips. Sin sincerely hoped the woman was blessed with a charming personality to compensate for her lack of physical attributes.

While Hiram and Cyrus were amusing themselves in the company of the fairest of the fair, Sin was doomed to dawdle with a woman whose face and figure could compel a man to weigh anchor for a two-year cruise—and never come back.

Spinning toward the far wall, Sin downed the last of his wine for courage. He reminded himself that it made no difference to him what Angelene Sheridan looked like. She was no more than the tool he would use to strike back at Charles for his part in the murder and mutiny. Sin only had to pretend interest in this chit to accomplish his purpose. In fact, anything more would complicate his plan for revenge. He should be grateful that he wouldn't have to spare Angelene any sentiment. It would make the task much easier.

Sin refilled his glass and drank it in three swallows. He was pretty sure why Charles doted over his supposedly intelligent but painfully homely daughter. Angelene Sheridan had a face that only her father could love.

"Dear Lord!" Hiram choked when he saw Sin approach the pitifully plain redhead who had been left alone beside the refreshment table. Small wonder why, Hiram thought. The poor woman's smile displayed buck teeth and the expression seemed to swallow up her pale features and put a squint in her eyes.

Hiram had been enthralled by the name Angelene, envisioning a veritable goddess who inspired masculine dreams. Watching Sin single out the weed among the gaily-adorned flowers of aristocracy indicated that this was none other than Angelene Sheridan and that Sin was prepared to begin his vengeful retaliation against Charles.

Reminded of the bleak tale Sin had confided, Hiram swore under his breath. He and Cyrus had pledged to do whatever they could to aid in Sin's mission. However, Hiram was still a mite uncomfortable about using a woman—even this woman—to repay Charles Sheridan for his part in the vile crime. Why couldn't Charles have had some other treasure besides his daughter? Why couldn't he have been obsessed with becoming the king of cotton, for instance?

Sighing, Hiram scanned the spacious ballroom to see Cyrus dancing the cotillion with Sarah Wilhelm. Hiram supposed he might as well amuse himself while Sin charmed the redhead he had cornered. By evening's end Sin might enjoy a measure of revenge, but it didn't look as if it was going to be as pleasant as Sin had hoped. Hiram predicted this particular method of retaliation was not going to taste as sweet as infuriating Kimball and Porter.

Setting his wineglass aside, Hiram adjusted his spectacles, manufactured a smile and shouldered his way through the crowd to introduce himself to the fetching chestnut-haired female who had captivated him from across the room.

# *Twelve*

Sin made his bowing introduction to the redhead, who blushed profusely, and she became so tongue-tied she couldn't utter her own name. Not that it mattered. Sin knew who she was after seeing her trailing behind Charles Sheridan in the receiving line. Since the chit couldn't find her tongue, Sin was forced to monopolize the conversation.

After exhausting all comments about the weather and the climate of Natchez, Sin rattled on about opening his hotel, describing—in detail—the decor and the menu. He nearly bored himself to death, even if his blushing companion appeared to be hanging on every word.

Small wonder Charles doted upon his daughter. And no surprise that she hadn't landed a husband yet. Sin was fairly certain that part of Hiram's information had been inaccurate. Angelene Sheridan had not, in fact, discarded several beaus; they had simply dropped her like a hot coal. Sin suspected that even the most dedicated wife-hunters had turned elsewhere to seek their fortunes. Sin wasn't sure that even Charles had enough money to purchase Angelene a husband. Talking to a wall would have been as stimulating as chatting with this chit . . .

Sin's dismal thoughts trailed off and his voice dried

up when familiar laughter wafted toward him. His gaze drifted across the tops of bejeweled heads to see a blinding vision of beauty beneath the center chandelier. Green eyes glistened in the light, and red-gold hair caught fire and burned.

Instantly, Sin remembered the bittersweet pleasure of a night cut short by two ruffians. He recalled the addicting taste of kisses that put Wilhelm's stock of imported wine to shame. Sin could almost feel the woman's body pressed to his!

He had told himself he could not properly pursue that lovely female and still satisfy his revenge on Charles Sheridan. Even now Sin was forced to associate with this blushing, tongue-tied redhead rather than seeking his own amusements with a woman who intellectually challenged him and physically set him on fire.

Sin tried to ignore the stunning beauty whose golden gown was molded enticingly to her figure, but his eyes fixed on her, and forbidden hunger gnawed at him. His gaze drifted down the column of her throat to the swells of her breasts, remembering the feel of her curves beneath his fingertips. His body reacted instantaneously and Sin cursed under his breath. The woman aroused him by her mere presence.

When Sin's attention shifted to the man beside the green-eyed goddess he silently scowled. There stood the same drunken dandy Sin had encountered at Mealy's Tavern Under-the-Hill. This enchantress in gold satin certainly appeared to have poor taste in men. Reginald Foster had made an obnoxious nuisance of himself while trying to bed the harlot he had singled out.

Sin frowned pensively, wondering if the overzealous

dandy might have been the one this elf had referred to that stormy night they had met in the meadow. If not, she would discover soon enough that her latest escort had arms like an octopus and all the tender sensibilities of a sting ray.

The laughter evaporated on her lips when her gaze locked with Sin's. He watched that pert chin elevate a notch before she turned away. No doubt, she regretted giving him an introduction that enabled him to move in the same circles she did.

When the music of the orchestra struck up a tune, Reginald made a sweeping bow and claimed his lady. Sin pivoted toward his homely companion, only to hear a *psst* from behind him. He swiveled his head around to see Hiram materializing from out of nowhere.

"I need to speak to you—*now*," he insisted.

Sin clasped his companion's clammy hand and brought it to his lips before taking his leave. The poor girl nearly dribbled down the wall into a faint. Still she couldn't get out one word, even when Sin bade her adieu.

"Do you have a problem?" Sin questioned as Hiram towed him to a vacant corner.

"No, *you* have a problem."

"Aye," Sin replied, flicking a glance at the wallflower. "Angelene Sheridan has the personality of a jellyfish. I'm having enough trouble drawing her father's attention to my supposed interest in his daughter without you interrupting."

"You've got more trouble than you know," Hiram muttered. "The jellyfish you mentioned is not Angelene Sheridan."

Sin glanced back at the redhead. "No?"

"No," Hiram confirmed. ''Angelene Sheridan just arrived with that besotted dandy we met Under-the-Hill. Of course, the man has his hands full keeping up with the lady. She has just been passed to a third pair of arms in two minutes and the line forms on the east wall. You'll be here all night trying to get a half minute's audience with her."

Sin felt his carefully controlled expression fracture like broken glass when he stared across the room. This was Angelene Sheridan? The elusive creature who had refused to divulge her name and asked such pointed questions about the reason for his interest in her, after he had dared to kiss her, and she had dared to respond?

All the comments The Elf had made about men with devious intentions and insincere interest came back to Sin in a jumbled rush. Now he understood why Angelene Sheridan was so wary of the motives of men. She was indeed a rare, beautiful jewel with the kind of money and prestige men would lie, steal and probably kill for. Hell's fire, Sin thought as conflicting sentiments swamped and buffeted him. What else could go wrong with his well-laid plans?

*This changed everything . . . and yet, it changed nothing . . .*

"Damn it to hell," Sin muttered to himself. Why had fate played such a cruel trick on him after all these years of surviving and thriving on his vow of uncompromising vengeance? Why did that captivating beauty have to be Charles Sheridan's daughter?

"I suggest we retreat so you can reevaluate the situation," Hiram advised. "In the first place, my conscience is starting to hound me about using a woman to exact revenge against Charles. In the second place, you might incite war if you try to cut into the line that is forming behind Angel. And in the third place—"

"Bloomin' hell," Cyrus interrupted as he surged toward his friends. "I've got bad news—the worst—Cap'n. That red-haired wallaby you thought was Angelene isn't—"

"So I have just been told."

Sin inhaled a fortifying breath and watched Angelene being passed to another eager set of arms. The woman would have more handprints on her than a glass door by the time the party ended. Sin's chances of gaining an audience with Angelene—after their last unpleasant encounter—were the same as spotting an iceberg in the tropics.

Charles Sheridan's precious daughter? Damn . . .

Sin needed time to collect his thoughts and recover from his shock. He couldn't proceed in his customary calm, composed manner when the jolting revelation had scattered his thoughts to kingdom come.

"I could use a stiff drink," Sin announced.

"I'll fetch it for you," Hiram volunteered. "I'll meet you on the gallery in five minutes."

"Bring the whole damned bottle with you," Sin requested as he spun on his heel.

Cyrus lifted an amused brow when he noticed the scowl that rarely claimed Sin's passive features. "Rattled, mate? Don't blame ya. From the gossip I've been hearin' from Sarah, nobody gets the best of Angel. Maybe you should steal Charles's pet dog or horse and call it good."

Sin did not find the comment amusing, nor did he respond to it; instead he headed toward the terrace.

Sentiment should not enter into his plans, he told himself. He should proceed as cold-bloodedly as Sheridan, Porter and Kimball had. None of those men had cared how Sin felt, cared what had happened to the twelve-year-old brother of the man they had murdered before they stole the *Annalee* and her heaping cargo.

*Eye for an eye,* just as Pearly Graham had said. *Take each man's obsession away from him and leave him to suffer, just as Sin had suffered all nine kinds of hell.*

Sin strode onto the gallery, his pearl-handled cane tapping restlessly against the tiled floor. Once he was out of earshot of the crowd, he proceeded to curse the air black and blue, and he didn't stop spewing oaths until he had gained some measure of his customary composure.

It took awhile.


Requesting the chance to catch her breath, Angelene slipped from the arms of her most recent dance partner and propelled herself toward the refreshment table. Besides being half starved from choking down the unappetizing meals served by the new cook at Sheridan Hall, Angelene was perturbed. She had hoped to discourage the wife-hunters who congregated around her, by agreeing to let Reggie Foster escort her to the party.

So much for good intentions. The scheme had served no useful purpose. And furthermore, seeing Nick Sinclair after their last encounter spoiled what was left of her good disposition. The man had trampled on her feelings when he'd raged at her for trying to save his worthless life. Her pride was still smarting from the painful knowledge that all she had been to him, despite the fact that she had kept her identity a secret, was a warm body that could provide him with physical pleasure.

Angelene was now thoroughly convinced that men were all alike. They only exploited women. Men offered no sincere respect and refused to treat women as their equals.

"Have you met Sin and his companions yet?" Sarah Wilhelm questioned as she planted herself beside Angelene. "Intriguing rakes, one and all, especially that blond Adonis who is managing Sin's plantation and horse stables." Sarah paused to flash Cyrus her most engaging smile when he sauntered past her on his way to the terrace.

After taking a sip of punch, Sarah leaned close to impart the latest gossip. "We're not certain just where Sin acquired his fabulous fortune, but he is said to be incredibly wealthy. He is opening a new hotel and plans to race his prize steeds at Pharsalia."

Angelene sipped her drink and cursed herself for being the slightest bit interested in what Natchez's most renowned young gossiper had to say.

"Some suggest that Sin and his friends were highwaymen along the Natchez Trace, stealing from travelers headed upstream after they had sold their goods in town. Others say that Sin was one of Jean Lafitte's pirates who preyed on ships in the gulf and along the Caribbean isles."

Angelene wouldn't have been surprised to discover that both speculations were true. After witnessing Sin in action during that appalling encounter a week earlier, she was prepared to swear Sin was involved with gambling houses Under-the-Hill. The man was undoubtedly living on credit to establish himself among the gentry. Fool that she was, she had given him letters of introduction.

It wouldn't be the first time someone had wriggled into the elite social circles on pretended laurels. Most of the fortune hunters who flocked to Natchez, in hopes of marrying wealthy planters' daughters, were the second and third sons of aristocratic families who couldn't inherit unless their older brothers died and left them the family fortune.

Angelene glanced around the crowded ballroom. Ah yes, the place was filled with cunning and deception.

"I wonder when Sin acquired that scar?" Sarah mused aloud.

"Probably in a duel of swords over his questionable honor. Or perhaps one of his robbery victims lashed out when stripped of valuables. And of course, there's the possibility that Sin caught the sharp end of a cutlass when he and his pirates overran a ship," Angelene spitefully speculated—and then wished she hadn't.

Sarah's eyes widened as she digested the juicy tidbits for gossip. "A gentleman bandit? How intriguing. And here he is in our midst. I must say, there is something devilishly different about those three men. I'm inclined to think they are reformed pirates, judging by the handsome blond's accent. As for Hiram Brodie—"

The name struck an unnerving chord in Angelene's mind. She instantly recalled her father telling her that Hiram Brodie had purchased their field slaves. Shortly thereafter, the overseer and cook had resigned. The butler had left the previous week. Angelene frowned suspiciously. She would bet the family fortune that it was actually Sinclair who had hired Johnston, Brownley and Agnes Ralston.

Why, that conniving scoundrel! He had taken the most competent hired help from Sheridan Hall and added them to his own staff. There was no telling who else in town had been victimized by such sneaky tactics.

"Have you heard that Sinclair hired away Jerome Kimball's clerk to manage the South Sea Paradise Hotel?"

"South Sea Paradise?" Angelene questioned, bemused.

Sarah flung her a withering glance. "Really, Angelene, you need to venture into town more often. The world is passing you by."

"The fact is that I have had several duties to attend at both our plantations since I returned from school. And Papa and I have been in New Orleans for more than a week," she answered.

"Well, I assure you that you have missed a very busy time here. Not only did Sin hire Kimball's trusted manager, but also waitresses, maids and several of the concubines who lounge on the upper floor of his hotel. And Owen Porter's trainers and jockeys have taken up residence at Raven's Hill. People are stampeding all over each other to work for the newest member of society."

Well, that answered one question, Angelene silently fumed. Porter and Kimball were probably beside themselves now that Sinclair had cut into their profits and undermined the working of the hotel and plantation. For certain, things at Sheridan Hall hadn't been running smoothly since Hiram Brodie began hiring the help out from under Charles's nose . . .

"Excuse me, Angelene," Sarah said, jostling her friend from her pensive thoughts. "I should play the good hostess and entertain Cyrus. We certainly wouldn't want him to feel unwelcome, and I might be able to discover which of the rumors about Sin are true while I'm at it."

Angelene appraised the tall, attractive blond who appeared at the terrace door. At six-foot-one, the man almost matched Sin in size and stature. His wavy, sand-colored hair and intriguing amber eyes drew several appreciative female stares. The red cummerbund, frock coat and flog cloak accentuated his rakish appearance.

Sarah Wilhelm wasn't wasting any time making her interest in Cyrus known, Angelene noted. The girl was fascinated and it showed. Sarah would get her foolish heart broken if Cyrus was anything like the darkly mysterious Nick Sinclair.

Angelene scrutinized the second man who appeared at the terrace door. That had to be Hiram Brodie, Angelene decided. Intelligent brown eyes gleamed behind wire-rimmed glasses. Hiram scanned the room before his gaze settled on her. He stared at her for a long moment before glancing back at the looming shadow that dominated the doorway.

*Sin in the flesh,* Angelene thought bitterly. That ex-pirate or ex-highwayman—or whatever he was—had probably decided to make fools of them all. The news that Sin had opened a hotel to compete with Jerome Kimball and had acquired horses and trainers to challenge Owen Porter suggested he was the kind of man who thrived on competition. The more difficult the challenge, the better, she suspected. Nick Sinclair had arrived in Natchez, not as a meek lamb but like an ominous lion.

When those onyx eyes focused on Angelene with an unreadable expression, she turned her back. With head held high, she marched off and latched onto the first dance partner who happened by. She was not a woman who repeated her mistakes. She was not going near Nick Sinclair again. She had granted him intimate privileges on two reckless occasions and had discovered, to her mortification, that there was nothing special about her to attract a man except her fortune and her body.

Until she met a man who wanted her only for herself, one who cared for and treated her as an equal, she would flit from one shallow fortune hunter to another. The wife-hunters who claimed she had been elusive in the past hadn't seen anything yet! They would grow very old waiting for her to share her family fortune with any of them.

As for Sin, he could sail straight to hell on his damned pirate ship and Angel would wish him a hearty good riddance!

## *Thirteen*

In silent amusement, Sin watched Angelene make a spectacular production of avoiding him. She definitely had a flair for the dramatic, he decided. It went with her feisty temperament. But despite her efforts, she couldn't hide from him for long.

Sin had stood on the terrace for a quarter of an hour, weighing his objectives and choices. After thorough deliberation, he had decided on his plan of action. Despite Hiram's and Cyrus's reluctance, Sin had come to the conclusion that Charles Sheridan could not be allowed preferential treatment, just because he had a devastatingly attractive daughter. The man had committed an unpardonable sin and he would pay, just like his cohorts. If Angelene Sheridan had to suffer a bit for the pampered life she had lived at Sin's and his brother's expense then so be it.

*An eye for an eye.*

And speaking of eyes, Sin mused as his gaze drifted to the latest arrival, Jerome Kimball was glaring daggers at him. Or was it pistols?

It was time that man discovered Sin was wise to the assassination plot that took Chester Wiffle's and Jonathan

Stanley's lives. With tormenting intent, Sin circled the dance floor to confront Jerome.

"I believe you were hoping to acquire my pearl-handled cane," Sin said for starters.

The group of men standing around Jerome peered curiously at Sin before focusing their attention on Jerome. The older man scowled.

"And what is that supposed to mean, Sinclair?"

"Only that the two agents you hired to *purchase* my cane at such an extravagant price were . . . um . . . surprised that I refused to give it up."

Jerome curled his stubby fingers inside his cravat where it closed around his throat. Those fathomless black eyes looked right through him. Jerome would be damned—literally—if he made the same rash mistake Owen had made by raising his quirt in impulsive anger.

"I'm sure I don't have the foggiest notion what you're talking about," Jerome said haughtily.

"I'm sure you do." Sin had the attention of every gentleman within hearing distance and he took advantage of opportunity. "Hiring those two ruffians to dispose of me before I opened my hotel to compete with your establishment was a waste of money, Jerome. You don't seem capable of handling friendly rivalry very well. I'm left to wonder how many other competitors you have disposed of in the past."

The congregation of men gasped and stared at Jerome whose face turned a fascinating shade of purple.

"If I should wind up dead, there will be no question on whose head the blame will rest," Sin shrewdly added.

"You sneaky bas—" Jerome slammed his mouth shut so hard his teeth rattled. Willfully, he battled for composure. "False accusations will earn you no friends in Natchez. Slinging mud at the competition is under-handed."

*"Mud* I could tolerate, Jerome. It's the assassination attempts by your henchmen that I object to." Sin's gaze drilled into the fuming entrepreneur. "A man who thrives on another man's misfortune is no man at all."

On that provoking comment Sin turned and walked away. Since he was feeling pleased with himself, he decided to drop a few grenades in Owen Porter's lap while the man was tooting his own horn among the horsey set.

Owen Porter frowned warily when he saw those obsidian eyes zero in on him, as if his measure was being taken down a rifle barrel. This time, no matter how much Sin provoked him, Owen was *not* going to lose his temper.

Jerome and Owen had made arrangements to rid themselves of Sin. Owen could endure a few more hours of the man. The strike was scheduled for tonight—a robbery by highwaymen during the return trip to Raven's Hill. Owen had suggested that one of the other attending aristocrats be targeted to ensure no suspicion reflected on them. A rather brilliant idea—Owen had congratulated himself upon it.

Vowing to bide his time, Owen awaited Sin's approach. He held his tongue while Sin introduced himself to the horse breeders and racers among the socially elite.

"I've heard it told that you have taken an interest in joining us at Pharsalia sometime in the near future." This from Robert Dunbar, a stuffy middle-aged gent who reminded Sin of a pig fattened for market. The man had close-set brown eyes, a sizable snout and ears that stuck out at a noticeable angle from the sides of his head.

"You have heard correctly, sir. I have purchased a racer that is showing great promise." Sin flicked a glance toward Owen. "Or so my new trainer says."

Owen counted to ten—backward—and held his tongue. He was not going to rise to the bait like a brainless guppy. He didn't have to. One of his blundering associates did it for him, damn the luck.

"I've heard Owen's ex-trainer works for you," Hubert King commented.

"Never thought Owen would give Alfred Ponds up. Best trainer around, next to my own trainer, of course," Robert Dunbar proudly boasted.

"Truly?" Sin replied. "According to Owen, there is none better than Alfred Ponds. Owen claims that's the reason he has been so successful on the track, and because he has a better eye for horseflesh than—" Sin paused, as if racking his memory to accurately quote Owen—"the dunderheads he races against. I believe that was the term Owen used."

The four aristocrats collectively sucked in their breath and glowered at Owen.

"I said nothing of the kind, you lying son of a—" Owen shut his mouth so fast he bit his tongue.

Sin nodded, unruffled by the insult. "You're right. My mistake, Owen. Now that I think on it, I believe the direct quote was 'horses' asses,' not 'dunderheads.' " He glanced around the shocked group who looked as if they would have liked to beat Owen to a pulp. "It was a pleasure meeting you, gentlemen. And by the way, I don't agree with Owen. You seem to be a likable lot of friendly rivals to me. I certainly won't let his low opinion of you influence me in the least."

"You bastard!" Owen exploded.

Owen's timing was terrible. The orchestra was between songs and his voice carried across the room like a discharging cannon. The crowd pivoted in synchronized rhythm to watch Owen's pudgy face turn the color of raw liver. When he struck out with a doubled fist, Sin stepped quickly to the side. The blow connected with Robert Dunbar's jaw, causing him to spill his drink down the front of his jacket.

"Call me a horse's ass, will you?" Robert raged, holding his injured jaw. "I've put up with your blustering boasts for more years than I care to count. And you can consider your name excluded from the guest list of my party next week. I'd bring a horse into my house before I would admit you!"

"That goes double for me, Porter," Hubert King sneered.

Leaving Owen and his ex-friends casting aspersions and drawing plenty of unwanted attention from the crowd, Sin wandered off. He was well satisfied with his work. Owen Porter would have a devil of a time returning to the horsey set's good graces.

Angelene had vowed to ignore Nick Sinclair as he strolled around the ballroom, but her traitorous gaze kept seeking out the tall, cloaked figure. She had seen Sin approach Kimball and then Porter. She had also witnessed the outcome of each encounter.

As usual, Sin's expression was carefully controlled, as

was his rich baritone voice. Kimball and Porter had made utter fools of themselves and raised the gentry's eyebrows. With very little effort—or was it meticulously plotted strategy?—Sin was turning the aristocrats away from Kimball and Porter and collecting support.

To the left and right of her, Angelene overheard remarks about how rudely Sin had been treated, simply because he was a newcomer who had become the subject of speculation and gossip. Porter and Kimball were being labeled as temperamental snobs. Sin was a shrewd, calculating individual, Angelene decided. Good thing she had realized what a devil he really was before she found herself hopelessly intrigued by him. Sin had been aptly nicknamed.

Angelene had once again been claimed by her escort, Reginald Foster. When she saw Sin approach, his impassive expression intact, she automatically tensed. She wondered if she could keep her wits about her to prevent herself from looking as ridiculous as Kimball and Porter. No doubt, this would prove to be an exercise in self-control.

The instant Reginald spotted Sin, Angelene felt him flinch. She wondered what sort of dealing Reggie had with the man. He tried to waltz away, but Sin tapped him on the shoulder with the blunt end of his cane.

"Good evening, Reginald. I'm glad we could meet under more civilized circumstances than we did the first time," Sin said blandly. "You've moved up the social ladder since I last saw you."

Reggie's fingers dug so tightly into Angelene's ribs that she grimaced. She watched the young dandy break into a sweat.

"What do you want, Sinclair?" Reggie gritted through his teeth.

"Only the chance to dance with the lady."

"You'll have to wait your turn in line." Reggie nodded his head toward the dozen suitors holding up the wall. "In this circle, gentlemanly patience is required."

One thick brow elevated questioningly. "Considering the *im*patience you displayed with a certain young lady whom I had to rescue from your groping clutches, I wasn't aware that you were familiar with such things."

Profuse color rose from Reggie's neck and bled along his hairline. "How dare you bring that up in front of a lady!"

"And the other female you were pawing so disrespectfully, against her wishes, was not a lady?" Sin placidly baited.

"She was just a whore—" Reggie clamped his lips together and cursed under his breath. He had committed a serious error. Angelene was very sensitive about the lack of respect men paid to all women. It was one of her pet peeves.

Angelene took an indignant step backward. *"Just?"* she queried. She well remembered the night when Reggie had tried to step over the bounds of propriety with her. "Did this incident occur after you tried to—?"

"So you were the cause of his frustration," Sin cut in. The thought annoyed him. Reggie definitely needed to be taken down a notch—or three.

"Just go take your place in line, Sinclair. I have nothing more to say to you," Reggie growled, attempting to reclaim Angelene.

"Nor I to you," she assured Reggie, dodging his out-stretched hand.

When Angelene wheeled away, Sin caught her trailing arm. "I beg a dance."

"Beg all you want," she said, glaring at the hand that held her captive with such ease.

Sin lifted a challenging brow. "Be careful that you don't find yourself lumped in the same category with the esteemed Mr. Kimball and the indomitable Mr. Porter," he calmly warned her.

Reluctantly, Angelene allowed herself to be entrapped in Sin's powerful arms. She considered whacking him over the head with the cane he draped over his elbow, but she expected she would find herself looking as much the culprit as Kimball and Porter. This scoundrel was proving to offer a challenging match of wits.

"You dance as superbly as you set fuses," she commented, as Sin glided in graceful rhythm with the music. "It leaves me to wonder if your previous occupation had anything to do with demolition."

Sin ignored the goading remark. He was not to be provoked. "Why didn't you tell me who you were, Angelene?"

She tilted her head to meet those penetrating black eyes that were set in a ruggedly handsome face. "Because, Mr. Sinclair, I prefer to be appreciated for myself. Obviously I am entertaining an unrealistic whim. Men are tiresomely unconcerned whether a woman has a brain in her head or whether she has the characteristics a man finds admirable. My plague is having a fortune at my disposal. Most men can look no farther than that."

Sin said nothing. He simply stored away the information and vowed not to let the slightest sentiment sway him from his objective. He was here for one purpose, he reminded himself. His physical attraction to Angelene Sheridan was simply an unfortunate stroke of luck. He could control his urges where she was concerned, knowing she was Charles Sheridan's daughter. She was no more than a pawn and he could not let himself forget that.

"No comment?" Angelene prodded him. "Perhaps I misjudged the depth of your mentality. Did you exhaust your incisive wit while dealing with Jerome, Owen and Reggie?"

Sin deflected the verbal blow and promised not to let her sharp tongue get the better of him. When the music ended, he wrapped an arm around Angelene's waist and shepherded her toward the refreshment table. "I prefer that you chew on a pastry rather than on me."

"And I prefer to take bites out of you. It's so much more satisfying," she replied. "Better to attack a highwayman or pirate than to be his victim, I always say."

Sin reached for a pastry. His hand stalled momentarily before he scooped it up. "Is that what you think I am?"

"Truth be told, I think you're a sly, sinister devil masquerading as a gentleman. I saw you in your deadliest form when you confronted your enemies from Under-the-Hill, and I have seen you play with the minds of both Kimball and Porter. You are dark, mysterious and dangerous and I have tolerated your company as long as I can stand to. Good evening, Sinclair."

When she spun around to make her exit Sin latched onto her arm. This encounter was not going as he'd anticipated. He was not in control here. That wasn't good.

It was also unusual.

"I said—"

"I heard you," Sin muttered. "Join me on the terrace, Angelene."

"For what purpose? Your *sin*fully *sin*ister pleasure?" Her green eyes flashed. "I assure you it will not be for mine."

"It *was* for your pleasure not too long ago, as I recall."

Her arm lifted reflexively, determined to retaliate. To her frustration, he caught her hand and dropped a kiss to her fingertips, even as her nails bit into the palm of his hand.

And then good fortune smiled on Sin. He sensed that he was about to find himself the culprit, spoiling the sympathetic sentiment he had accumulated after encountering Porter and Kimball. But before the spirited beauty could force Sin into a difficult situation, Reggie Foster showed up. Now here was a man who could—and deserved to—become a scapegoat.

Sin smiled to himself and pressed another kiss to Angelene's wrist, even though she was still flexing her sharp claws in his hand.

"You have overstepped yourself, Sinclair," Reggie blurted out. "Angelene happens to be my companion for the evening, and I will not tolerate your slobbering all over her!"

"I beg to differ," Sin countered with infuriating calm. "Slobbering is what you were doing to the defenseless female you were chasing around the upstairs room at Mealy's Tavern. You told me to mind my own business rather than assist the damsel in distress. Though I am not a woman, I was certainly offended by your behavior.

Otherwise, I would have had no reason to pin your lusty hide to the floor while the girl locked herself in her room for protection."

The descriptive account drew a glowering look from Angelene. Like a fool, Reggie tried to save face. He needed the Sheridan fortune badly, and quickly. His dwindling funds were making it difficult to keep up any kind of pretense. "You have pestered Angelene and insulted me for the last time, Sinclair. Take yourself off with your pirate friends and leave us alone."

Damn, what did it take to thoroughly provoke this pretentious aristocrat into battle? Sin wondered. By the minute, his desire to square off against Reggie was escalating.

"I wouldn't throw stones, my friend," Sin said blandly. "Your occupation of romancing fortunes for personal gain through flattery and deceit is a form of piracy, after all."

"You have gone too far, Sinclair!" Reggie blared furiously.

"And you have not gone far enough in performing a hard day's work for a hard day's wage. Indeed, you spend more time pondering ways to avoid work than breaking a sweat."

Reggie was trapped and he knew it. His voice had carried around the room while Sin's controlled tone was barely more than a whisper. To redeem himself, Reggie had to lay blame on Sinclair and call him out. Reggie was a fair shot, after all. From all indication, the only way for him to live down the tale Sinclair could spread about the unpleasant fiasco at Mealy's Tavern was to shut the man up—permanently. If Reggie didn't challenge

Sinclair to a duel, it was going to look as if he was everything Sin claimed him to be.

"I trust you know how to find your way to the dueling field at Vidalia, Sinclair," Reggie sneered. "You shall pay for offending me and the lady."

"Don't be ridiculous," Angelene put in.

Reggie drew himself up to proud stature. "You heard the man. He has offended my honor and your respectability."

"Oh, for heaven's sake, he did no such thing," Angelene sniffed. "If you had any brains you would realize you had only been baited."

"Obviously the lady sees you for what you are," Sin remarked. "There is hardly the need for you to defend your honor to impress her when she is aware that you have no more honor than you have brains."

While Reggie sputtered and cursed, Sin calmly stood his ground. This situation was taking the twist he had anticipated and welcomed. Reggie was easy to read, even if Angelene wasn't. Luckily, it was out of her hands now—which was exactly the way Sin wanted it.

Angelene silently groaned when the glibly uttered provocation struck Reggie's sensitive nerves. The fool had fallen into the same trap that had ensnared Kimball and Porter. Reggie was doomed, and to those within hearing distance, the altercation appeared to be over her. Curse it!

"That does it, Sinclair. I challenge you with whatever weapon you choose," Reggie declared.

"You wish to fight me for the right to court the lady?" Sin questioned the flustered dandy.

"Hell yes!"

Angelene tried to object. "Now wait just a minute—"

"Tomorrow at dawn, Sinclair."

"And where do you expect to find a second on short notice? Sin asked placidly.

The crowd was closing in and Reggie's face turned scarlet with fury. He was being mocked in front of the gentry. "I have more friends in Natchez than you."

"Blast it, Reggie, you are no match for Sinclair," Angelene hissed at him. "I have seen him in act—"

Her gaze swung to Sinclair and she swore she saw his lips twitch in a guarded smile, as if she had somehow played right into his hands. She truly wished she could read that quick and alert mind of his.

"Until tomorrow," Reggie snapped as he grabbed Angelene's arm and towed her away.

The crowd parted to let the couple pass and Sin stood there, his expression as calm as if he had been discussing a preference in wine rather than a duel. As Sin had always maintained, those who flew off the handle usually landed in the skillet. Sin now had all his fried fish exactly where he wanted them—evenly seared on both sides.

# *Fourteen*

Owen Porter eased up beside Jerome Kimball while Reggie was spouting his challenge. "Perhaps we were hasty in plotting Sinclair's demise," he murmured. "We could let Reggie fill the bastard full of buckshot and save ourselves some money."

"Reggie is no match for Sinclair," Jerome insisted.

"How can you be sure?"

Jerome didn't explain. He preferred to have no one else know about his first attempt to dispose of the unwanted competition. "I have the feeling it will take more than one man to bring Sinclair down," was all he said before he strolled off.

Cyrus leaned leisurely against the terrace door, grinning wryly as Sin approached. "You've had a busy evenin', mate."

"Productive," Sin amended.

Cyrus chuckled. "I do admire your ingenuity. You've made your enemies look foolish in front of their peers. And you claim I have devilish charm and an ornery streak that goes bone-deep? I consider myself a distant second to you."

Sin shrugged nonchalantly and motioned for Hiram to join them. "Since I'm scheduled to be at Vidalia at dawn, I think I'll call it a night."

Cyrus smirked at that. "I can think of other things I'd call it besides a night. A bloody *circus* is more like it."

When the threesome paid their respects to their host, Aubrey Wilhelm apologized all over himself for the disruptions and rude behavior.

Sin dropped into a gallant bow. "You cannot be held accountable for the behavior of some of your guests. For some reason, those who find themselves in competition with me feel compelled to pick fights. Even the civilized gentry seems to be plagued with unsporting rivals."

"Well, you can be sure that Kimball and Porter will be excluded from future guest lists. They behaved abominably while you conducted yourself as a gentleman."

With a polite nod, Sin ambled away, bookended by his friends. He pulled up short when red-gold hair glistened in the porch light. From the look of things, Angelene intended to make her own way home and Reggie was refusing to let her. The dandy was scuttling after her, demanding that she halt. Angelene, of course, did nothing of the kind.

Now why didn't that surprise him?

Very soon Angelene would learn to obey Sin's command, he promised himself. She would have no choice. In fact, he had devised a way to appease his need for revenge, and to satisfy the craving she aroused in him. The idea had struck him the moment Reggie marched up, looking like a man on the verge of issuing a ridiculous challenge. It had taken little effort to twist the man's words in Sin's favor.

Angelene was going to find herself in a most compromising position because of Reggie, Sin predicted. Her protest to the challenge suggested as much. And when she tried to attest to his skills in self-defense Sin had seen the jaws of a very clever trap opening to his advantage . . .

The instant Reggie grabbed Angelene and whirled her around, Sin's thoughts evaporated. He charged forward to intervene. His reaction was so natural that he didn't stop to consider what it suggested—refused to consider it, in fact.

Hiram and Cyrus took immediate note of Sin's impulsive action, however.

"So much for the best-laid plans," Cyrus chortled as he watched Sin rush to the rescue. "The woman he swore to ruin is the same one he's going off to save. It's going to be difficult rowin' if he plans to do both at the same time."

"It's just as well he realizes that sooner rather than later," Hiram replied. "Sin would not have been proud of himself if he struck such a low blow, even in the name of revenge. Besides, I'd say he's going to have one hell of a time keeping a step ahead of Angelene Sheridan as it is."

"Aye, mate." Cyrus grinned broadly. "According to the earful of gossip Sarah Wilhelm unloaded on me, Angel is as difficult to pin down as a loose sail in a brisk wind."

Hiram frowned as Sin advanced on Reggie. "Do you think we should lend Sin a hand?"

"Why? He's still got two hands, doesn't he? One is usually enough, with a spare for good measure."

* * *

"I believe the lady prefers that you make yourself scarce, Foster," Sin said as he broke the man's hold with well-placed pressure to the back of his neck. The ancient Chinese art of unarmed combat was a skill Sin had found effective on mules, and fools.

"I can speak for myself, thank you very much," Angelene muttered, massaging the arm Reggie had nearly wrenched off.

"I have no doubt of that," Sin assured her. To Reggie he said, "Your time would be better spent taking target practice. As Angelene has already indicated, you are definitely going to need it, come dawn."

Snarling, Reggie lurched around and stamped off.

"If you intend to project a gentlemanly air for the gentry, your conscience—provided you have one—won't let you kill Reggie," Angelene insisted.

Sin's face closed up and his eyes glittered dangerously. "You might be surprised to discover just how many so-called gentlemen hereabout have no conscience when it comes to killing, especially when fortunes are involved."

Angelene studied the slight twitch that tightened the scar on his cheek. "What does that imply?"

"I'm afraid you'll find out sooner than you prefer . . ." His voice trailed off when he caught sight of Charles Sheridan approaching. A knot of suppressed resentment twisted in his belly, just as it had when he'd encountered Porter and Kimball.

"Angel, I think you should ride home with me," Charles suggested. He paused to stare at Sinclair in the faint light that splayed through the window. "Don't I know you from somewhere, Sinclair? Although we haven't been formally introduced, I feel as if we have met before."

*On a dark night on board the* Annalee *perhaps?* Sin silently asked.

Charles smiled pleasantly and extended his hand in introduction. "Charles Sheridan. I regret those ridiculous outbursts you endured tonight."

*Not as much as you'll regret it later, I'll wager.*

"But I'm inclined to agree with my daughter about the challenge. Dueling with Reginald will hardly serve your purpose if you wish to become a respected member of the gentry. Dueling is a barbaric method of resolving conflicts."

*So is outright murder. Always has been,* Sin silently added. "You don't believe your daughter is worth fighting for?"

Charles blinked at the question. "Well yes, but there are more appropriate ways of gaining a woman's attention than leaving dead bodies strung out behind you."

Sin looked past Charles, drawn by the flaming tendrils of red-gold hair, waiting to hear Angelene second that opinion. She agreed with her father, just as Sin expected she would.

"My father has a valid point," Angelene put in.

"Then I will have to ponder the challenge," Sin shrewdly remarked. "Perhaps I'll change my mind by dawn. But at present I'm inclined to let Reggie back up his insults and boasts with a pistol."

Nodding slightly, Sin strode off to join Hiram and Cyrus in the coach. His thoughts were troubled by Charles Sheridan's gracious manners. Sin expected him to mention the loss of his plantation overseer, cook and most recently his butler. Charles had portrayed the sophisticated gentleman, much to Sin's dismay. Perhaps . . .

*Don't let tender sentiment sway you. Sheridan was part of an assassination plot. He committed a crime and profited greatly.*

The man would lose his charm when confronted with his personal brand of torment, Sin assured himself. Charles would show his true colors, just like Kimball and Porter.

The thought soothed Sin's nagging conscience—or at least he convinced himself that it did.

While Hiram was lounging on the seat of the landau and Cyrus was humming a ditty, Sin cut his way through a jungle of conflicting thoughts. The crack of a pistol brought all three men to attention and had them swearing profusely. The carriage skidded to a halt when a booming voice reverberated in the darkness.

"Step yourselves down, gents. We're taking charity collections for the poor."

Sin glanced grimly at his companions. "I don't suppose either of you brought along hardware."

Cyrus nodded his blond head and gestured toward his boot. "I never leave home without it, mate."

Hiram patted the pistol strapped to his calf. "You warned us to be prepared after your encounter with Kimball's henchman."

"Hurry up, gents. This ain't no time to be getting contrary or tightfisted. I only want to see my poor mother comfortable in her dotage."

The sarcastic remark drew several chuckles from the highwayman's cohorts.

"There are at least three of them," Sin calculated. "Maybe four."

Cyrus peered out the window. "And here you've been tellin' me society was civilized. There looks to be as many pirates on land as at sea. Now how are we going to handle this pickle, mate?"

Sin reached for his leather poke and hurled it out the window. He doubted the thieves would be satisfied. More than likely his hide was what they were ultimately after. Kimball was said to have a slew of friends from Under-the-Hill. Sin had to give his nemesis credit. Staging a robbery would ensure that Kimball didn't take the blame since he was hardly in need of cash—yet.

"Not good enough, gents," Jim Calloway said gruffly. "Step down so we can see if you're as generous as you could be."

Sin sighed audibly and reached for the door latch. "At the risk of sounding like a poor sport, if I take a bullet through the chest, shoot the one responsible."

"Done," Cyrus promised.

Despite Sin's order that his friends remain inside the coach, Hiram and Cyrus stepped down behind him.

"Since when did you start disobeying commands?" Sin questioned quietly.

"Since you insisted we call you Sin instead of Captain," Hiram whispered back.

Cyrus boldly stepped forward and stared at the silhouettes that lurked in the shelter of the cedar trees. "My name is Sinclair and I assure you I won't report this incident if you take the cash and let me and my friends continue on our way."

"Damn you, Cyrus," Sin grumbled, edging forward. *"I'm* Sinclair," he told the brigands.

"I don't need either of you impersonating me," Hiram declared, striding forward. *"I* am Sinclair."

Whispers were exchanged in the trees, confirming what Sin assumed to be true. This was not an ordinary everyday robbery. It was another assassination attempt, arranged by Kimball and maybe even Porter. He had seen both men deep in conversation several times during the evening—plotting, no doubt.

The thieves went into conference, trying to decide which of the identically dressed men was Sinclair. Sin leaped forward to scoop up the money pouch, drag attention and gunfire. Flames glared in the darkness, spotlighting the four horsemen. Musketballs danced in the dirt beside Sin's shoulder as he rolled into the ditch.

Meanwhile, Hiram and Cyrus were diving beneath the coach and returning fire. When Sin's pistol breathed flames, yelps resounded among the trees. The bandits scattered like pheasants and Sin gathered his legs beneath him, listening to the sound of fading hoofbeats.

"Kimball seems to be having a helluva time acquiring good help these days," Sin commented as he dusted himself off. His gaze lifted to the wide-eyed groom who sat atop the coach. "Are you all right, lad?"

"N-no, s-sir," the young groom stuttered.

"Did you take a shot?"

"N-no, s-sir."

"Then what's the problem?"

"I believe I had a bit of an accident."

Cyrus camouflaged a chuckle behind a cough while Hiram's shoulders shook in silent amusement.

Sin opened his pouch and tossed the lad two gold coins. "And I believe in extra pay for combat duty. You responded exactly as you should have. You held steady. We are most grateful."

"T-thank you, s-sir."

"No need to thank me," Sin replied before he stepped into the coach. "You're the one who reacted prudently."

"Aye, mate," Cyrus chimed in. "It was this damnfool Sinclair who flirted with disaster. I had half a mind to shoot him myself when he purposely drew fire so we could see where the highwaymen were hidin'."

When the coach lurched off, the two men concealed in underbrush cursed mightily.

"I swear you can't kill that devil," Owen scowled as he crawled toward his horse.

"There are ways," Jerome assured him. "But we are going to have to get that bastard alone to do it."

"I think Sinclair needs to have an accident," Owen advised. "I don't want folks getting suspicious of us. If we're linked to his death, we'll defeat our purpose."

Jerome muttered at the second failed attempt, knowing Owen was right. Sinclair had cleverly set both men up to shoulder the blame if he wound up a murder victim. An arranged accident was the only solution. Jerome was going to have to devise the perfect catastrophe to plant that bastard six feet deep. His devil's luck couldn't hold out forever, Jerome convinced himself. What Jerome needed was a foolproof method.

* * *

Dressed in men's breeches and a shirt, Angelene trotted her mount through the darkness, with only scant moonlight to guide her up the twisting passageway that led to Raven's Hill. Almost perpendicular walls, twenty feet high, rose on either side of the sunken trail. Angelene likened her late-night journey to a trip through a three-sided tunnel that was choked with gnarled tree roots, tangling grapevines and underbrush. She swore there were a thousand ravens roosting in the shadowed reaches, all warning her that seeking out Sin was not one of her brighter ideas. Unfortunately, Angelene felt a moral obligation to save Reggie from his own foolishness.

Inhaling a courageous breath, Angelene nudged her reluctant steed through the gloomy corridor, determined to talk some sense into Nick Sinclair before the duel which was scheduled at dawn.

It would not be an equal match, mentally or physically. Reggie was a relatively harmless fortune hunter who had allowed blustering pride to spur him into a battle. He would be a dead man if Angelene couldn't persuade Sin to remain in bed and ignore the sunrise appointment at Vidalia. Angelene knew that Sinclair was dangerous because she had witnessed his combative skills. Why, the man was as cool as an iceberg and as unerring as one of King Arthur's legendary knights.

Moonlight speared down like the beacon from a lighthouse when Angelene emerged from the sunken trail and topped the hill. Massive shadows of oaks and pines lined the rolling acreage that had once belonged to an eccentric old bachelor. Angelene had visited the mansion in her youth and explored it with a child's fascinated curiosity, while her father visited with the old gent. But to her amazement, the outward appearance of the mansion had changed dramatically since the last time she'd seen it. Angelene couldn't believe what she was staring at!

Why, the house looked more like a landlocked schooner than a southern plantation. There were even large portholes where windows had once been. The wrought-iron railings on the second and third story galleries had been replaced with teakwood. Stern lanterns hung at either end of the wide monstrosity. The upper level reminded Angelene of a quarter deck, and elaborately carved and gilded motifs and figureheads made of brass and copper ornamented the "stem" and "stern" of the home.

Sin had definitely been a buccaneer in a previous life, she concluded. He had brought the sea with him—and probably several chests of stolen treasure—when he'd relocated in Natchez.

Angelene was grimly aware that she knew little about the mysterious rake she found herself unwillingly attracted to—and for no logical reason she could think of. Well, that did not matter, she told herself firmly. She had come to persuade Sin to spare Reggie's life.

Hopping to the ground, Angelene strode toward the widespread magnolia tree that she had climbed as a child. She avoided the back steps and any traffic she might encounter there. If memory served, the tree's long limbs dangled above the second-floor gallery. The master suite was in a wing to the left, where Rudolph Fifkin, the previous owner, had been known to lounge by a wide row of windows that overlooked the cove. Rudolph had fancied himself a playwright—the next Shakespeare, in fact. But his works had never been performed, on account of his lack of creative talent. Angelene ought to know. She had sneaked into the sunlit chamber during her father's visits and read them.

Angelene latched onto a branch and swung up to climb to the master suite, wondering if a woman who purposely went in search of *Sin* wasn't asking for more trouble than she could handle. Much she was loath to admit it, Angelene knew that her formal education and proclaimed intelligence were no match for Nick Sinclair's astute mind. He was the most resourceful creature she had ever run across. Watching him deal with Kimball, Porter and Foster reminded her of a chess game in which Sin was the only player and the other men were his pawns.

She would have to avoid falling into the same trap.

## *Fifteen*

Ensconced in the corner chair of his darkened room, Sin came to immediate attention when he heard the muffled creak of the door. When a shadowed figure, garbed in breeches, appeared, Sin automatically reached for the pistol on the nightstand. A rare smile tugged at his lips when he noticed the shapely curves and swells that filled out the man's clothing. He had been expecting a late visitor, via the front door, dressed in conventional attire. A slight miscalculation on his part.

In attentive silence, Sin watched the curvaceous silhouette tiptoe toward his bed. He wondered if Angelene was packing a weapon and intended to use it on him if he refused to agree to the demands he predicted she would make. That would save Kimball and Porter the trouble of disposing of him.

"A visit from an *Angel*. How divine."

Startled, Angelene whirled toward the bland voice that drifted from the corner. "Why aren't you in bed?"

"Because I have grown tired of sleeping by myself. Have you come to remedy the situation?"

Up went that delicate but defiant chin. "Hardly. Since you have sauntered around Natchez, gathering the best servants, field hands, cooks and trainers to be had, I wouldn't be surprised to hear you have filled the position of mistress as well. How fares our ex-cook, by the way?'

"Agnes? She is blithely content here, as are all the other servants. As for my mistress, the position is still open. Would you like to apply?"

Angelene's gaze landed on the shiny barrel of the pistol lying on the nightstand. "Perhaps I should do Reggie, Jerome and Owen the grand favor of blowing you to smithereens," she muttered at him. "Putting you out of everybody's misery is beginning to have tremendous appeal."

"I'm sure it does, considering your high-spirited temperament."

A wary frown knitted Angelene's brow as she stared at the massive figure—a shadow among the shadows. "If I didn't know better, I would swear you were expecting me."

"Would you?" he questioned glibly.

"Yes I would. I'm also discovering that dealing with *Sin* is proving to be a very exasperating business."

"Even for an Angel who delights in walking where mortals fear to tread? I think not," Sin said nonchalantly. "We both know you thrive on challenge. And I'm reasonably certain that you will find sharing my bed to be an enlightening endeavor."

"I am *not* here to apply for the position of your mistress!" she assured him crisply. "I have come to persuade you to avoid this preposterous duel."

"I am aware of that," came the bland voice from the shadows.

Sin was also aware that beneath Angel's lively spirit and independent nature beat a very tender and generous heart. She was a champion of lost causes, a defender of underdogs. She had risked her life to save Sin from assassins and she was risking her reputation to spare Reggie's life. Angelene's noble traits were also her vulnerabilities, and because of them, she had played right into Sin's hands. He had her exactly where he wanted her . . . Well, not quite . . .

"Aware of what?" Angelene persisted. "Aware that I don't wish to be your mistress, or that I want this farce of gunplay stopped before it starts?"

"Both."

There was a moment of silence while Sin rose and emerged from the shadows. Angelene swallowed uneasily when she noted the pensive expression upon his rugged features. "When you are immersed in deep thought it never bodes well for the subject of your contemplations. You are too cunning and analytical by half," Angelene grumbled resentfully. "I swear I have never met anyone who can so accurately predict reactions. You always seem to know what response to expect and plan accordingly. My intuition tells me that coming here wasn't the smartest thing I've ever done, even if it did seem a noble mission when I left home."

Sin ventured close, coming to stand an arm's length away from delectable temptation. "It *is* a noble crusade, Angel," he assured her.

"Then you will spare Reggie."

It wasn't a question, Sin noted. It was a command.

"That depends."

Angelene gnashed her teeth. "Depends on what?"

"On the reason you want to see Reggie alive and well," he calmly replied. "Are you in love with the man?"

"That is an absurd question, especially coming from one with your incisive wit," Angelene scoffed. "You know better than that. I am in love with no man."

"Then why would you risk your sterling reputation by coming here in the dark of night and sneaking into my bedroom to plead for his life?"

"Because killing Reggie would not only be exceptionally bad for him, but it would be a poor reflection on you."

"You are concerned about my respectable reputation, Angel? I'm touched."

It truly amazed her how the man could get his sarcasm across without employing smirks, scoffs or sneers. And how, she would like to know, could anyone maintain such incredible self-possession? Only once had Angelene seen Sin exhibit roiling emotion. In that instance he had shouted at her because she had nearly gotten her head blown off trying to help him.

"I came here to discuss this disgusting duel, not how *touched* you are," she insisted. "I demand that you leave Reggie in one piece."

"Demand, Angel?"

"Yes," she boldly affirmed.

"And what are you prepared to offer if I spare Reggie's life and subject myself to the inevitable gossip? I will be labeled a coward if I fail to appear on the dueling field at Vidalia."

Angelene blinked, annoyed at herself for failing to consider the flip side of this two-headed coin. Sin was right. *He was damned if he did accept the challenge he could easily win and damned if he didn't.*

"I will ensure that any speculation as to your reasons

for declining the duel exemplify your wish to avoid bloodshed. I will inform the gentry that you are an expert marksman, one of the best I've ever seen, in fact, and that you would find no sporting challenge in Reggie Foster."

"And how do you intend to do that without confessing to our secret rendezvous?"

"It was not a rendezvous," she qualified.

"No? Then what would you call it?"

"A mistake."

"Nonetheless, gossipers would have a field day with that information. I took great pains to keep the incident off public record and ensure no one knew of your involvement in the fatal scuffle. If you boast of my skills in self-defense, you will need to explain how you know that I am quite capable of taking care of myself."

Angelene grumbled to herself. He had stumped her with that one.

"I have a suggestion," Sin casually announced.

"I figured you would," Angelene muttered. "You always seem to be one step ahead."

Sin moved a step closer to peer down into her moonlit features. His male body came to immediate alert. The powerful physical attraction he felt for this spirited beauty grew more pronounced by the day and had—he did admit—played an influential role in the alternative scheme he had devised. He was going to give Angel no way out . . . because he had no wish to let her go. There was no reason why he should, either. She was, after all, Charles Sheridan's daughter.

"Well?" Angelene prodded impatiently. "What is this brilliant suggestion of yours?"

Sin yielded to the temptation then. His forefinger traced her velvet-soft lips, craving the delicious taste of her, the arousing feel of her supple body molded familiarly to his. "If you agree to become my mistress, I will spare the foolish dandy."

His outrageous bargain triggered Angelene's explosive temper. She launched herself at him, teeth and claws bared.

Sin caught her easily, applying pressure to her wrist until she hissed a curse at him. While Sin had trained himself to become the epitome of self-control, Angelene Sheridan was the personification of living, breathing fire—his exact opposite. Watching her react to his baiting and teasing provided plenty of amusement.

"You bastard!" she spat furiously.

"I believe we have already discussed the legitimacy of my birth," he calmly reminded her. "As to my suggestion of declaring your preference for me, it will assure Reggie and everyone else that there is no need for a duel. That's all that will save me from being verbally crucified by those who are anxious to claim I am a coward for refusing the challenge."

Angelene was so outraged and incensed that she could barely see straight. "I came here to spare a man's life and you seek to repay me by soiling *my* reputation to save *yours?* You are beneath contempt. And furthermore, you have the morals of a pirate, because you are a pirate!" she raged at him. "You have practically turned this house into a ship and you hired the best servants in the area and paid them wages with your stolen treasures. I wouldn't climb into your bed, even if we were the last of an endangered species and life as we knew it was doomed to extinction!"

"Not even to save your father from the same social ruin that Jerome Kimball and Owen Porter now face?" he questioned with deliberate calm.

Angelene went utterly still, her gaze narrowing on that infuriatingly impassive face. "What do you mean?"

"I mean, that since I am as human as the next man—"

"*That* is debatable."

"—I find myself attracted to you," he continued in an ingratiating tone. "Enough, in fact, to make this situation play to my advantage—"

"You play every situation to your advantage," she bitterly accused.

He didn't debate that. "Unless you agree to my wishes, Reggie will be pushing up daisies and Charles Sheridan's plantations will come tumbling down around his ears. He will find no labor force to plant and harvest his cotton, no market for his crops, and no servants to tend his needs. In short, your father will become a pauper, a social outcast, just like Kimball and Porter."

In all her twenty years Angelene had never felt such killing fury pulsate through her! "I have never encountered a man who would stoop so low as to bring about the downfall of influential men whose reputations and incomes had been secure until you worked your devilish voodoo. You are the undisputed master of evil cunning."

"Thank you, Angel. I am especially fond of you, too."

"I despise you and your distorted sense of humor!" Angelene spewed. "You are the most dishonorable, ignominious man I have ever met!"

"My code of ethics is not the issue," Sin said evenly.

"And your personal feelings need not enter into this. Emotions can be controlled."

"Yours obviously, but not mine," she flashed.

"But the question is: Will you agree to become my mistress to spare your foolhardy dandy's life and save your father's reputation and his fortune?" he persisted.

"Why are you doing this!" Angelene inhaled a fortifying breath and clamped an iron grip on her temper.

"I am attracted to you."

Angelene could have kicked herself for being the least bit flattered by his admission. She must be as insane as he was. Of course, she was still furious with him for maneuvering her into a corner. She stood there, staring up into that expressionless face, wondering how she could extricate herself without bringing Sin's wrath down on her father.

"Come here, Angel," he commanded softly.

Angelene remained rooted to the spot. "No. I want to know why my reputation is the sacrifice I am expected to make to save my father and Reggie—a man I wouldn't marry on a bet."

Sin stared at the bewitching vision whose trim-fitting clothes clung to her alluring feminine figure like a glove. He could easily visualize how she would look, lying naked beneath him. That tantalizing thought sent heat spiraling through his blood. His body clenched with repressed need and he silently acknowledged that his plan of revenge was a two-way curse.

"Because Angel, although you are the last woman I should want, you are the woman I desire. It is as simple and as complicated as that."

The softly uttered remark left Angelene floundering to

understand his meaning, but the glitter in those black diamond eyes was spellbinding.

Sure enough, Angelene thought to herself, she had ridden to hell to face the devil. He had craftily played her like his pawn. If she followed the irate voice of pride, it could cost her father his fortune and Reggie his life. If she followed the forbidden whisper of feminine desire it would ruin her reputation and shame the family name.

*It seemed that she was damned if she did and damned if she didn't.*

Angelene resorted to compromise—one she never would have offered if not faced with such unacceptable alternatives. "What if I agree to marry you?"

Sin inwardly grimaced as he watched Angelene wrestle with the dilemma he represented. Up until now, Sin swore he knew what all nine kinds of hell were like. What was to have been one of his great moments of revenge against Charles Sheridan was also Sin's torment. He felt no satisfaction in forcing this fallen Angel to succumb to his command. Marriage would salvage Angelene's pride, but it would lessen the degree of Sheridan's initial torture. First and foremost, Sin wanted to see Charles raging furiously. Anything less would defeat Sin's purpose—for the present, at least.

*An eye for an eye,* Sin forcefully reminded himself. The three murdering mutineers hadn't allowed sentiment to deter them eighteen years ago. They only considered the end result of their actions—acquiring wealth. The means to that greedy end had been of no concern. Lost lives had been a sacrifice they didn't hesitate to make. Why should he compromise when he had vowed to give every bit as good as he had gotten?

Sin had survived treachery by a stroke of fate. Why should he waver, now that he had finally attained the powerful position that enabled him to crush the men who had killed his brother and left him to die?

"I do not need a wife, only a mistress," Sin replied belatedly. "Other men hunger for your fortune, but I only desire the pleasure we can give each other."

His declaration shattered her every hope. This ruthless devil didn't care enough about her to spare her when she had risked her life to spare him from would-be assassins. Sin had a heart of stone, no conscience to speak of and no soul whatsoever. How could she have ever found herself attracted to this blackguard?

Sin lifted his hand to wipe away the tears he saw glistening in Angel's eyes. A riptide of unwanted emotion warred inside him and he very nearly knuckled under. He thought he would enjoy bringing this fiery beauty to her knees and crushing Charles Sheridan in one fell swoop.

He did not.

And yet, Sin had made a solemn vow to his brother, a promise that if he did survive, he would track those murderers down and repay them. And with his dying breath, Joshua Montague had accepted his young brother's promise, whispering that he would be there on that day of reckoning, if not in body then in spirit.

Angelene peered into the shadowed face that hovered a hair's breadth away. Her decision would affect her father's life, Reggie's life and her own. She remembered the way her father had doted over her mother, the way he doted over Angelene. Charles would do anything for her, Angelene was confident of that. Although she would never know that kind of unfaltering devotion from other men, Angelene was prepared to sacrifice to protect her father, just as he would lay his life on the line for her. As for Nick Sinclair, Angelene pitied him. He would never understand what selfless love was.

"While you may become the master of my body, you will never become the captain of my soul. *That* you will never have. And while you may come to be known as Angel's *Sin*, I will never become Sin's *Angel*. I will be your mistress from hell."

Angelene stared at him with fierce determination. "I will not fight you in bed, only because I want to save my father from the ruin you have brought down on Kimball and Porter. But Natchez will become a battleground of our wills, every livelong hour of every livelong day. On that you may depend."

"I expected no less from you," he murmured, losing himself in her alluring fragrance, to those green eyes that bespoke of unbreakable spirit. "All I want is what I've craved since the first night I saw you racing the storm, since I first touched you. I want to feel your fire in my blood and fan the flames . . ."

# *Sixteen*

When his raven head dipped toward hers, Angelene dodged his intended kiss. "Expect to be disappointed," she warned him.

"Disappointed?" He couldn't imagine how that could be!

"I have never endeavored to pleasure a man—" Her voice quavered as his hand glided up her hip to swirl over the swell of her breast. "I have no inkling how to start, even if I wanted to, which I don't."

There was an uncharacteristic smile on his lips as he moved deliberately closer. "I'll show you everything you'll need to know, Angel. Trust me."

Reluctantly, she allowed him to settle her hands on the broad, muscular wall of his chest and draw her into the circle of his arms. "As surely as I will fulfill the bargain I have no choice but to accept, I will *never* trust you . . ."

It was not her trust that was driving him to complete distraction, Sin realized as his lips settled upon hers. It was her. He wanted Angelene Sheridan. He had known that as an undeniable fact the first time he met her. Even discovering the truth of her identity hadn't stopped him from wanting her in ways he had wanted no other woman. Angelene aroused him, challenged him. That was the only reality Sin could understand when he lost himself to the spark that had ignited between them the first time they had touched.

Sin made a solemn vow to himself when he felt Angelene reluctantly yet instinctively respond to his tender kiss. Even in these corridors of hell he had designed for himself, there would be one corner of heaven. He would employ every seductive technique he knew, to awaken Angelene's passion. She might battle him on every front during their waking hours, but he would make her desire him as much as he desired her. Tonight, he promised himself, she would not submit as demanded by their bargain, but rather surrender to rapture.

To that dedicated end, Sin treated Angelene to gentle caresses that pleasured rather than demanded, to kisses that savored rather than devoured. He heard her breath catch when his hand tunneled beneath her shirt, when he teased the beaded peaks of her beasts. Slowly, he unbuttoned her shirt. His lips drifted down her satiny throat to greet every inch of skin he exposed.

When her breath tore out on a quivering sigh Sin knew it was pleasure she experienced, not repulsion. Each touch was a new experience for her, an erotic response that mesmerized him. He would cherish her, memorize every luscious inch of her flesh until she willingly welcomed him. She would find no fault when she was in his arms.

Sin told himself these things, but his utter fascination in exploring her with kisses and caresses became a hopeless distraction. He absorbed the alluring scent of her, memorized the silky texture of her skin. He marveled at the way she instinctively arched into his hands and lips.

He heard the muffled cry she couldn't contain when pleasure overshadowed her resentment. He watched, beguiled, as moonbeams streamed through the window, spotlighting the waterfall of red-gold hair, outlining her shapely figure.

All she knew of desire would be what she learned from him, and in turn, he would learn each place where she liked to be touched and how she liked to be touched while she was discovering it for herself.

Without taking his eyes off her, Sin scooped her into his arms and laid her on his bed. He could see the fearful quiver in her eyes mingling with the sparkle of desire he had aroused in her. It was as if she were expecting to be ravished, and her own bravado was all that kept her from attempting to escape what she didn't understand . . .

The thought caused Sin's hands to falter on the buttons of his shirt while he undressed. Although tonight would be Angelene's first experiment with intimate passion, it would also be his first experience with an innocent. He prided himself in iron will and self-restraint, but, given the hungry need that presently throbbed through him, Sin wondered if he had the patience this naive beauty needed.

It was not Angelene's humiliation he sought, it was her answering desire. This wasn't about his personal feud with Charles Sheridan, Sin realized. It was only about the fierce attraction he felt for this intriguing woman he had met on a darkened meadow one stormy night.

But damn it, why did the woman he desired and the one he planned to destroy—to enrage her father—have to be one and the same?

Amusement twinkled in Sin's eyes, scattering his troubled thoughts, when Angelene scooted to the far side of the bed and buried herself beneath the quilt like a butterfly in a cocoon. She was definitely wary of what she was feeling and what would happen next. He would have to proceed slowly, gently.

With fingers that trembled from barely restrained need, Sin shed his shirt and tossed it toward a nearby chair . . .

Sin had never given his masculine prowess much thought . . . until Angelene's wide green eyes focused on his hair-roughened chest, flooded over the washboard muscles of his belly and dropped to the waist band of his breeches. He considered himself a man with a man's needs—period. But Angelene's gaze, so full of feminine speculation and curiosity, made him feel very desirable, whether she intended it or not. He wondered how she would react when he doffed his breeches.

He proceeded to do just that.

"Dear L——" Angelene's voice fractured when her gaze drifted below Sin's lean waist. "It is physically impossible to——" She forgot to breathe when that powerful mass of masculinity stretched out beside her, dwarfing her—and the bed that had seemed roomy enough moments before.

"Sh . . . sh," Sin whispered as he reached over to close her gaping jaw with a tender caress. He could feel the hot blush that stained her cheeks, see the moonlight reflecting off her luminous eyes. "Let's take this one step at a time, shall we?"

"I agreed to submit, but I hadn't expected the torture of——"

His forefinger pressed against her lips, shushing her.

He eased closer, battling the ravenous hunger gnawing at him. "This is not about torture, Angel."

She gulped nervously. "Forgive me if I'm doubtful, Sin."

"Have I hurt you yet?"

"No."

"Nor do I intend to." Sin didn't say that he *wouldn't* unintentionally. He decided there were some things better left to be discussed when the moment was upon them.

When his hand drifted over her hip to swirl over her belly, he felt Angelene tense and then relax beneath his feathery touch. Her skin was like the finest Chinese silk. Her figure rivaled the greatest European sculptures. Exquisite, he thought as he sought her lips, dying of thirst for a sip of heaven's nectar.

Her quiet gasp provoked his satisfied smile. He could feel her quivering beneath his adventurous caresses. Need clenched inside him and Sin battened it down. He wanted to relish each new phase of passion he introduced Angel to. It gave him an unexpected sense of pleasure knowing he was the first man to enjoy such intimate privileges with this much-sought-after heiress. Although Angel resented him, they were going to share the most private of secrets about each other before this night was out.

Ever so gently he measured the trim indentation of her waist, the flair of her hips. He feasted on the taste of her lips. When his hand trailed across her thigh to nudge her legs apart, he felt the heat of her response tempting him. A shudder went through him as he traced the satiny flesh of her inner thigh, imagining how it would feel to have that sultry flame burning around him until it consumed them both.

Sin couldn't remember enjoying a woman quite so much and torturing himself to such extremes in the process. Taking the innocence of this spirited female demanded that he give something of himself in return. He wasn't certain why he felt the need to be sensitive and gentle, it just seemed as natural and inevitable as breathing. He wanted Angel to want him to the same profound degree he wanted her.

Angle's breath caught in her throat when his questing fingers delicately traced her, delved deeper . . . and wildly aroused her.

"Sin?"

"Perhaps," he whispered as his lips drifted across her collarbone to hover over the rising bud of her breast. "But it's also delicious pleasure."

He stroked her slowly, tenderly, feeling the hot rain of her response bathing his fingertip.

"Oh . . . God!" Angelene groaned when unexpected sensations rippled through her like waves of flames.

She was so warm, so fragile, so responsive that Sin's senses reeled. He wanted to burn alive in the soft liquid flames he had ignited in her.

His stroking hand incited another trembling response and Sin nearly moaned aloud when he felt her contracting around his fingertip in a secret caress. He had vowed to take his time with Angel, but he had already deprived himself too long. He needed her—now—wanted to become the pulsing essence within her, wanted to be close enough to share the same flesh, the same breath, the same thoughts.

When he eased her legs farther apart with his knee and braced above her, he stared down into the shadowy face that he had seen so often in forbidden dreams. Angelene instinctively moved toward him and Sin forgot how crucial this moment could be. When he thrust forward, responding to pure male instinct, Angel stiffened beneath him, her breath escaping in a hiss of pain.

She was so small by comparison, Sin realized—a moment too late. This was supposed to have been the instant that he was most attentive to her needs, but he had been blinded by his own ardent desire.

"You lied to me," she whispered, afraid to move for fear of intensifying the unfamiliar pressure he inflicted.

Sin forced himself not to move, though it was the most natural reaction. "I'm sorry," he rasped hoarsely.

"It doesn't help." She inhaled a courageous but shallow breath. "At least it's over."

Sin felt the outrageous urge to burst out laughing—or yell in frustration—he wasn't sure which. He found her naïveté as refreshing as it was tormenting. "Angel?"

Her breath wobbled as she held herself taut against the unfamiliar pain. "W-what?"

"It isn't over yet. It has only begun."

Wide green eyes searched his craggy features as he loomed over her. "It . . . gets . . . worse?"

Sin cringed at the question. He would make her enjoy him as much as he was enjoying her, he vowed determinedly. He was going to teach her the meaning of life's most sensual sensations, even if it damned near killed him—and it felt as if it would.

He withdrew slightly and bent to take her lips beneath his. As he glided toward her again, his tongue mated with hers. With more patience than he even realized he possessed he set a slow, gentle cadence. His greatest reward came in feeling her untried body yield to him, accept him, respond to him. With each penetrating thrust he felt her arch to meet him and heard her cry of wonderment.

Sin drew her legs around his hips and gave himself up to the passion that pounded through him like a storm engulfing a hapless ship. He had definitely been too long between women, he decided. That was why this vivacious beauty had him thinking that her first time was his first time. Only that, Sin assured himself before passion churned over him like high-rolling breakers. Only that . . .

Or was it . . . ?

Sin had come close to drowning once before, but never as close as this! Indescribable rapture swamped him as he moved in ageless rhythm, feeling Angelene match him, feeling her become trapped in the same engulfing tidal wave of ecstasy that drenched him.

And then he was catapulting through a dark universe where time knew no measure, where pleasure so intense expanded until it knew no boundary. His body pulsed in wild release and he felt Angelene tremble in answering response, felt her nails digging into his shoulders, as if to anchor herself in a dizzying world that spun into oblivion.

Sweet mercy, Sin thought when numbing rapture burgeoned inside him. This kind of breath-robbing intensity could kill a man! Or maybe it already had and Sin just was just too numb with pleasure to realize it yet.

"Sin?"

"Not in my book," he said on a ragged sigh.

"We really are going to have to do something about your sense of humor," she playfully admonished.

He smiled rakishly. "Doing *this* on a regular basis would probably help."

"That's what I want to talk to you about." Angelene wrapped her arms round him, amazed at the wild hunger that raged through her body, even after Sin shuddered and collapsed above her. The unexplainable sensations refused to subside. "Can we do that again . . . now?"

Sin raised his ruffled head when he felt her moving sensuously beneath him. To his recollection, he had never been asked to engage in a repeat performance, nor had he wanted to. He had simply gotten up and walked away . . . until now . . .

He could feel himself rousing in response to her provocative movements, and he wondered if this sweet fire that burned between them would always demand constant feeding. If tonight was anything to go by, the greatest task he encountered would be prying himself out of bed.

When her adventurous hand slipped down the slope of his back and drifted over his hip, Sin instantly responded. In no more time that it took to draw breath, they were moving as one, discovering another dimension of mindless passion. Sin had the feeling that he hadn't just seduced an innocent, but he had awakened a passionate tigress.

Good thing he had become conditioned to rigorous physical activity, he mused with a raffish smile. Angel was proving to be a very engaging and responsive lover. Not that he would think of complaining. Indeed, he could name a dozen envious fortune hunters who wished they could exchange places with him tonight. And all those frustrated husbands who ventured to brothels, when their wealthy, sophisticated wives proved a little too ladylike, would be scowling resentfully if they knew how wildly passionate this rare jewel was. Angel was, Sin decided, every husband's dream come true—lovely, sophisticated and incredibly responsive . . . And she belonged to him in ways no other man could claim . . .

That was the last thought to flit through his mind before inexpressible passion consumed him. Sin felt the shimmering sensations coursing through him again, growing even more intense than the first time.

It was unnerving to feel so lost in a woman. Angel represented the kind of danger Sin had never confronted. She could trigger the outpouring of emotions he had become conditioned to suppress. He could no more restrain the wild pulsations that whipped through his body and vibrated through hers like a gale pelting a canvas sail than he could hold back a devastating typhoon.

As before, Sin felt the earth wobbling on its axis, tossing him farther off balance. His heart nearly beat him to death as need sent him thrusting harder, deeper, seeking breathless release. His arms contracted as desire surged through him, exploding out of control.

Sweet mercy was right! Sin thought. There was no way to appease the phenomenal need he and Angel awakened in each other, at least not for more than a few minutes or hours at a time. Sin had never experienced anything like this, and the only thing he could compare it to was riding the wild waves of a storm at sea. But this, ah . . . this voyage granted unbelievable ecstasy.

Even when he felt himself drifting down from sublime

heights to catch his breath, he felt insatiable need assaulting him again, felt Angelene shifting restlessly beneath him. Neither of them seemed able to get enough of each other.

Was this normal? No, Sin decided. This was an obsession.

"Sin?"

His lips grazed her cupid's bow mouth and he smiled to himself. "I know, Angel. I wonder who said lightning didn't strike more than once in the same place. Whoever it was made a miscalculation." And so had Sin . . .

"Dear Lord," Angelene whispered, bewildered by the wild urge to experience every fantastic sensation again. "What is wrong with me?"

"That's the problem," Sin murmured as he settled above her. "Everything about you is perfectly right . . ."

Sin gave himself up to the inexhaustible craving they aroused in each other. He wondered if his stamina would last the night, for it appeared it was going to require the entire night to cure this incredible addiction.

It was a good thing Sin planned to decline the duel at Vidalia. He wasn't sure a tugboat could have towed him away from this passionate beauty at the break of dawn. He should have known Angel would test him to his very limits. She was a woman brimming with vitality and boundless energy. She was the kind of woman a man had trouble handling, Sin thought with a smile, but then a man wouldn't mind dying *trying,* either . . .

# Seventeen

"Sin!" Cyrus called from the hall. "It's time to leave. Are you ready?"

Cyrus, with Hiram on his heels, barged into the darkened room. Both men came to a screeching halt when they heard a muffled gasp that sounded nothing like Sin's baritone voice.

"What the devil—?" Hiram squinted into the shadows when the bed creaked and incongruous forms shifted beneath the quilt.

Cyrus grinned wryly, knowing *what* if not *who* was in Sin's bed. A woman, no doubt about that. "Hate to interrupt, mate, but you have a duel to fight at dawn. Hardly a match for your fightin' skills, I admit, but Reggie needs to be put in his place."

Sin scowled to himself. He had been jolted awake by the patter of rain and the sound of unwelcome intruders. The night had provided little sleep, though he was hardly one to complain. He had intended to crawl out of bed and inform his seconds of his change of plans.

So much for good intentions. As for humiliating Angelene—as he had planned to do when he'd originally devised his revenge for Charles Sheridan—Sin couldn't bring himself to shame her in front of his men. Angelene was mortified as it was, if her attempt to bury herself beneath the blanket was any indication. She was plastered so tightly against him to avoid discovery that it was damned arousing. Lord! After the night they'd shared, one would have thought he would have been too tired to respond.

Apparently not.

"I have decided to forgo the duel."

"Not fightin'?" Cyrus parroted as his gaze circled from the shadowed forms in bed to the discarded men's clothes on the . . . Men's clothes? His wide amber eyes leaped back to the bed. "Cap'n?"

Sin expelled an exasperated breath when both Cyrus's and Hiram's astounded gazes fell to the garments on the floor. Things were getting worse by the second. "I believe you'll find a mount tethered on the east side of—"

"West," came a mumbled voice from the pile of quilts.

"West side of the house," Sin calmly continued. "I would appreciate it if you would saddle a horse for me and bring both horses around to the front of—"

"Back."

"Back of the house."

"What about Reggie Foster?" Hiram inquired.

"You need not saddle a horse for him," Sin said blandly.

A giggle broke out beneath the quilts and Sin bit back a smile. He was glad Angel appreciated his droll sense of humor. Most people simply didn't understand it—Hiram and Cyrus, for instance.

"Come again?" Cyrus questioned.

Sin didn't think he had the energy left for *that*. "We needn't contact Foster. I'm sure it will occur to him sooner or later that we aren't coming. And close the door on your way out, please."

Hiram and Cyrus took their cue and trooped off.

"You aren't coming with me," Angelene insisted as she wormed toward the edge of the bed to pluck up her clothes.

Sin smiled appreciatively at the shapely figure revealed by the drooping quilt. "Now what kind of gentleman would I be if I didn't accompany you home, especially in the rain."

Angelene fastened her shirt and flung him a withering glance. "We have already established the fact that you aren't much of a gentleman, so don't delude yourself in thinking you must live up to noble expectation."

"No? If I'm so ignoble, then what sort of woman cavorts with the likes of me?" he mocked glibly.

"One who has no other choice," Angelene muttered as she bounded from bed and wiggled into her breeches.

When she had dressed, she turned to fling another well-deserved barb at Sin, but her gaze fell to the dark stains on the sheet. Humiliation blossomed on her cheeks. Of all her impulsive escapades this was positively the most disastrous. She had come to save Reggie's foolish neck and lost her virginity in order to save her father from the same catastrophe that had struck Kimball and Porter.

Sin winced uncomfortably when he noticed where Angel's gaze had strayed. He hadn't intended to carry things quite so far and he certainly hadn't expected his conscience to nag him so relentlessly.

While Angelene pulled on her stockings, Sin grabbed his clothes and hurriedly dressed. The silence, broken only by the thump of raindrops, was as thick as the coal tar used to seal the hulls of ships.

"How long will it take for you to gather your belongings?" Sin queried.

Angelene's hand stalled as she reached for her boots. "My belongings?" she repeated cautiously.

"I expect you to take up residence here, of course," he said in a neutral tone.

Angelene groped for the reins of her temper and came up empty-handed. "There are limits to what I will do to protect—"

"I don't believe in setting limits. It only gives one an excuse not to test his full potential."

Green eyes flared like torches. "You are a genuine—"

"Bastard," he calmly finished for her. "Yes, so I have been told on a number of occasions."

"And most deservedly."

Sin's massive shoulders lifted in an indifferent shrug. "That is neither here nor there. You will find your suite at Raven's Hill comfortably furnished. You will be provided with all the luxuries your father's home afforded." When Angel stared at him as if he were insane—or she was and she couldn't decide which—Sin nearly broke into a smile. "I think you will be able to rejoin me here by tomorrow evening."

"You may not survive until tomorrow evening," Angelene muttered spitefully.

Sin curled his arm around her elbow and escorted her to the door that adjoined the master suite. Angelene stared at the spacious room that had been remodeled and decorated with ivory statues, teakwood totems, bronze dragons and priceless keepsakes that looked as if they had been collected from every corner of the world. She had the unshakable feeling the room had been prepared for her beforehand.

Angelene stared speculatively at the brawny giant beside her. She would have given her fortune to know what Sin was planning.

"If the accommodations are not to your liking, they can be altered," Sin assured her as he ushered her toward the terrace.

"I demand to know what is going on."

"Demanding again, Angel?"

"Have my father, Owen Porter, Jerome Kimball and Reggie Foster done something to become your personal targets?" she wanted to know.

Refusing to reply, Sin opened the door to the gallery and headed toward the back staircase.

"I am waiting for an answer," Angelene prodded.

"What makes you think that has anything to do with you and me?"

"Because nothing you do is without motive. If I have learned nothing else about you, I have learned that."

Sin drew Angelene to a halt at the head of the steps. An unexpected surge of emotion pulsed through him as he peered down into sharp emerald eyes and a wild tangle of red-gold hair. "Whatever else happens, Angel, believe that my attraction to you—"

Scoffing bitterly, Angelene wormed loose from his grasp. "Your *attraction* comes without feelings attached," she countered. "You are a man without a heart or soul so don't insult my intelligence by trying to convince me that I mean more to you than you do to me."

For some reason that defiant comment struck deeper

than Sin thought it would. As usual though, he shrugged sentiment aside. After all, he had ceased feeling eighteen years ago and had isolated himself from sentimental emotion.

"Very well then," he replied as he shepherded Angelene down the steps. "Think whatever you prefer. Just be here tomorrow night."

"Rest assured that I do not need your permission to think what I want!"

Sin felt the makings of a grin upon his lips. Angelene was true to her word. She had vowed to give him hell every chance she got. However, Sin was accustomed to dealing with hell.

Angelene paused on the landing of the steps and glanced at the sinewy rake. "Since you have left me with no alternative, I will accept this defeat—as a momentary setback."

"And you have accepted defeat so graciously, too," Sin added.

Angelene gnashed her teeth and promised herself she would invent a way to outfox this clever rascal. That would become *her* ulterior motive . . .

The mumble of voices jostled Angelene from her bitter deliberations. She glanced down to see Hiram and Cyrus gaping at the flowing mass of blond hair that descended to her waist. The two men stood in the rain, staring up at her as if they had seen a ghost—or something to that effect.

Sin felt Angelene tense beside him and he told himself to repress that angry nip of conscience that was taking bites out of him. It was obvious that his friends did not approve of what had transpired. He also knew Angelene was cringing with mortification, even as she marched down the steps with as much dignity as the situation permitted her.

"Take my rain slicker, Miss Sheridan," Hiram generously offered.

Angelene murmured a subdued thank-you and accepted the poncho. Without waiting for Sins assistance, she bounded onto the saddle and trotted off, leaving Sin to follow—or not.

"How did you . . . ? Why is she—?"

"Later," Sin cut Cyrus off. He stepped into the stirrup and leaned down to accept the jacket Hiram handed to him. "I have a request. Consult our new servants as to the whereabouts of Kimball's, Porter's and Sheridan's important documents—property deeds to be specific."

"What are you plannin' now?" Cyrus queried, bewildered.

"We'll discuss that later, too," was all Sin said before he nudged Turk into a canter and rode into the downpour.

Charles Sheridan was beside himself with distress. There were times when his rambunctious daughter sailed off into the night to ride that spirited steed of hers, but she always returned home. This time, however, she had not. When Charles summoned Angelene to breakfast, the maid appeared to report that Angelene was not in her room and it didn't look as if she had been all night. Charles paced his study, frowning in concern. He could imagine all sorts of calamity befalling Angelene. There was always the threat of robbery and abduction, around

Natchez. In fact, news had arrived earlier that two coaches had been attacked after Wilhelm's party.

The steady rain intensified Charles's distress. According to the stable boy whom Charles had contacted an hour earlier, the creeks in the area were already running full. Angel could have been stranded anywhere.

The unsettling thought caused Charles to wheel toward the foyer. He couldn't wait any longer. He had to send out a search party. He would drive himself crazy worrying if . . .

Before Charles could snatch up his jacket and head to the stables, the front door creaked open to reveal his daughter and . . . Charles's concern transformed to indignation when he recognized the darkly clad figure looming behind Angelene.

"What is the meaning of this, Sinclair!"

Sin was hardly surprised that Charles had never considered wrongdoing on his precious daughter's part. In Charles's eyes, Angel was guiltless. She was, after all, his treasured possession. Sin, however, was another matter entirely.

"Considering the inclement weather, I thought it best to accompany Angelene home," Sin replied placidly.

Charles glanced from his daughter's averted gaze to the towering figure of a man behind her. Sinclair was as impenetrable as rock.

"Angel, go up to your room immediately!" Charles demanded.

"No, I—"

"Now!" Charles bellowed.

"I would like a private word with you, Charles," Sin insisted.

"And you'll get it," Charles muttered furiously. Wheeling about, he stormed into his office and gestured for Sin to step inside. The instant he did, Charles slammed the door.

"You bastard!"

Sin calmly doffed his rain slicker and draped it over the hook beside the door. "For some reason, everyone around Natchez seems to question my legitimacy. I wonder why that is?"

Sin's dry sarcasm flew over Charles's head. Charles gritted his teeth and clenched his fists. "You have threatened my daughter's reputation by showing up on my doorstep like this and you damned well know it! My God, man, do you think my servants are deaf and blind?"

"I assume they must be, considering the way you're shouting," Sin nonchalantly inserted.

"Rumors will be flying and not even this downpour will slow the gossip down! How dare you take this serious matter so lightly!"

Charles's visible outrage indicated his deep affection for his daughter. The man was at the end of his tether, Sin noted. He wondered if Charles was feeling half the billowing frustration and anguish he'd endured while drifting in a skiff, watching his last family member die. No, Sin decided, Charles Sheridan didn't know what vindictive fury really was—yet.

"Where did you find my daughter? And why couldn't you have had the decency to let her make her own entrance?" Charles raged.

"I can hardly be held accountable for your daughter's actions, now can I?" Sin parried. "The fact is that she came to Raven's Hill of her own free will."

The remarks took the wind out of Charles's sails. "She *what?*"

"Did I stutter?"

Charles bolted forward, seething with fury. "Are you implying that Angelene, who has never—"

"I suggest you keep your voice down. You loudly announced earlier that the servants were neither deaf nor blind."

"I'll see you burn in hell for this, Sinclair," Charles snarled maliciously.

"I have decided I want your daughter," Sin said calmly.

Charles jerked up his head and glowered flaming daggers. "Just as you wanted the horse Porter says you bought out from under him? Just as you have gone into competition against Kimball and turned his peers against him?"

Sin wondered if any of the three mutineers would ever make the connection. Obviously not. Sin had changed drastically in appearance the last eighteen years. The mutineers would have to be prompted, especially once Sin irritated them to the point that they couldn't see or think past their fury.

"You better think again if you believe I will give my consent to a marriage between the likes of you and Angel!" Charles raged.

Black diamond eyes bore down on Charles's reddened face." I don't recall mentioning marriage."

Charles's jaw fell off its hinges. He stood there, speechless, at a complete loss as to how to deal with a man who never raised his voice or altered expressions. Sinclair truly was a walking rock, damn him!

"I have decided, however, to be extremely discreet in

our affair," Sin continued. "My servants will not breathe a word about this . . . um . . . connection that has developed between Angel and me. I hope you have the same control over the situation at Sheridan Hall. If not, word of the liaison will spread through Natchez like an epidemic and you will have only yourself to thank for it."

Charles struggled to inhale a breath and locate his tongue. It took considerable effort. "I refuse to allow you anywhere near my daughter again!"

"Angelene has shown her preference and I have shown mine," Sin countered. "This is not your concern."

"Damn you, I wish Reggie had—" Charles stopped short. "Where is Reggie? Dead?"

"I haven't a clue. Angelene convinced me to refuse the challenge. She insisted it wasn't in my best interests. Of course a man would be an utter fool to disregard recommendations from an Angel, wouldn't he?"

Charles's brown eyes narrowed. "She sought you out to save that blundering fob's neck and this is how you repay her? Dear Lord, what kind of man are you, Sinclair? Have you no conscience whatsoever?"

"As much as you do, I expect."

Sin kept waiting for Charles to strike out in demented fury, but he appeared to have more self-control than his cohorts. No doubt, when Charles recovered his wits, he would resort to the treacherous tactics Kimball and Porter employed—bushwhacking. After all, Sin reminded himself, they were three of a kind.

"For the record," Sin said as he pulled on the rain slicker, "I am the kind of man who knows what he wants and how to get it." His gaze transfixed on Charles's puckered frown. "I'm sure you can relate to that."

"Why are you doing this?" Charles hissed.

Sin leaned against the door knob and glanced over his shoulder at the third mutineer. "You will discover the answer to that question soon enough," he promised before he closed the door behind him and walked away.

# Eighteen

Angelene cringed when her bedroom door crashed against the wall and dust dribbled from the woodwork. She had been dreading this encounter. The look of disappointment and outrage on Charles's features was like a knife through the heart. Nick Sinclair was going to be eternally sorry, she vowed stormily. She was holding him accountable, and somehow she was going to foil his attempt to wreak havoc on the lives of the people he had singled out for some clandestine purpose.

"Angel, how could you!" Charles burst out miserably.

Angelene said the only thing she could say. "Papa, I'm sorry. I know I have disgraced you, but Nick Sinclair is . . ." She paused, called upon her acting ability and chose her words carefully. "I have never met a man who makes me feel the way he does."

That was certainly the truth! Sin had her wondering how many ways she could murder him without getting caught.

"He treats me the way no other man ever has and he recognizes my intelligence and does not resent it."

That was a half truth. Nick Sinclair had obviously given a great deal of thought as to how to entrap her. No other man had accomplished the feat. Only Sin had taken her intelligence into account and proceeded accordingly. The clever rascal!

Charles peered incredulously at his daughter. "Are you telling me you have actually developed a fond attachment for that man? There are scads of eligible bachelors hereabout who have ten times more scruples than he obviously does. Why him, Angel?"

"Because he challenges me instead of patronizing me," she answered in all honesty.

Despite her annoyance with that rake, Sin had stirred feelings in Angelene she had never expected to experience with a man. No matter how furious Sin made her, that was the one truth Angelene could not deny.

"Don't you think this is rather short notice, Angel? Dear Lord, you only just met the man last night!"

"Actually, we have met several times, while I was exercising my mount before returning home from Oak Gables," she informed her father. "We have been acquainted since Sin arrived in Natchez."

Charles dropped into the nearest chair and raked his hand through his crop of red hair. "You are telling me that you went willingly to Nick Sinclair, that *he* is the one you have chosen over all other suitors?"

"Yes, Papa, he is the one I have chosen." *As the one she would like to strangle,* she silently tacked on. Angelene couldn't tell her father the whole truth, not without inciting a clash between the man she had loved her whole life through and the one who fascinated her, against her better judgment.

After a long moment, Charles heaved an audible sigh and nodded his head. "Very well then, if you are sure he is the one you want, I will agree to a wedding, despite these awkward circumstances."

Angelene swallowed hard and prepared herself to leap another difficult hurdle. "I prefer to handle the details of that myself, should I decide . . . should *we* decide to wed . . . eventually."

Charles snapped up his head. "No daughter of mine is going to shame herself like that, no matter how she feels about a man. I expressly forbid it!"

"Very well then, we . . . um . . . will discuss marriage arrangements when I see him again."

"When will that be!" Charles persisted.

"Tomorrow night."

Another strained moment passed while Charles scrutinized Angelene from beneath puckered brows. "Do you love him so much, Angel?"

Angelene met her father's intense stare and sent a repentant prayer heavenward. "As much as you loved Mother. I want to be with Sin. Can you understand that, Papa? After encountering so many men who are *not* right for me, it didn't take long for me to realize who *is*."

When Charles strode over to press a kiss to her cheek, Angelene silently cursed Sin for forcing her into this frustrating predicament that had her twisting truths to pacify her father.

After witnessing Sin's confrontations with Kimball, Foster and Porter, she dreaded the prospect of her father squaring off against a man who thought so far ahead of everyone else. Sin's shrewdness and intellect were without compare. Angelene admired that about him as much as she resented it.

"Well, I hope Sinclair proves to be worthy of your

affection," Charles murmured before he turned around and walked out.

When the door clicked shut, tears misted Angelene's eyes. She was a fool to waste even one ounce of emotion on Nick Sinclair—at least not useless tears. She prided herself on her intelligence, didn't she? Well, by damn, she was going to devise a way to thwart Sin's plans. She would employ some of his methods. Somehow, she was going to counter that rascal and teach him a lesson he would not soon forget.

Angelene ambled over to the window and watched rain pour down in torrents. She'd had the presence of mind earlier that morning to assure Sin that he had left her no choice but to comply with his commands. Hopefully, he had accepted her at her word. Now all she had to do was puzzle out a solution that he might not be able to predict.

Pensively, Angelene stared at the rain and contemplated every bit and piece of gossip and tidbit of conversation referring to Nick Sinclair. She quickly recalled how Sin had provoked Kimball and Porter into losing their tempers and lashing out at him in front of an audience of peers. Then she reviewed the events leading up to Reggie's stupid challenge. That sly rascal had twisted the situation until Reggie found himself declaring a challenge over *her*. That had been another of Sin's clever tactics.

And then there was that remark her own father had made the previous night about seeing something familiar about Nick Sinclair. Had Charles previously met Sin, years ago perhaps? What could Charles possibly have done to provoke Sin into attempting to ruin him financially and socially?

Angelene frowned in deep concentration. It stood to reason that Nick Sinclair could have drastically changed in appearance if her father had met him in his youth. Angelene had been a small child when they'd arrived in Natchez. She knew her father had been at sea when she was born. Her mother had told her that much, though Charles never discussed those years as a sailor. Angelene definitely needed more information to resolve this perplexing puzzle.

In the meantime, she had to find a way to avoid further humiliation that might reflect on her father. She had pacified and temporarily put Charles off by insisting she would discuss marriage with Sin. But Sin had made it clear that he wanted no permanent ties, only physical satisfaction . . .

Angelene squeezed her eyes shut and cursed her own vulnerability to a man who held such a strange power over her. For that reason alone she had to avoid Sin.

Sweet merciful heavens, he could transform her into a wanton with his sinfully tantalizing seduction. No telling how great a fool she would make of herself if she fell beneath his devilish charm—on a regular basis.

On that unsettling thought, Angelene reminded herself that she had until the following evening to conjure up a way to avoid Sin before he destroyed her completely.


Sin sipped his glass of Madeira, declining the invitation to join Cyrus and Hiram in a game of cards. He was oddly restless after being confined indoors for the better part of two days. It reminded him of storms at sea.

He would take his turn at the helm and then tuck himself in his cabin while waves crashed and rolled and rain poured over the decks and down the companionway.

Angelene was probably laughing to herself right about now, thinking she had been granted a reprieve. Sin had considered every variable when dealing with Kimball, Porter and Sheridan, but it was inclement weather that now stood between him and something he suddenly wanted very badly.

Odd, wasn't it, that he found little enjoyment in dealing with the arrogant Reggie Foster and those three mutineers. Entrapping them provided no challenge. They had fallen into his hands so easily that it had taken most of the fun out of revenge. Angelene, however, was more than he had originally anticipated—and then some.

Now there was the real challenge—a spirited, intelligent and very defiant female who provided him with more passion than he had thought possible.

A knot of remembered pleasure coiled inside Sin when he allowed his thoughts to drift to the night they'd shared. Sin had gotten more than he had intended to claim when he designed Charles's personal torment. Angelene had been the unexpected factor that compelled Sin to seek more than the ruination of Sheridan's daughter's reputation. Sin had wanted her—simply because he wanted her.

Since Sin had decided to change the rules in the game he played, Hiram and Cyrus had been noticeably cool and distant. They didn't approve of his dealing with Angelene. Of course, they would change their tunes if they had been the ones who had reveled in a night of . . .

Sin squirmed uncomfortably in his chair beside the blazing hearth. Had it not been for the endless rain that turned creeks into raging rivers, he could have been matching wits with that green-eyed elf. Instead, he was substituting wine for intoxicating kisses and the warmth of the fireplace for the heat of desire.

Hardly adequate substitutes, Sin thought. In fact, he was quickly losing his taste for wine. And the hearth only provided outer warmth . . .

The rap at the front door drew Sin's curious frown. He was not expecting company on such a rainy night. Kimball and Porter had been forced to take the entire day off in their never-ending crusade to kill him. Sheridan still had his precious daughter under his wing, so there would be no reason for him to be out and about. As for Angelene, she had enough sense not to venture out when the river and creeks were at flood stage.

Sin set his glass aside and strode into the vestibule, shadowed by his two curious friends. To Sin's disbelief, Charles Sheridan, looking like a drowned river rat, stood on the stoop.

"I fear something horrible has happened," Charles said without preamble. He stepped inside, leaving puddles around his feet.

A deep sense of foreboding settled over Sin. He didn't appreciate surprises or miscalculations. "Where is Angelene?"

Charles fidgeted nervously with his hat and the sleeves of his drenched coat. A look of pure anguish settled on his features. "My groom came to the house to inform me that Angelene had ridden off with two satchels strapped to her saddle." Charles inhaled a shaky breath and plowed on. "The horse returned, half covered with moss and mud, dragging one satchel behind it. I've had every able-bodied servant combing the area in search of Angel, but we have turned up nothing."

Sin felt a chill slither down his spine. The look in Charles's eyes was like staring into an eighteen-year-old mirror. Only now was the man remotely close to experiencing the anguish Sin had suffered. That same tormented feeling rose from the cold depths where it had been stored, and Sin inwardly cringed at the implications.

Dear God in heaven! Sin's nagging conscience would never let him hear the end of it if Angelene had struck out on such a treacherous night to keep the promise Sin had wrenched out of her. Did she think him so heartless and insensitive that he expected her to keep her evening appointment on a night unfit for man and beast—and certainly not for a mere slip of a woman!

"I fear the worst," Charles choked out. "I hadn't wanted to believe what Angel told me about her deep affection for you. But if she risked her life to come to you on such a night—"

Sin felt as if the hatchet buried in his spine had been given a painful twist. He had forced Angelene to lie to her father to protect him from Sin's threats of financial and social destruction. And worse, she had braved a flood for fear of his ruthless retaliation.

When Sin turned to fetch his coat, two pairs of narrowed eyes riveted on him. Cyrus and Hiram didn't have to say a word. Condemnation was written on their faces in bold letters. Revenge, Sin was quickly discovering, often demanded excessive prices, and he was losing his taste for it faster than he was for the wine.

With fiendish haste, Sin shrugged on his rain slicker

and propelled himself out the door. The other three men were a few steps behind him.

"I don't know what I'd do if I lost her, too," Charles mumbled half aloud. "I almost did once . . . not again . . ."

The cold wind whipped beneath Sin's poncho as Turk splattered through the rivulets of water that poured off the steep slopes lining the path down Raven's Hill. The road stood six inches under water and feeder creeks along the route were flooding their banks.

The torch Sin carried hissed and sputtered in the rain, making it difficult to navigate through the shifting shadows. He should have brought along a compass. Tracking in a downpour through unfamiliar terrain was worse than charting a course in storm-tossed seas. At least at sea Sin was accustomed to natural hazards. Floods, he was learning, were not his forte.

With every moment that slipped past, Sin felt a sense of hopelessness seep into his bones. Guilt and regret hounded him every plodding step. He had not been content to tarnish Charles's daughter's reputation. Oh no, Sin had let his fascination for that lively female influence him to the point that he bartered for the most intimate of privileges. He had wanted Angelene any way he could get her and the only way had been to blackmail her into saving her father. But damn it, he had not intended Angel to sacrifice herself because of his compelling obsession!

"Cap'n. I don't think—"

Sin flung up a hand to halt Cyrus's discouraging words. "If you don't wish to participate in this search, then go back to the house. I'm not giving up if there is a remote chance of finding Angel."

Charles glanced from the raging floodwater to Sinclair. "You really *do* care about my daughter then? She does mean something to you?"

"How could anyone not care about a woman with so much fire and spirit?" Sin replied as he searched through the dim torchlight for some sign of Angelene.

"Over there!" Charles shouted suddenly. "I think I see something."

He was off his horse in a flash, charging toward the object among a clump of trees that was half-submerged in the swirling stream. Water hissed and gurgled dangerously, but Charles splashed forward, battling the current, refusing to overlook any possibility in hopes of rescuing Angelene.

"He can't fight the force of all that water," Hiram muttered, swinging down from his mount.

Sin was off his steed in a single bound, focusing on the flash of gold that glistened in the torchlight. It appeared Charles had spotted something among the tangled limbs that bobbed in midstream.

The current had become an uncontrollable tide. Huge trees had been sucked into the creeks. Smaller trees that had been jerked loose and sucked into the current had tangled in the sawyer. And all around the swirl of limbs and brush, was an undercurrent that could tow a man into its perilous depths before he could snatch a breath of air.

Charles's chances of fighting the fierce current decreased by the second. He had reached deep water, making footing nearly impossible. When the impact of floodwater engulfed him, Charles yelped and teetered backward. Nothing but his feet were visible as he som-

*Now, for the first time...*

You can find Janelle Taylor, Shannon Drake, Rosanne Bittner, Sylvie Sommerfield, Penelope Neri, Phoebe Conn, Bobbi Smith, and the rest of today's most popular, bestselling authors

*...All in one brand-new club!*

Introducing KENSINGTON CHOICE, the new Zebra/Pinnacle service that delivers the best new historical romances direct to your home, at a significant discount off the publisher's prices.

## As your introduction, we invite you to accept 4 FREE BOOKS worth up to $23.96

details inside...

# *We've got your authors!*

If you seek out the latest historical romances by today's bestselling authors, our new reader's service, KENSINGTON CHOICE, is the club for you.

KENSINGTON CHOICE is the only club where you can find authors like Janelle Taylor, Shannon Drake, Rosanne Bittner, Sylvie Sommerfield, Penelope Neri and Phoebe Conn all in one place…

…and the only service that will deliver their romances direct to your home as soon as they are published—even before they reach the bookstores.

KENSINGTON CHOICE is also the only service that will give you a substantial guaranteed discount off the publisher's prices on every one of those romances.

That's right: Every month, the Editors at Zebra and Pinnacle select four of the newest novels by our bestselling authors and rush them straight to you, usually *before they reach the bookstores*. The publisher's prices for these romances range from $4.99 to $5.99—but they are always yours for the guaranteed low price of just *$3.95!*

That means you'll always save over $1.00…often as much as *$2.00*…off the publisher's prices on every new novel you get from KENSINGTON CHOICE!

All books are sent on a 10-day free examination basis, and there is no minimum number of books to buy. (A postage and handling charge of $1.50 is added to each shipment.)

As your introduction to the convenience and value of this new service, we invite you to accept

# 4 BOOKS FREE

The 4 books, worth up to $23.96, are our welcoming gift. You pay only $1 to help cover postage and handling.

To start your subscription to KENSINGTON CHOICE and receive your introductory package of 4 FREE romances, detach and mail the postpaid card at right *today*.

# We have 4 FREE BOOKS for you as your introduction to KENSINGTON CHOICE

To get your FREE BOOKS, worth up to $23.96, mail the card below.

## FREE BOOK CERTIFICATE

As my introduction to your new KENSINGTON CHOICE reader's service, please send me 4 FREE historical romances (worth up to $23.96), billing me just $1 to help cover postage and handling. As a KENSINGTON CHOICE subscriber, I will then receive 4 brand-new romances to preview each month for 10 days FREE. I can return any books I decide not to keep and owe nothing. The publisher's prices for the KENSINGTON CHOICE romances range from $4.99 to $5.99, but as a subscriber I will be entitled to get them for just $3.95 per book or $15.80 for all four titles. There is no minimum number of books to buy, and I can cancel my subscription at any time. A $1.50 postage and handling charge is added to each shipment.

Name _____

Address _____ Apt. _____

City _____ State_____ Zip _____

Telephone (____) _____

Signature _____

(If under 18, parent or guardian must sign)

Subscription subject to acceptance. Terms and prices subject to change.

KC1194

We have
4
**FREE**
Historical
Romances
for you!

(worth up
to $23.96!)

*Details inside!*

ersaulted with the tumbling current that sped through the winding creek.

Sin scowled to himself as he braced himself against the rush of cold water. He plowed forward, trying to gauge where the frothy water was taking the upended man. The torch that Hiram held high reflected on a hand that skimmed the rippling surface. Sin lunged forward, asking himself why the hell he was risking his own neck to save a man who had caused him years of untold torment.

This was one of the three men Sin had vowed to destroy. Charles could easily drown, just as Sin almost had that horrifying night. What could be more fitting than that?

Sin's hand stalled in midair when Charles's face momentarily popped to the surface. Charles wore an expression of terror and desperation, an expression Sin knew all too well. Though bitterness and resentment churned inside him, Sin snaked out a hand and grabbed Charles by the collar of his coat, jerking him up so he could steal a breath of air.

The overpowering force of racing water and Charles's panicky floundering threw Sin off balance. He went down like an anchor, grimacing as renewed pain shot through his mending leg.

Then as now, it was sheer will to survive the difficult odds that compelled Sin to battle for footing, while keeping a hand clamped on Charles. Years at sea provided the instinct and experience needed to navigate toward calmer water. "Dead reckoning," Sin thought. The nautical term was becoming more appropriate by the second.

Sin relied on all his experience and instinct to save

him. He could feel the current decreasing with each powerful stroke of his arms and legs and he followed the path of least resistance. He towed Charles's limp body behind him, refusing to surrender to impending disaster.

After countless dives off the coast of Polynesian islands and Australia, Sin had learned to hold his breath for extended periods of time. When Sin tried to surface for breath he was met by gallons of water. He surged forward in hopes of locating the shallows so he could brace his weary legs beneath him.

The instant he found solid footing he burst to the surface to hear wild shouts in the distance. Clenching his fist in Charles's coat, Sin hauled the lifeless body up beside him and struggled toward shore.

Hiram and Cyrus skidded down the bank and waded into the current to relieve Sin of his waterlogged burden. Above the sound of rumbling water, Charles coughed and choked and chanted Angelene's name.

Sin glanced toward the shiny object that had sent Charles recklessly dashing into the raging waters. The glimmer of gold was still visible in the torch light. Sin surveyed the area, searching for a less treacherous route to reach the gnarled clump of trees that clogged the channel.

Wading ashore, Sin retrieved the rope from his saddle and walked upstream. With one end of the rope tied around his waist and the other end secured to a tree, Sin let the force of the water carry him downstream to the sawyer. Curling an arm around a broken stump, Sin snatched up the satchel that had been wedged in the sawyer by its golden handle. He groped in the water, expecting to find Angelene's body somewhere below, but his hand only bumped into tangled roots and broken branches.

A pang of guilt and regret hammered at Sin's conscience as he felt his way around the tree limbs in search of Angelene. Sin finally gave up his futile search. He wasn't sure he even wanted to find her, knowing what condition she would be in if he did. The lodged satchel indicated Angel had been here for a time, but the force of the water had obviously dislodged her and taken her downstream.

God only knew where she was now . . . but Sin knew he had sent her there . . .

When Sin shouted to his men, they towed him to higher ground. He glanced up at the powerful stallion called Turk and smiled grimly. Wouldn't Owen Porter be furious if he knew his valuable steed had not only been exposed to unfavorable weather conditions but was also being used like a plow horse?

Shaking himself off, Sin came ashore with the satchel clasped in his hand. A string of muffled curses tumbled from his lips when realization crashed down on him like broken masts tumbling in a destructive storm. He had saved the life of a man he had come to Natchez to destroy and had practically ordered the watery execution of the woman he had used as a gambit.

Sin swore at the bitter irony of his own method of revenge. He, who had learned to detach himself and proceed with logical calculation, had succumbed to sympathy for a man he had sworn to hate until his dying day. And he had manipulated Angelene because of his selfish desire for her.

Hell and damnation! Sin was learning that each stroke of revenge came with a biting backlash.

Cyrus outstretched a hand to assist Sin to level ground. "I suppose you realize what you just did, mate," he murmured. "You saved the man you came here to ruin."

"Don't remind me." Sin inhaled a fortifying breath and stared at the satchel.

"Charles is having a bad time of it," Hiram reported, gesturing toward the shadowed figure that was propped against a tree. "He's still chanting his daughter's name. She wouldn't have been out on such a night if you hadn't—"

"Don't remind me of that, either," Sin interrupted.

His conscience was flaying him alive. No need for Cyrus to snatch up the whip.

Hiram removed his spectacles and tucked them in his pocket since he couldn't see through them anyway. "Satisfied, Captain? You came here to take what those three mutineers treasured most. It looks as if you have succeeded where Charles Sheridan is concerned."

"The horse and hotel were different," Cyrus added disparagingly, "but the lady was something else again. Don't mind tellin' ya I had my reservations about that since the night when I clapped eyes on Angel. You of all people ought to know how unfair it is for innocent victims to become sacrifices."

When Cyrus and Hiram strode off, Sin stared down at the soggy satchel and wondered if Kimball, Porter and Sheridan had ever come to regret taking his brother's life to satisfy their greed. Sin was beginning to think he had more heart than Angelene had given him credit for. He was certainly suffering all the torments of the damned right now.

*The only life Sin had intended to spare in his quest for revenge was the one that had been lost . . .*

As Sin limped toward his horse, a haunting vision of green eyes, red-gold hair and bewitching smile rose before him. He predicted that wherever Angel was, she was well pleased with herself. She had inadvertently forced him to spare Charles Sheridan, just as she had done when she agreed to Sin's uncompromising terms.

Fate, Sin decided, had a nasty way of complicating the best-laid plans. Sin would have given the world to have Angelene back. She had become the one bright and entertaining spot in his life. He hadn't realized just how much he was going to miss her . . . until after she was gone . . .

# Nineteen

Angelene dragged her muddy self up another steep incline to reach the cottage below Raven's Hill. The feigned death she had cleverly arranged for herself had very nearly become reality. She hadn't expected the raging waters to be so violent. Of course, the methodical Nick Sinclair wouldn't have made such an error in judgment, Angelene thought resentfully.

Inhaling an exhausted breath, Angelene trudged toward the secluded cabin. With any luck, she could take refuge until the flood waters ebbed and then sneak back to Sheridan Hall to assure her father that she had survived.

When she had devised her original plan, she had intended to take one satchel of clothes and enough cash to sustain her while she remained hidden for a few weeks. So much for her ingenious scheme to avoid being used as leverage against her father. Now all Angelene had was the clothes on her back and not one red cent to pay for food and lodging.

Well, at least no one would think to search for her at the cottage, she consoled herself. She would remain safe, right under Sin's nose—the last place he would look for her, if he bothered searching for her waterlogged body at all. Which he probably wouldn't. All she was to him was a pawn in his mysterious games. Sin certainly wouldn't be crying a river of tears for her. More than likely he wouldn't even change expression.

When Angelene opened the door to the darkened cabin, a parrot squawked like a doorbell.

"Who's there?" came a gravelly voice.

Angelene shrank back, cursing another miscalculation. Someone was living in the cabin at the bottom of Raven's Hill. Damn.

"You may as well come in out of the rain and close the hatch," Pearly Graham invited as he levered up on his bed. "Ain't a good night to be about."

Fiddler chirped in agreement.

Hesitantly, Angelene stepped inside and closed the door. She heard the click of a pistol's hammer and froze to her spot.

"Now get yerself over here, mate, so I can have a look at ya. If it's more than a port in a storm yer lookin' for, I'll know now."

Light flared from the south side of the room and shadows shrank into the corners. Pearly's eyes popped when the clinging clothes revealed a woman's shapely figure and a cascade of wet hair.

"Well, I'll be damned," Pearly croaked.

"I'll be damned," Fiddler repeated.

"Shut yer mouth, ya ball of feathers," Pearly snapped at the parrot. Setting the pistol aside, he motioned Angelene into a chair and tossed her the quilt from the end of his bed.

Shivering uncontrollably, Angelene wrapped the blanket around her and surveyed the crusty older man and his pegleg. He looked just as she imagined a pirate would look. A friend of Sin's, no doubt.

"Lass, ye'r either incredibly brave or incredibly foolish to be out and about. Water's risin' faster than a tidal wave."

"Incredibly foolish applies," Angelene muttered.

Pearly's brown eyes narrowed speculatively. "Runnin' *to* somebody or *away* from 'em, lass?"

"Both," Angelene hedged.

"Makes for difficult navigation when yer headed two directions at once, I'd guess. Lucky ya didn't slip yer cables and slide into Fiddler's Green." Pearly surged onto his good leg and hobbled across the room. "Agnes left a couple of slices of mincemeat pie. Hungry, lass?"

"No . . . thank you."

"Well then, I reckon I'll snack alone. Ya don't know what yer missin' though. Agnes is the best cook I've ever come across on all the Seven Seas. Now there's a woman who knows the way to a man's heart—and she sure enough found mine."

Angelene was well acquainted with Agnes's incomparable culinary skills. She hadn't had a decent meal at home since Sin hired Agnes away. "Maybe I will have a slice of pie."

Pearly grinned and limped over with a plate. "Ya got a name, lass?"

Angelene had no intention of divulging her identity. This man was obviously associated with Sin. Having Sin know she had survived would defeat her purpose. He would simply use her to pressure Charles again.

"Jane," she murmured before taking a bite of pie.

Pearly chuckled as he sank down at the table to devour

his tasty snack. "Well, nice to meet ya, Jane. Pearly Graham at yer humble service. My daddy named me Beauregard after himself, right before he shoved off to sea. Never did like him or the name much. The nickname suits me better."

"Because of your fascination with jewels?" More likely a pirate's booty, Angelene cynically concluded.

"Pearls mostly," he specified. "Nothin' fascinates me more than openin' a shell and pluckin' one of them little beggars out. Mother Nature's jewelry boxes, those oysters. Found a pearl big as yer thumbnail—off the coast of Polynesia. A black pearl, the rarest jewel of all the seas. Would ya like to take a gander at it, lass?"

Angelene nodded her wet head.

Pearly finished off his pie and reached over to retrieve a tin box from his trunk. He plucked up the shiny jewel and then leaned out to drop it in her hand. "Many a man has died for the want of such a prize. Legend says these gems hold a powerful mystique. Men even battle sharks to steal treasures like this one from the sea, and some men pay dearly. My friend Sinclair nearly lost the use of his leg when retrievin' this little beauty."

Angelene jerked up her head, noting that Pearly was watching her with wise and experienced eyes. Her reflexive gesture must have given her away, for Pearly was studying her even more closely.

"Ya know Sinclair, I see. But of course, I doubt there are those around here who don't know him by now. The man always did make a great splash wherever he went. Just because he's landlocked won't make no difference. He's a rare breed, that one."

Angelene rolled the luminous silver-gray pearl between her thumb and middle finger, pondering what it had cost Sin to acquire it. That certainly explained his limp and testified to his fearless daring. As Sin said himself: Setting limits only deprived a man from exploring his potential—or something to that effect.

Pearly handed Angelene a glass of wine, which she automatically accepted. "This should warm yer innards, lass." He gestured his bushy gray head toward the pearl while Angelene sipped freely. "Pearls are always cool to the touch, even against warm skin. Like a woman's heart, I always said."

"A woman's heart?" Angelene sniffed and took another sip of the drink. It had an unfamiliar taste but it provided the warmth she desperately needed. "I can think of certain men whose hearts are as cold as this pearl—"

Her voice dried up when Fiddler unexpectedly swooped down to perch on her arm.

"Get back, you damned bag of feathers!" Pearly barked. "You've already made a feast of one of these gems. You'll not get that pesky beak around another!"

Fiddler squawked indignantly when Pearly thumped his head. The parrot hopped back to his perch with feathers ruffled.

"Damned bird," Pearly muttered. "I'm gonna insist that Sinclair take Fiddler to the main house. These pearls ain't Fiddler's grit. He's lucky I didn't reach down his craw to fetch the last gem he swallowed. It took an oyster several years to form that priceless jewel and that cacklin' feather-brain devoured it in one gulp."

Casting a murderous glance at Fiddler, Pearly plucked up the jewel and stashed it in the tin box. His hand stalled as he glanced back at the bewitching young woman whose mere presence had added a radiance to the cabin. Impulsively, Pearly reached for the gold chain that held a flawless white rosé pearl.

"Here, lass, this one is yer perfect match."

Angelene stared at the lustrous jewel suspended from the chain. "I can't accept such a priceless treasure."

"'Course ya can. This treasure is mine to give. I want ya to have it. Go on, take it."

When Angelene glanced speculatively at his peg leg, Pearly chuckled. "No, I didn't lose my leg divin' for this pearl. It was a bloodthirsty swashbuckler who did this to me. Sinclair sent him to hell in a seine shortly thereafter."

"So you owe him your life," she concluded.

"Actually we decided to call it even—one good turn for another, ya see. I fished Sin from the ocean and took him under my wing. Turned out to be one exceptional sailor, he did."

Pearly twisted around to refill Angelene's wineglass and then handed it to her. "We saw the world together, Sin and me. From Cape Horn to the Cocos, across the South Seas to Calcutta and to the hongs of Canton." He smiled, revealing the gap between his teeth and raised his glass in a toast. "What Sin and me ain't done ain't worth doin'. You can name any port the world round and I can spin a yarn about it. In fact, I recall the time we creeped through the Straits of Sunda, outfoxed Malayan pirates and found ourselves droppin' anchor off the coast of Papua in search of the gold lip pearl. Sin tied a fifty-pound stone around his waist to get to the bottom of the cove. He came up with a basket of oysters that turned out to be one of our best finds ever."

When Angel's eyes drifted to half-mast, Pearly took

the glass from her hand and kept talking. "Some of those East Indian divers can hold their breath for six minutes. Most amazin' thing I ever saw. Sin can manage a couple of minutes and he works fast when he's down there. One load of oysters he brought up on the coast of one of them nameless reefs proved to be another priceless treasure. The mandarins in Canton paid handsomely for those perfect gems Sin fished out. A man can make a fortune peddlin' pearls and tradin' ginseng in the Far East. Could and did, in fact. Some say Sin has the Midas touch, but it's shrewd calculation on his part . . ."

Pearly smiled wryly when Angelene's head sagged against her shoulder. With considerable effort, Pearly eased her off the chair and onto the bed. The combination of wine, gin, and a good lacing of laudanum—often used to render men unconscious so they could be shanghaied and hauled aboard ships as unwilling crewmen—had left her oblivious to the world.

Pearly knew all about medicinal curatives and exotic remedies. In fact, his first experience with them was the night he had unknowingly ingested a potion and found himself dragged off to a privateer's ship. Since that time, Pearly had become an apothecary who collected herbs and curatives from around the world.

"Can't have ya sittin' there shiverin' in yer timbers, lass," Pearly lectured his sleeping companion. "And can't take the risk of havin' ya sneak away, either."

Fiddler ducked his head, pranced on his perch and squawked.

"Well, what did ya expect me to do, bird brain?" Pearly snorted at the parrot. "Let the lass catch the grippe?"

"Catch the grippe"—squawk!—"Catch the grippe," Fiddler chattered.

Pearly cast the parrot a dour glance and grabbed his coat. "And don't eat anything while I'm gone. You've got enough jewels in yer gizzard to tempt me to slit you wide open as it is."

Leaving Fiddler to keep tabs on "Jane", Pearly hobbled out into the rain and sidestepped up the hill. He had the feeling Sinclair might be interested in this late-night visitor.

Sin was halfway through a bottle of Madeira wine when Pearly's pegleg thumped against the flagstones outside the study. The creak of the door confirmed the old mariner's arrival and a draft of cold wind chilled what was left of Sin's soul.

"I'm surprised to see you out on a night like this. You usually chose to stay below deck when rain storms clouded the seas," Sin remembered.

Pearly raised an eyebrow at the slur in Sin's deep voice. "Drinkin' away yer troubles, lad?" He chuckled as he shook off the rain and made his way toward the warmth of the hearth. "I always told ya that troubles have fins and gills and know how to swim."

"It's been a bad night." Sin gestured toward the empty chair that faced the dancing flames. "The conscience I recently discovered I still have has hung me out to dry."

"Then yer the only thing dry around here. Even the frogs have had enough of wet." Pearly plunked into the chair and tossed Sin a discreet glance. "A conscience can be a damned nuisance at times, can't it? Always tellin' a man what he should do instead of agreein' with what he wants to do." He stared toward the foyer. "Where's them two overgrown shadows that usually follow ya around?"

Sin leaned his head back against the chair and watched the golden flames devour the log, as thoroughly as remorse was engulfing him. "Hiram and Cyrus accompanied Charles Sheridan home after his near drowning."

"You tried to shove the swab into floodwaters?" Pearly fluted.

Sin displayed rare emotion by scowling. "No, I pulled him out and have been asking myself why ever since."

"Does this have somethin' to do with the man's most coveted possession?" Pearly inquired.

Sin squirmed uneasily in his chair. "Everything, in fact," he murmured. "I'm afraid Sheridan's daughter perished because of me. I demanded she return this evening if she wanted to save her father from the same ruin that threatens Kimball and Porter." He sighed audibly and turned tormented onyx eyes toward Pearly. "I never dreamed Angel would brave the floods to obey my command."

"You didn't take into consideration that the girl's father could mean so much to her, because he means nothin' to ya other than an object of revenge," Pearly predicted. "It's damned hard to calculate the variables of human emotion unless ya experience 'em yerself, lad. I'm afraid ya stopped feelin' the night they cast ya into the sea."

Sin nodded grimly. "Watching your brother bleed to death in your arms does that to an impressionable young boy."

"And the lost lass? Angel, ya say?"

Sin's breath gushed out and he downed another swallow to numb the anguishing knot in the pit of his belly. "Angel turned out to be the same woman I told you I met when we first came to Natchez. I didn't know her by name then, because she wouldn't tell me who she was. She was the fascinating green-eyed elf that I couldn't pursue because of my plans for Sheridan's daughter."

Pearly groaned. "Helluva twist of fate. So she turned out to be one and the same, did she?"

Sin nodded his dark head and took another sip of wine, staring sightlessly into the fire. "Suddenly, what I personally desired and the revenge I craved were tied in a Gordian knot."

"You had a problem for sure," Pearly agreed.

"If my brother's death weighed as heavily on the mutineers' consciences as Angel's does on mine, it's a wonder those bastards still have their sanity."

"Why's that?"

"Why's what?" Sin questioned the question.

"Why does Angel's loss weigh so heavily?" Pearly wanted to know, appraising Sin through narrowed eyes. "She was just a woman, wasn't she? The world is full of 'em. I thought nothin' in life was as important to ya as settlin' yer grudge. I thought this Angel was no more than a means to a vengeful end—with nothin' in between."

Sin found himself revisited by the enchanting vision that had haunted him for hours on end. "It seems my attachment was stronger than I'd thought. Either that or I'm not accustomed to dealing with this rusty conscience. But for certain, I'm left with a bad taste in my mouth and all of China's finest imported wine can't wash it down."

"She was pretty, huh?"

"Breathtakingly so."

"And witty, I expect." Pearly added, smiling slyly while he lounged in his chair.

"Definitely a mental challenge," Sin reported.

"And the lass fell in love with ya? Despite yer plans for her papa?"

"No." Sin chugged his drink and set the empty glass aside. "I gave her no reason to feel anything except humiliation and resentment. I suspect the reason my ears are ringing right now is that she heaped curses on me with her last breath . . ."

The tormenting thought put another uncharacteristic scowl on Sin's rugged features. The scar flashed white against his tanned cheek. His heart felt as if a hole the size of the Pacific Ocean flooded through it. Emotions were warring inside him. He wanted to throw something, though never in all his thirty years had he resorted to a temper tantrum—except once . . .

Sin squeezed his eyes shut, remembering the night he had railed at Angelene when she nearly got her fool head blown off trying to save his life. He had never thanked her for her assistance. His roiling temper had bubbled the pitch in his seams and he had lashed out like a frayed sail snapping in the wind.

That feisty female had the knack of wrenching emotion from him, even when he was determined to hold it in check.

"And you'd give most anything to have the lass back?"

Pearly's voice intruded into Sin's troubled thoughts. "Aye."

"Just to ease yer naggin' conscience, I s'pose?" The crusty old mariner questioned.

Sin was accustomed to keeping his own counsel. He had said more than he preferred already. But then, he reminded himself, Pearly Graham knew him better than any man alive. Indeed, Sin wouldn't be alive now but for Pearly.

Pearly hoisted himself out of his chair and grabbed his pea jacket. "Come with me, Sin. I've got a rare jewel I want ya to see."

"I'm not in the mood for that tonight," Sin grumbled.

"Oh, I think you'll like the looks of this particular gem, lad. Haul yerself up."

Reluctantly, Sin followed in Pearly's wake. The rain had finally tapered off into a fine mist that left Raven's Hill surrounded in a dense fog. The sound of rushing water and homeless frogs serenaded the night.

"Nothin' like a good flood to stir up the cove and provide nourishment for yer oyster bed," Pearly said optimistically.

True, Sin thought. Unfortunately, only the oysters and mollusks he had collected and placed in the cove were enjoying the flood. At the moment, even his fascination with practicing the ancient Chinese art of seeding oysters to produce pearls didn't lighten his black mood. Nothing filled the empty coil in his belly. Certainly not the wine he had consumed in hopes of rendering himself senseless . . .

When Pearly opened the door of the cottage to reveal the sleeping beauty on his cot, Sin stumbled to a halt.

Red-gold hair glistened like flames in the lantern light and cascaded over the pillow, trailing to the floor. The damp breeches and shirt clung to Angelene's figure like second skin.

"Now there's a gem worthy of bein' fished from flood-waters." Pearly studied Sin astutely. The bronzed face that rarely displayed emotion softened in visible relief. Pearly smiled knowingly as Sin surged across the room to kneel beside the bed.

"I gave her the white rosé. That's what the lass is, I'd say. She's got a luster about her, don't ya think? O'course, I had to doctor her drink to ensure she didn't sneak off into the night."

Tenderly, Sin traced Angelene's lips and brushed his thumb over her cheek. "She's cold from exposure."

"I told her pearls were as cold as a woman's heart," Pearly snickered as he eased closer. "She claimed it was a man's heart that never warmed. Wonder why she'd say a thing like that? I also wonder why she told me her name was Jane and why she couldn't decide whether to run toward or away from the man with the cold heart."

Sin glanced up at the bushy-haired mariner who grinned slyly at him. "How did you know who she was?"

"How does any man know when he's been visited by an Angel? He just does, that's all." His grin widened noticeably. "Besides that, Agnes described her to me when I asked about Sheridan's daughter."

Sin scooped Angelene up in his arms and pivoted toward the door. "I owe you, Pearly."

"Not hardly. I'm moored in a roundhouse befittin' a grand cap'n. I've got all the time in the world to mix my curatives and toy with my jewels—thanks to you.

Besides, Angel found me." He winked playfully. "That's how angels work, ya know. When a man needs a little sparkle in his life, that's when angels show up."

Sin strode off, pausing on the porch when Pearly called after him.

"A few words of advice, Sin. The way yer goin' at this now forces the lass to choose between you and her papa. Think about that. There's another way, ya know. If she were to know the truth, it would go worse for Sheridan and better for you. Have a care that ya don't set yerself up to lose what ya find yerself desirin' most. And ya might discover that what ya stand to lose—to enjoy yer revenge—don't equal what ya have to gain."

Sin stared down into the flawless face that matched the priceless white rosé pearl that lay against her neck. He battled the maelstrom of emotions that assaulted him.

"I made a promise to my brother, Pearly, and Joshua accepted it on his dying breath. What would you have me do? Forget my vow to him?"

"It's a real dilemma, Sin, truly it is. I wish ya luck with it. I'll be the first to admit them three men deserve to pay their debts, but this lass . . ." He sighed heavily. "Well, I don't know that I could find it in my heart to make her pay for her papa's sins. Don't seem right, does it?"

Sin walked off, grappling with Pearly's words, wondering why he felt so protective of this fiery-tongued female who had promised to give him hell for backing her into a corner. Sin had been so determined in purpose before he encountered Angelene. Now he wavered in indecision. But at least the oppressive weight that had settled on his shoulders like an anchor had lifted when he discovered she was still alive. No doubt, divine intervention was all that had saved her. This was one lucky Angel, he decided.

Sin strode into the study to find Hiram and Cyrus pouring glasses of wine. Both men wheeled around in surprise when they saw the woman draped over Sin's arms.

"My God! Where did you find her?" Hiram questioned. "Is she still alive?"

Sin nodded his raven head as he veered toward the staircase. "Pearly gave her one of his potions. Send word to Sheridan that his daughter survived."

"Lettin' your landed fish off the hook?" Cyrus inquired.

"Only for the time being. Sheridan has suffered enough for one night," was all Sin said before he walked away.

# Twenty

Sin peeled off his wet clothes and Angelene's. That turned out to be pleasure in itself—as fascinating as opening a shell in search of a pearl. He stared down at the beguiling beauty who lay on his bed, oddly content to portray the handmaiden, while Angelene fought her way through the drugging effects of Pearly's potion.

Pearly was right, on several counts, Sin decided. Angelene was like the white rosé, a flawless, lovely gem. And having come so close to losing her, Sin found himself weighing and measuring the influence she had over him. This woman had been blessed with the face of an angel and the luscious body of a goddess. Her rare courage and irrepressible spirit were incomparable. Those were the losses that grieved Sin most of all when he'd imagined that he would never see her again.

And of course, there were those dramatic outbursts of temper that provided a constant source of pleasure and amusement. Sin had known little of such things. Except through Angelene. But allowing her to matter so much had put Sin between the devil and the deep—and kept him there.

When Sin glided a warm cloth over her icy skin, Angelene was roused to another level of consciousness. Her body reflexively arched toward his stroking hand. Her heavily lidded eyes fluttered open to stare at him, and Sin wondered if she knew where she was or who she was with. When Sin removed the warm cloth and dipped it in the basin, Angelene moaned in objection.

"Mmm . . ." Angelene stretched and twisted drowsily as Sin dragged the cloth over her cool flesh.

Sin felt a smile tugging at his lips—the same contented smile he had worn while he and Angelene were discovering sensual paradise. This intriguing creature pleased and appeased him in more ways than he could count.

That could be as dangerous as it was satisfying.

Sin frowned pensively when Pearly's words came back to him. While Sin monitored the leisurely stroke of his hand over Angel's supple flesh, he considered the old sailor's advice. True, there were other ways to have his revenge on Charles Sinclair without destroying the fragile bond developing between him and Angel. But confiding the truth to her was a double-edged sword. Pearly had pointed out what Sin had to gain, but the old mariner neglected to take into consideration what Angel stood to lose. Sin, however, weighed cause and result carefully. He could see past the simplicity of Pearly's advice to predict complications that would lie ahead. As Sin had heard, the solution to one problem was usually the beginning of another . . .

When Angelene rolled sideways, her hand went gliding over Sin's bent knee. His thoughts drifted off course. And when she instinctively snuggled up against him he wanted nothing more than to test again the unbelievable sensations she aroused in him. This woman set him aflame without even trying. Sin hated to hazard a guess as to how he would fare if Angel realized the kind of power she could hold over him if she *did* try.

"Angel?"

"Hum?" she answered groggily.

"Do you know where you are?"

"With you."

He grinned at that. His hand glided over her hip to pull her against his naked contours. "Then you remember who I am?"

When his moist lips skimmed the column of her throat and hovered over her lips, Angelene moaned softly. "I would recognize that deep voice anywhere," she rasped.

Sin knew he was taking unfair advantage, but he couldn't help himself. The harrowing events of the night had put him back in touch with his emotions. Drinking hadn't filled the hollow ache. Only holding Angel could do that. She was fast becoming an obsession to all five of his senses, not to mention that sixth sense he often relied upon. He wanted to absorb her, to enjoy her until nothing mattered to either of them except feeding the kind of fire that could burn down the night.

With tender care, Sin reacquainted himself with every delectable inch of her flesh and reveled in each uninhibited response. Sin felt a hard knot of desire coiling inside him when Angel returned each caress. He groaned when slender fingers cruised over the dark matting of hair on his chest and descended to his belly.

"Do you like that?" Angelene asked, a slur in her voice.

"I'm not sure. Maybe if you do it a half-dozen more times I can decide," he said hoarsely.

Her soft laughter tickled his senses and he stirred hungrily beneath her roaming hand. "Mmm, I definitely like that," he assured her.

"What else do you like?"

"Are you sure you want to know?"

"Show me how to make you burn—the same way you set me aflame."

Sin wasn't sure Angel knew what she was doing or saying. In fact if he hadn't known better, he'd have sworn Pearly had added a pinch of aphrodisiac to the potion. Angel had become too adventurous and daring by half. Her hands were swirling lower, making stimulating contact with his ultrasensitive flesh.

He groaned out loud.

His response evoked her throaty laughter and made her bolder still. Sin didn't know whether to thank Pearly or curse him.

Sin felt his body clench when her hand enfolded him, measured him, teased him almost beyond bearing. He had never granted such intimate privileges to a woman. He preferred to be the captain of passionate voyages. But then, having Angel as copilot was beginning to have tremendous appeal . . .

Sin's breath hissed out when she stroked him twice, thrice. He involuntarily arched toward her. Sensations— like thunderbolts—sizzled through him. "Don't . . . Stop . . ."

"Whatever you wish," she murmured as her kisses drifted down his belly to explore the sensitive flesh of his thighs.

Sin choked on his breath when his heart threatened to pound his ribs to slivers. "That's not what I meant, elf."

"You feel like satin," she mused aloud. "And you taste like the sea."

When she drew him into her mouth and flicked her tongue against the hard length of him, Sin came unraveled like a tattered sail in a high wind. His very thoughts were being cast wildly about, scattered by one inexpressible sensation after another. Each time her hands and lips moved over his rigid flesh he clung desperately to self-control. But patient restraint was slipping its moorings, caress by tantalizing caress.

"A man has his limits," Sin groaned in unholy torment.

Angelene chortled playfully. "Some men perhaps. But not you. Challenge yourself."

"I already have," he moaned in reply.

"Then expand them, because I find myself incredibly curious."

And Sin was sure he was going to be incredibly *dead* if she didn't cease her bold explorations! Damn, Pearly hadn't realized what he was doing when he doctored Angelene's drink. The old mariner had transformed Angel into a seductive siren. Her adventurous nature, added to the effects of the potion, proved to be a lethal combination. And worse, Sin had tipped the bottle one too many times that night. The wine had taken the edge off his willpower, leaving him highly susceptible to Angel's power.

A groan of splendorous torment rumbled in his chest when Angelene glided upward in an erotic caress. The peaks of her breasts brushed across his belly and chest and Sin trembled in barely contained need. When her petal-soft lips whispered over him, Sin tasted his own need for her. His senses reeled as she deepened the kiss, using the techniques he had taught her. Sin felt another wave of intense pleasure battering his self-control when her restless hands drifted down to stroke the throbbing length of him, again and again. Sin valiantly battled for restraint—and lost. Although he had intended to return every sensation of pleasure she bestowed on him, fervent passion was making impossible demands.

Sin needed her desperately and he needed her *now.* He ached to slide into that silken fire and lose himself to the turbulent sensations that swept him away like a ship on a wind-tossed sea.

"I'm sorry," Sin whispered as his hands clamped urgently on her hips. He arched instinctively toward her as he drew her down upon him, sheathing himself in her softest flesh. "You've cost me my control . . ."

Her lips came back to his as he thrust against her. She was satisfying the burning need that caressing him had aroused in her. "And I like you best of all when you're out of control. Only then can you know how you make me feel. At least in this, I'm not your pawn. We're fools together . . ."

Her voice fragmented into a wild gasp when his ardent lovemaking dragged her into the churning depths of passion beyond measure, sensation beyond description. Firebursts of rapture billowed and blazed as they moved as one, discovering new dimensions of passion.

When he felt her shimmering around him, clinging as tightly to him as he clung to her, Sin muffled a groan of ecstasy against her lips. Pleasure pulsated in an endless current between his body and hers and back again. Sin gasped for breath as shudder after shudder racked his body. And then he was floating in a hazy mist, suspended for eternity . . .

It was a long, breathless moment before the fog of passion evaporated. But Sin had no desire to release his grasp on Angel.

"Pearly was right," Angelene whispered, nuzzling her cheek against Sin's sturdy shoulder. "I can't seem to decide whether to run toward you or away from you . . ."

Sin was certain Pearly's potion was working like a truth serum, freeing Angelene's most private thoughts. "And now, Angel?" he murmured huskily.

"Now there is no place I'd rather be than next to you . . ."

Sin felt her breathing like a soft caress against his neck. He expelled an exhausted but contented sigh. There wasn't any place on land or sea he'd rather be. At least not until morning dawned and Angel remembered this was the last place she wanted to be . . . and why she was forced to be here . . .

Sin grimaced when sunlight blazed through the row of windows. His every timber was groaning from the exertion of battling floodwaters to save a man who didn't deserve such consideration. He glanced sideways to see a mass of curly blond hair glistening with sunbeams. The quilt had drifted down Angelene's back, baring her physique to his gaze. Sin reached out to trail his forefinger over her shoulder. He asked himself what it would be like to awake every morning to such simple but satisfying pleasure.

Not likely that was going to happen, Sin reminded

himself. Not with this particular woman, not under the present circumstances.

The very reason Angel was in his bed now was the same reason they would be torn apart later. Despite what Pearly advised, Sin believed the greater cruelty would come in turning Angel against her own father by revealing the events of the past. Perhaps Charles deserved that, but Angelene would suffer the most if Sin told her the whole truth. At least this way, she could direct her fury and resentment at Sin. That was the price he had to pay to have his revenge and spare Angelene what she really didn't want to know.

When Angelene stirred beside him, Sin braced himself for the worst. Now that Pearly's potion had worn off, Sin expected this Angel would turn hellion. He predicted she would have plenty to say—none of it as flattering as the words she murmured last night.

Angelene lifted droopy eyes, glanced momentarily in Sin's direction and dropped her head back to the pillow.

"Good morning," Sin greeted complacently.

"Is it?"

Angelene's head popped up and she stared around the room as if she had just realized where she was. Her wide-eyed gaze landed on the masculine form beside her and then she glanced down to note that she was wearing nothing but the pearl teardrop the old mariner had given her. The last thing she remembered was listening to Pearly spin his adventurous yarns.

"How the blazes did I get here?"

"I carried you."

"That traitor," Angelene muttered, modestly pulling the quilt around her. "What was in that drink?"

"Besides the wine?"

"Besides the wine," she grumbled irritably.

"A love potion?" Sin ventured glibly.

"No medication could perform *that* miracle."

"I beg to differ. According to legends of the South Seas—"

"I was being sarcastic."

"So was I."

"Then you'll have to be more obvious about it, at least until this potion wears off," Angelene insisted. "Try changing tones of voice and expressions, for once."

"Would you like me to think slower, too, until you have time to catch up?" Sin asked.

"You're being sarcastic again."

"If you figured that out then you must be feeling better than you thought," he teased, straight-faced.

Angelene braced her elbows beneath her and glared at him. A frown knitted her brow when fuzzy flashbacks darted through her mind in disarray. Her frown intensified when more defined fragments of memory floated to the surface. She had the oddest feeling . . .

"Oh God!"

"I prefer that you call me Sin." He chuckled inwardly at the appalled expression that claimed her animated features. Angelene was beginning to recall the intimacies they had shared, some of which she had brazenly instigated. He wondered if she remembered that, too.

"Never doubt that I have called you that—and worse— several times, to your face and behind your back."

"Except last night," he casually corrected.

Angelene blinked owlishly. "What did I say last night?"

"That you could think of nowhere else you would rather be than with me."

Her cheeks flamed when black diamond eyes twinkled at her. "I wasn't myself last night."

"I'm aware of that."

"Then you must also be aware that I do not expect to be held responsible for anything I said or did."

"I expected as much."

Sin rolled from bed, thinking he'd gotten off easier than anticipated. It must have been the lingering effects of the potion that prohibited Angelene from returning to peak fighting form.

Angelene's unguarded stare roamed over Sin's powerful physique, noting the mending wound on his leg, remembering what Pearly had told her about battling a shark. There were other scars, too, she noticed, souvenirs from battles he had won—or at least he'd emerged in better condition than his foe.

The realization of the differences in the lives she and Sin had led left her studying him speculatively. Was it any wonder he had learned to switch his emotions off, to react with instinct and condition himself to dealing with a world that had proved dangerous and sometimes violent? Perhaps if she had endured the experiences Pearly had only hinted at . . .

"I have decided to send you home, Angelene," Sin abruptly announced as he pulled on his breeches. "I have decided that is best."

Angelene should have been relieved, but she felt an odd sense of disappointment. Despite everything, this man was beginning to matter a great deal to her. Embarrassed though she was about the liberties she had taken with him the previous night—and she was beginning to remember each and every bold touch—Angelene knew herself well enough to know she would have dared no such thing with any other man.

Dear God in heaven! Was she falling in love with Sin? She had vowed that he wouldn't touch her heart, but that was exactly what had happened. Angelene groaned miserably.

"Are you all right?"

"No—yes." Angelene heaved a frustrated sigh.

"Which is it?"

"More to the point, *why* is it?" she mused aloud.

"Excuse me?"

Angelene flicked her wrist in a dismissing gesture. "Never mind."

"Would you prefer to stay here with me?" Sin studied her astutely, hoping . . .

Oh hell, he was not a man who lived on false hopes. He was a man of calculated action. He knew wishing made nothing so. If it did, the world would run according to his whims and specifications. It didn't.

Angelene sat up, clutching the quilt, though why she bothered she didn't know. Since she had seduced Sin, there was no call for modesty now. "Of course I wish to go home where I belong." She eyed him warily as he shrugged on a fresh shirt. "But how is this going to affect my father?"

"I imagine he will be greatly relieved to see you. He worried himself sick last night, thinking you had drowned."

"That isn't what I meant."

"I realize that."

"Then stop tormenting me, damn it! I already told you my wits aren't what they should be."

Sin glanced at her sideways. Angelene was back in form—whether she thought so or not.

Angry at Sin and at herself, Angelene bounded from bed to retrieve her clothes. Sin smiled in approval when Angelene stamped around the end of the bed, wearing nothing but the white rosé pearl necklace Pearly had given her. She was utterly breathtaking, from the top of her tangled blond head to the soles of her feet.

"I swear you are the most exasperating man I have ever met." She jerked on her shirt and thrust a bare leg into her breeches—backward. Grumbling, Angelene began the process again. "If I decide to marry one day, I am going to seek out some cotton-brained idiot who cannot read my every thought and predict my actions before I've decided upon them myself."

"You won't be satisfied with a man you can tow around like a barge, Angel."

She jerked up her head and glowered at him. "At least I won't be one mental step behind him all the blessed time!" she flung back.

Sin ambled over to tilt her face to his. "Don't be so hard on yourself, elf. You're only a half a step behind me and I feel very fortunate to remain even that far ahead of you."

For some reason that comment pleased her immensely. It implied that Sin respected her intelligence. He saw more in her than a warm body to ease his very passionate needs.

"Sin, I . . ." She compressed her lips, hesitant to make

a commitment to a man she still didn't understand, despite the tender emotions she had begun to feel for him.

"Yes, Angel?" he prodded.

"It was nothing important," she hedged. "And don't annoy me by telling me you know what I'm thinking."

He peered into those luminous green eyes and felt a strangely sentimental tug on his heartstrings. Odd, for almost two decades, he hadn't thought he had strings—or a heart to go with them.

Impulsively, his head dipped down to treat himself to the sweet nectar of her lips. "There are times, elf, when I very much wish your name wasn't Angelene Sheridan. You are making life very difficult for me."

Riding a wave of impulsive sentiment herself, Angelene wrapped her arms round his neck and kissed him soundly. She silently conveyed what she felt awkward voicing aloud. She had come to care a great deal for Sin, more than she should have. He was rapidly developing the power to hurt her as no other man could. She wondered if he knew that. Probably. The rascal possessed mental powers that bordered on phenomenal.

Before she embarrassed herself further, Angelene retreated into her own space. Whirling around, she propelled herself toward the terrace door.

Pondering the reason for Angelene's amorous embrace, Sin watched Angel walk away. The woman had become a habit he found difficult to break. He didn't want to send her away, but she would exert far too much influence on him if she stayed. Every time he looked at her, touched her, he would be questioning the long-held vow he had made to his brother. The men responsible *had* to be punished, Sin thought resolutely.

"I'll have Cyrus accompany you home."

"It isn't necessary. I can find my own way," she said without a backward glance. "All I need is the loan of a horse and the promise that I won't be accused of stealing it at some future time when you decide to use that as leverage over me."

When Angelene disappeared from sight, Sin permitted himself a chuckle. The lady's mind did work at a swift rate. She was almost as good at predicting cause and effect as he had trained himself to be.

Sin heaved a sigh and forced himself to concentrate on his primary purpose. It was time to put phase two of his plans into motion. Kimball, Porter and Sheridan had each endured their individual torment. Now they would endure collective fear and desperation. And last but hardly least, they would be punished for the crimes they had conspired to commit and conceal for eighteen years—to the day. And that, Sin reminded himself as he ambled downstairs to join Hiram and Cyrus was exactly as he had planned it.

When Sin ambled into the dining room, two pairs of curious eyes zeroed in on him. "I sent her home to her father," Sin responded to the unspoken question.

Two sets of broad shoulders slumped in relief. It was obvious that Hiram and Cyrus had sentimental soft spots. Loyal and devoted though they were, his friends did not approve of his dealings with Angelene. But neither did they comprehend the driving need that hounded Sin, because they had not endured the hellish nightmare first-hand.

True, Sin was having a difficult time where Angel was concerned, so he could appreciate Hiram's and Cyrus's reluctance to see an innocent victim caught in crossfire. Yet, one important point gelled in Sin's mind. With premeditated forethought, Kimball, Porter and Sheridan had killed Sin's brother and had stolen the cargo and the ship for personal gain. The crime had gone unpunished for almost two decades, but retaliation should be no less severe. Those three mutineers were living off money acquired as a direct result of a violent crime. And by damn, justice *would* be served, Sin vowed fiercely.

Hiram plucked up a fluffy biscuit and smothered it with jelly. "We've been hearing reports of flood damage around the area," he said after swallowing a morsel of biscuit. "Several small farms are standing underwater."

"Kimball's and Porter's as well, I hope," Sin said as he poured himself a cup of tea.

"No, they settled on high ground," Cyrus replied.

"What a pity."

"Some of the hired help and their families had to camp out," Hiram continued. "Backwater is keeping several unfortunate farmers out of their homes."

Sin mulled over the thought while he ate his meal. "Hiram, how close to completion is the remodeling project at the hotel?"

"The carpenters finished yesterday morning and I sent them on their way before rising water left them stranded."

"Gather our men," Sin requested, rising from his chair. "Send them out to tell the flood victims that South Sea Paradise is providing accommodations until the waters ebb."

Hiram blinked. "You're opening the inn to the needy? What about the grand opening?"

"I still intend to have the grand opening this weekend. Kimball, Porter and Sheridan will receive their own private invitations to join me." Sin stared down at his stunned friends. "And please do not plan anything for this evening. We have a task to perform."

"We do?" Cyrus questioned.

Sin picked up a biscuit. "We do. You did learn from our new staff of servants where the mutineers stashed their important documents, I hope."

"Yes, their ex-employees were very cooperative in providing that information," Hiram assured him.

"Good. We will be paying midnight visits to our neighbors."

With that provoking remark, Sin walked out, leaving Hiram and Cyrus to stare at each other.

"Swear to God," Cyrus mumbled. "Even after all these years together I still can't figure out how that man's mind works."

"That's because Sinclair operates on a higher plane. I'm sure we'll find out what the devil is going on when Sin is ready for us to know," Hiram insisted before he strode off to gather the crew.

"Some things never change," Cyrus said as he followed Hiram out the door.

Hiram didn't argue with that. Sin was a man who knew exactly what he wanted and how to get it. It wasn't the devil's luck that gave Sin the edge. He left nothing to chance and did very little on impulse or whim. Sin knew where he was going, long before he ever walked out the door.

## Twenty-one

Jerome Kimball stood at the hotel office, scowling as he watched displaced farmers and their families file into South Sea Paradise. Stories of Sinclair's benevolence had spread through town like wildfire. The man who had been surrounded by wary suspicion was gaining in prestige by the day. Meanwhile Kimball and Porter were losing ground fast.

Jerome had been approached by several outspoken aristocrats who had seen him explode in bad temper at Wilhelm's ball. They had inquired as to why Jerome—a wealthy, influential, long-time resident of Natchez—hadn't opened *his* hotel to the needy. Then his associates had chastised Jerome for making a scene at Wilhelm's party. While Jerome's and Owen's names were being deleted from future guest lists, Sinclair was being praised as a hero and practically handed the key to the city.

"Do you see what he's doing?" Owen Porter muttered as he stalked into Jerome's office. "Not only are Sinclair and his pirate crew transporting flood victims to the hotel, but he has that prize piece of horseflesh hitched up to a wagon! That stallion should belong to me."

Owen thrashed back and forth for a full minute before halting beside Jerome. "That man has got to go, I tell you. He's making us the laughingstocks of Natchez. And I just heard that Sinclair is having his grand opening Saturday. He'll probably be dragging our names through the mud during dinner. I think we should—" Owen clamped his jaws shut when a young lad appeared at the open door.

"Well, what is it?" Jerome demanded impatiently.

The lad scurried forward to hand one message to Jerome and the other to Owen. Without a word, the boy scuttled off.

"Damnation, what do you suppose this is all about?" Jerome muttered aloud.

Owen read the invitation requesting his presence at the conference room of South Sea Paradise on opening night. "We're probably being summoned to another slaughter," he predicted. "Sinclair will undoubtedly accuse us of plotting his demise after the robbery attempt. The devil certainly believes in keeping things stirred up, doesn't he?"

"And if we don't accept the invitation given by Natchez's latest hero, it will be another bad reflection on us," Jerome grumbled sourly. "I wish I could recall where the hell I've seen that man. I detest the advantage he has over me."

"I experienced the same feeling myself," Owen said, staring musingly at his invitation.

"A pity that Reggie Foster didn't do us the courtesy of gunning Sinclair down at Vidalia. The only bright spot is that Reggie has been making his rounds, declaring Sinclair to be too much the coward to square off on the dueling field. Too bad Sinclair's sudden generosity for the flood victims has overshadowed the accusations of cowardice."

"I dread this upcoming conference," Owen mumbled. "I find it impossible to curb my temper when Sinclair provokes me. Thanks to that bastard I've been blacklisted at Pharsalia Race Track. For that reason alone I'd like to tear that him limb from limb."

"Better to let some underling do it for you," Jerome advised.

Owen sniffed sarcastically. "If the ruffians from Under-the-Hill don't have better luck, we may never get rid of that pest."

"Even a devil cat only has nine lives," Jerome reminded him as he stared out the window, watching Sinclair direct traffic in front of his hotel. "Rest assured that Sin's time is coming. But we have to strike before he gathers more alliances with the gentry."

When Owen strode oft, Jerome was still staring at the refurbished hotel, wishing the flood had washed Sinclair out to sea and saved Jerome the trouble of disposing of him.


"Angel! Thank God you're all right." Charles gathered his daughter in his arms and squeezed the stuffing out of her.

"I'm sorry I worried you. That wasn't my intent."

And it hadn't been. Angelene had planned to get word to Charles before the night was out. Unfortunately, her staged death had almost become reality. And all for naught, as it turned out. Sin had quickly tired of her and sent her home. Angelene should have been relieved, but it hurt to know that the only man who intrigued her had lost interest when the challenge she presented had been conquered.

What Angelene feared in the beginning was disappointingly true. All that attracted men to her was the prospect of a hefty dowry and simple physical satisfaction. It must be her flighty temper and impulsive antics that put men off.

"I owe Sinclair a great deal," Charles said as he ushered Angelene through the foyer.

Angelene froze. Owing Sin was not a good thing. Suspicion rose like an incoming tide. "What do you mean you owe Sinclair?"

"Didn't he tell you?" Charles asked, surprised.

Angelene was growing more apprehensive by the second. "No, he didn't."

"Sinclair saved my life last night. I rode to Raven's Hill to tell him you'd disappeared, and he joined in the search. I spotted your satchel lodged on a sawyer and blundered into the floodwaters in hopes of finding you. But for Sinclair I would have drowned."

Angelene frowned pensively, at a loss to explain why Sinclair would rescue the man he had threatened to ruin socially and financially, for reasons she still couldn't fathom. But knowing Sin, he had his secret motives. Everything he did had a purpose. Even sending her home. This was not a good time to be a half a mental step behind Sin.

When a knock sounded on the door Charles pivoted around. "I'm going to have to hire another butler before I wear myself out," he grumbled.

Charles opened the door to find a lad who extended

an envelope. Mission accomplished, the boy turned on his heels and walked off. Charles read the invitation and smiled. "We have been invited to South Sea Paradise for the grand opening on Saturday, and Sinclair requests my presence at a conference. Perhaps he wants to discuss arrangements for a wedding."

Angelene knew better, and she couldn't share her father's enthusiasm. The nagging feeling that there was some connection between Sinclair and her father had grown steadily worse since Wilhelm's ball.

"Papa? How long were you at sea before you settled in Natchez?"

Charles grew very still and dodged her probing stare. "Several years. Why do you ask?"

"I was just curious."

The fact that Charles glanced in every direction except at Angelene didn't bode well. Before she could probe into her father's past, looking for some connection between him and a man her father found vaguely familiar, Charles strode off.

"I have to check on the flood damage in the cotton fields," he insisted on his way out the door. "I may not be back until late."

It was apparent that her question had struck a sensitive nerve. Angelene watched Charles go, wondering what he was hiding from her and what it might possibly have to do with Nick Sinclair. And what did Kimball, Porter and Reggie Foster have to do with anything? Angelene threw up her hands in frustration. It was impossible to put a puzzle together that had too many missing pieces.

\* \* \*

With the silence of a shadow, Sin crept toward the darkened study in Sheridan Hall. According to the servants who had previously worked at the plantation, Charles kept his important documents stashed in the bottom drawer of his desk, locked in a metal container.

Kimball and Porter had similar habits, Sin had learned. And at this very moment, Hiram and Cyrus were making midnight visits to secure the documents Sin intended to have on hand for the conference he had scheduled.

The locked window of the study posed little problem for Sin. He wedged a strip of metal between the sills to release the latches. In the space of a breath he was inside the room, inching toward the desk. The skeleton key he had brought along gained him access to the bottom drawer. The lock on the metal container proved to be a bit more difficult, but hardly impossible.

Once the document box clicked open, Sin tiptoed back to the window to make use of the moonlight. He thumbed through the papers until he located the ones he needed. A deep sense of satisfaction flooded through him as he replaced the container and secured the drawer. With documents in hand, Sin exited the same way he came in.

His gaze lifted to the outside gallery above him, stifling the impulsive urge to pay Angelene a visit. As busy as he had been during the day, his betraying thoughts constantly turned to that lively green-eyed female. God, how he wished Angelene were someone else, anybody else!

Very soon, she would discover what vindictive force drove him. And with that knowledge, the wild, sweet pleasures they had discovered in each other's arms would come an end.

Before Sin realized it, his footsteps had taken him to the winding outer staircase that led to the upper gallery. Almost by instinct he moved toward Angelene's room, drawn by the dim candlelight of an otherwise darkened floor. He paused beside the window and smiled as he watched Angelene pace the suite like a restless cat. With her unbound red-gold hair flowing around her she did indeed appear angelic, proving that appearances could be deceiving. This was one Angel who possessed more lively spirit than she knew what to do with.

A pang of regret tormented Sin as he turned away from temptation. He had made his choice. He was obliged to keep his vow to his brother, no matter what the personal sacrifice.

After Sin's conference with the three mutineers, Angelene would hate him.

Charles Sheridan glanced up in surprise when he spied Jerome Kimball and Owen Porter lounging at the foot of the hotel stairs. They were the last two men Charles expected to see at South Sea Paradise after the disruption at Wilhelm's party.

Thus far, Jerome and Owen hadn't noticed Charles. A throng of excited guests clogged the lobby. A jauntily dressed pirate was serving champagne to the line of patrons who eagerly awaited entrance to the restaurant.

Across the street, Kimball Hotel stood empty and quiet. Everyone who was anyone in Natchez was at South Sea Paradise. Judging from the fascinating decor of the lobby, Charles predicted that this unique establishment would draw clientele like flies. Sinclair's name was on every tongue these days. The man had proved to be a business genius. Charles was impressed.

Despite his previous confrontation with Sinclair, Charles had gained respect for the man. With any luck, the announcement of a marriage would preserve Angelene's reputation and tie her to the man who had acquired status and an exceptionally high profile in Natchez.

In good spirits, Charles threaded through the crowd to reach the steps. Before he could greet Kimball and Porter, Sinclair appeared on the landing above them, elegantly attired, except for that red sash and flowing black cape that had become his trademark.

"If you gentlemen will join me in the conference room, we can attend to a matter I wish to bring to your attention."

"What the blazes is this about?" Kimball demanded as he stalked up the steps.

Sin did not dignify the harsh question with an answer. These men would discover soon enough what purpose this meeting served.

Charles Sheridan stumbled to a halt when Sin strode into the conference room. Above the doorway hung a sign that sent memories avalanching upon him. "Dear God . . ."

Jerome Kimball glanced up to see *Annalee* etched on the gold plate above the door. His face lost all color. Beside him, Owen Porter choked on his breath and stumbled off balance.

All three men stared uneasily at the interior of the room that resembled the quarterdeck of a schooner. The wooden railing around the dais was reminiscent of a helm. Canvas sails, attached to polished spars, hung on the wall. It was if they were stepping back through time, into a closed chapter of a past they had made a pact never to mention or discuss.

Sin's two junior officers were dressed in similar attire and they stood on the dais, watching recognition dawn on the three men's blanched faces.

"Come sit down, gentlemen," Sin insisted in a neutral voice. "Welcome aboard the *Annalee.*"

With the enthusiasm of doomed prisoners walking the plank, Kimball, Porter and Sheridan sank down at the table. Sin derived immense satisfaction from watching the mutineers squirm in their skin. The past had caught up with them and they were being vividly reminded of the incident they had conveniently chosen to forget.

"What nonsense is this?" Kimball burst out, the instant Cyrus Duncan closed the door to ensure privacy.

"I assure you, Jerome, this is far from nonsense. Perhaps you have had difficulty recalling what was familiar about me. Do you remember a voyage from Boston, bound for New Orleans. The *Annalee* had encountered two British frigates and, at her captain's skillful hands, she eluded capture."

Sin strode leisurely around the table, his voice as calm and controlled as ever. "We were at war with Britain, if you recall. There were those among the crew who preferred to engage in battle and reap profits from goods that could be confiscated from enemy ships and sold for personal gain. According to the heated debate on deck, other merchant ships had turned to privateering during those times, and fortunes were being made, if a man didn't mind stooping to piracy now and again."

Sin paused behind Porter whose white knuckles were clamped around the goblet of wine provided for him. "The captain—Joshua Montague was his name—refused the demands of his money-hungry crew," Sin continued neutrally. "His objective was to sell the cargo in Louisiana and make the return cruise, dodging the British blockades."

In casual strides, Sin came to stand behind Charles Sheridan. "Greed, it seems, can drive a man to drastic measures to ensure his financial security."

Sin paused behind Kimball whose face was puckered in a black scowl. "In fact, the want of wealth can prove to be such an obsession that the means seems to justify the end—in some men's minds."

Sin returned to the head of the table and braced his hands. He stared into one peaked face and then another. "Taking my brother's life may have been of small consequence to you, but not to me." His voice hit a frigid pitch that was barely above a whisper. "All that you have acquired the last eighteen years was bought and paid for with my brother's blood. And while you sailed away to enjoy your profits, I was suffering through living hell, drifting at sea with a dead man."

"Jacob Montague . . ." Charles whispered in disbelief.

Owen Porter stared at the scar that gleamed white against Sinclair's bronzed cheek, remembering the night he had drawn his cutlass to knock the pesky brat aside . . . His hand jerked backward, upending the goblet. Wine dribbled across the table like spilled blood.

Jerome Kimball's face lost all color.

"Were you aware that in Europe, captured pirates are castigated by setting them adrift in a skiff with one of their dead comrades? It is said that the experience is so tormenting that it drives men insane," Sin continued in a tone that sent chills down every spine. "All that kept that young body from losing his sanity was his defiant vow to survive to see justice served, no matter how long it took, no matter what it cost . . . No matter what . . ."

Sin battled for hard-won composure when horrible memories rose like ghastly monsters from the deep. He reaffirmed his solemn pact with his departed brother and stared down at the three apprehensive men.

"I have not punished you *for* your sins, but rather *by* them. I have let my vengeful end justify my means, as you have done. I have taken from each of you what you hold dear, just as you stripped my one and only treasure from me. Joshua was all the family I had left and the *Annalee* was our inheritance. Joshua did not wish to turn to profiteering, yet I spent six years aboard just such a ship whose crew didn't blink twice at killing and plundering for the almighty coin.

"And speaking of the almighty coin, gentlemen, everything that you have acquired in life is mine. I am calling in the long-standing debt." He glanced toward his somber-faced friends. "Hiram, Cyrus, give these mutineers their documents."

All three men gasped in unison when the deeds to their property were placed in front of them.

"You stole these papers!" Owen exploded. "You broke into our homes. How dare—"

"Dare?" Sin lifted a challenging brow. "I have dared nothing. I simply asked the employees who once worked for you and now faithfully serve me where my documents were located. You can hardly cry theft or trespassing on what you have so graciously endeavored to amass for me over the last eighteen years. Let's not forget that the initial downpayment for the hotel, plantations and stables came from the sale of the *Annalee* and her heaping cargo."

Sin's voice dropped like an anchor into icy depths. "You will either sign the deeds over to me in payment of the long-standing debt or I will contact the proper authorities immediately and have you arrested for murder and mutiny."

Sin retrieved the pens from the middle of the table and presented one to each man. "Sign the deeds or sign your own death certificate," he ordered. "Kimball Hotel will be my gift to Hiram Brodie—a true and loyal friend. Owen's stables, horses and plantation will belong to Cyrus Duncan—a man who would never betray his captain the way you three men did. Sheridan Hall and Oak Gables I will keep for myself."

Hiram and Cyrus blinked, stunned by Sin's unexpected announcement, but they said nothing to break the silence that sizzled through the room.

"You seem to forget that Limestall was there, too," Owen muttered.

"I haven't forgotten," Sin calmly replied. "Limestall, however, did me the discourtesy of dying from a bullet wound before I could locate the four of you and strip away your fortunes, just as you stole the Montague fortune from Joshua and me. But according to reliable sources, Limestall's son has been doing a grand job of squandering all the money his father acquired. His poor business management will destroy what his father built on blood money."

"How did you find us?" Charles questioned, head downcast, shoulders slumped in crushing defeat.

"You have Owen Porter's obsession for horses to thank for that," Sin said blandly. "I was the captain of the ship that Owen's agent contacted in New Orleans to purchase and transport the Byerley Turk from the Far East to Natchez. I had searched every port in hopes of locating the four of you, but Owen and the Turk were gracious enough to come to me. That's why I have grown so fond of that horse. The Turk delivered you to me."

He paused to stare at the three men. "Now sign the property over to us, if you please, so we can conclude our business. I have a lobby and restaurant teeming with patrons I wish to greet. I intend to do them the courtesy of making them feel welcome at our grand opening."

Cursing under his breath, Owen Porter took pen in hand and scrawled his name on the deed and signed the property over to Cyrus Duncan. Charles and Jerome transferred their deeds and slumped back in their chairs.

Wine dribbled off the edge of the table and onto the floor like the ticking of a clock that marked the time of reckoning.

When Sin had collected the deeds and handed them to Hiram, he pivoted toward the condemned men. "I have only one demand left to make to you. I want you to deliver to me the man who shot my brother and shoved him overboard before I could mount the companionway steps to intervene that fateful night. Joshua's murderer and I have unfinished business to transact. The other two men will walk away and attempt to begin again—by their own devices, not with blood-money secured by fatal sacrifice."

"And how do you know Limestall wasn't the one who shot your brother?" Owen challenged.

Sin picked up his wineglass and took a sip, leaving the men hanging on tenterhooks. "Because Limestall was the only one I could see clearly when I dashed up the steps. The three of you were huddled around my brother like a pack of wolves before you tossed him overboard."

Setting the glass aside, Sin gestured for Hiram and Cyrus to follow him to the door. "You have until tomorrow to produce the name of my brother's killer, gentlemen. And *do* consider the consequences if you *don't*."

## Twenty-two

When the door whined shut behind Sin, all three men half collapsed in their chairs.

"How the devil did that little bastard survive?" Owen questioned the world at large.

"This is certainly an unexpected twist of fate," Kimball muttered dismally.

Charles Sheridan raised his head and stared straight ahead, seeing nothing but the grim memories that had caught up with him. "That's why each of us has been targeted with our own private brand of torture," he mused aloud. "Owen lost his prize steed and stable of horses because those were his obsessions. For Kimball it was the hotel. And my torment was knowing that—"

Charles squeezed his eyes shut. He had the haunted feeling that Angelene's loss of innocence and threatened reputation were the prices he paid because his daughter—the beguiling image of his wife—was his most precious treasure.

Angelene was nothing but a gambit Sinclair had used to avenge his brother's death. Sinclair had preyed on her innocence and tainted her reputation to spite Charles. The only reason Sinclair had assisted in the search for Angelene was to rescue his pawn for further tormenting ploys against Charles. And the only reason Sinclair had dragged Charles from the floodwaters was to inflict the second phase of torment.

"What did Sinclair take from you?" Kimball demanded when Charles's voice dried up.

"My daughter," Charles whispered brokenly.

"That son of a bitch won't live through the night," Kimball snarled. "I'll have his head and our deeds back if it's the last thing I do!"

"What makes you think you'll be successful?" Owen muttered bitterly. "We tried to dispose of that scoundrel after Wilhelm's party, for all the good it did."

Charles jerked up his head. "What are you talking about?"

"Jerome hired some ruffians from Under-the-Hill to stage a robbery and have Sinclair shot. But as you can plainly see, the attempt failed."

"And it wasn't the first time, either," Jerome admitted. "I sent two men to dispose of Sinclair after our first confrontation. Our only chance of survival against him is to combine forces."

Charles adamantly shook his head. "I'm not going to be a party to another killing. The first one has been weighing on my conscience far too long. Sinclair lost his brother because of us and he was left to scratch and claw his way through life."

"Have you lost your wits, Sheridan?" Jerome spluttered. "Do you honestly believe Sinclair is going to forgive and forget after he has his brother's killer served to him on a platter? If you do then you're a fool. He'll go straight to the authorities and have the two survivors arrested. The murder case will be the biggest scandal this city has ever seen. If you value your daughter you won't leave her with the shame she'll have to face. Not only will she be stigmatized because of her association with Sinclair, but she'll be ostracized because she's your daughter."

Owen leaned close, holding Charles's tormented gaze. "You've got no choice, man. If you don't agree to this alliance to save your own neck then you have to do it for Angelene's sake."

Charles picked up his wineglass in a shaky hand and downed a sip. Yes, he knew Angelene would suffer, but she would not be penniless. She would inherit her grandparents' trust when she wed. She could relocate and begin again—away from the scandalous gossip. Angelene would survive, even if Charles didn't.

"I will not condone the murder," Charles said emphatically.

"Then you intend to give the name Sinclair demands?" Jerome questioned in a gritted growl.

Charles focused his full attention on Jerome. "You are the one who pressed Joshua Montague to turn privateer. You were also the one who shot him and flung him overboard. Would you have Owen and me pay for the crime you committed?"

Jerome swore violently when Owen stared at him. "Don't delude yourself, Owen. You were the one who struck that young whelp with your cutlass when he flung himself at us. Sinclair knows perfectly well that you are responsible for his scar and for flinging him into the sea in his brother's wake. Do you really think he'll let you live when you marked him for life? Mark my words, Sinclair will come at you with another proposition, and then another. He intends to turn us against each other before he deals with each one of us separately, just as he did when he first arrived in town. He'll see us all dead, I tell you!"

Jerome's glittering hazel eyes focused on Charles. "Perhaps you didn't fire the shot or wield the cutlass, but you were a part of the mutiny. You profited as much as we did. If you think you can convince Sinclair you were an innocent bystander then you are foolishly mistaken. I'll tell him it was your idea, if not your hand that held the pistol."

Owen sighed heavily. "I would dearly love to know how Sinclair survived and how he found time to cut the skiff loose before I knocked him into the sea."

Charles rose from his chair and headed toward the door. "Whatever I deserve I will accept." He pivoted to face Jerome's disgusted snarl. "If you don't surrender yourself to Sinclair, I will be forced to give your name."

On that grim promise, Charles walked out.

At the time of the incident Charles had what he thought were legitimate reasons for pressing the captain to turn privateer. He had been desperate for money to support his wife and child after they had been disowned by Emily's strict and spiteful father.

The situation had gotten completely out of hand when Jerome lost his temper and resorted to threats of violence. But when the appalling deed was done, Charles had been hounded by excessive guilt. He had lived with the awful secret for eighteen years. He was glad his wife wasn't here to discover the truth. It was bad enough that Angelene would have to be told what had happened, told that she had been a tool of revenge, told that all her misery was the result of her father's secretive and shameful past.

Dear God, the world was about to come tumbling down and there was nothing Charles could do to spare his daughter, nothing except commit another crime against a man who had suffered untold injuries and hardships. *That*, Charles could not permit. He would point an accusing finger at Jerome Kimball first, despite the vow of silence the men had made that fateful night.

Jerome guzzled down his wine, expelled several foul oaths and stared grimly at Owen. "We have to take immediate action," he insisted. "You and I are both dead men if we don't."

"Charles will betray us," Owen prophesied. "He has no stomach for violence—then or now."

Jerome was on his feet, pacing the length of the room. "I need a chance to think this through. Sinclair sprang this surprise on us to catch us off guard, so we wouldn't have time to regroup."

"Either that or he is providing the guilty party time to pack up and attempt escape so he can run him down," Owen said bleakly. "Sinclair and that gang of pirates he calls friends would probably enjoy that. First you, I suspect, and then me. The swamps around Natchez tell no tales, after all. We could be tortured, slaughtered and no one would know what became of us. We would conveniently disappear and never return."

Jerome reversed direction and headed for the door. "I'll be in touch later, Owen," he murmured, distracted.

Owen didn't waste time escaping from the confines

of the room. He needed time alone to consider *his* alternatives—what few Sinclair left available. Damn that man! Sinclair was proving to be a ruthless curse that wouldn't go away.

First had come high water and then hell. Owen shuddered to think what the last plague of Sin was going to be!

Sin halted on the staircase landing to inhale a purifying breath. He stared at the milling crowd that filled the hotel to capacity. After eighteen long years he had the chance to savor the satisfaction of the moment. Watching recognition dawn on each guilty face had been gratifying. All three men were partially aware of what Sin had felt back then—shock, fury and immeasurable grief. But no matter what Sin did to those three men, they would never fully appreciate the torment he had endured, because even his methods of revenge couldn't adequately recreate the horrors of that dreadful night.

Those murderers could never see the world through the eyes of a twelve-year-old boy who had lost everything, except his own life. During those next two days of drifting on open sea, Sin had feared he would lose both his sanity and his life. It had been indescribable hell . . .

Excited voices wafted up to Sin, jostling him from his pensive reverie. Smiling faces greeted him as he scanned the crowd.

"Utterly fascinating, Sinclair!" Aubrey Wilhelm called up to him. "My wife and I feel as if we washed ashore on an enchanted tropical island."

When a waiter, dressed in pirate's garb, ambled past, Aubrey scooped up a glass from the tray and lifted it in toast. "To Sinclair and the success of South Sea Paradise."

Arms lifted and smiling faces focused on Sin. He nodded graciously and started down the steps. His gaze landed on the stunning vision in green satin and his breath caught when sparkling emerald eyes settled on him. The man in him instantly responded to the fetching young woman who was truly the finest jewel Natchez had to offer.

Sin longed to share Angelene's company one last time before the bond between them was severed completely. When she returned home tonight, her father would divulge the truth before disaster brought him to his knees. Sin wanted—needed—this last night, one more delicious memory before Angelene was given answers to questions she would be wishing she hadn't asked.

Before Sin could descend the steps, Hiram tugged at his cloak. "What you did for Cyrus and me was incredibly generous, but we can't accept."

"Aye, mate, Cyrus chimed in. "As you said, it was your inheritance that was stolen."

"And it is also mine to give away," Sin countered. "We have been together for years, guarding each other's backs, fending off pirates and battling raging seas. Because of your unswerving faithfulness, you will share the fortunes. I expect Hiram will have his own ideas about redecorating his hotel and estate. And you, Cyrus, will enjoy the competition of racing against the gentry at Pharsalia—in between taking your leisure at the plantation, of course."

When Hiram opened his mouth to voice a second protest, Sin flung up a hand to forestall him. "Consider this your payment for the weeks of legwork required to gather the information I needed. And do not argue with me, either of you," he ordered. "You, after all, have seen first-hand how vengeful I can be. And right about now, I predict Kimball, Porter and Sheridan are regretting that they've gotten on my bad side."

"I'll wager that's the truth," Cyrus agreed. "Good thing those blokes weren't wearin' false teeth. They would've dropped their dentures when you lowered the boom on them."

When Sin descended the steps, his attention fixated on the eye-catching beauty by the door, Hiram dismally shook his head. "And I'll wager Sin is having a devil of a time soothing his conscience about Angelene. He wasn't expecting her to matter quite so much when she got trapped in the middle of this bitter feud."

Cyrus's smile evaporated. "Aye, it will be difficult to give up such a prize as that stunnin' lady. Every time she walks into a room, it's as if the red moon rose on a black sea. Sin knows he can't make that lovely Angel choose between him and her own father, especially not now, not even after the truth is out in the open."

Hiram nodded in bleak agreement as he watched Sin thread through an enthusiastic crowd that heaped glowing compliments on him. "I imagine that grim knowledge is eating Sin alive right now. He'll have the full measure of his revenge, but he'll pay a high price for it," he predicted.

Angelene felt her heart twist in her chest when her gaze met Sin's from across the congested foyer. Despite her disappointment and confusion, her fierce reaction to seeing Sin revealed her affection, one-sided though it proved to be.

Her heart always skipped several vital beats at the sight of this swarthy rogue. Their secret memories were enough to put a blush on her cheeks. Sin had become her greatest weakness and she wondered if he knew it. Probably. Sin always seemed to know how she would react before she did. Surely he was aware of how his glib humor and seductive charm affected her. How could he not? She had come apart in his arms too many times.

Despite Sin's attempt to maintain his self-reserve, he felt a smile tug at his lips when he halted in front of Angelene. Her eyes were sparkling more brilliantly than the gems Pearly meticulously polished. When she cocked her head to the side, her lips pursed in teasing amusement, Sin felt his knees wobble.

"I do believe that's the first honest smile I've seen you wear, Mister Sinclair. You should smile more often. It becomes you."

"Does it? Perhaps it's the pleasurable memories of late that provoke my smile."

Bystanders who overheard their conversation glanced from her to Sin. A blush crept up her cheeks. "Pleasurable memories, sir?"

He took her hand, bringing her fingertips to his lips. His obsidian eyes twinkled before he bent his head to brush a kiss to her wrist. "Memories of dancing with a lovely young lady at Wilhelm's ball. I was hoping you would remember a time that I find impossible to forget."

Angelene breathed a quiet sigh of relief. Sin had shrewdly set himself up to humiliate her and he could have instigated scandalous gossip if that had been his wont. Instead, he chose to compliment rather than mortify. She could have hugged him for that.

"Well, well, who do we have here?"

The smirking voice that came from starboard was as expected as it was unwanted. Sin rose to full stature to look down at Reggie Foster. The proud dandy had allowed the cancellation of the duel to go to his head—and obviously not for safekeeping. Reggie had come from the old philosophical school that believed honor must be salvaged at all cost. It was as idealistic as it was unrealistic. In Sin's estimation a man had to *acquire* honor before he could *defend* it. This young pup still had a lot to learn.

"I thought you would postpone your grand opening until talk of your cowardice died down," Reggie declared in a voice that carried across the jammed lobby. "A man who refuses to appear for a duel usually doesn't have the gall to show his face for at least a week."

"Consider yourself lucky Sinclair didn't bother with you," Angelene snapped at the idiotic fool.

Reggie clasped his hand around Angelene's elbow to lead her away from Sin. "The very fact that he didn't make an appearance at Vidalia testifies that he values his life above your honor—"

His voice dissolved when his shoulder bumped against the immovable wall of Sin's chest. How Sinclair had maneuvered himself so agilely and swiftly Reggie couldn't say, but he was there, blocking the way as effectively as a rock wall.

"I had no need to rise at dawn to compete for the lady's attention," Sin said nonchalantly.

Angelene held her breath, wondering if Sin was going to announce *why* he hadn't risen at dawn. She wished she had a hole she could crawl into.

Sin's gaze darted momentarily to Angelene, noting her apprehension. *"The very fact—"* Sin began, tossing Reggie's words back at him, "—that Angelene is here as my honored dinner guest indicates her preference and mine."

Reggie faltered, his gaze bouncing from Sinclair to Angelene. "You prefer the company of a coward?"

When Reggie loudly posed his question, all conversation in the lobby ground to a halt. Angelene felt as if she were standing in the spotlight on center stage. All eyes keyed on her, waiting, watching.

Her gaze lifted to Sin's rugged face. Obsidian eyes bore down on her and thick black brows lifted inquisitively. Angelene followed her heart, no matter how foolish that would probably prove to be.

"I'm sorry, Reggie," she said without taking her eyes of Sin. "But I much admire a man who can shrug off unjust accusations against him to spare another man's life. *The very fact* is that I was the one who pleaded with Sinclair to leave you in one piece." She cast Reggie an absent glance. "I was reasonably certain that your combative skills were limited only to your ability to shoot off your mouth. That is hardly effective on a dueling field, against such an invincible opponent as Sinclair."

The comment sent snickers rippling through the crowd.

"Angelene!" Reggie crowed, highly affronted.

"I do not advise calling the lady out," Sin warned as he tucked Angelene's hand around his elbow. "I would feel obliged to stand in her stead on the dueling field.

And rest assured, Reggie, that I would not turn the other cheek a second time. I can tolerate insults against me, but I will not permit one unflattering word to be spoken about such an enchanting young lady as this."

"I absolutely refuse to let you—"

Sin interrupted before Reggie stuck his foot in his mouth with another reckless challenge. "However, I do admire a man who would rise at the crack of dawn to fight a duel he was destined to lose. That suggests a certain degree of bravery. As a reward, Reggie, I am offering you employment—an *honorable* day's wage for an *honorable* day's work. Report to Raven's Hill at the crack of dawn tomorrow and this unfortunate incident will be forgotten."

While Reggie stood there, his mouth opening and shutting like an unbattened hatch, Sin ushered Angelene toward the restaurant. "I hope you find the decor and cuisine to your liking, Miss Sheridan. I have been anxious to hear your opinions on our renovations."

"I find South Sea Paradise as fascinating as the man who created such an enthralling atmosphere."

One dark brow elevated at the unexpected compliment that was heard around the crowded lobby. Angelene had publicly given Sin her vote of approval. He wondered if she would retract it when her father divulged his version of the meeting that had taken place in the conference room.

Sin glanced down into dancing green eyes that reminded him of legends about mischievous leprechauns. He could feel irrepressible spirit radiating from her to him, igniting flames of remembered moments, remembered pleasures.

Burning hunger claimed him—a hunger that all the succulent cuisine in the restaurant couldn't appease . . .

The words Pearly had spoken came back to Sin like the tormenting refrain of a bittersweet melody. *Have a care that you don't lose more than you win to satisfy your revenge.*

If Sin had nothing else to look forward to, he would at least have this amicable night with Angelene. They would set all conflicts aside and enjoy each other's company. For sure and certain, this pleasurable truce would be broken by evening's end, Sin bleakly reminded himself as he shepherded Angelene to the secluded corner table.

# *Twenty-three*

Jerome Kimball and Owen Porter halted on the steps to watch the encounter between Sinclair, Reggie and Angelene. When Sinclair led Angelene into the restaurant, leaving Reggie's jaw flapping in the wind, Jerome muttered under his breath.

"Angelene . . ." Jerome's voice evaporated when an ingenious thought flitted through his mind. "Come on, Owen, I have an idea that can solve our problem."

Owen shook his head in disgust when Angelene walked off on Sinclair's arm, making her preference publicly known. "That girl always did have more adventurous spirit than a woman rightfully ought to have. She'll get more than she bargained for when she realizes Sinclair is playing her for a fool. If Charles hadn't doted upon that girl to such idiotic extremes she would have already been married and she wouldn't find herself at Sinclair's mercy."

Jerome smiled wickedly as the scheme unfolded in his mind. Very soon Sinclair wasn't going to cause anyone problems, and Charles Sheridan would no longer be dragging his feet. Jerome was convinced he could end this nightmare and save face and fortune.

Jerome's gaze darted to Cyrus and Hiram. As for Sinclair's lackeys, they weren't going to reap the benefits of Jerome's and Owen's years of labor. They would end up as deep in hell as Sinclair would be, he promised himself fiercely.

Angelene nodded her thanks when the waitress filled her wineglass, at Sin's request. She glanced around the busy restaurant and recognized several of the women who tended the tables. They were the courtesans Kimball had once employed.

A wry smile pursed Angelene's lips, as she wondered how many of the gentlemen in attendance were squirming uneasily while their former mistresses waited on them—and their wives.

"Pearly was right. You do have a tendency to make a great splash," she said, her eyes sparkling with impish amusement.

Sin lifted his drink, meeting her mischievous gaze over the rim of his goblet. "I have always been fascinated with ironic justice," he assured her. "And by the way, I'm paying my waitresses a decent wage so they aren't forced to rely upon the world's oldest profession to support themselves. As for the husbands who have strayed from home in the past, they will have to make an effort to regain favor with their wives."

The comment brought both amusement and pain. "I hadn't realized you were so interested in preserving the sanctity of marriage."

Sin stared her squarely in the eye as he set down his goblet. "I believe in honoring solemn vows, Angelene, no matter what they are."

Angelene had the inescapable feeling they were having a double conversation. Unfortunately, she was unsure of Sin's underlying meaning. But Sin was an enigmatic man who kept his private thoughts to himself. There were times—like now—when she wished he would speak openly.

She flicked Sin a quick glance before her gaze dropped to the amber liquid in her glass. "The beverage you're serving to your guests doesn't happen to be one of Pearly's potions, I hope."

"No, but you have called my attention to an oversight that I will correct. In my noble effort to restore aristocratic marriages, I will ask Pearly to mix up one of his love potions."

Angelene blushed profusely when reminded of their intimate conversation on that subject and the effects the potion had on her.

Sin noted her heightened color and reached across the table to trace the elegant line of her jaw. "Before you become defensive, Angel," he whispered quietly, "I was not being sarcastic."

She met his obsidian gaze. "No?"

"No. I can think of no stronger potion than the enchanting sight of you. I fully understand why you have been nicknamed the Natchez Jewel. Your mystical inner sparkle challenges and intrigues a man. You will always outshine the most precious of gems."

Angelene peered into that rugged bronzed face and felt the last corner of her heart crumble. Sin's tender touch could double her pulse rate in the space of a breath. His quietly uttered compliment sent riveting pleasure through every fiber of her being.

Angelene had been able to cast off other men's flattery with a shrug. But Sin had developed an unconquerable power over her that made her responsive to all he said and did. It was dangerous and alluring.

It was . . . love.

The vibrating tension that surrounded the secluded table shattered when the attractive waitress set their plates in front of them. Angelene stared down at the filet of chicken with truffles, diced potatoes and snap beans, knowing the succulent entrees weren't going to appease her appetite. She craved the forbidden. It was disheartening to realize—and over dinner no less!—that she had become a fool in love.

"The meal doesn't appeal to you?" Sin questioned, studying her odd expression.

Angelene snapped out of her trance and manufactured a smile. "The food is fine, I'm sure." She darted him a quick glance and picked up her fork. "It's just that I've suddenly acquired a taste for love potions and their special effects. I don't think this meal is going to measure up . . ."

Her voice trailed off when Sin dropped his fork. It clattered against his china plate like a gong. Angelene could think of nothing more gratifying than catching Sin off guard. It was a rare moment—solace for the realization that this man had stolen her heart and soul. She would be his for the taking, even if he was not taking for the right reasons.

Sin placed a stranglehold on his fork and ignored the curious glances that came his way. Angelene's comment had caught him by surprise, not to mention what it had done to vital parts of his anatomy. Need—inappropriate and untimely though it was—had become more essential than nourishment.

God, how he wished he could snap his fingers and make the restaurant patrons disappear in a puff of smoke. He knew the enchantment of this evening would shatter, the instant Angelene returned home. Her father would inform her of the loss of Sheridan Hall and Oak Gables and Angelene's green eyes would glitter with fury. And as Pearly prophesied, Sin would be counting the cost of what he would lose in the name of revenge.

The staggering fortune he had amassed in the Far East trade and by pearling could not foot this bill, Sin decided. No amount of money could buy the one treasure beyond his reach.

Sin couldn't have it both ways and he knew it. Turning his back on this bewitching beauty was a steep price, but he had made a promise to his brother, a dying wish that must be honored.

*There will be other women who will intrigue you,* Sin tried to reassure himself.

*But not another Angel who is the personification of living fire and tangible spirit,* came that annoying voice deep inside him.

*I made a vow to my brother and I'm obliged to keep it,* Sin furiously insisted.

*And you will destroy this unique, remarkable woman in the process. You are sentencing her to the years of hell you endured.*

"Angel, I—" Sin caught himself before he apologized for something she had yet to understand. He would not destroy the companionable pleasure they shared. It would end too soon as it was.

Angelene regarded him curiously. The tense lines bracketing his mouth emphasized the scar on his jaw. She waited while he wrestled with whatever he had intended to say—and didn't. The emotion that battled its way to the surface had once again been suppressed and Angelene felt the defeat as if it were her own.

They ate in silence, each one lost to private thoughts. When Sin escorted Angelene through the crowd, she felt dozens of eyes turn toward them, silently linking her name to his. Seeing Sarah Wilhelm waiting in line, assured Angelene that the news would be all over town in two days. Sarah had the fastest tongue in Natchez. The gentry who had yet to arrive at the grand opening would be informed of who was seen with whom and of the incident with Reggie Foster.

Well, there was a consolation, Angelene reminded herself. The fortune hunters who pursued her would back off. But little did the aristocrats and wife hunters know that Nick Sinclair had no interest in wedlock. He only wanted the temporary pleasure a woman could provide. In that, nothing had changed.

Angelene smiled ruefully, struck by the ironic thought that the one man she wanted didn't need her in his life—only in his bed on occasion. This, she decided, was her punishment for rejecting so many undesirable suitors . . .

When Sin glided his sinewy arm around her waist to steer her out the door, her depressing thoughts scattered. They stepped onto the street to see the line stretching down the boardwalk.

"It looks as though the expenses of refurbishing will

be collected in a single night," Angelene speculated. "All of Natchez has become bedeviled by Sin."

"And what of you, Angel?" he questioned as they strolled toward her carriage.

"I also fell beneath the spell of South Sea Paradise," she hedged, striving for a light, breezy tone. "Who can resist the lure of being transported to a tropical island?"

Sin was aware she had artfully dodged the subtle question. He lifted Angelene's hand to his lips, wishing he could sweep her into his arms and drink his fill from those dewy lips. After tonight she was going to feel as if she had been forsaken and betrayed, and there wasn't a damned thing Sin could do about that.

Angelene peered into those dark eyes that bore into her with vivid intensity. She craved the taste of him desperately. His light but compelling touch was all but turning her knees to jelly.

"Good night, Miss Sheridan," Sin said politely. "I'm pleased that South Sea Paradise meets with your approval."

Angelene resisted the urge to fling her arms around his neck and kiss his lips passionately, right in front of God and anyone who cared to watch. "Thank you for a most enjoyable evening, Mr. Sinclair. You have my sincere wish for your continued success."

Turning away, Angelene stepped into the coach, feeling her flesh sizzle beneath Sin's assisting hands. She wasn't anticipating the cold bath she would have to take to cool the flames that seared her from inside out.

As the coach rolled away, Sin stood in ponderous silence. *Why her?* he asked himself tormentedly. Why did he want the one woman he couldn't have?

He pivoted around to greet the guests lined up outside the hotel and silently reminded himself that life had two great and torturous tragedies—getting one's heart's desire and not getting it. And revenge, Sin had learned, was a cutlass that could also wound the one who wielded it.

Another form of torment, Sin thought grimly. He was very well acquainted with that. More was the pity that he confidently assumed hell had nothing else to teach him that he didn't already know.

And the irony of it was that visitations from an Angel had proved him wrong . . .

Reggie Foster slumped down at the table in the men's club and stared at the man who had barely acknowledged his presence. Charles Sheridan was too busy doing hand-to-glass combat with his ale to pay Reggie the slightest attention. Reggie, however, intended to be seen and heard. He needed Sheridan's assistance.

"I think you should have a talk with your daughter," Reggie advised before swallowing several gulps of grog. "Cavorting with Sinclair will bring her nothing but trouble. Her reputation will be ruined when the gentry finally come to their senses and realize that Sinclair is making fools of them all."

Charles stared into the contents of his mug, wishing the blond-haired dandy who had invited himself to the table would vanish into thin air. Reggie Foster was the fool. Sinclair had let him off easy and the idiot didn't even know it.

"I have done everything possible to make my interest in Angelene known." Reggie took another drink and blotted the foam from his lips with a napkin. "I implore you to give your consent to our marriage before Angelene is ruined forever."

Charles glanced up then. Reggie was a fortune hunter who ran a distant second in comparison to the wit and wiles of Nick Sinclair. Or rather Jacob Montague, Charles gloomily amended. The ugly past had overtaken Charles and he was wise enough to know it, even if Kimball and Porter were determined to scramble for survival. They would ultimately lose, Charles predicted. Sinclair was far too clever to be caught unaware.

"Charles?" Reggie prompted when the crestfallen aristocrat refused to reply. "It is your daughter's future we are discussing. I'm offering salvation."

Charles grunted and sipped his drink. His fourth, but he no longer cared to count. "You are trying to form an alliance with the wrong man, Reggie. Time will prove that I am powerless against Sinclair. He pulls my strings like a puppeteer. You would be well advised to accept the job Sinclair offered you, despite your foolhardy insults. When the world comes tumbling down I guarantee you'll prefer to be standing beneath the shelter Sinclair provides."

Reggie frowned at Charles's cryptic remarks. "You're accepting defeat and allowing Sinclair to destroy your daughter's reputation? He will, you know. Whatever Angelene thinks she sees in him is an illusion."

Charles polished off his drink and levered out of his chair. Hands braced on the table, he stared bleary-eyed at Reggie. "Take my word for it, young man. Sin is no mirage. He is *very real*. He is an indestructible force. Align yourself with him and thank your lucky stars that you did. He has granted you a favor that I wish were mine."

With that obscure comment, Charles pushed himself upright and wobbled toward the door. He had been sipping bottled courage for two hours. Now it was time to face his daughter and confess the awful truth about his not-so-honorable past. He wanted Angelene to understand how and why she had become mixed up in Sinclair's private feud, why Charles had been brought to his knees in humiliation and financial ruin.

Charles had come to the bleak conclusion that he would have to send Angel away immediately—tonight. By this time tomorrow all of Natchez would know Charles's shame. He had to spare Angelene by providing her with enough cash to relocate elsewhere. She would have to be made to understand that only a hasty marriage in a distant city would protect her from scandal. Only then would she receive the inheritance her maternal grandparents had left to her.

Charles was tormented by the knowledge that Angelene would not have time to search for a man she could love. She must settle for one who would ensure that she received her inheritance. He had wanted to see his daughter happily wed, to know she had discovered the meaning of the mutual affection Charles and Emily had shared, in spite of his in-laws' glaring disapproval.

Charles's worst torment came in knowing that his daughter had actually fallen beneath Sinclair's spell. It was in her eyes, her smile. Angelene had risked her reputation to seek out Sinclair. She had declared her preference—loudly and clearly—tonight. Angelene was on a collision course with catastrophe and Charles—God forgive him—was the one who had paved the way to hell for her.

Charles cursed colorfully, wishing Sin had let him drown in those turbulent floodwaters. But then, Sinclair had no intention of letting Charles do him the discourtesy of dying before facing the full measure of revenge. Limestall didn't know how lucky he was. He had gone to his grave, blithely unaware that his past was waiting to settle over him like a black cloud.

Tears misted Charles's eyes as he plopped into his coach and signaled to the groom. By morning, Charles would no longer have a home to call his own and Angelene would be forever beyond his reach. She would have to make her own way as best she could, aware that her father was not what he seemed.

Charles knotted his fists and cursed his own weaknesses, his drastic mistakes. He was doomed. All that had been important to Charles was being stripped away.

And nothing short of murder could save him.


Owen Porter lashed out with his riding quirt when one of the scalawags on Silver Street made a grab for him. Before the would-be thief could regain his balance, Jerome Kimball rammed the man with his mount. Yelping, the thug fell facedown in one of the muddy puddles left by the flood.

"May you rot in hell," the man snarled as he crawled upon hands and knees to watch the twosome ride off.

Jerome spat a suitable rejoinder at the would-be thief and then focused his attention on the stone and timber tavern that was nestled between the bawdy house and shabby dance hall Under-the-Hill.

"I hope this scheme works," Owen grumbled uneasily. "I don't enjoy rubbing shoulders with these snakes Under-the-Hill. They'll turn on you in a minute if the price is right."

"Then we'll ensure our price is right," Jerome insisted. "We have only one hope of countering Sinclair and very little time to spare. Jim Calloway and his brigands are our only hope."

"Calloway? The burly highwayman we hired to stage the robbery?" Owen snorted disdainfully. "He and his men already failed to dispose of Sinclair. We wasted good money and we can't afford another bungled attempt."

"But Calloway and his cohorts won't be squaring off against Sinclair and his sidekicks," Jerome reminded him as he reined to a halt. "I have someone else in mind to dispose of Hiram and Cyrus. Stop fretting, Owen. By the time the night is out we will have the situation in hand. There is an army of cutthroats at our disposal. Sinclair and his pirates will be no match for the lot of scavengers Under-the-Hill."

Owen swung down from his prize steed, wondering if his horse would still be there when he emerged from the smoke-filled tavern. Damn, he should have ridden a worthless nag!

Jerome watched Owen double-tether his horse. "Come on, Owen," he muttered impatiently. "Losing your mount is the least of your concerns right now."

Sighing heavily, Owen slopped through the mud. "You're right. I have to save my own neck and my stable full of valuable steeds. I just wish I didn't have to put my life in the hands of scoundrels like Calloway," Owen groused.

"Then consider your other option," Jerome grunted as he reached for the door latch.

Owen did, finding himself choosing between the least of two evils. In grim resignation he strode inside the tavern to locate Calloway and set Jerome's plot in motion.

## Twenty-four

Angelene ducked beneath the archway of snagging limbs that covered the trail leading to Raven's Hill. She had returned home to find herself incredibly restless and yearning for something as compelling as it was forbidden—Sin.

Having accepted the truth of her emotions, Angelene garbed herself in men's clothes and left Sheridan Hall before her father returned home. In years past, Angelene had idealistically claimed she wanted to be needed just for herself, not for the luxury her father's money could provide. And conversely, she wanted the one man who had become essential to her happiness—despite everything—to want *her*—despite everything. No matter what, she was going to confess what was in her heart.

*And you'll probably get your heart broken in the process,* came the voice of stubborn feminine pride.

Well, Angelene was in love with Nick Sinclair and she was going to be completely honest in her feelings. For all the times she had *not* been in love she would admit her affection when she *was.*

*Angel's greatest Sin,* the nagging voice came again.

"Clam up," Angelene muttered. "I want him to know the truth."

*So he can bind you in another of his clever schemes? More than likely that's what will happen.*

Inhaling a determined breath Angelene zigzagged through the trees. She had not come to Raven's Hill to propose bargains or issue demands, she had come to follow her heart.

Angelene tethered her mount and surveyed Sin's unusual home. She grinned, thinking the mansion looked a great deal like Noah's arc setting on high ground. Knowing Sin's phenomenal ability of prediction, he had probably forecast the flood and had prepared for the worst by transforming his new home into a ship.

She wondered if Sin was expecting her. The man had an amazing knack of predicting her reactions before she reacted, after all. But hopefully, she would be one step ahead of *him* tonight.

Angelene approached the magnolia tree that would again serve as her makeshift ladder. This time she would be waiting for Sin to return from the grand opening of South Sea Paradise. Even if all he wanted was the pleasure of a feminine body he would receive more than he bargained for.

Pride be damned, Angelene told herself. Sin probably couldn't return her deep affection, but he would accept it—at the very least.

A mischievous smile pursed her lips as she eased a leg over the gallery railing and tiptoed toward Sin's private suite. Even if she met with disappointment she would dearly love to shock that self-disciplined expression off his handsome face—just once. That in itself would be quite an accomplishment. Even if Sin didn't possess the capacity to love, she would like to startle him. Ah, if she could only provoke a smile like the one he had smiled earlier in the evening.

A smile at the very least, she promised herself as she slipped through the terrace door to become engulfed in shadows. If she couldn't have Sin's love then she would have one smile and one last pleasurable memory before he turned his interest to a new conquest.

If only . . . Angelene squelched the whimsical thought and sank into the chair in the corner, anxiously awaiting Sin's arrival.

Sin stepped down from his coach and stared up at the massive house he now called home. He heaved an audible sigh. This should be his finest hour, the delicious fruit of his tireless labors. He should be flying as high as a moonraker sail.

The grand opening of South Sea Paradise had been a smashing success. The unique decor of the hotel and restaurant had earned him compliments galore. Sin's conference with the three mutineers had unfolded exactly as he had anticipated. So why was he feeling like a rudderless ship slatting in a wind-blown sea?

Because his dealings with his brother's killer had severed all ties with Angelene.

"Good evening, sir," Johnston cheerfully greeted his new employer. "I hope your new business venture went well this evening." Johnston took Sin's cape and pearl-handled cane and offered him a smile. "I prepared you a glass of wine when I saw your coach arrive. It's waiting in the study."

Sin murmured a quiet thank-you and ambled into his

office to down the drink in three swallows. It didn't curb the craving that gnawed at him. He hadn't expected it would.

Halfway up the stairs Sin was stung by the impulse to reverse direction and seek out Pearly. The crusty old sailor had always been a welcome distraction. Sin pivoted around and then halted indecisively. On second thought, Pearly was probably entertaining Agnes. Those two enjoyed each other's company immensely. Sin wished he could savor . . .

He turned and headed for his room. First thing tomorrow he would deal with his brother's killer. He needed to be well-rested and mentally prepared. After all, he had spent eighteen years waiting for this day.

Revenge was all that mattered, Sin told himself firmly.

Sin opened the door to his room and shucked his jacket. His shirt and sash promptly followed. He had just reached for the fastening of his breeches when a silky voice floated from the shadowed corner.

"I was wondering when you would return."

His hand stalled and he glanced toward the darkened corner.

"Don't let me stop you from undressing."

There was a seductive smile in that sultry voice that Sin could envision without even seeing. The image aroused him instantaneously.

"I rather enjoy the scenery," Angelene added provocatively.

Sin became very still as suspicion warred with hungry need. He hadn't expected a visit from the forbidden Angel—now or ever again. Knowing what she must know by now, he wasn't certain of her motive. If anything, Sin had anticipated a flash of inflammable temper, not provocative seduction. This unexpected visit, he was sorry to say, caught him completely off guard.

"I thought I had made it clear that you were no longer under any sort of obligation," he said as he ambled toward the corner.

Angelene rose from her chair, bringing up her hand to his chest. Her fingertips explored the bands of muscles on his streamlined torso. She savored the delicious textures of his flesh.

Sin's muffled moan vibrated against his teeth. This bewitching Angel possessed the ability to stir him with a mere touch. She filled his male body with throbbing desire and emptied his mind of the suspicious questions he should have been asking himself. Sin didn't really want to know why Angel was here, only that she was here. All he wanted was to lose himself in her intoxicating kiss and drift off to rapturous paradise . . .

His breath clogged in his throat like sea foam, when petal-soft lips skimmed his chest, pausing to tease his male nipples before venturing off to explore flesh that Sin hadn't realized was so receptive to burning sensation. Featherlight caresses swept over his rib cage and whispered down his hips. Instant and complete arousal gripped him and his pulse roared in his ears as she knelt before him.

When he curled his arm around her waist, desperate to hoist her upward and press her into his hardened contours, she laughed softly and pushed his hand away.

"You once played the lady's maid and undressed me. Now I intend to return the favor. I'll let you know if I require an extra hand, Mr. Sinclair."

"Angel, I don't—" His voice frayed when her hand trailed over the fabric of his breeches. Tender caresses grazed the swollen ridge of male flesh and Sin found it impossible to contain the groan that escaped his lips. "I—"

His breath evaporated when she pushed his breeches down past his hips. Her moist lips brushed over his arousal and Sin forgot how to speak. Need surged through him, forcing him to concentrate on keeping upon his feet when the shadows were spinning furiously around him.

God! She was devastating him, one kiss and caress at a time. He should have objected when his breeches pooled at his feet, but when her hands glided from ankle to inner thigh and she savored him with her tongue, teeth and lips he could do nothing but revel in pleasure that expanded until it sizzled through every fiber of his being.

His breath hissed out when her tongue glided over the length of him, measuring him, arousing him by feverish degrees. The brush of her lips was as light as the flutter of butterfly wings, but it burned like glowing coals. A silver drop of need betrayed him and every nerve and muscle in Sin's body trembled in response. His willpower definitely wasn't as good as he believed it to be—at least not when it came to this playfully seductive elf. She made him come unfurled like a high flying sail when she cupped him, tasted him, enfolded him with caressing fingertips.

"Angel, I can't stand—"

"Then perhaps you should sit down," she whispered against his inner thigh.

"You misunderstand—" He groaned. "Angel, please—"

"Am I not?" she asked with an impish smile in her voice.

"Unbearably so." He moaned when the satiny whip of desire flayed him—again.

"Pleasing you pleases me. I get dizzy just touching you, breathing in the scent of you," she whispered, urging him into the chair.

Sin sank down more quickly than intended when talons of ungovernable passion raked over him, destroying his equilibrium. Each time her lips and teeth grazed his potent flesh and her slender fingers traced him, pleasure coursed heavily through him. Sin felt his accelerated heartbeat pounding down his resistance. His senses reeled when her warm breath misted over him. He needed her like a flame needed to burn, and ah, this was the sweetest kind of fire imaginable.

Sin considered the irony of his own surrender. He couldn't even count all the times he had staved off Malayan pirates and Chinese sea robbers, not to mention a vicious shark attack, without even considering the possibility of defeat. But this vibrant, uninhibited woman had the power to destroy him with her gentle touch. He wanted her so badly that he ached from eyebrows to ankles. He would lay his fortune at her feet if she would appease the wild, pulsing need that dragged him to the crumbling edge of abandon and left him dangling over the wide expanse of oblivion

"Angel, come here," Sin groaned hoarsely. "I need you . . ."

"You don't need me enough—yet," she insisted as her hands skimmed over his thigh.

Sin sucked in his breath when she playfully nipped at

him with her teeth and circled him with her tongue. She discovered every masculine texture and secret contour until she knew him better than he knew himself.

Arms shaking, Sin drew her up until she was straddling his hips. Her lips settled on his and Sin shuddered when she offered him the taste of his desire. He needed to feel her encasing him like a warm velvet glove, holding him deeply, intimately. Not having her seemed the most maddening kind of torture ever devised. But this? Sweet mercy, he had never known such frantic desperation, such intense pleasure that it rivaled all-consuming pain.

Sin fumbled to release the fastenings on her breeches and cursed his shaking hands. There were times—like now, most especially now—that he wished this unconventional female would stick to wearing conventional clothes. But then, Sin reminded himself, that was part of Angelene's intriguing lure. She dared to be different, dared to live by her own rules, just as he did. And that was another reason he was so susceptible, so wildly attracted to Angel. She defied restrictions.

When Sin had finally freed Angelene from her clothes and resettled her over his thighs, his hands glided over the crowned peaks of her breasts, marveling at the feel of her silky skin. When her breath tore out on a ragged sigh, Sin lifted his head to take her nipple in his mouth, suckling, flicking, teasing her until another moan of pleasure escaped her lips.

His hand drifted down the flare of her hips and swirled over the smooth flesh of her inner thighs. The trembling sensations he aroused with his languid caress had them moaning in unison. Over and over, he traced her heated softness with his thumb, teasing dewy responses that offered secret invitations. But Sin wanted her to ache for him, to burn for him as he burned for her.

He had never been able to take from Angel without giving in return. Having her want him to the point of mindless frenzy had been essential since the first night they had become lovers. Sin had accepted that without analyzing why it was so necessary to him. It was simply an instinctive reaction. With Angel, passion was meant to be shared, never taken for his own selfish need, no matter how wild and hungry he was for her.

The slow deep penetration of his fingertip caused Angelene to grip Sin's shoulders, anchoring herself against her own intense need. Her nails scored his taut muscles and he relished the outward display, smiling at her uncontrollable response. The greater the pressure her biting fingers exerted, the more profound her pleasure. And her passion became his own as he intimately aroused her, returning the same tender, tormenting rapture she had bestowed on him.

Sin held her quivering in his hand as he eased her hips exactly upon his. He yearned to feel her lush body molded so closely to his that each erratic breath, each shivering convulsion was a shared ecstasy.

Sin's hips moved hungrily, though he fought the savage needs that spurred him. It took dedicated effort to be gentle and patient when his body cried out for wild, reckless abandon. He glided within her, caressing her with each sensual stroke, until her breath shattered on a muffled whimper and her arms slid over his shoulders to hold him as if she never meant to let him go.

With one penetrating thrust Sin buried himself in the

very core of her fiery desire. He moved her hips against his, setting the ancient, but timeless rhythm of passion. He pressed her body to his until he could go no deeper, could hold her no closer. His lips devoured the taste of her as they blended into one essence and charted the most intimate of journeys into ecstasy.

He caught Angelene's wild cry of fulfillment and clung to her as passion shattered the last fragments of conscious control. Even after his heart returned to a reasonably normal rate Sin could still feel the lingering effects of untamed passion thrumming through him. He asked himself when was the last time he had been so thoroughly devastated by the woman in his arms, when he had become so powerless that he transformed into a creature driven only by his body's fierce demands.

*The last time was when he had been with Angel, always when he was with Angel,* Sin reminded himself.

Hearing Angelene's shattered sigh, Sin cradled her possessively in his arms. She nestled contentedly against his shoulder, her breath caressing him like a gentle breeze. When she kissed him so tenderly, Sin felt his body stirring, as if it had been days rather than minutes since he had made love to her. Lord, he barely had the strength to drag himself away from her and already he wanted her again—even in this confining chair, of all places. Sin would never be able to sit down in the corner of his room without remembering what this night had been like.

"I love the taste and feel of you, Sin," Angelene whispered against his lips. "I . . . love . . . you . . ."

The haze that clouded Sin's mind evaporated in the space of a heartbeat. Wary trepidation climbed up his spine and cleared his senses like a gusty wind scattering fog.

So that was what this unexpected visit was all about, he surmised. The question he had refused to pose earlier had just been answered. He could have cursed Angel for speaking words he knew perfectly well she didn't mean. Damn her! It hurt to hear such sweet lies flowing from those honeyed lips.

Sin may have been bewitched and beguiled, but he knew what Angelene was up to. Just as she had first come to Raven's Hill to beg for Reggie's life, she now came to save her beloved father from ruin. Charles had obviously told Angelene that Sin had stripped away the Sheridan fortune with the stroke of a pen. Upon hearing Charles's slanted version of the story, Angelene had undoubtedly made this personal sacrifice for her father— the only man she claimed to love and respect. She had consented to become Sin's mistress and had braved flood waters to protect her father. Why should Sin be surprised that she professed to love him, in order to shield Charles from disaster?

There was no question in Sin's mind that Angel had come to seduce him, plying him with empty phrases of love, hoping to prey on his sentiment so he would go easy on Charles. But Sin was no one's fool, not even Angel's. Empty words could not erase Sin's resolute vows of revenge for Sin's lost inheritance and the unspeakable horror of watching his brother bleed to death.

Sin had known heartache and disappointment—so much of it that his heart and soul had very nearly stripped away. But he had never been so outraged as he was now. Angel's tender loving lies ignited the fury that Sin had managed to control while he dealt with Kimball, Porter and Sheridan. She alone had the ability to splinter the spars attached to his temper and put him in a full-blown rage.

Abruptly, Sin set Angelene away from him and surged to his feet. She blinked at the instantaneous metamorphosis that overcame him. The snarl that captured his rugged features reminded her of the very devil emerging from the fiery pits. Angelene instinctively retreated apace, clutching at her discarded clothes.

"Love?" he hurled back at her, his lips curling with disdain. "And what were you expecting me to say in return? That whatever you asked of me I would give it? Blindly? Freely? Unconditionally?"

"No, I—"

Sin raged on, refusing to allow her to make excuses and pleas that would infuriate him all the more—if that were possible. At the moment he doubted it was. He wanted to strangle her.

"I told you from the beginning that all I wanted from you was the pleasure of your body when the mood suited me. Don't think your sentimental declaration will grant you favors with me, *Angel.*" Sin hissed her name as if it were a foul-tasting curse. Indeed, it was. "Nothing has changed and nothing will ever change, no matter what sweet words trip off your tongue."

"But, I only wanted—"

"I know perfectly well what you wanted from me," he sneered into her blanched face. "And what you want is the one thing you cannot have, the one thing I will not give you, no matter how many words of love you whisper to me."

"Sin, you—"

He snatched her to him; his hands dug into her forearms, his harsh breath was burning her cheeks. "I can tolerate lies from others, but not from you, Angel. I could have even understood if you had come here in a fit of temper, making demands. But I never expected you to crawl, to manipulate like scheming females who use sexual pleasure to gain control of men. You just proved you're like the whores who will do and say anything to get what they want for their price."

His vicious words caused every last ounce of color to drain from her face and put a mist of tears in her eyes. Hurt and shame were clearly visible on her features, assuring Sin that he had cut deep.

Sin spun away. "Get out of my sight! And if you ever again ply me with love words to bend me to your will, I will make sure that all of Natchez knows you spread yourself beneath me like a common whore. Now get out of here and don't set foot on Raven's Hill ever again. Do you hear me!"

Who couldn't? Angelene stared at the raging dragon who was breathing the fires of hell at her. She had prepared herself for Sin's silence when she dared to confess what was in her heart, but she had never expected him to come apart at the seams as if she had committed some unpardonable crime.

Tears burned her cheeks as she wormed into her clothes and grabbed her boots. Sin refused to even look at her while he gathered his own garments. He kept telling her to get out of his sight and he hurled curses that shattered what was left of her pride.

Muffling a sob, Angelene burst through the terrace

door and considered throwing herself off the balcony to end the shame and agony that buffeted her. With a shaky hand, she raked the tangle of hair from her face and scurried toward the staircase, uncaring who saw her make her exit.

So long as she lived, she would *never* tell another man she loved him. She was *never* going to give any other man the power to hurt her the way she was hurting now. And she wouldn't come near Raven's Hill again unless she were dragged there by a team of horses! And Sin could go to hell and burn to a crisp for all she cared.

The spiteful thought was followed by the realization that this devil was immune to hell's flames. Sin was indestructible, unconquerable, because he had no soul, no heart, no emotion.

Angelene wished she were protected by the same invincible shell that shielded Sin. She had never realized there were so many ways to hurt without actually experiencing physical pain. She felt as if she had died inside and was forced to go on living. With every torturous step the horse took as she rode into the night the hurting became more pronounced. She would always hate him for that . . .

Tears poured down Angelene's cheeks. She let her horse guard its own steps while she cried until there was nothing left but the demoralizing knowledge that the only thing about her for a man to love was the lure of her father's fortune, and of a body to be used to appease lusty need.

There was only one man who cared for her, really cared for her, Angelene reminded herself as she thundered through the darkness that seemed to span forever.

Only her father loved her for who she was, despite all her flaws and failings. And as for the other men on the planet, they could burn in hell with Sin!

# Twenty-five

Sin slammed down the back steps of his mansion. He didn't have the slightest idea where he was going . . . until he found himself standing at Pearly's cabin door. Tittering laughter drifted from the cottage and Sin cursed the joyous sound. He was furious; he was never furious. Well, hardly ever, he amended with a scowl. He was a man in control of his mind, body and instincts, a man in control of himself. Or at least he had been until those three little words had tumbled off Angel's lying lips and ignited his temper like a blazing torch. Sin was so irate that he needed to talk to someone. Pearly was the only close friend available. Hiram and Cyrus had yet to return from the hotel or men's club or wherever the blazes they were.

Just as Sin spun around to leave, the door opened and Agnes sauntered out. She pulled up short when she saw the looming shadow blocking her path. She shrank back, her face flushing with embarrassment.

"Don't worry," Pearly gently assured her. "Sin carries no tales." He surveyed the puckered scowl, trying to re-call when he had seen so much emotion gathered on Sin's rugged features. "And he don't usually look like this, either, Agnes. Got a thorn in his paw, I'd say. But

I've got a potion to soak it loose." He gave Agnes an encouraging nudge. "Thank ya for bringin' me that delicious white raisin puddin'. Best I ever ate."

Agnes ducked her head and sidled past Sin. When she disappeared into the trees, Sin stalked inside and flung himself down in the nearest chair.

"Need a drink?" Pearly questioned as he hobbled to the cabinet.

"Only if it will render me unconscious until dawn."

Pearly did a double take when Sin fairly growled out the words. "My goodness, boy. You do have somethin' stuck in yer craw, don't ya? You and Fiddler both. That damned bag of feathers pecked up another pearl. I hope he chokes on it, too."

While Sin thrashed in his chair, Pearly mixed a drink that would calm Sin down. He hobbled over to hand him the glass. "Here, drink up. It'll cure what ails ya."

Sin downed the drink in one gulp and thrust the glass back at Pearly. "That's a start. Now finish it."

"You wanna fall off yer feet right here? Drink too much of my shell shock potion and you'll never make it back to yer own room."

Sin shrugged carelessly and shifted in his chair. He accepted the second glass of Pearly's concoction, hoping it would take the edge off the frustration that was eating him alive.

"Wanna talk about it?"

"No." Sin clamped his mouth shut and breathed deeply. "Yes."

"Make up yer mind." Pearly extended the third drink to him. "Go easy with this one. Its a double shot. You'll be crawling home like a seasick landlubber."

Sin sipped the brew and stared at the parrot. He was chattering to himself and practicing some sort of ritualistic dance to attract the mate he didn't have. Lucky damned bird. Fiddler didn't know how good he had it.

"Didn't yer conference with the mutineers go to yer likin'?" Pearly prodded as he levered into his favorite chair.

"It went fine, just fine," Sin said in a clipped tone.

Pearly raised a bushy brow. "Kimball and Porter tried to take a few more potshots at ya?"

"No, they were too busy trying to gather their wits for that."

"Well then?" Pearly demanded impatiently. "What the devil is eatin' on ya?"

Sill was up and pacing in less than a heartbeat. "She came here to sweet talk me into giving Sheridan a suspended sentence," he exploded in bad temper.

"The Angel?"

"No, the witch," Sin amended sourly. "She fed me whispered words, thinking I would fall to my knees like every other moonstruck beau who chases after her. Well, I'm not like the rest of them, damn it!"

"Certainly got that right," Pearly murmured through an amused smile.

Sin ranted on as if he hadn't heard. "Her temper and feisty retaliation I could have handled. Indeed, I expected that. But this!" He threw up his hands and let them drop to his sides before he switched direction to pace from stem to stern.

"What'd she say?"

Sin wheeled on Pearly, as if this were all his fault. "She said she loved me, damn it to hell!"

Pearly shook his head to ease the ringing in his ears. Sin's booming voice was worse than an exploding cannon at close range. Battling a grin, Pearly watched the brooding giant pace from port to starboard, wearing tracks on the imported rug. When Sin stalked past, Pearly handed him his glass and retrieved it when Sin made his return stalk from the far side of the room.

"Now let me get this straight. Yer madder than a beached whale because the lass said she loved ya."

Sin spun like a water spout. "Yes! The lying little witch! What kind of fool does she think I am?"

"A rantin', ravin' fool?" Pearly offered, smothering a grin.

The glower Sin leveled on Pearly would have sent a shark into retreat. It didn't faze Pearly, though. He was too amused to be afraid.

"Well, I am not going to cut Charles Sheridan any slack!" Sin bellowed.

"Nobody says ya have to," Pearly calmly patronized him.

"In fact, the bastard just made things worse for himself by sending his daughter to me. I'll never forgive him for stooping so low. Charles is beneath contempt and so is Angel for agreeing to it." Sin wheeled around to stomp in the other direction. "And if that lying female ever shows her face around here again, I'll—" His voice trailed off into inarticulate curses that Pearly was thankful he didn't have to hear.

"As well ya should." Pearly handed Sin the glass once again, watching the fuming man gulp the brew with every step he took. "Feelin' better yet?"

"No." Sin slammed the empty glass down on the table

and staggered when the potion hit him like a beam between the eyes. "Pearly? Where the hell'd you go?"

"I told ya to go easy on that drink." A chuckle burst
from Pearly's lips when Sin's knees caved in and he hit
the floor with a groan and a thud. Fiddler hopped from
his perch and landed on Sin's chest, pecking at the
mother-of-pearl buttons.

Heaving a sigh, Pearly hoisted himself out of his chair
and shoved a cushion under Sin's head. "Sorry, but even
this drink won't cure what's really ailin' ya, boy," he said
to his unconscious friend. "And believe me, I've never
seen a worse case than the one you've got. Incurable, I'd
say. I wonder if ye'r too stubborn to realize it. Probably
so."

Pearly snuffed the lantern and stretched out on his cot,
still grinning broadly. "You handled every crisis that ever
blew yer way on every sea in every port. And here ya
are yammerin' like a lunatic over the tender words of a
woman. But don't think too ill of yerself, m'boy." He
leaned out to pat Sin on the shoulder. "You ain't the first
man who split his seams over a woman and I doubt you'll
be the last.

"The shame of it is, smart as ya are, ya still can't
figure out what turned ya so sensitive and temperamental
all of a sudden. You've got yerself a real problem, Sin.
I wish ya luck figurin' it out." Pearly closed his eyes and
fell asleep with a grin playing on his lips.


Jim Calloway smiled wickedly when he saw the wild
mane of red-gold hair waving like a banner. The rider
who thundered across the meadow at breakneck speed

didn't know she was riding into a trap. All the better for Calloway and his kidnap brigade.

"The little lady we were sent here to abduct is saving us a lot of trouble," Calloway declared.

The other three riders stared at their victim and licked their lips in anticipation.

Calloway snickered when he detected the gleam in his men's eyes. "I was thinking the same thing myself. Kimball and Porter said we were to keep our hands off the miss, but it won't be easy. First thing we have to do is get her surrounded. Those two gents don't want anybody to see the miss until they come to fetch her themselves."

Calloway gestured his head, sending his men off in different directions. Angelene Sheridan wasn't going to realize she was in trouble until it was upon her. She would be trussed up, gagged and draped over her horse before she knew what happened.

The mimicking hoot of an owl sent riders charging toward Angelene. She jerked up her head and reined sideways the instant she saw the man racing toward her. Before she could urge her horse west, another cloaked figure closed in. Angelene was in an extremely reckless frame of mind and refused to submit. She gritted her teeth and gouged her steed, galloping directly toward the nearest rider. She would have made good her escape, too, if the hooligan hadn't grabbed his pistol and slammed it against her head as she rode by.

Pain cracked through Angelene's skull. Physical pain. She almost welcomed that. It was more tolerable than the aching emptiness that filled the cavity where her heart had been. When darkness closed in like a suffocating fog, Angelene groped for the reins. She felt nothing but air slipping through her fingers like the shattered pieces of a dream. She collapsed on the ground, uncaring if she awoke, at least not in this lifetime . . .

"Damnation, Rigley, you weren't supposed to crack her skull open," Calloway growled at his confederate.

"She was about to get away," Rigley countered as he tucked his pistol in the band of his breeches.

Calloway muttered under his breath and dismounted. "Well, I suppose this will take the fight out of her. Help me get her bound and tossed over her horse."

Within a few minutes, Angelene was tied tighter than a mummy and hoisted over her steed. In silence the procession rode off into the night, following Kimball's and Porter's instructions.

"Don't know why we have to row her across the river while it's in flood stage," Pearsall complained. "There's abandoned shacks all round Natchez where we could hide her for days on end."

"We're following Kimball's orders," Calloway insisted. "Besides, nobody can sneak up on us unaware while we're holed up on that shipwrecked steamboat that's stuck in the oxbow lake. We can blow unwanted guests out of the water."

"I'd feel safer with firm ground under me rather than a rocking tub that's only half afloat. With the current running so fierce, that boat is liable to be stabbed in the hull by debris and sink under us. Besides that, there's gators in those swamps."

"The *Natchez Empress* has been stuck in that sandbar for three years and no floodtide has sunk her yet," Calloway snorted. "Quit your fretting, Pearsall. We're getting

paid plenty to keep the lady company, so you can just
sidestep across those uneven decks."

Pearsall shut his mouth and stared at the river that
shimmered in the moonlight. He reckoned Calloway was
right. For the price Kimball and Porter were paying them
to keep their captive out of sight, he could battle his
squeamish belly. He smiled devilishly, imagining pleasurable ways of taking his mind off his dislike of boats.
Having his turn with the fancy lady would go a long way
in distracting him.


Sin awakened with a groan at the crack of dawn. He
dragged himself onto hands and knees and shook the
cobwebs from his brain. When his vision cleared, he
found himself staring down at the Belgium carpet where
Fiddler stood watching him with unblinking black eyes.
When the parrot squawked, Sin grimaced uncomfortably.
His head was a mite sensitive.

A sigh escaped Sin's lips as he floundered to his knees
and then surged to his feet. The room careened and then
gradually settled into place, allowing Sin to get his bear-
ings. Pearly, the ex-apothecary on the *Siren*—resident
medicine man was more like it—had mixed a potent
brew that had put Sin out like a doused lamp. True, Sin
had demanded a sedative to take the edge off his uncus-
tomary burst of temper and exploding frustration, but he
preferred to come to with a clear head.

Raking the strands of midnight hair from his eyes, Sin
glanced toward the bed. No Pearly. How the peglegged
mariner had thumped past Sin to make an early morning
exit he couldn't imagine . . .

Several double shots of sleeping potion, Sin reminded himself. That would do it.

Sin was still standing in the middle of the room, one hand braced on the table and the other holding his sensitive head when Pearly came whistling along the flagstone walk and thumped into the cottage. Fiddler let out a loud squawk of greeting and began to perform his high-stepping, head-ducking ritual. With both hands, Sin began massaging his temples. They were pounding like bongo drums.

Pearly set his basket of gathered herbs on the table. "Found yer feet, I see."

"Did I lose them last night?" Sin asked in a scratchy voice.

God, he felt as if he'd slept on the floor. He stared down at the cushion that belonged on the chair. Damn, he *had* slept on the floor. No wonder every muscle complained.

Pearly chuckled as he plucked the leaves off three separate herbs and ground them in a wooden bowl. "Aye, yer feet went the same way as yer temper. First full-fledged tantrum I've seen ya throw since you were a kid. Highly amusin', it was."

Sin snarled, and battled for composure. Last night he had held an angel in his arms and she had made him come undone before she turned into a lying, scheming witch. The thought provoked Sin to growl like an ill-tempered bear.

"Here, better drink this." Pearly shoved a concoction of juice and herbs at Sin. "You'll need a clear head if ye'r gonna confront those mutineers again."

Sin accepted the glass and took a sip. "Pearly, this is horrible." He choked on the chalky underbite.

"It ain't the taste we're after, it's quick results." Pearly grinned at the awful face Sin made as he forced down the medicinal brew. "I swung by the oyster bed in the coves on my way back to the cabin. Some of the buoys and panels pulled loose durin' the flood. The shells are gonna have to be cleaned off."

Sin nodded mutely and swallowed the last of the foul-tasting curative. But within a few minutes the dull thud behind his eyes eased and his vision cleared. Sin began to feel like his old self again, though he was still mad as hell at Angelene and her sniveling father. He still couldn't believe that Charles had the nerve to send Angelene to seduce him and then ply him with false words of affection . . .

Hell yes, he could, Sin decided. Angelene had been born with more gumption than a woman rightfully ought to have. Why would she give a thought about whispering empty words in hopes of saving her father's fortune?

She wouldn't and she hadn't, damn her.

As for Charles Sheridan, Sin lost what little respect he had for the man. The selfish bastard was doing everything he could to save himself—even asking his daughter to whore and lie for him. The man had no conscience, no scruples. But then, what did he expect? Sin asked himself sourly. Sheridan was one of the mutineers, after all.

An impatient rap at the door jostled Sin from his frustrated musings. In two long strides he was at the door, glaring at the humble-looking Reggie Foster.

"The butler said I might find you here," Reggie murmured, casting Sin a quick glance before studying the toes of his own boots. "Um . . . about the job you offered me . . . um . . . last night."

Sin inhaled a purifying breath and stepped onto the porch. "We'll discuss the details over a cup of coffee." He glanced back at Pearly, nodding his appreciation for the medicinal brew. "I'll check on the matter you mentioned when I have time."

Issuing a saucy salute, Pearly hobbled over to return the misplaced cushion and gave Fiddler a whack when he pecked at the mother-of-pearl buttons on his cuff. "Damn nuisance of a bird. I ought to make a pillow out of ya."

While Pearly and Fiddler fussed at each other, Sin led the way to the house. Reggie was at his heels. "How do you feel about working in a hotel?"

Reggie jerked up his head and parroted, "Hotel?"

"We purchased another one recently and will be beginning renovations," Sin explained. "Hiram Brodie will be your employer. You have the obvious good breeding and polished manners to serve as host and manager, provided you can be satisfied with your salary—a fair one, of course—without dipping into the profit as less honorable men are sometimes prone to do."

"I wouldn't steal from you," Reggie hastily assured him.

"Good," Sin said evenly, "Because the next duel you arrange will be your last. I won't tolerate embezzlement."

"No, sir."

"And every guest entering the hotel will be treated with equal importance and courtesy."

"Yes, sir."

Sin slanted the handsome down-on-his-luck aristocrat a stern glance. "And there will be no courtships of eligible plantation owners' daughters while on duty."

"I—"

Sin repeated the order slowly and distinctly. "There will be no courtship on duty. Your first and foremost obligation will be to the hotel, to Hiram and to me. Are we clear on that point, Reggie?"

"Yes, sir."

"Good. Considering the extremes to which a certain young lady went, in an effort to preserve your life, I would rather not have to shoot you. But if you cross me, I can easily be persuaded."

Sin opened the back door for Reggie who halted to peer up at him.

"Can I ask you a personal question, Sinclair?"

"You can ask," Sin replied. "But I will decide whether I choose to answer it."

Reggie glanced up at the stern lanterns and brass decorations that transformed the stately mansion into a land-locked ship. "Were you really a pirate once upon a time?"

"I was close enough to being a pirate at one time to know it wasn't the life I wanted," Sin confided as he motioned Reggie inside. "I did confront my share of sea robbers and cutthroats during my voyages to the Far East. They were a ruthless lot. The man you saw at the cottage lost his leg to a bloodthirsty buccaneer."

"And you walked the scoundrel off the plank?" Reggie inquired as he surveyed the ivory statues and Oriental urns that graced Sin's office.

"No I carved the bastard into bite-size pieces and fed

him to sharks," Sin casually reported. "I never could tolerate seeing my friends offended or thieves stealing what
didn't rightfully belong to them. I've become very sensitive about that sort of thing." He gestured toward the
hall. "Right this way, Reggie."

While Sin led the way through the foyer to the dining
room, Reggie gulped and followed behind. He had the
inescapable feeling he was indeed lucky to be in one
piece and in the employ of a man who made a better
friend than a formidable enemy. Reggie was thankful he
had had the sense to take Charles Sheridan's advice and
align himself with Sinclair. It would prove to be much
healthier, he speculated.

## Twenty-six

Angelene stifled a groan when she awoke to a hellish headache. Her skull was throbbing with every heartbeat. When she tried to roll to her side, she found herself trussed up in enough rope to hang herself twice. She lifted dull eyes to study her surroundings.

The bunk on which she lay stood in the corner of what once must have been a passenger's stateroom. Tarnished brass molding dangled from the ceiling in the midst of hundreds of spiderwebs. The slanted floor and irregular shifting and swaying indicated to Angelene that she had been stashed on one of the unfortunate steamboats that had been trapped in sawyers and sandbars. The Mississippi was notorious for snaring ships. There were dozens of them lodged in the swamps and oxbow lakes that had been formed when the river cut a new channel.

Although Angelene knew where she was, she couldn't fathom why she was being held captive. She frowned past her headache to contemplate her predicament. More than likely, the ruffians who had swooped down on her intended to "sell" her back to her father for an astronomical fee. That was an unfortunate but common hazard of living near Under-the-Hill. When hooligans were short of funds they resorted to kidnapping to replenish their cash.

Angelene rolled her head to the side and saw a tray of stale bread and moldy cheese. She wondered how her captors thought she was going to eat the unappetizing rations when her hands were tied up. Not that she was hungry. Indeed, she felt nothing except a nagging headache and an emptiness that food couldn't fill. She would be cursing Sin with her dying breath for being so cruel and heartless. The man had stripped her pride, spirit and emotion. Dear Lord, what woman would want to give her heart to a man like that? What woman would want to endure this kind of humiliation?

Angelene made a firm pact with herself. Love, now a four-letter word, would never pass her lips again. And furthermore, she would never allow a man to have any advantage over her—emotionally, physically or intellectually. For sure and certain, no one could hurt or devastate her the way Sin had. In comparison, nothing would be that bad again. Angelene vowed to hate Sin every bit as much as she had thought she had loved him.

"Angelene!" Charles Sheridan sent a call down the hall, announcing his arrival at his daughter's bedroom door. He had fully intended to bare his soul the previous night, but Angelene hadn't returned home before Charles's bout with ale left him asleep in his chair where he unintentionally spent the night. He could procrastinate no longer. Angelene had to be told the dark secrets of his past and the inevitability of the future. He had to see Angel packed and fleeing from the scandal and gossip that would be circulating in Natchez before the day was out.

"Angelene, I must speak with you at once—" Charles skidded to a halt when he spied the empty bed. "Sinclair," he muttered bitterly.

That man held some sort of wicked power that lured Angelene to him, even at the risk of her reputation. Even while that rascal was demanding payment of a long-standing debt and preparing to cut Charles's throat a dozen different ways, Sinclair was still using Angelene for his lusty pleasures. Damn the man!

Charles cursed himself for bringing such humiliation on his daughter. But as much as Charles resented this situation, he knew he only had himself to blame. He didn't expect Angel to forgive him once she knew the awful truth. Indeed, she would be eager to make a new start—away from the mortifying past and a father whose secret sins turned his daughter's world into shambles.

Heaving a heavy-hearted sigh, Charles switched direction and trudged downstairs. The servants would have to be notified they were under new management. That should please them, knowing the almighty Sinclair would see them well-paid and content, just as all the former servants had been when they'd defected to Raven's Hill.

Before Charles could summon the servants, a loud knock rattled the door hinges. Charles swung open the portal to find Jerome Kimball and Owen Porter standing grimly before him.

"We need to talk privately," Jerome insisted as he barged into the vestibule.

Uneasy sensations slithered down Charles's spine as he watched Owen and Jerome veer into the study. Judging by their expressions, both men had arrived at some sort of plan to extricate themselves from Sinclair's clutches.

Charles inhaled a determined breath and closed the office door behind him. Whatever this drastic ploy, Charles was not going to be a part of it. As he had declared the previous night, he intended to tell Sinclair what he wanted to know and to accept his punishment. There was nothing Jerome or Owen could say to change his mind.

"I have already told you that I will not be a party to another senseless killing," Charles insisted. "I deeply regret my part in the first and I refuse to consent to a second killing."

"Sit down, Charles," Jerome gritted out.

Charles lifted his chin and sank down in the chair across from Jerome. "Nothing you can say will change my mind. I am going to accept the consequences of what I've done."

"I'm glad you feel that way," Jerome smirked, "because you are going to turn yourself over to Sinclair, naming yourself as Joshua Montague's murderer."

"What?" Charles hooted in disbelief. "You expect me to take the blame for what you did, because I'm the only one of us who seems to have any semblance of conscience?" Charles gave his red head an adamant shake. "I have kept my silence as we agreed eighteen years ago, but I won't hang for you, Jerome."

Jerome smiled sardonically. "Not even to spare your own daughter's life, Charles? Not even to save your most cherished possession?"

Icicles formed on Charles's heart. His owl-eyed gaze bounced between Jerome and Owen.

"I presume you have noticed your daughter's absence," Jerome remarked.

Charles had assumed Angelene was with Sinclair. Obviously he was mistaken. "Where is she?" he snarled, brown eyes glittering.

"She is being held captive by the men Owen and I hired. She will only be released upon our command." Jerome leaned forward, unflinchingly meeting Charles's virulent glower. "Either you confess to the murder and hand yourself over to Sinclair or your daughter will find herself at the mercy of our henchmen." He wagged a finger in Charles's livid face. "If you betray us, Angelene will die. Do you understand, Charles? No matter what else happens you will never lay eyes on your daughter again. She is the price you will pay if you betray us."

Charles sat stiffly in his chair, battling his rage. "Bastards," he spat.

*"Live* ones," Owen snorted. "I prefer to keep it that way, too. This could have been settled in a more acceptable manner if you hadn't dragged your feet and voiced threats. You left us with no choice, Charles."

"And how do you propose to counter Sinclair when he finishes with me and comes looking for you? You said yourself that you don't expect him to keep silent about the crimes against him and his brother."

"You are going to serve Sinclair up to us," Jerome elaborated. "After you confess to the killing, you will inform Sinclair that we wish to meet with him to hand over our ready cash to ensure continued silence."

When Charles frowned dubiously, Owen took up

where Jerome left off. "We will meet Sinclair this afternoon at the abandoned roadhouse on Natchez Trace and let him think we are on our way out of town."

"And ambush him," Charles guessed. "And you expect to have more luck than last time?"

"This time Owen and I will personally see to the matter."

"And what if Sinclair brings his friends along for protection?"

Jerome smiled craftily. "His friends will have their own problems to resolve by noon. They will be dealt with separately and we will all have our property back by nightfall. If things go as anticipated, you will survive to see your daughter released and our lives will resume where they left off before that devil showed up."

"There are too many variables to consider," Charles muttered. "Not the least of which is Sinclair himself. The man has proved himself to be astute and cunning. If something happens to you and Owen during the confrontation by Natchez Trace, my daughter risks death because of your poor judgment. I will not agree to this!"

Jerome rose to his feet, motioning for Owen to follow him. "You have no choice, Charles. If you have any desire to see Angelene again, you will do exactly as you have been told and you will make certain Sinclair doesn't think he has anything to fear from us. Convince him that we have accepted our fate and are prepared to leave Natchez for good."

Charles felt a terrifying snare closing around him. He had no alternative. If he confessed all to Sinclair, Jerome and Owen would have their revenge by never allowing

Angelene to escape her captors. And knowing Jerome and Owen, they had tucked Angelene in some remote, out-of-the-way cabin, making it nearly impossible to locate her before disaster struck.

"I suggest you ride to Raven's Hill immediately," Owen said on his way out the door. "You wouldn't appreciate the company Angelene is being forced to keep, especially if this drags on for more than a day. Those hooligans from Under-the-Hill can only be trusted so far with a woman as lovely as Angelene. She could lose more than her life to them—several times over."

On that repulsive threat, Jerome and Owen filed out. Charles cursed the day he found himself in league with two men who proved they would stop at nothing to save their hides and their fortunes.

Dear God in Heaven! Charles didn't wish to live if Angelene was going to be punished for his disastrous mistakes.

Charles inhaled several cathartic breaths and struggled to compose himself. He had to get his story straight before he offered his confession to Sinclair. The man was extremely intelligent and an expert at gauging reactions. Sinclair always seemed to know what to look for in a man's face, in his eyes. Somehow, Charles was going to have to look and sound convincing or Sinclair would become suspicious.

Charles cringed, knowing that his daughter's life depended on his ability to deceive Sinclair. Considering his track record with that crafty rascal, Charles had grave reservations about the forthcoming encounter.

\* \* \*

After a reviving bath, a fresh set of clothes and several cups of coffee, Sin was prepared to deal with the day. He had foisted Reggie off on Hiram who was listing Reggie's expected duties at the new hotel. Cyrus had strode off to check with the plantation overseer before taking his riding lesson. Now that Cyrus had become the owner of a stable full of prize horses, he decided he should become an accomplished rider. Thus far, the ex-sailor simply managed to keep his seat while astride a horse. Cyrus had less experience in the saddle than Sin did.

Sin checked his timepiece, wondering when one—or all—of the mutineers would show up. He rather hoped the threesome had done so much squabbling among themselves that they had strangled one another. Nothing would be more satisfying than having them turn on each other. It would prove that the three mutineers were no more than they had ever been—heartless cutthroats who would betray each other to save themselves.

As for that lying little witch . . . Sin bit down on a curse and sipped his coffee. He was not going to allow bitter memories to distract him. Not today.

The knock at the door put Sin on full alert. He set his cup aside and ambled to the study door to watch Johnston greet the guest. One thick black brow lifted when he saw Charles Sheridan standing on the porch.

"I wish to speak to Sinclair."

Johnston made a courtly bow and motioned his previous employer inside. "Right this way, Mr. Sheridan. I will inform Sinclair of your arrival."

"Mister Sinclair has been informed," Sin said as he stepped into view. His astute gaze measured Sheridan's stance and the expression in his brown eyes. The man was doing his damnedest to remain calm and self-assured, but Sin could detect the slight crack in his composure. The bastard, he should be shot for putting his daughter up to last night's deceptive seduction, or at the very least agreeing to it. Damn him!

When Sin gestured for Charles to join him in the office, the older man shook his head. "I prefer absolute privacy. Perhaps we could take a tour of your estate."

Sin glanced down, wondering if Sheridan were heavily armed, intent on a quick murder and hasty escape. If Charles thought he could pull that off he was the world's biggest fool.

"As you wish." Sin grabbed his pearl-handled cane with its retractable dagger and led the way outside.

He was careful to stay abreast rather than a step ahead of his enemy. This was not a good day to catch a dagger or bullet in the back.

# Twenty-seven

Sin came to a halt on a knoll of ground that overlooked the cove. "Is this private enough?"

Charles nodded bleakly. Crosscurrents of emotion warred inside him. His overworked conscience was wreaking havoc with his desperate need to ensure Angel's safety. Charles inhaled a fortifying breath and expelled the confession he had rehearsed a dozen times during his jaunt to the plantation.

"You demanded the name of your brother's killer." He darted a quick glance at Sin and then focused on a distant point beyond the creek. "I was the one who convinced Porter, Limestall and Kimball to confront your brother about turning privateer to make extra profit during the war. We approached Joshua with the idea that night and he loudly objected. Words were bandied about and tempers flared. When push came to shove I pulled a pistol on your brother, demanding that he agree or find himself bound and stuffed in the hull until we could put him ashore."

Charles paused to inhale a nervous breath and flicked another glance at Sinclair. The man was an absolute marvel. He stood there with the wind in his face, staring across the meadow, listening. There was nothing about his manner or pose that indicated any emotion. Sinclair merely digested the confession and waited for Charles to continue.

"Joshua defied the pistol trained on him. When I made the mistake of glancing toward one of the other men, Joshua pounced on me. The pistol discharged and I panicked when I realized what had happened. I shoved him aside and he tumbled overboard."

Charles half-turned to study the profile beside him, thinking Sinclair gave a fine imitation of a stone mountain. "I came here to turn myself over to you. I would ask for a few hours to get my business in order before you do your worst. I will make no attempt to escape."

"And what of Kimball and Porter?" Sin questioned without glancing at Charles. "Have they also accepted their fates and the loss of their property?"

The lies were becoming more difficult to voice. Charles's conscience nipped at him when it came time to deliver Sinclair to Porter and Kimball as he had been ordered to do. Reluctantly, he continued. "They are willing to offer you financial compensation before they leave town, if you agree to keep their part in the conspiracy silent. They will pay you what money they can collect."

"They are offering to be blackmailed? How generous of them." Sin turned his head slightly, his expression inscrutable.

Charles nodded bleakly and looked away. "Yes."

Sin swore under his breath. He was beginning to see all too clearly that the three mutineers had spent their evening scheming. All three men were probably hoping that he had taken the bait last night and would agree to go lightly on Charles since he was Angel's father.

Did they think him such a weak, love-sick imbecile
that he would dismiss past crimes because he had acquired the supposed love of the bewitching Natchez
Jewel? These three mutineers were the fools!

Very slowly, Sin pivoted to face Charles. "You didn't
kill my brother. Why are you lying to me?"

The quietly uttered words caught Charles completely
off guard and he stumbled back as if he'd been struck.
"But you said you didn't know who killed Joshua. How
can you—?"

Sin knotted his fists in the lapels of Charles's coat and
dragged him close. "I said I wanted the three of you to
give me the name of my brother's killer," he snarled into
Charles peaked face. "I did not, however, say that I didn't
know who it was. I have always known. After I fished
my brother from the sea and hauled him into the lifeboat,
he told me who fired the shot."

Charles hung in Sin's merciless grasp, startled by the
thunderous scowl and glittering black eyes. He had never
seen Sinclair change expression before and wished he
hadn't now. The look that claimed Sinclair's craggy features held a deadly promise that he could do much worse
than snarl, if be cared to.

"And don't think for one minute that you can prey on
my sympathy because of your daughter. I grant you no
favors because of her," Sin growled venomously.

Charles blinked, stunned with the thought that Sinclair
knew Angel had been abducted. "You know? How—?"

"Of course, I know," Sin snapped brusquely. All vestige of control escaped him. He had never been more
furious than he had been the previous night and again
this morning. He was outraged and he didn't care who

knew it. "You've just signed your death warrant with your scheming and lying. You and your so-called little Angel can both roast in hell for all I care!"

Charles clasped both hands on the fist that twisted his shirt around his neck like a hangman's noose. "Do what you will with me. I don't care," he croaked on what little breath Sin granted him. "But I beg you to spare my daughter. I will not have her death on my conscience, too. Anything but that! She's all I have, all I care about!"

Sin snapped back to his senses and eased his fierce grip, lowering Charles back to the ground. A wary frown plowed his brows. "Her death? What do you mean?"

Charles gulped and wheezed for breath. His gaze locked with Sin's puzzled expression. "What do *you* mean? I thought you said you knew what happened to Angel."

"Explain yourself, Sheridan," Sin demanded, refusing to step away and lose his intimidating advantage.

"I can't." Charles inhaled a shaky breath and uplifted his chin. "Do your worst to me."

"I want Kimball first," he growled. "His head on a platter, then Owen's for leaving me with this scar as memory and for tossing me into the sea. And then—"

"No!" Charles was almost frantic now. If Sinclair and his men hunted down Porter and Kimball, Angelene would be as good as dead. "Let me be your scapegoat."

Sin appraised Charles's frenzied reactions. Something was very wrong here. Somehow Sin had miscalculated, leaving himself susceptible to complications. There was something Charles wasn't saying. The man's uneasiness was vibrating through him like a tuning fork, warning

Sin that it was essential to probe deeper for the truth—all of it.

With an ominous snarl, Sin jerked Charles off the ground, leaving his feet dangling. "Tell me exactly what is going on or I swear I'll cut you to ribbons, Sheridan."

"I can't," Charles whispered.

"Can't you?" A menacing smile curled Sin's lips. "You might be surprised to find that you can, given the right incentive."

Charles's eyes widened when the clicking sound revealed the dagger concealed in the blunt end of Sin's cane. With a flick of his wrist, Sin laid the razor-sharp blade to Charles's throat. He bothered with no further threat; he simply pricked flesh and drew blood. Sin twisted his fist in Charles's collar, cutting off air until the man's face turned purple. Still Charles refused to speak.

"Believe me, Sheridan, I have learned torture techniques from uncivilized native islanders and imperial Chinese crusaders that will have you squealing like a stuck pig."

Sin's frigid voice indicated that he would spare no mercy in gleaning the truth. Charles would probably experience so much torment that he started to blurt out the truth without even realizing it. This looming giant had proved himself to be a formidable adversary already. Now there was something wild and dangerous in those dark eyes that promised and delivered hell to anyone who dared to cross him.

With a broken cry of anguish Charles slumped in defeat, held upright only by Sin's fist clenched in his shirt.

"All right, I'll tell you what you want to know . . . on one condition."

"There are no conditions. There is only the truth," Sin sneered as he unleashed his captive, still keeping the dagger against Charles's neck.

Charles panted for breath and hurriedly formulated his thoughts. "Jerome and Owen took Angelene captive because I refused to agree to a murder attempt on your life. They ordered me to take the blame for your brother's death or lose my daughter."

Sin muttered a vile oath. "Go on, Sheridan."

"They wanted me to persuade you to meet them at an abandoned shack by Natchez Trace under the pretense of delivering blackmail money before they supposedly fled from Natchez to avoid scandal and humiliation."

"So they could ambush me?"

Charles nodded—carefully. The dagger was still resting beside his jugular vein. "Your friends are to meet with the same fate at another location this afternoon. Jerome and Owen hired henchman from Under-the-Hill to deal with them while they dispose of you."

"And Angelene?" Sin prompted.

"She will only be released by Owen's and Jerome's command, and by no one else."

"Where are they holding her?"

"I don't know. They wouldn't tell me for fear of being double-crossed."

"And so the only way to ensure your daughter's safety was for you to take the blame for murder and for me to perish at your comrades' hands. Is that the gist of it?"

Charles nodded and expended a shuddering sigh.

"And you sent Angel here last night in hopes that I

might reduce your sentence before you confessed to the crime, didn't you?"

Charles jerked upright, frowning in confusion. "Reduce my sentence?"

Sin scowled at him. "I already have one parrot, Sheridan. I do not need another. Don't repeat the question; answer it!"

"I haven't even spoken to Angel since I left the house to attend your conference last night. I wound up at the men's club to drown my troubles. Four mugs of ale later I rode home to explain to her why the world was about to come tumbling down. I fell asleep before she returned home or before she was taken captive—I don't know which. She knows nothing about my past because I have had difficulty finding the opportunity and the nerve to tell her."

Sin closed his eyes and swore viciously. No wonder Angelene had looked so stunned and hurt last night when he began raving so cruelly at her. She hadn't known what had occurred at the conference. She had not been a part of any conspiracy against him.

She had actually fallen in love with him when he had done nothing to deserve her affection, had done nothing but use her for his own vengeful purpose.

Sin cringed when memories from the previous night avalanched on him. Dear God, what had he done? Angel had come to him, despite further risk to her reputation. She had come to bare her heart and he had . . .

Sin felt his insides twist into aching knots. He had shredded Angelene's pride and had sneered at her declaration of love, thinking she was deceiving him to save her father. He had been too furious to allow her to explain, for fear that he would be fed another round of lies.

And because he had lost his temper and hurled cruel insults, Angelene had ridden off into the night and found herself abducted for reasons she didn't even understand. And worse, if Sin hadn't shouted her out of his house, she would have been with him through the night. It was his fault she had fallen into the hands of Jerome's and Owen's ruthless henchmen.

Scowling, Sin wheeled around and stalked toward the house.

"What are you going to do?" Charles demanded as he scurried after him.

"Get myself killed to save your precious daughter, of course," Sin muttered. "What other choice do I have?"

"I don't expect you to follow through, knowing what you know. I will find a way to deal with them and rescue Angelene if at all possible. You owe me nothing—" Charles pulled up short when Sin abruptly lurched around to stare grimly at him.

"One question, Sheridan."

"Yes?"

"Why did you cut the lifeboat loose that night?"

Charles was flabbergasted by the question that had come out of the blue. "I—" He swallowed audibly. "I—"

"A token gesture provoked by a guilty conscience perhaps?"

Charles dropped his head and nodded gloomily. "And because I regretted what happened," he added. "I've always been sorry that I let myself be dragged into that disaster. At the time I thought I had a justifiable reason for demanding that we turn privateer. But the reasons weren't worth the lives lost and years of remembering what I couldn't forget." Tortured brown eyes lifted to Sin. "How did you know it was me?"

"Yours was the only face I didn't see above me while I floundered to grab my brother. The other men were watching to see if we both sank before the ship swept past us. The freed skiff came from the port side of the *Annalee.*"

Sin stared at Charles long and hard. "That one act of kindness, however, does not excuse you for being a part of a deadly conspiracy. Your act was a token effort at best."

Charles sighed heavily and nodded. "I realize that."

When Sin wheeled away, Charles followed dismally after him.

Sin sent a call to arms to his former crew. Weather-beaten sailors appeared from the stables and the line of cottages that flanked the cove. They came with cutlasses, blunderbusses and pistols—like a swarm of pirates answering the signal to charge. They were seasoned fighters, one and all, and Sin needed their assistance. He assembled his men in the meadow and quickly organized his thoughts.

"What's going on?" Hiram and Cyrus questioned in unison.

Sin repeated the scheme as Charles had told it to him. Then he divided his crew into two forces to trail after Hiram and Cyrus—who were destined to become the sitting ducks for a bushwhacking.

"Not one of the hired brigands can be allowed to escape," Sin ordered. "If Kimball and Porter get wind of the failed attempts on Cyrus's and Hiram's lives, an innocent victim will be lost. There can be no miscalculations. Do I make myself clear?"

Every member of the crew nodded resolutely.

"But how are you supposed to survive if Kimball and Porter have to be allowed to walk away in order to lead us to Angelene?" Cyrus wanted to know.

Sin smiled rather bleakly, but refused to elaborate.

Hiram grumbled under his breath. "I realize you're accustomed to keeping your own counsel, captain, but in this instance—"

"This instance will be no exception," Sin cut in. "I will deal with Kimball and Porter as I must. It is your duty to keep from getting yourself shot before our men can surround and capture your would-be assassins."

When the crew trooped off, only Pearly remained. His narrowed gaze probed into Sin like a scalpel. "Ya know I can be of no use in a battle where speed and agility are required. But what is to be my duty?"

Sin ambled over to turn Pearly around and propel him back to the cabin. "You, my friend, are going to have to mix a potion that will make me bullet-proof."

Pearly snorted at that. "You know there ain't no brew for that."

"Sinclair?"

Sin glanced over his shoulder to see Charles Sheridan standing alone on the hill.

"How can I help?"

"Go pour yourself a drink to steady your nerves," Sin suggested. "I'll join you shortly."

"I'm not sure you have enough whiskey in stock to calm my nerves." Charles lifted his shaking hands in testimony of his uneasiness. "My daughter's life is at stake.

How much whiskey does a man have to drink to forget that?"

Sin strode off with Pearly, leaving Charles to make his way to the house.

"Are ya sure ya can trust that one?" Pearly questioned as Sin shepherded him toward the cabin.

"The only thing I'm sure of is that my life seems to be the sacrifice needed to spare Angel," Sin replied.

"That's a pretty steep price to pay to save a woman you were ready to strangle last night. What do you care if she survives?"

Sin opened the door and shoveled Pearly inside. "I didn't come here for questions, old man."

Pearly expelled a gruff snort. "And as usual, yer intentions are as clear as muddy water."

# Twenty-eight

Angelene decided she had stared at the ceiling and felt sorry for herself long enough. It was time to act. She had every intention of surviving this calamity for no other reason than to have the chance to *never* speak to Nick Sinclair as long as she lived. Sin could hardly be aware of how much she despised him if she were dead, now could he?

Now then, Angelene said to herself, what would Sin do if he found himself in this predicament?

Angelene rolled sideways to estimate the distance to the door. It would take three hops to get there. By standing with her back to the door, she might be able to maneuver into position to twist the knob—provided it wasn't locked. She frowned pensively and methodically pondered the possibilities. This was a shipwrecked boat. There was a chance that her captors had located keys to the stateroom . . .

Angelene shook her head and tried again, focusing on her main objective and working backward from there. Her ultimate goal was freedom. The means was escaping this room. Since she couldn't swim to safety, trussed up in rope, she had to devise a way to escape confinement and locate an improvised weapon.

In pensive deliberation Angelene reviewed her options. She should be reasonably good at getting her captors to play into her hands. After all, she had watched Sin operate for weeks. He was a master at predicting responses to his actions.

There were two logical reasons why she might ask her captors to free her—to eat and to see to her personal needs. She would use both as an excuse.

Angelene wriggled and squirmed until she was sitting upright. Surging to her feet, she hopped to the door. With her hands bound behind her, she pivoted to twist the knob and she discovered the door had not been locked. That indicated her captors were confident of themselves or hadn't bothered to search for a key—maybe both.

Maneuvering around the opened door, Angelene stared at the abandoned boiler deck. Knowing the layout of most steamboats, she guessed her captors were lounging in the main dining cabin. She hopped along the promenade toward the wide windows, shouting muffled demands for assistance. She saw shadowed silhouettes leap up inside the dining cabin and she smiled to herself. She had startled the four men into action. With pistols aimed, the scraggly men burst out the door and advanced on her.

Jim Calloway scowled as he pulled the gag from Angelene's mouth. "What the hell are you doing, woman? Trying to scream for help?" He flung his arm in an expansive gesture. "There's nobody out here to save you. Nothing but snakes and a few gators in this overgrown swamp."

Angelene looked him squarely in the eye and said as calmly as Sin would have done. "I have to see to my needs and I want something to eat before I faint from starvation. I would like to be free of these ropes." She flung him a withering glance. "I can't imagine why you saw the need to bind me up so tightly in the first place, unless you are afraid one woman is going to wrestle four men to the deck and confiscate your weapons."

Calloway smirked at that. "Hardly, miss."

"Well then, at least provide me the freedom of movement to do what I need to do. All I'm asking for is common courtesy."

It sounded like a reasonable request to Calloway. He circled behind Angelene and untied the ropes.

"I really would appreciate something to eat besides stale bread and cheese. Is there something else I could have?"

"Go fetch the miss something decent to eat," Calloway ordered Pearsall.

"I assume I'm being held for ransom," Angelene continued. "How long do you expect the negotiations to take?"

When the men glanced at each other and refused to reply, a flash of panic claimed her, but she brazened it out. Perhaps she had made another miscalculation. Damn. Maybe she had provided too much food for thought. Double damn.

While Calloway accompanied her back to her cabin to use the facilities, Angelene pondered over other reasons that she might possibly have been taken captive. She came up with nothing. If not for ransom, she had no earthly idea what this was all about. But that didn't matter, she reminded herself. Escape was all that mattered.

Angelene appraised the small niche in the corner of

her cabin. The chamber pot, pitcher and basin were not what she called effective weapons of defense, but they might have to suffice. When she reentered her room, Calloway's bulky body blockaded the door. Meager rations of dried ham and sea biscuits replaced the bread and cheese.

"Thank you. I appreciate the consideration," she said politely.

Calloway regarded the fetching female curiously. He had expected blubbering tears and tantrums. What he got, instead, was calm acceptance.

"You aren't going to put up a fuss?" he asked.

Angelene looked up from her tray and munched on the sea biscuit before replying, "For what practical purpose? As I see it, my only recourse is to be patient. Whenever you and your men have concluded whatever business you are conducting at my expense, I will be released. Since I am without funds and have done nothing to invite your anger I can only assume I am a pawn for financial gain. And I can hardly swim ashore, now can I? In the first place, I can't swim a lick. In the second place, this swampy lake looks as if it's infested with vile creatures."

Calloway's fuzzy brow climbed into a high arch while he listened to Angelene ramble conversationally.

"I would request some reading material to while away the hours, if you can locate some. If I'm not mistaken, the steamboat should have a library in the ladies' cabin beside the barroom. I would appreciate it if you would fetch some books for me."

Calloway found himself doing as she requested before he realized it. When the door creaked shut, Angelene bounded to her feet. Carefully, she eased open the portal and moved in the opposite direction to survey the promenade and paddlewheel that was buried in mud, moss and snarled roots. She muffled a curse when she saw no sign of a skiff on the blind side of the steamboat.

A distasteful shiver ricocheted down her spine as she stared at the tangled vines and trees that clogged the abandoned river channel. Water rippled with unseen predators that lurked in the depths. It was not, Angelene decided, going to be a pleasant swim. And despite what she told Calloway, she could most certainly swim—if she had to. Hopefully, it wouldn't come to that.

Resounding footfalls prompted Angelene to scurry back to her stateroom before she was discovered roaming about. She sank down by her tray and crammed a sea biscuit into her mouth before the door swung open. An uneasy tingle assailed her when the man named Pearsall sauntered toward her. Although the filthy scavenger had two books in his hand, Angelene decided he had something else on his mind.

A frightening thought assailed her. Perhaps she wasn't here for ransom, but rather to be molested and then tossed into the swamps. Dear Lord! She couldn't afford such serious miscalculations if she intended to survive to hate Sin for years to come!

Charles Sheridan was as jittery as a jackrabbit, even after he had poured himself two drinks to take the edge off his nerves. Sin had grilled Charles with questions, most of which seemed irrelevant. Charles had been asked to describe the terrain around the abandoned inn at the end of Natchez Trace.

What kind of trees? The location of creeks? Was the path overgrown? Was the trail similar to the tunnel of vines and brush that led to Raven's Hill? Was there a meadow nearby? Were there gators in the waterways? Venomous snakes? Charles had no idea what those things had to do with the present situation.

Sighing shakily, Charles watched Sin rein his dark bay horse to a halt beside a forest of pines. They were a half mile from the spot where Sinclair was to meet Kimball and Porter.

"This is as far as I dare to ride with you," Charles whispered. "I'm sure Kimball and Porter are lying in wait. If they see us together, they'll become suspicious and Angelene won't have a prayer of surviving."

Sin reached down to pat the Turk's muscled neck, feeling the high-spirited animal shift impatiently beneath him. The horse had been chomping on its bit during the ride, anxious for a run. Sin shared the animal's need to explode into action to release nervous energy. But recklessness was not the order of the day, Sin reminded himself. Precaution, good timing and calculation were. He needed to keep Porter and Kimball alive—temporarily at least.

Charles pointed toward the grassy knoll to the east. "There is the bluff you were asking about. It's a thirty-foot drop to the creek."

"A drop through a tangle of underbrush?" Sin questioned.

"No, the bluff is nearly perpendicular, like the one on Silver Street that leads to the wharf."

"And the depth of the creek?"

More questions, Charles thought in frustration. He had given up asking Sin why he wanted all this seemingly impertinent data. Now he had resigned himself to responding to the befuddling questions. Whatever Sinclair planned to do was between him and God—or the devil. Charles wasn't prepared to say which.

"The stream is usually only about six foot deep, but with the flood waters I estimate a depth of twice that much, maybe more."

Sin studied the landscape for a long, deliberate moment, assessing every insignificant detail. Finally, he focused penetrating black eyes on Charles.

"When this encounter is over, I will come back here to you," he said slowly and succinctly. "No matter what happens, do not leave the shelter of these trees. No matter what you *think* has happened, do not alter your position or attempt to intervene. Is that clear, Sheridan?"

Charles nodded bleakly.

"I may be gone a few minutes or as much as a half hour, but no matter how long, you will remain in this position and make no contact with Kimball or Porter." Sin pinned Charles with a stony stare. "If you disobey me or betray me—"

"I'll be here," Charles promised. "My daughter's life hangs in the balance. What you might do to me is nothing compared to the anguish I would suffer if I lost Angelene."

Sin studied Charles critically, wondering if he could trust this man not to falter. Charles could double-cross him and rejoin Kimball and Porter. After all, Charles himself admitted that saving his daughter was his fore-most concern.

"Remember one thing, Sheridan," he said in a decep-tively quiet voice.

"What's that?"

Sin turned away and nudged Turk forward. "You thought I was dead once. Don't make the mistake of thinking I won't find a way to come back and haunt you again . . ."

Charles swallowed hard and watched Sinclair offer himself as an easy target when he trotted the prize steed across the meadow. Charles didn't really think he had a right to pray, considering his unpardonable sins. But he prayed nonetheless, if only for divine intervention to save Angel from disaster and Sin from the hell he had boldly ridden into.

Jerome Kimball smiled in fiendish anticipation when Sinclair emerged from the shadows of the trees and rode across the meadow in his usual attire of black cape, dark breeches and red sash. He watched Sinclair pause on the knoll above the creek and glance around, as if unsure where he was supposed to be going.

"Charles must have been convincing," Owen Porter whispered.

"To save Angelene's life, what choice did he have?" Jerome murmured as he shook himself loose from the underbrush. "If Charles survived Sinclair's fury, he'll thank us for this."

Owen followed Jerome to their tethered horses. He cast greedy eyes on the Turk. When this battle was over,

Owen would have that strapping bay stallion. For certain, Sinclair wasn't going to need it where he was going.

When Sinclair made no move to leave the crown of the bluff, Jerome muttered in annoyance. "Charles obviously didn't give directions worth a damn. Sinclair can't seem to find the shack."

"Maybe Charles didn't live long enough to relay all the information," Owen ventured grimly.

"Whatever the case, I would have preferred to deal with that devil at the obscure inn instead of out in the open."

"Damn it, he's turning back," Owen grumbled. "We have to confront him on the hill. If Sinclair returns home and discovers what happened to his sidekicks, he'll come after us with arrest warrants. That mob of pirates he refers to as his staff will be all over us."

Scowling, Jerome nudged his mount into a trot to block Sinclair's route down the bluff. He automatically touched the concealed pistol beneath his jacket and heard the jangle of coins in the pouch he had brought along. "It has to be here and now," he muttered. "When we fish into our pocket for the blackmail money, we'll open fire."

Owen nodded grimly. "With two to one odds and the element of surprise, we shouldn't have trouble with that scoundrel. All we have to do is aim and fire at Sinclair's bright red sash. The bastard will be dead before he knows what hit him."

Sin schooled his expression while he watched the two riders approach. As Charles had indicated, the men had been monitoring his activities. But Sin had no intention of going near the shack Charles had described. He had pretended disorientation to lure Kimball and Porter out where he could keep an eye on them—and they on him.

The windy bluff was also as Charles had described it—a plunging drop into the swollen creek. Keeping his back to the cliff, Sin swung from the saddle to greet his enemies.

"Where's Charles?" Jerome asked without preamble.

Sin shrugged nonchalantly. "Enduring his first phase of torture for killing my brother. He was screaming in agony last time I saw him."

Owen winced uncomfortably while he sat upon his mount, staring down at the unflappable devil. He wondered what his fate would have been for scarring Sinclair's face. With any luck Owen wouldn't have to find out. The torture Sinclair planned would die with him.

"We brought all the ready cash we could collect to ensure your silence," Owen blurted out, his voice not quite as steady as he hoped. Fortunately, Sinclair didn't seem to notice. Owen suspected the rascal was too busy gloating over his seeming success.

"I'm sure your first payment will suffice . . . until you have time to collect the second," Sin replied in a placid tone.

He discreetly studied Kimball's and Porter's position in front of him and then he leaned casually against Turk's shoulder. Knowing Porter's weakness for prize horses, the man wouldn't risk nicking Turk when the gunplay began. Kimball would be the only one with a clear shot. That was exactly the way Sin wanted it.

"You realize, of course, that Owen and I will have to leave Natchez to find work," Jerome grunted.

"There are always ships in need of crewmen. I'm sure the two of you still remember the ropes. Sailing isn't something a man forgets, or what can happen on ill-fated ships," he added meaningfully.

"When are you expecting the second payment and how much?" Owen questioned as he tried to shift his steed to a better vantage point. As it was, the Turk's broad head stood between him and Sinclair.

"I think three months would be ample time for you to resettle and deliver the payment." He stared calmly at Jerome. "I'll be in need of extra cash to refurbish the other hotel for Hiram and to renovate Owen's stables." Sin derived immense satisfaction in watching the men gnash their teeth. "Now if you'll hand over your payments, I have other business to conduct. Sheridan should be ready for phase two of his torture—"

Sin stepped back apace when the sunlight reflected off the pistol barrel half-concealed beneath the leather pouch in Jerome's hand. Sin had no clear view of Porter. He did not need it. His main concern was Jerome.

The crack of the discharging pistol sent Sin spinning like a top. He gouged Turk in the hip as he stumbled back. The animal bolted toward Kimball and Porter, forcing their horses to prance sideways. Even as Sin plummeted over the edge of the bluff he could hear the snarls above him.

Jerome and Owen charged their horses up the cliff to see Sinclair land spread-eagle in the creek. His limp body hung on the surface for a few seconds before it sunk from sight.

"Damn it, Owen, why didn't you fire at him?" Jerome snarled. "I'm not sure my shot will prove fatal."

"The Turk was in my way," Owen answered. "If Sinclair doesn't resurface soon, he has to be dead."

They waited in silence, and then waited some more. Random air bubbles were dancing on the sunlit surface of the creek.

"You must have gotten him good," Owen declared after a full minute had elapsed.

His gaze circled to the opposite shore, looking for some sign that Sinclair might have gathered the strength to swim to safety. He glanced over his shoulder to see the powerful stallion halt and drop his head to graze.

"I'm going after the Byerley Turk."

While Owen trotted his mount toward the riderless steed, Jerome kept his gaze trained on the spot where Sinclair had gone down. A half minute later Owen returned with the Turk and Jerome glanced at his companion.

"Surely you realize you can't keep that horse," Jerome snorted. "It would cast suspicion on you when people start asking what has become of Sinclair."

"I will not have this valuable animal treated like a nag," Owen objected. "I've spent two years waiting for this horse."

"And said horse carries a curse," Jerome assured him harshly. "If it were not for your obsession for the Turk, Sinclair might never have located us. You'll have to let the horse run loose."

"Run loose?!" Owen howled. "Are you mad?"

Jerome cast one last glance at the churning creek, assured that Sinclair had met his most timely end. "All right then, tether your precious horse and we'll come back for it later. We'll release it near Raven's Hill. You can purchase the steed when the furor dies down."

Keeping a tight grasp on Turk's reins, Owen trotted over to the skirting of trees to tether the steed. "I suggest we release Angelene immediately." Another thought surfaced and he frowned at Jerome. "What are we going to do about Charles?"

"Nothing," Jerome replied. "He made his choice when he threatened to name names. Whatever Sinclair did to Charles was deserved."

Charles watched the two men trot over the hill, overwhelmed by the need to follow. They might lead him to Angelene immediately. Heaving a frustrated sigh, Charles glanced toward the bluff. He had witnessed the shooting and the subsequent fall and he could not imagine how Sinclair could possibly have survived the gunshot. Jerome and Owen had stood on the cliff for what seemed forever, ensuring that their dastardly deed had been accomplished.

Charles inhaled a steadying breath and reminded himself that Angelene would be released sooner or later and that he had to be content with that. He couldn't follow Kimball and Porter because Sinclair's quiet words kept whispering through Charles's mind.

*Do not make the mistake of thinking I won't find a way to come back and haunt you again.*

The menace in Sinclair's voice kept Charles frozen to the spot, even if he was certain the man had miscalculated this time.

# *Twenty-nine*

Angelene forced herself to remain calm as Pearsall swaggered toward her, smiling wolfishly. "My friend says you'd be wantin' something to entertain you."

Her gaze darted past the lean, bearded ruffian who grinned like a hungry barracuda. Angelene needed an improvised weapon and she needed it now. The lusty gleam in Pearsall's deep-set eyes suggested his disgusting intention.

Her only recourse was to plow over the man, hoping to knock him off balance. Angelene came off the bunk like a shot, catching Pearsall in mid-swagger. When she rammed her shoulder into his midsection, he doubled over, grunting in pain.

Frantic, Angelene clutched the pistol that was tucked in the band of his breeches. When Pearsall hit the floor with a thud and a snarl, Angelene swooped down to slam the butt of the pistol against his skull. She knew exactly what that felt like. She was still sporting a dull headache after Rigley had whacked her on the head.

Once Pearsall was unconscious, Angelene scurried out the door. She grasped the promenade rail and swung a breeches-clad leg over the edge. The gingerbread scroll-work of the railing provided footholds, allowing her to step down until she reached the splintered beam on the main deck.

Angelene winced when she heard a ferocious roar above her. She ducked down beside an overturned deck chair and cursed herself for not having taken the time to level a second blow to Pearsall's thick skull for good measure. The man was back on his feet, bellowing like a moose, alerting his confederates to her escape.

Now she would never be able to reach the skiff before the other men gave chase. That was the first place they would look, she predicted. Angelene glanced hastily around, seeking a hiding place that would grant her time to gather her wits.

Pearsall had forced her hand sooner than she had planned. Now she was trapped on board the half-sunken steamboat with four men who wouldn't ignore her again. And worse, she couldn't expect preferential treatment if she were caught. More than likely Pearsall would be the first of several unpleasant ordeals.

Angelene stared at the slimy swamp and decided, there and then, that if worse came to worst, she would take her chances with the alligators and snakes. But she prayed it wouldn't come to that, because the thought had her cringing in her skin.

Feeling the burning throb in his chest, Sin burst to the water's surface and gasped for air. He quickly submerged again, using the force of the current to propel him downstream, away from Jerome's and Owen's watchful eyes. The underwater swim in cloudy depths left Sin bumping into objects he preferred not to spend time wondering about. Considering the inhabitants of the creek, Sin deemed himself lucky to be wading ashore with all body parts attached.

Drawing the dagger from his soggy boot, Sin cautiously cut through the reeds toward dry ground. He didn't have time to waste. He couldn't allow Kimball and Porter out of his sight longer than necessary. Sin didn't trust those two murderers and he especially didn't trust the ruffians hired to hold Angelene hostage. There was no guarantee that Kimball's henchmen wouldn't devise their own money-making scheme with Angel as bait. Kimball and Porter could find themselves double-crossed, and Angelene would suffer because of it . . .

A whiplike shadow flashed toward Sin's leg as he slogged through the reeds. Reflexively, Sin swung his arm in an arc, beheading the water moccasin he had disturbed in his haste to follow his enemies. Sin had been intimately acquainted with enough venomous snakes during his extensive travels to know most pesky vipers preferred to swim in schools like fish. He was ready and waiting when the second and third strikes came from the three-foot long snakes sunbathing on the creek bank.

Hauling himself to solid ground, Sin inspected the bullet hole just below his heart. He sidestepped up the hill, thanking Pearly for the lightweight but protective vest he had designed. A full set of armor had been out of the question. Sin would have sunk into the muck and drowned before he could peel off weighted protection. Thanks to Pearly's inventiveness, Sin was able to return from the dead to torment Kimball and Porter.

And Sheridan perhaps? Sin asked himself. He still wasn't sure he could count on the man not to betray him, but Sin would find out soon enough if Sheridan had acquired any trustworthiness these past eighteen years.

"I'm rather surprised to see that you're still here."

Charles nearly jumped out of his skin when he heard the remarkably calm voice echoing out of nowhere. He swiveled on the saddle to see Sinclair—his wet clothes dripping with moss and twigs—emerging from the trees. His gaze fell to the ragged hole in Sin's shirt and to what appeared to be shiny gray flesh beneath it. His astounded glance leaped back to Sin's rugged, impassive face.

"Are you part fish, Sinclair?" Charles asked as Sin swung up behind him. "How did you . . . ? What is that—?"

"We better catch up with Kimball and Porter," Sin cut in quickly. "I don't want to take a chance on them being double-crossed by their own henchmen. Angel might find herself held for ransom."

"I hadn't thought of that. I wish you hadn't mentioned it. I was just beginning to relax," Charles grumbled as he trotted across the pasture to retrieve Sin's mount.

With one lithe move, Sin shifted onto his horse and reined around. He watched in pensive silence as Kimball and Porter split up at the edge of town. He hoped they were simply being discreet rather than delaying contact with their henchmen. The more time that elapsed, the more difficulties Angelene might encounter.

Sin smothered the guilt and frustration that hounded him and focused on his objective. He had become conditioned to expecting the worst and planning accordingly.

This was no time to be sidetracked by emotion—like regret, and a few others he didn't dare name.

As much as Sin wanted to skin Kimball and Porter alive, he had to let them lead the way to Angelene. It was simply a matter of necessity and effective use of time. Although torturing the information out of Kimball and Porter had tremendous appeal, it could cost precious minutes that Angel might not be able to spare. Knowing how daring she could become when catastrophe struck, Sin was compelled by a sense of urgency.

"Where the devil do you suppose Owen is going?" Charles murmured.

"I wish I knew."

When their route took them through the middle of town, Sin stopped at South Sea Paradise Hotel. While Charles kept an eye on Porter, Sin put a courier en route to Raven's Hill to gather a strike force that would be waiting at the hotel for further instruction. Sin intended to have a seasoned cavalry of fighters at his disposal.

When Sin caught up with Charles a few minutes later, Porter had turned north to rejoin Kimball. The two men veered down the hill where they were swallowed up by the thick underbrush and choking vines that lined the river.

"Where the blazes did they stash her?" Charles muttered.

Within a few minutes the answer became alarmingly clear. Kimball and Porter had dismounted and piled into the dinghy that had been concealed in the bushes.

"Ride back to the hotel and bring my men down here," Sin ordered as he watched the sunlight sparkling on the ripples Kimball and Porter made as they rowed away. "I'll see what I can do about transportation."

"Let's just wait to see if Kimball and Porter bring her back to shore," Charles insisted. "I want to be here—"

"We have to be prepared for anything," Sin interrupted. "We have to have reinforcements and boats."

Sighing in resignation, Charles wheeled around and thundered up the steep incline, leaving Sin crouched in the brush, monitoring the men's progress toward the gnarl of trees and swamps that lay beyond the channel.

Damn, Sin thought as he remounted his steed. Surrounding a secluded shack was one thing. Rowing across the river in broad daylight was something else. He had noticed the pilot house of the shipwrecked steamboat among the trees when he first arrived in town. The pilot house made a perfect lookout tower. Angelene's captors could see unwanted guests arriving with far too much advance notice.

If Sin followed Charles's advice and waited, hoping for the best, Angel might not be returned in good condition—if at all. If Kimball's and Porter's scheme went awry, waiting could prove disastrous.

Hell and damnation, Sin thought as he thundered toward the wharf. How he wished Angel could unfold her wings and flit away from the boat that was half-afloat in the oxbow lake beyond the river channel. Getting to her wasn't going to be easy, even with seasoned sailors to back him up!


Angelene wormed her way into the cabinet in the ship's galley when she heard the echo of footsteps on the main deck.

"Damn you, Pearsall," Calloway scowled. "I sent you

to deliver a book, not take your turn with the woman. You heard what Kimball and Porter said, so back off. Until we decide how to deal with those muckamucks and turn this situation to an even better advantage you'll have to show a little patience."

Angelene stopped breathing when the names were mentioned. Kimball and Porter? They had a part in her abduction? But why?

"Well, I don't know why we should bother with those two pettifoggers anyway," Pearsall grumbled. "We've got half our money. We could sell the girl back to her pa after we've pleasured ourselves with her."

Angelene swallowed with a silent gulp. She hadn't done herself any favors by voicing her speculations. She was going to have to take a risk and escape this ship quickly. If not by boat then under her own power, distasteful as that would be in a swamp!

Calloway slammed into the galley and glanced around the empty chamber. "She could be anywhere. With all these nooks and crannies on this ship we'll be lucky to find her by dark."

"Rigley is checking the hurricane deck and Conners is staying with the skiff in case she tries to row off. We'll find her sooner or later," Pearsall said.

When the men started opening cabinet doors in systematic order, Angelene knew it would take a miracle to prevent herself from being recaptured. She stopped breathing altogether when she heard the hinges creak on the cabinet beside her. This was it. Her time of reckoning. She would be dragged out by the hair of her head, molested and then tied up, dreading the hellish nightmare that would begin all over again.

And she was going to curse Kimball and Porter with her dying breath, she vowed. Only God knew their reasons for using her as a pawn, but sure as the sun rose, those two men were going to be the death of her!

Sin maneuvered his skiff, and the other vessels he was towing behind him, to the spot where Kimball's and Owen's horses had been tethered. He had just stepped ashore when the rescue brigade arrived in full force. The sailors were clamped onto their horses for dear life, better acclimated to ships than four-legged modes of transportation. The crew was armed with an assortment of weapons and enough supplies to counter whatever trouble they encountered.

Perhaps it was a stroke of luck that this siege would take place on the water, Sin mused. A wild chase on land by sailors inept in the saddle might have proved disastrous.

Sin breathed an inward sigh of relief when he spied Hiram and Cyrus. "Did you meet with much difficulty?"

Cyrus and Hiram shook their heads. "Those clowns who were hired to ambush us played right into the crew's hands," Cyrus reported. When Sin stared at Hiram, Cyrus grinned mischievously. "Well, with the exception of Hiram gettin' a new part in his hair. He needed one anyway, in my opinion."

"It was only a scratch," Hiram said with a shrug. "We'll be burying my would-be killer tomorrow. The rest of the thugs were herded off to jail before we received your note."

Sin shifted his attention to the silvery glare on the

river. The light was nearly blinding with the afternoon sun beaming down.

"Where is she?" Cyrus questioned, staring across the river.

Sin pointed toward the clump of cypress trees that were partially submerged in the river. "There looks to be a steamboat mired in sand. That would be my guess," Sin replied. "Kimball and Porter just rowed around the trees before you arrived. We're going to have to come upstream against the current to reach the swamp if we are to make use of the glare on the water. It's going to be difficult rowing, but drifting downstream to the ship will make us easy targets and prevent us from reaching the cover of the vines and trees."

"Dear God." Charles stared at the pilot house visible above the canopy of trees. "We'll never get to Angel without being spotted. I still think we should wait here."

Sin flashed the man a stony glance. "They won't bring her back and risk being identified," he assured Charles. "Even if Angelene was blindfolded, she would recognize Kimball's and Porter's voices. Considering the flood stage of the river and floating debris, there might be a need to speak in order to negotiate around obstacles. Kimball and Porter won't take that risk, and their henchmen might use Angelene for their own protection if they sense trouble."

Cyrus handed Sin a cutlass and flintlock and then stared at the choppy water. "You have a plan, I hope."

Sin stepped back into the lead skiff and unfastened the trailing rope. "I hope to have one by the time we have a closer look at our surroundings. Did you bring plenty of rope and grappling irons?"

"Right here, Cap'n," one of the sailors called.

When Charles tried to climb aboard, Sin waved him back. "We'll handle this, Sheridan."

"Like hell you will!" Charles blustered as he made a spectacular display of planting himself in the rowboat. "That happens to be my daughter out there and I'm not so old that I have forgotten how to handle myself on the water—" His guilty gaze lanced off Sin's imperceptible stare. "I haven't forgotten a lot of things, Sinclair."

"What the hell are you wearin' under your shirt?" Cyrus questioned when his gaze landed on the bullet hole, powder burns and peculiar gray shadow where Sin's skin should have been.

Sin didn't bother replying. He grabbed the oars and eased into the swift channel, letting the force of the river carry him downstream before battling the strong current to approach the boat with blinding sunlight at his back. Sin concentrated his thought on the jungle of trees, moss and twisted vines that formed a barrier between the river and swamp to the west.

This was no time for miscalculation, he reminded himself. He would just as soon not be the reason Angel went spiriting off to the pearly gates. He wasn't sure his newly revived conscience could deal with that. He had yet to ask forgiveness for the cruel and brutal words he had hurled at her. Would that Angel lived long enough to accept his humble apology.

* * *

When Jim Calloway opened the door of the cabinet beside her, Angelene wished herself invisible and then begged divine forgiveness for every failing grace, every loss of temper, every unkind word . . .

A wild shout came from somewhere on the hurricane deck.

"Rigley must have found her." Calloway spun on his heels and charged out the galley door with Pearsall hot on his heels.

Angelene sagged in relief and disbelief. Her prayer had been answered, and not a second too soon, either!

Like a mouse scurrying from its nest, Angelene crawled on hands and knees and climbed into one of the cabinets that Calloway and Pearsall had already checked.

Think! Angelene demanded of herself. Cause and reaction, that's how Sin made his calculations—damn his hard-boiled heart. If she made a dash toward the skiff while the other three men were distracted, Conners would send up a call for assistance. But if she could debilitate Conners and row off in the skiff, she might have a sporting chance before a volley of bullets pelted her.

Angelene inhaled deeply and told herself it was now or never. Easing herself from the bottom cabinet, she slithered across the floor until another thought occurred to her. Angelene rose up on her knees and opened the drawers above her.

A satisfied smile pursed her lips as her hand folded around a rolling pin. Her makeshift club might prevent Conners from raising an untimely shout. The pistol she had confiscated from Pearsall would be her last resort.

Armed and determined, Angelene crawled out the galley door and wormed across the deck toward the skiff . . .

# Thirty

Before Calloway could voice his question, Rigley's brawny arm shot toward the rail. "It's Kimball and Porter," he grumbled.

Calloway swore colorfully as he wheeled to see the rowboat circling the steamship to moor by the paddlewheel. "That's it then," he instantly decided. "We don't need to have our ears chewed off because we misplaced the chit. We'll send off a ransom note to Sheridan and feed Kimball and Porter to the gators, soon as we pick them clean of valuables."

With pistols drawn, Calloway and Rigley crept across the promenade. Pearsall followed behind. Having been disarmed by Angelene earlier, he could do no more than cheer his cohorts on.

From their vantage point on the hurricane deck, the three men could see Kimball and Porter maneuvering their skiff into position to climb up the paddlewheel. When Kimball and Porter swung over the railing to the main deck, Rigley and Calloway opened fire. Their scheme was better than their aim. Bullets thudded against the railing, splintering wood, only winging Porter in the arm before he could dive for cover.

Calloway spewed a curse when he heard footsteps

clicking against the deck below. Lurching around, he charged toward the steps to gain a better vantage point on the boiler deck.

"Pearsall," Calloway hissed over his shoulder. "Keep them pinned down. Don't let them climb back into that skiff until we can unload on them."

"Pin them down with what," Pearsall snorted. "I don't have a pistol."

"Then heave deck chairs. Anything!" Calloway ordered before he dashed down the steps, two at a time.

Sin heard the shots explode in the distance and he rowed toward the island in the swamp with fiend-ridden haste. He didn't like the unnerving visions that leaped to mind. All of them had to do with Angelene making some foolhardy escape attempt and getting her lovely head blown off after she hadn't succeeded the first time she tried. Damn it, she had better not get herself killed!

Sin broke his rowing motion long enough to signal to his men to go ashore. The instant his skiff ran aground, Sin bounded over the gnarled roots and crouched in the curtain of moss and vines to assess the situation.

He did not like what he saw.

Two familiar silhouettes, with pistols drawn, were backed against the wall on the main deck. One of the henchmen stood on the hurricane deck, hurling chairs down at them. Sin wondered if Kimball and Porter appreciated the irony of the mutiny that was taking place on board the half-sunken steamboat. They, who had murdered for greed, were being betrayed by the men they had hired. The two burly henchmen, both of whom looked suspiciously like the gang members who had staged the robbery and murder attempt on himself two weeks earlier, were on the boiler deck, leaning over the rail, taking potshots at Kimball and Porter.

Oddly enough, Sin realized with a start, he was more concerned about rescuing Angelene than having his final revenge on Kimball and Porter. He had nearly come unglued when she launched an attack on the hooligans Kimball had sent to dispose of him a month earlier. This was far worse, because Sin had yet to determine where Angelene was. She could have been anywhere on the ship and he didn't have a clue how to protect her . . .

Just then, Sin spotted a flash of red-gold among the shadows at the bow of the steamboat. His gaze darted toward the henchman who stood on the deck near the rowboat, pistol aimed and waiting.

"Good God," Sin groaned aloud.

He knew what Angelene was planning to do. Hell, he could almost hear her *thinking* it from here! The woman obviously had no regard for that lovely head of hers, seeing how she was practically asking to get it blown off a second time. She was trying to use the distraction at the stern of the boat to make her escape, but the henchman with the loaded gun had other ideas. Damn it to hell! Sin thought in exasperation.

Shoving Cyrus and Hiram out of his way, Sin dived back into his skiff. "Climb in with the other men and circle the island on the north side," he hurriedly ordered.

Hiram frowned, baffled. "Where are you go—"

Sin was already rowing away before Hiram could finish his question. Sin gritted his teeth and rowed like a windmill. Hell, he wasn't going to be able to reach Angelene before she made her daring escape attempt. If he sent off a shot at long range, it would only draw attention to the bow of the ship. His men hadn't had time to close in on Kimball and Porter who had their own problems with double-crossing henchmen.

Sin needed five more minutes. Hell's fire, was that asking so much?

Angelene was short on patience, Sin mused. Probably always would be until the day she died—which was going to be today if she didn't watch out!

Sin had just swung around the tip of the island when catastrophe struck. His heart turned over in his chest when he saw the sandy-haired henchman jerk up his head and wheel toward the blur of red-gold hair that charged toward him. Sin felt as if he were holding his breath when Angelene—carrying a . . . rolling pin? Christ!— launched herself at Conners.

Sin noticed the pistol tucked in the band of Angelene's breeches and he also noticed that she had opted for the rolling pin. Heaven forbid that she defend herself with a pistol, against a pistol, Sin thought sourly. Angel was too damned tenderhearted to charge her enemy with a loaded gun.

The pistol in Conners' hand discharged and Sin expected to see Angel's head roll. Miraculously, she had managed to put a hatchet chop to Conners' wrist, deflecting the shot. Conners erupted in a furious snarl and backhanded Angelene before she could level a blow to his skull with her rolling pin.

In helpless frustration Sin watched Conners take a second swing that sent Angelene staggering backward. Her momentum caused her to flip over the railing, knocking her head against the hull.

It was as if Sin were watching calamity in agonizingly slow motion. He heard the dull thunk, and saw Angelene's head whiplash. Her body immediately went limp and she dropped into the water like an anchor, disappearing in the muck.

Sin couldn't honestly remember rowing the rest of the distance to the steamboat. It was if that space in time and fragment of memory had been deleted from his mind. His gaze was fixed on the spot where Angelene had gone down. He was no more than vaguely aware that Conners had spotted him. Water splattered in his face when Conners fired.

Shouts were erupting from everywhere at once, but Sin heard little more than his own rapid pulse hammering in his ears. Before Conners could reload and fire, Sin dived into the swamp, feeling his way through an underwater maze of roots and vegetation, hoping to locate Angelene before she drowned. Each time he thought he had grasped her arm, he yanked upward to find himself holding a thick vine. Sin knew time was running out. If he didn't find her soon, he wouldn't be able to revive her . . .

A flashback from his past picked a miserable moment to assail him. Suddenly Sin had reverted to being a terrified boy of twelve who had been shoved over the railing after his injured brother had been tossed overboard. Sin had fought the sea to reach his brother. He could hear his own sobbing screams as he latched onto Joshua's arm and pulled him to the surface, relying on strength he didn't even know he had, hurling obscenities at the men who unsympathetically watched him from the deck.

Sin had wrapped his arm around his brother's limp body, trying to sidestroke toward the *Annalee*. Through blurred eyes he had stared up at the stern lantern, seeing the lifeboat drifting across the water.

Towing Joshua beside him, Sin had plowed through the waves to reach the skiff. His lungs had burned from overexertion by the time he wrestled Joshua into the skiff and dragged himself onto the seat. The dim light had glared on the grisly wound on Joshua's chest and the very soul of Sin's existence had drained out of him. They had only been granted a few minutes together before Joshua sagged lifelessly against the edge of the boat. Time enough for Sin to demand the name of the man who took Joshua's life, time enough to damn them all to hell, time enough to hiss a fierce vow of revenge . . .

Emotion—wild and haunting—surged through Sin, now as then. An innocent life had been stripped away, a young boy's childhood had been tormented and destroyed . . . And it was happening all over again, like a recurring nightmare . . .

Not again! Sin inwardly screamed when the vision of Angelene falling overboard replaced the ghastly vision of his brother.

In panic, Sin thrashed through the tangling obstructions, praying for all he was worth. *Not this time,* he chanted as he groped through the darkness. He would sell his soul to the devil if he could be granted the chance to spare this one innocent life!

\* \* \*

Jerome spluttered furiously when he spied the two skiffs approaching from the north, filled to capacity with that pirate crew, led by the two men who were supposed to have been killed hours earlier. A shocked gasp burst from his lips when he spotted Charles Sheridan's red head. Jerome swore the world was closing in on him when grappling irons and tailings arched through the air and dug into the gingerbread scrollwork. Pirates swung across the swamps on tailings and pounced on deck, armed to the teeth.

Shots exploded around Jerome and he spewed curses when Cyrus charged at him. Jerome swung his empty pistol like a club. Before he could render a blow, Cyrus's steely fist caught him in the soft underbelly, doubling him over. Jerome wasn't allowed time to snatch a breath before the second beefy fist struck his chin and sent him stumbling against the wall. Jerome sagged onto the deck, his head pulsing, his eyes blurred. He slumped sideways when Hiram's punishing blows knocked Owen off his feet and left him sprawled atop Jerome.

Shouts and gunshots filled the air. Footsteps resounded, but Jerome was pinned to the promenade, struggling to recover his wits. He heard a scream and a splash somewhere in the near distance. One of his backstabbing henchmen, no doubt, had succumbed to these vicious buccaneers who had been under Sinclair's command.

When, at least that devil Sinclair had been sent back to hell, Jerome consoled himself groggily. Jerome had had the pleasure of launching Sinclair back whence he had come.

"Get on your feet, you bastard."

Charles shoved Owen aside and latched onto the lapels

of Jerome's coat, jerking him upright. "Where's my daughter?"

Jerome wrestled with his tongue, but he couldn't formulate the curse he was so eager to spit in Charles's flushed face. This was all Charles Sheridan's fault. None of this would have happened if that stupid fool hadn't turned soft-hearted.

"Where is Angel?" Charles demanded viciously.

Jerome's head snapped back against the wall when Charles tried to shake him to his senses. It didn't help. The world was a fuzzy blur and Jerome could do no more than fall to his knees.

Scowling, Charles latched onto Owen, but he proved as incoherent as Jerome. Charles shoved Owen back against the wall, as if touching him were unbearably repulsive. He glanced up when he heard footsteps on the deck above him.

"Has anyone found my daughter yet?" Charles roared in frustration.

"The crew is searching for her now," Hiram assured the distraught man. "Sheridan . . . ?"

Fear and exertion had Charles gasping for breath. When his eyes rolled back in his head, Hiram snagged his arm and levered him into a deck chair.

"We'll bring Angelene to you," Cyrus assured the older man. "Just sit tight, mate. No need to fret."

Charles told himself to breathe, to get himself under control, but it was easier said than done. Swallowing, he closed his eyes and waited, refusing to buckle to exhaustion until Angel appeared. He had to remain conscious long enough to beg forgiveness for bringing this hellish curse down on the one precious treasure he had left.

Hiram glanced worriedly at Cyrus. "The crew can't find Angelene," he murmured. "I swear the old man is about to have a seizure."

Cyrus studied Charles's wan features, wondering if he would last long enough to be reunited with his daughter, provided she could be located. The man had been living on sheer nerves for too many hours. That, compounded by his insistence on rowing against the fierce current, was catching up with him.

"Where the hell is Sin?" Hiram muttered at the world at large.

"Damned if I know," Cyrus said, staring bleakly at Charles. "But we better get Pearly and his curatives over here quick. This bloke doesn't look too good."

Hiram glanced down, watching the color drain from Charles's face and his head roll lifelessly against his shoulder. "Damnation. Pearly! We need you—quick!"

Sin felt air bubbles caressing his cheek. With arms outspread he dived downward, frantically groping for human flesh rather than the leathery tangle of roots and debris he kept finding below him. His hand brushed across slick skin and his fingers closed around a limp arm.

In a burst of speed, Sin shot upward, dragging his sunken treasure behind him. He surfaced on a choked gasp and dragged air into his burning lungs. He gave a hard yank, bringing Angelene up for precious breath, but her head rolled against his shoulder, her eyes closed, her parted lips a terrifying shade of blue.

Stark horror thrummed through every nerve and muscle in Sin's body when he stared into the ghostly face that rested on his shoulder. While he sidestroked toward the bow of the ship, he pressed his mouth to hers, giving her his breath, silently demanding that she respond.

Sin lifted his head and let loose with an enraged growl that shook the surface of the swamp like a tidal wave. By God, she would not die! Sin told himself. Unholy memories of a dark night on an open sea crested over him. Sin cursed foully. He could see his brother lying there as Angelene was now. He could hear a child's scream hovering over the water like a black cloud.

"Don't you dare die on me, damn you," Sin snarled before his lips came down hard on Angelene's, forcing her to breathe, to absorb his strength, his unrelenting will.

His arm contracted around her ribs, pumping her chest, demanding that she obey his order to live, to breathe. In one powerful stroke, Sin surged toward the bow, frantic to drag Angelene on deck. And all the while he gave her his own panted breath, silently chanting commands to defy the darkness that enshrouded her.

Hiram and Cyrus came to attention when they heard Sin's wild cry. Leaving Pearly to tend Sheridan, they charged around the corner and dashed toward the bow.

Hiram's gaze swept across the slimy waters, searching for ripples. When he spotted them, his breath froze in his chest. There, off port bow, he could see Sin thrashing toward the ship. A mane of red-gold hair trailed over his shoulder and a face as white as salt glowed in the sunlight that filtered through the trees. But it was the log-shaped object that traveled in Sin's wake that had Hiram dashing madly toward the rail, groping for his blunderbuss.

"Sin! Gator!" Hiram bellowed.

"Holy Mother of God!" Cyrus gasped as he dashed toward disaster in the making.

The shouts of alarm prompted Sin to glance over his shoulder. Beady black eyes and a long snout surged toward him. Sin spewed obscenities, wondering why his life had become a succession of trials and challenges that tested him until he knew all his own secrets, his every strength and weakness.

Other men's greed had left him facing unspeakable tortures no one should have to endure, had robbed him of his childhood. The fickle charms of the sea had pelted him with howling storms and blistering calms that carved weather-beaten lines in his features and put calluses on his hands. He had explored every boundary of his own courage and will, time and again, and still there was always another impending disaster waiting to happen. Would it ever stop?

With a furious oath, Sin dug a little deeper into himself, fought all that much harder to reach the ship, even when his body ached from frantic exertion.

The shot Hiram fired into the water did more to enrage than discourage the vicious creature that followed its prey. The gator slid sideways in the water, its spiked tail lifting like a whip to flay its victims.

Sin called upon every hidden reserve he possessed and lifted Angelene's lifeless body up and out of reach of the sea dragon that had come to feed. Out of the corner of his eye, Sin saw Cyrus extending himself over the rail, struggling to clamp hold of Angelene any way he could, giving Sin the time he needed to meet disaster head-on . . .

# Thirty-one

When the gator's tail slammed against his legs, Sin felt Angelene's weight lifted from his arms. Spinning free, Sin grabbed the dagger he had tucked in his sash and backstroked out of reach before the gator could switch direction and come at him with those deadly jaws.

Another spray of buckshot splattered the water, but the reptile advanced with single-minded purpose. Inarticulate oaths exploded from the deck above Sin and he felt them rolling over him as if they were his own. A deck chair cartwheeled through the air, splashing between Sin and the jaws of death. In one powerful surge Sin heaved himself upward to cling to the railing. When the gator cut through the water, Sin curled himself into a ball, hanging on by one clenched fist, not daring to turn his back during attack.

Black eyes clashed with black eyes as the eight-foot-long monster bore down on its prey. A steel blade flashed and glinted in the sun and blood spurted, mingling with the muck of the swamp. Scaly flesh parted on the monster's head—once, twice, thrice. Sin struck like a maniac, spewing curses, expending fury and vengeance that had been bottled up inside him for eighteen years.

This creature had become the scapegoat for every anguish, every pain and frustration Sin had ever encountered. It was another lethal challenge met—the sum of roiling hatred, of every emotion that had been buried deep inside him. He attacked every cruelty in life, every disappointment, every shattered dream with a ruthless vengeance.

Angelene regained consciousness long enough to hear the muffled growls and throttled curses of a familiar voice, but the sounds didn't belong to the blurry face that loomed over her. She felt the heels of Cyrus's hands digging into her chest, forcing her to breathe. Her head turned sluggishly toward the snarling growls that rose from the swamp.

Her gaze fixed on the raven-haired man who hung onto the railing, striking out with his dagger clenched in a fist of iron, slashing the monster that writhed in the water. *Vengeance personified,* Angelene thought groggily. Beast battling beast to the death.

When water gurgled in her throat, Angelene spluttered and wheezed and found herself shoved facedown on the deck. Images exploded around her and curses hovered in the air. Angelene fought to keep her wits, but the forceful, repeated blows to her spine left her feeling as if she was being turned inside out. Her lashes fluttered against her ashen cheeks and she lost the battle she fought, and drifted aimlessly in the inky depths of silence . . .

Hiram stood on the deck, his jaw gaping wide enough for a sea gull to roost, watching Sin practically skin the

gator alive with the swipes of his dagger. Twice Hiram
had tried to pry Sin's fist loose and hoist him onto the
deck. But it was as if Sin's hand was forged to the scroll-
work, his muscles frozen in a stranglehold that a crowbar
couldn't loosen.

It wasn't until the mutilated mass of spines and scales
sank into the swamp that Sin sagged against the hull of
the ship. But he was still cursing with each panted breath.

When Hiram heard the methodical thump of Pearly's
pegleg approaching, he pivoted to stare helplessly at the
crusty sailor. Pearly's gaze was focused on the man who
hung on the railing, spewing oaths that singed ears.

A wave of memories splashed over Pearly as he hobbled toward Sin. He stared down at the raven head of
the man—and the boy—who had known more hell in his
lifetime than any mortal rightfully ought to know. Pearly
spoke the same encouraging words now that he had spoken the day the skiff had capsized, sending Joshua's rigid
body into the depths of the sea, leaving a young boy
clinging to the boat for dear life.

"Up with ya now, lad," he said kindly, softly. "That's
it, slow and easy. Roll yer clew-garnet and close up yer
sails. A man's got to change tack now and again. Come
on, lad, we're runnin' before the winds and everything's
gonna be all right. You'll see."

Sin lifted his ruffled head, the knife still locked in his
fist, the gator's blood soaking the sleeve of his shirt. The
red glaze faded from his onyx eyes as he focused on the
gray head and ruddy face above him.

"I know yer timbers are groanin', lad, but you'll be
fit to fiddle soon enough. Come to ole Pearly. You were

thrown on yer beam's end, but yer gonna be just fine. I swear it, lad."

Hiram stepped back apace when Sin hoisted himself up by one arm and rolled over the rail. His eyes were still wild with the residue of unleashed fury when he braced himself on his feet.

Through all the difficult times and endless years Hiram had sailed the Seven Seas under Sin's unerring command, he had never seen this skillful captain transform himself into such a mass of crazed rage. Always before, Sin had been a stalwart, the epitome of calculation and self-control. Now he seethed, as if the very fires of hell blazed inside him.

"Sin?" Hiram whispered apprehensively.

Sin didn't hear his name being called. He saw nothing but the limp form and trailing mane of red-gold hair that splayed across the deck. The knife dropped from his fingers and clanked on the planks. His chest heaved like a swelling breaker at sea as he shouldered past Cyrus and sank down beside Angelene. He took up where Cyrus had left off, forcing the water from her lungs. Sin didn't know where he found the strength to administer to the half-drowned elf, but he refused to give up the battle.

"Come on, Angel," Sin muttered at her, his fingers shoving rhythmically against her shoulder blades. "Give up your gills and fins. The sea is no life for a lady."

While Sin turned Angel over and bent to breathe life into her, Hiram stared dismally at Pearly. Angelene's face was the color of a frothy wave. Hiram swallowed visibly and shook his head.

"Don't give up on the lass yet." Pearly opened the

leather satchel he had brought along and retrieved a dram of amber liquid.

Folding his pegleg beneath him, Pearly laid the potion to Angelene's parted lips. "Here, lass. I gave yer papa a potion to calm him down and this one will perk ya up. Come on, be a good lass and swallow ole Pearly's brew."

When the liquid dribbled down the side of her face, Sin growled and gave Angel a fierce shake. "Listen to Pearly," he commanded. "You'll swallow it down for him, if not for me."

Sooty lashes fluttered up to stare through Sin as if he were invisible. His heart shriveled up inside him like a raisin.

"Take the potion, Angel," he growled. "Do you hear me? Take it!"

Again Pearly pressed the cup to her bloodless lips and again the curative didn't reach her throat.

"Cyrus, come help," Pearly instructed. "Give her a few breaths and press on her chest—"

"I'll do it," Sin insisted. "I'm not leaving her until she breathes on her own accord and takes the potion. She's doing this to spite me. And even if I deserve it, she's not going to lie here and die. I forbid it, I handed my brother over to God, but not her, not ever!"

Pearly scooted away, watching curiously as Sin forced life into Angelene's limp body. The seconds dragged into minutes without encouraging response.

"Sin?" Pearly said grimly. "She's not comin' around enough to give her the brew. I'm afraid—"

Blazing black eyes seared the words to Pearly's tongue. "Give me the potion," he snarled.

Pearly did as ordered. He watched Sin take a sip of

the curative before lifting Angel's face and pressing his lips to hers, feeding her the brew as he massaged her neck. He repeated the process twice more, his lips covering hers, his fingertips soothing the liquid down her throat.

Charles staggered around the corner to see Angelene sprawled lifelessly on deck and he fell to his knees. "Oh God. I almost lost you once. I can't bear to go through that agony again!"

Sin momentarily glanced sideways to see tears pooling in Charles's eyes. He wondered what Charles meant, but he had no time to interrogate the distraught man. Angelene demanded his full concentration.

Pearly's eyes widened in surprise and relief when he saw Angelene's chest swell and her fingers contract. "Well, I'll be damned."

"And so will the two men who put her through hell and left her hanging on by a frayed thread," Sin growled when he came up for air. "Where are Kimball and Porter?"

"Bound up on the stern," Cyrus answered. "Our men are keepin' an eye on them for you."

Sin carefully laid Angelene on the deck. Then he peeled away his shirt to cushion her head.

Hiram blinked when he spied the peculiar breastplate that had been strapped around Sin's midsection.

Pearly's eyes twinkled when Hiram and Cyrus studied the odd contraption of doubled sharkskin separated by rows of triangular shark teeth. "A lightweight, bulletproof vest," he informed the befuddled men. "Shark teeth are damned near as hard as diamonds and the shagreen is near tough as elephant hide. More flexible than a coat of armor, too. Rather ingenious, if I do say so myself."

After Sin unstrapped the breastplate and tucked it under the shirt to elevate Angel's head to a more comfortable angle, he rose to his feet. For a long moment he stared down at her, watching a hint of color work its way up from her throat to her hairline. Satisfied that she would survive, Sin scooped up his discarded dagger.

"Hiram, take Angelene and her father to Raven's Hill for safekeeping. Cyrus, march these criminals off to jail." He turned to the crusty mariner. "See that Angelene is resting comfortably under the influence of one of your sleeping potions."

"And what are you goin' to be doin' while we're tidyin' up around here, mate?" Cyrus asked.

Eyes as cold as the Arctic Sea zeroed in on Cyrus. "I'm going to give Kimball and Porter the full measure of my revenge."

The murderous look on Sin's face made Hiram and Cyrus believe in hell. Every breath Sin inhaled, every movement indicated bottled fury looking for a place to explode again.

When Sin stalked off, snatching up a coil of rope that lay on the deck, Hiram turned grimly to Cyrus. "Well, I've learned one important lesson today."

"Aye, me, too, mate," Cyrus murmured as he watched Sin disappear around the corner. "Don't ever make Sin killing mad . . ."


Jerome Kimball gasped in disbelief when the bare-chested devil who refused to die stalked toward him. Ev-

erything inside Jerome snapped. No matter what he tried
to do, no matter how he plotted and schemed he couldn't
destroy this bastard. Sin just kept coming back—like a
recurring nightmare.

Enraged, Jerome leaped to his feet. He took a wild
swing with his bound hands, but Sin deflected the on-
coming blow with his forearm. His free hand, clenched
around the butt of his knife, landed squarely on Jerome's
chin. With a dull groan, Jerome stumbled against the
wall. Blood trickled off his bitten tongue and pain exploded in his skull.

"Any man who would sacrifice an Angel deserves the
worst tortures ever devised," Sin sneered as he jerked
Jerome onto wobbly legs. "For killing my brother you'll
know all the torments hell can teach you. For nearly destroying Angel you will die a slow, agonizing death, right
alongside your worthless friend."

Owen Porter was still screaming for mercy when Sin
shoved him into the skiff. Jerome was hissing curses out
the side of his mouth that wasn't quite so swollen from
the punishing blow.

Charles Sheridan braced himself against the rail and
watched the skiff disappear into the tangle of trees and
vines beyond the wrecked steamboat. He chanted words
of repentance and murmured the beatitudes, when two
spine-tingling screams rose up from the shadows of the
swamps, sending birds from their perches. The sounds
were reminiscent of the howls of the newly damned.

And then a furious roar, guaranteed to make the devil
quake in his boots, echoed through the tangle of moss-
draped trees.

Every soul on board the half-sunken steamboat shriv-

eled when two more bloodcurdling screams splintered
the air. The wretched sound stretched across the swamp
and shivered through the shadows. The warble of birds
ceased. The creaking timbers of the ship were muffled
by the haunting shrieks that hovered like a fog.

And then came the kind of eerie silence that had the
men on board the steamboat shifting restlessly in their
skin and sending silent prayers heavenward.

Charles Sheridan stared into the distance, wondering
what his private cell in hell was going to be like when
Sin turned his devastating brand of revenge on *him* . . .

# Thirty-two

Pearly leaned against the gallery railing at Raven's Hill. When lightning flared he could see the restless pacing of the silhouette on the grassy knoll in the pasture. The wind swept across the landscape, lifting the flowing black cloak and swirling it around the tall, dark figure that prowled the night like a lost and tormented soul.

Pearly knew that Sin was wrestling with deeply-embedded emotion. He hadn't seen Sin retreat so far into himself since those first weeks after he had been hoisted out of the sea, carrying the weight of his brother's death on his young shoulders.

Eighteen years of repressed feelings had come bubbling up like molten lava. But Pearly knew it was more than the past colliding with the present that troubled and haunted Sin . . .

Pearly glanced skyward when the silvery claws of lightning spiked the low-hanging clouds. When thunder rumbled, he muttered under his breath.

"Damned fool. He'll get himself struck down, sure as the devil."

Pearly chuckled at the thought. Sin had been nothing short of a devil since the previous night when he had returned from the swamp to check on Angelene. Pearly had faithfully administered a potion to ease Angelene past the nightmare that roused her before she fell back into fits of coughing and restless sleep. Charles Sheridan, who had been ushered into one of the rooms in the north wing, had come to sit with his daughter, watching her thrash and sputter and then drift back to sleep.

"What is he doing out there?" Charles asked as he ambled up beside Pearly.

"Fightin' the shadows within the shadows," Pearly replied, his gaze fixed on the wind-whipped silhouette. "They're warring with each other."

Charles sighed heavily. "Because of me, I suspect."

"Partly," Pearly clarified.

"I've tried to explain to him why, but—"

Pearly waved him off. "He has to come the full circle and decide if and when he should forgive ya, Sheridan. A precious life was lost to him, a way of existence, a heritage of what he had once been. His family was pure aristocrat from Boston before he became a vagabond adrift at sea. He existed for only one purpose—to gather enough funds to send you and the other three men so deep into hell you'd never find yer way out."

Charles grimaced, instantly reminded of the horrified screams and growls of rage that had been unleashed in the swamp. "And now Sinclair is tormented because I'm still alive and he can't decide how to go about torturing me."

Pearly frowned and glanced back toward the room where a dim lantern held the darkness at bay. "It's more than that, I'll wager," he mused as he studied the sleeping form on the bed. "If Sin destroys you he will destroy yer daughter. And Sin knows full well how innocent victims can suffer."

Charles inhaled a determined breath and strode toward the steps. He walked up the hill toward the formidable silhouette and went down on his knees in a gesture of humble regret.

"All I have is yours, Sinclair, because I owe you that and much more for what I did in a moment of foolishness and desperation. I deserve what Kimball and Porter received."

Sin stared down at the crestfallen man. When he looked at Sheridan, he should have felt the same fury he experienced when he lashed Kimball and Porter to the trees in the swamp and tossed water moccasins on their sprawled bodies, provoking the vipers to strike until the victims had suffered numerous bites and succumbed to the potent effects of the venom. But Charles Sheridan was Angelene's father . . . Angelene's beloved father . . . Angelene . . .

The melodic name whispered through Sin's troubled mind and he inwardly winced. He had pulled Angelene from the dark tangles of the swamp and demanded that she survive. But for what? To watch her father be sent to hell with his co-conspirators? To learn the meaning of excessive grief and mortifying scandal?

Charles doubted Sin would be receptive to what he had to say, but the words ached to fly free. "I almost lost Angel when she was a child," he said brokenly. "She was so frail, so desperately ill, as lifeless as she was on deck of that old steamboat."

When Sin didn't stop him from offering the explanation, Charles continued. "At the time, my in-laws refused to speak to me, banished me and my wife from their family. I wasn't good enough for their aristocratic daughter and she was disowned because of me. They refused to accept our messages, my pleas for monetary assistance when Angel first became ill with what the doctors diagnosed as rheumatic fever."

Charles paused, swallowed audibly and then forged ahead in a tormented voice. "I had to remain at sea to earn a living, but my heart and soul were with my wife and child. I used part of the . . . blood money . . . to save my little girl. I needed all the cash I could acquire, and privateering seemed the fastest way to collect it. I was ready to do whatever was necessary to save Angel from the debilitating disease that struck her."

Charles inhaled slowly, deeply, struggling for composure. "When I returned from the sea, my wife and I stayed at the hospital night and day with Angel while the doctors treated her. At first they gave us little hope of recovery, but after six months she had regained enough strength to rise from bed. And for another two years she was restricted from physical activity that might cause a relapse."

Sin remembered what Hiram had told him about the Sheridans arriving in Natchez six months after the other three men appeared. *That shouldn't matter,* Sin reminded himself sternly. What Charles Sheridan had done was wrong, even if he had been driven by desperation. Joshua Montague's life was the sacrifice made to save Angelene with the best medicine and physicians the blood money could buy.

"And that is why I've spoiled Angel, pampered her and allowed her to run wild and free. There was a time when she didn't have the strength to turn over, much less sit up. Seeing her become so vibrant and alive is like a daily miracle and I could never force myself to restrain her in any way," Charles murmured. "When I saw Angel lying so pale and lifeless on deck yesterday, it was like living through hell again. My torment comes in knowing that when she is back on her feet I will have to confess to her what I've done to you and your brother. I'm so very sorry, Sinclair, more sorry than words can ever convey . . ."

When Charles's voice shattered on a sob, Sin said nothing. He merely stood his ground while Charles climbed to his feet and skulked back to the house. Sin wished he didn't understand or care what the man was enduring. But while Sin had been groping through the murky depths of the swamp and battling to revive Angelene, he had discovered and wrestled with the feelings Charles had described. Sin had been prepared to sell his own soul in order to ensure Angel survived.

Now, when Sin peered into that wan face, surrounded by a cloud of red-gold hair, his heart turned inside out. He had treated Angel abominably—as cruelly, in fact, as Sheridan had treated that young boy left at sea. Angel had come to Sin, offering him unconditional love and he had ground her pride beneath his bootheel, railing at her for deceptions she hadn't committed.

And now, what was Sin willing to sacrifice to compensate for the hurt and humiliation that he had seen glittering in those vivid green eyes? What price would he have to pay to restore Angel's faith in him, to assure her that loving him was not the curse of her life?

Sin stood at a most difficult crossroads and stared

across the storm-tossed meadow. He had done a great deal of soul searching that day. He had wrestled with his conscience and grappled with the solemn vow he had offered his brother.

If Sin brought charges against Charles, Angelene would suffer more than she already had. If he told Angelene the truth about the mutiny and murder, he would bring her the kind of anguish that he only wished on his worst enemies.

And the hell of it was that Sin had begun to like and respect the man Sheridan had become. Charles could have betrayed Sin at several turns, but the man had been dependable and steadfast while Kimball and Porter were plotting to kill him.

Sin smiled ruefully when the answer he had tried to ignore whispered in the wind. He was a man who had studied and analyzed cause and reaction as if they were a science. He knew how to restore Angel's spirit and he knew what he wanted—and what price he had to pay to have it.

In order to give one promise Sin had to retract another. Sin heaved a sigh and watched lightning flicker through the clouds of the churning storm that matched his turbulent mood. He had known the minute he encountered the Sheridans at Wilhelm's party that he would not be able to have it both ways, though he had tried—at Angel's expense.

*Always at Angel's expense* . . . Sin groaned, knowing he was as guilty as the mutineers when it came to his unjust dealings with Angel. He had not cost Angelene her life, but he was indirectly responsible for her abduction and near brush with death.

As lightning streaked from cloud to cloud and thunder rolled, Sin inhaled the scent of rain that saturated the breeze. Resolutely, Sin turned and walked toward the house. He hoped his brother would understand and release him from the vow that had been Sin's driving obsession for almost two decades. He could no longer live in the past, not when he found himself reaching out to the future, longing to make amends for the hurt he had caused Angelene.

Pearly watched the darkly clad figure stride across the covered gallery, accompanied by a flare of lightning and drumroll of thunder.

Pearly chuckled. "Nothin' like a dramatic entrance."

"I want you to give Angel a potion to rouse her," Sin requested.

Graying brows arched in surprise. "I thought I was supposed to be givin' her sedatives to help her sleep."

"I need to speak with Angel," Sin declared on his way by. "I'll meet you in her room in five minutes."

With no more explanation than that, Sin marched across the portico and barged into Charles's chambers without invitation. Charles recoiled when the wind swept inside and the somber-faced man in black filled the terrace door to overflowing.

It was apparent to Charles that Sinclair had arrived at a decision. There was a strong sense of purpose about him. Charles knew his time of reckoning had come. Sin had arrived to exact punishment for Charles's part in the mutiny. Charles made his peace with the Lord and prepared to face his doom.

"I have decided what price I demand to keep your secrets buried," Sin announced in an impassive tone.

Charles winced as he studied Sin's expressionless features. He was stung with the grim feeling that death would probably be the more acceptable option. "As I told you earlier, I will offer no resistance. As for my daughter—"

"That is what I'm here to discuss," Sin broke in. "Your final punishment will be the loss of your daughter, your most cherished possession. It is fair and it is just, Sheridan. A life for a life."

Charles could accept anything but that! "No, Sinclair. You have my property and you can take my life, but I refuse to have Angel suffer for her father's sins. Before you have me hanged or skinned alive, I have to tell Angel what I've done. Indeed, that will be worse punishment than a noose around my neck, Chinese thumbscrews or whatever hideous brand of torture you have designed for me."

Brown eyes misted over as Charles met Sin's dark, penetrating gaze. "Know this, Sinclair, for it is the truth. I would not have been a party to what happened that awful night if I had known it would evolve into murder and abandonment."

Charles glanced away, battling to compose himself. "Before Kimball fired the shot, I was the one who distracted him with protests. Your brother made a grab for the pistol, but Kimball retaliated too quickly. Then it was too late for me to stop what had gone too far. Porter made it worse by lashing out at you with his cutlass and heaving you overboard. And I did cut the lifeboat loose, but I was too afraid of what would happen to me if I voiced another objection to leaving you behind. Kimball and Porter had already been provoked to violence and they wouldn't have thought twice about killing me if the need had arisen. I knew they would turn on me and I would be thrashing against the waves, right along with you, and never have the chance to see my wife and daughter again."

"You did what you felt you had to do and so must I," Sin told him flatly. "I still intend to have your daughter on whatever terms I so name. Your objections count for nothing."

Charles blanched, knowing he was not being asked, but rather told of Sinclair's plans. He carefully formulated his question. "You expect me to serve my daughter up to you carte blanche to save myself?"

"Yes," Sin replied. "And you will voice no protests whatsoever, no matter what I say and do concerning Angelene. Do you understand me, Sheridan?"

Charles's eyes widened in alarm. "That would be a punishment worse than death," he muttered. "I will not agree to this!"

"If you refuse to hold your tongue while I'm dealing with Angelene, I will tell her of your past transgressions and the hell I lived through because of it. I guarantee that my version of the story will turn her completely against you, because I will explain—in vivid detail— what horrors and torments I endured. She will watch you become a pauper who will never be able to outrun scandal and I will ensure she offers you nothing, not even pity or forgiveness."

"I am to sell my soul to you, and give you my daughter?" Charles asked bitterly. "Just so I can go on living? It isn't worth it. I'd rather die first!"

The slightest hint of a smile pursed Sin's lips. Although Charles wasn't aware of it, he had uttered the magic words and passed the subtle test. "You realize, of course, that I do not feel the least bit inclined to request your permission. I am stating what is going to take place and warning you to hold your tongue unless you prefer to lose it. This is to be your punishment and your salvation. You will live but you will sacrifice Angel."

"Now hold on, Sinclair—"

"Come with me, Sheridan," Sin cut in before spinning on his heels. "This is not the time for you to speak, only to listen. In exchange for my plans for your daughter, the deeds to Sheridan Hall and Oak Gables will be returned to you. If you voice so much as one objection to anything I say to Angelene, you will be even more sorry than you claim to be now. On that you can depend."

Bemused, Charles followed Sin across the gallery. He had no inkling of what Sinclair intended. But then, that was hardly unusual. The man was always several mental leaps ahead of everyone.

# Thirty-three

At Sin's command, Pearly jostled Angelene awake and stuffed an Oriental curative down her throat. In less that five minutes, her lashes swept up and her face flushed in reaction to the stimulant Pearly had given her.

Sin planted himself at the foot of the bed. "We are going to be wed in two days, Angelene."

Her dull eyes widened in astonishment.

"I have discussed arrangements with your father and he is anxious to see the matter concluded. I do not wish to hear any objections from you so do not test my good disposition by voicing them."

Charles struggled to conceal his look of stunned disbelief and swallowed the protests Sinclair warned him not to make while he lorded over Angelene.

Bottled rage brought Angelene upright. She was most thankful for whatever potion Pearly had poured down her throat. It gave her the needed strength to defy the dark-eyed demon who was rapping out orders left and right.

"I have no intention of marrying you, much less speaking to you again," Angelene told him hoarsely.

"You just did," Sin pointed out in a glib tone.

She glared at him. "That didn't count."

"This is not a proposal, but rather a business venture

and mutual arrangement," Sin told her impersonally. "I have acquired several business holdings in Natchez. Kimball Hotel and Porter Stables, as well as a shared interest in Pharsalia Race Track, are under the management of my men. The inheritance from your grandparents is yet another acquisition I intend to obtain when we marry."

Sin clasped his hands behind his back and paced around to the side of the bed to peer down into Angel's suddenly animated features. "As my wife, I will expect you to be the perfect hostess for my guests and business associates. You will be agreeable at all times, no matter what demands are placed on you. When we attend parties, you will constantly remain at my side, not in the arms of other men. I expect you to assure our peers that you are completely devoted to me and I will make it clear that you are off limits to fortune hunters who might scheme to attach themselves to you in hopes of monetary gain, or whatever else they might want from you."

Angelene stared at him as if he were insane. The last time she recalled speaking to Sin he had demanded that she get out of his sight—and stay there. He had wanted nothing to do with the love she offered him. He swore he needed no more than physical appeasement of his needs and that he considered her to be nothing but a whore.

If Sin thought for one minute that she was going to let herself be treated like a second-class citizen and ordered about like a lowly servant, just because she had made the blundering mistake of admitting her affection for him, then he had damned well better think again! Hell would be encased in a glacier for centuries before she doted over this heartless scoundrel!

"The only devotion you will receive from me is a devotion to making your life miserable," Angelene choked out, eyes blazing.

Sin leaned down, his face only inches from hers. "Hear me well, my betrothed. You will become Sin's Angel," he said for her ears only. "And furthermore, there will be no more wild races on spirited horses that raise aristocratic eyebrows and set gossipers' tongues wagging on both ends."

*Sin's Angel?* Angelene remembered throwing those words at him the night she had come to beg for Reggie's life. She, however, insisted she would never be anybody's angel, especially his. This man was inviting all-out war. If this marriage took place it would become a battleground. Sin had to know that. So why was he imposing these unacceptable demands on her? He knew perfectly well that she balked at orders and defied restrictions that offended her free, independent spirit.

"Two days, Angel," he declared. "The ceremony will take place in the lobby of South Sea Paradise. And it *will* take place. On that you can depend."

"No!"

"Yes," he contradicted. "You will agree to love, honor and obey in front of witnesses and that is exactly what you will do. You have been hailed the most sought-after jewel of Natchez and I have decided that I wish to claim you. You will become one of my acquisitions, an attractive decoration to grace these halls."

"I hate you," she hissed at him.

"No, you love me," he whispered, flashing her a small but wicked smile. "And after thoughtful consideration I realize that your feelings can work to my advantage. And

I, after all, am known to be a man who always plays to his advantage."

Pushing away, Sin turned his back and strode toward the door. The delicate model of a schooner that sat on the nightstand sailed across the room. The missile missed his shoulder by inches and shattered against the door in a thousand pieces. Slowly, he pivoted to see her livid green eyes flashing and her cheeks blossoming with color. Angel, it seemed, was beginning to regain her fighting spirit.

"I will return first thing in the morning to inform you of the arrangements I have made for the ceremony."

The glass of water on the nightstand sprouted wings and flew across the room, catching Sin squarely in the chest.

Sin did not even give Angel the satisfaction of flinching. He was as self-contained as usual.

"And there will be no more of these dramatic temper tantrums, either," he added, straight-faced. "You are going to become the epitome of genteel behavior, Angel. I expect you to live up to your heavenly nickname."

"Then you better expect to be disappointed," she hurled at him.

"No," he nonchalantly countered. "I expect you to change your wild and reckless ways and become a credit to the Sinclair name."

"And you can drop your anchor in hell, Sin!" she all but yelled at him, her outrage in full bloom.

Sin's gaze darted to Charles who was studying him with a bewildered frown before he refocused on Angelene's irate expression. "And I keep telling you there is no need to recommend me to the place I'm very familiar with. Instead, I intend to spend my life in paradise with you, Angel."

"Papa, I demand a word with you," Angel muttered furiously.

"No," Sin absolutely refused. "Charles is not at your disposal. He has already spoiled you too much. I intend to do nothing of the kind. It seems to me that you are in dire need of rehabilitation to ensure you behave like a proper lady at all times."

"And you think you're man enough to reform me?" she sniffed caustically.

Sin met her mutinous glower. "Yes, I believe I am."

"Then you delude yourself," she flashed defiantly.

He smiled a challenging smile. "It only takes one Sin to de-wing an Angel."

"Just try it, and you'll find that a devil can be de-horned while he is trying to pull his pitchfork out of his back," she returned.

Sin chuckled to himself, for he dearly loved to fence words with this spirited female. No one burned with the kind of inner fire Angel possessed, not in passion, in temper or zest for life. She was one of a kind.

Motioning for Charles and Pearly to precede him out the door, Sin cast Angel one last glance. "Good night, Angel. May all your dreams be as sweet as your disposition."

"And may all your dreams become nightmares," she flung at his departing back.

When the door clicked shut, Charles rounded on Sin. "What the sweet loving hell are you trying to do?"

Pearly chortled at the red-faced man who was glaring poison darts at Sin. "He just gave Angel a sure-cure po-

tion that will put her back on her feet and keep her there."
His knowing gaze shifted to Sin's unreadable expression.
"Hatred and anger are powerful stimulants. I 'spect Angel
will be up on her feet and in prime condition, come
mornin'."

"And this is *my* punishment?" Charles questioned
when he heard a resounding crash inside the room. "I
think you outsmarted yourself this time, Sinclair. From
the sound of things, Angel has declared war. She has a
fierce aversion to being told how to act, what to do and
when to do it."

"Really? I was not aware of that."

It was not until Sin had strolled into his suite and shut
the door that Charles realized Sin was being ironic. As
usual, Charles was several leagues behind the workings
of the man's incisive mind.


As promised, Sin rapped on Angelene's door early the
following morning. And as he had also anticipated she
was up and dressed and glaring at him when she opened
the door. It was difficult to beep from chuckling when
she elevated her chin to a militant angle and greeted him
with defiance.

"I brought you flowers, for our betrothal—"

The door slammed shut, snapping the blossoms off the
colorful assortment of roses and azaleas. Sin bit back
another snicker, opened the door and calmly sauntered
inside, carrying his beheaded stems. "I have selected a
fashionable wedding gown from the garments I sent
Charles to fetch from Sheridan Hall."

"Fine, then you wear it," she smartcd off. "As for myself, I won't be here. I am packing to leave."

Sin glanced over her tangled blond head to see her satchel perched on the end of the bed. "You can put your things in my suite, because that is where you will be staying tonight and every other night for the rest of your life."

Angel cocked her arm, itching to slap that phlegmatic expression off his bronzed face. Sin caught her fist and brought it to his lips. Angelene wormed her hand loose and tilted her chin a notch higher.

"I don't know what hold you have over my father, but you have no hold over me."

"Don't I? I have your love—"

"What you have is my hatred, my contempt," she bit off.

"What about your undying gratitude? Perhaps you don't recall that I saved your life. You would have drowned if not for me."

"I would have preferred drowning to suffocating in this ridiculous marriage that you have arranged for your own advantage."

Sin remained unruffled. "Nevertheless, our marriage will enhance my good standing in the community. I have decided to project a respectable image to counter the uncomplimentary gossip that circulated when I first arrived in town. The story spreading around Natchez claims you have made your preference to me known and that I have made mine to you. It is also being said that I was so possessed by cold fury when Kimball and Porter sought to deprive me of what I held most dear that I went after both men in a killing rage, prepared to do whatever was necessary to get you back."

Angelene sniffed at that ludicrous rumor. "I wonder who started that farce of a tale."

"I did," Sin replied blandly. "It is to my advantage for my neighbors and associates to think we are hopelessly enamored with one another. And since I have already trained you to satisfy my basic needs, you are the logical selection as my bride."

"Trained me?" Angelene's temper exploded. Weak though she still was, she found the strength to lash out at him.

Unfortunately, Sin possessed superior strength, not to mention lightning quickness. He grabbed her arms and pinned them to her sides, turning her attack into an embrace.

Angelene swore she hated Sin all the more when her betraying body responded to the feel of his masculine length. When his lips came down on hers, fragments of half-forgotten memories invaded her mind. She vaguely recalled warm lips breathing life back into her when she had been so cold and too feeble to draw breath. Quiet words whispered to her as he deepened the kiss, coaxing a response that she had vowed never to give again.

Sin held himself in check, though need buffeted him at first touch. It was vital that he remind Angelene of the magic they created, the passion they ignited in each other. He had already taken possession of her body and she had put her brand on his. But he had yet to reclaim the key to her heart and gain control of that stubborn mind so he could soothe her injured pride. In this, he had to proceed very carefully, so as not to tip the scales that weighed heavily with disillusioned bitterness and love-turned-to-hatred.

Just as Sin had come to terms with his feelings about Charles Sheridan, so must Angelene deal with her own sentiments and the emotional wounds he had unintentionally inflicted on her. He had provided plenty of stimulant to allow her to exercise her temper, to purge the hurt and frustration he had caused her. Sin knew all too well that this was part of the healing process. Suppressed emotion had to be released before the wounds could heal. Otherwise, they would fester continuously. Once Angelene had aired all her anger they could begin again.

And Sin wanted that more than anything—a new and better beginning.

When he felt her reluctant yielding, he set her away from him, leaving her with food for thought. "You may defy me, Angel, but your body still belongs to me. There will always be that and you cannot deny it."

The man made her so furious she wanted to throw something again. "I warned you when you cornered me that I would become your mistress from hell, but that was mere child's play compared to the undutiful, belligerent and contrary wife I will make," she assured him hotly.

He shrugged a broad shoulder. "There are ways to make you agreeable."

"The same techniques you used on my father?" she shot back. "Psychological warfare? Threats? Blackmail?"

"Possibly. Charles has come around to my way of thinking and so will you, eventually."

"Don't bet on it. I can teach stubborn to a mule when I feel like it."

Sin spun toward the door before he broke into an amused smile. He casually stepped over the beheaded flowers and closed the door behind him. It was remarkable how quickly Angelene had recovered her energy and strength when she had nourishment to feed her fiery temper. Of course, that spontaneous temper was one of the things he adored about her. She was vibrant and alive and he fed on her irrepressible spirit.

The anger and frustration Sin had provided was pouring out of Angelene by the second. Whether she realized it or not—and obviously she was too peeved with him to reason it out—he had generously supplied a target on which she could vent her irritation. He knew he was getting what he deserved. He had caused her plenty of anguish and heartache . . .

Sin jerked himself to attention and strode down the hall at a faster clip. He didn't have time to dawdle in thought. He knew what Angelene's reaction would be and he needed to ensure she wasn't allowed to do what she had made up her mind to do.

Still fuming, Angelene plucked up the satchel of clothes and supplies that had been retrieved for her from Sheridan Hall. She breezed out the terrace door, refusing to remain under the same roof with that infuriating devil. Despite what Sin said, there would be no marriage, no sharing of a bed. No nothing!

Angelene stomped down the back steps and jerked to a halt when she found Sin nonchalantly blocking her escape route. Damnation, how could she have forgotten his irritating knack of predicting what she was going to do before she did it.

"If you are restless, I suggest a short ride in the fresh air," Sin said as he climbed the steps. He paused in front of her to take the satchel and toss it back to the portico. "I was just on my way to the cove. You can join me."

Angelene muttered under her breath. Sin could read her like a map and she resented it. Well, he wasn't going to second-guess her a minute longer. She would fire off a few of the questions that cluttered her mind. After she had some answers, *then* she would make a discreet exit.

"I demand to know what my abduction was all about," she blurted out. "What did Kimball and Porter have to gain by holding me hostage? And what is the *real* reason you came to rescue me—?"

"Kindly keep your voice down, Angel—"

"I will not keep my voice down if I don't feel like it and I don't feel like it! And I insist on knowing what mysterious leverage you are holding over my father," she railed at him. "Something strange has been going on around here for weeks and I intend to find out what it is, if it's the last thing I do!"

Sin muttered to himself when Angelene's booming demands drew the attention of her father, as well as of Hiram, Pearly and Cyrus. All three men emerged from the terrace doors, staring curiously at the wild-haired hellion who had practically shouted the house down.

Angelene wheeled around. Her gaze was pinning her father to the wall. "Papa, I have the feeling that Sinclair has somehow placed you and Kimball and Porter under his thumb. I insist on knowing why. What have you done that affords him the power to lord over me as well as you? If you won't tell me, I'll find someone who will. Kimball and Porter, for instance. Where are they? In jail?"

"They're dead."

The hollow voice came from so close behind Angelene that she flinched. She wheeled to face Sin's expressionless stare. "You killed them? Why?"

Sin lifted his hand to trace the elegant line of her jaw. Although Angelene's eyes flashed, she didn't back away, for she was too intent on receiving answers to her questions. "They are dead because they tried to use you to lure me into a death trap." It was a half truth, but it was the only answer Sin could provide in order to protect Angelene from what she wouldn't want to hear.

"And my father?" she demanded. "Why has he agreed to a marriage I don't want?"

Sin stared over Angel's tangled blond head to see Charles fidgeting uneasily. Sin had the power to destroy Charles by implicating him. But the need to create rather than destroy prevented Sin from voicing absolute truths. His gaze darted to the other three men who waited in apprehensive silence.

Pearly's gaze settled on Angel and he nodded approvingly, as if to reassure Sin that he had made the right choice.

"The fact of the matter is, Angel, that during my past and present dealings with Kimball and Porter, your father saved my life twice."

Charles sagged visibly, his head dropping against his chest, his eyes closing on a silent prayer.

"As for the marriage," Sin continued, "Charles feels confident that I am exactly what you need."

"I need you like I need a hole in the head," she huffed.

"Ah," Sin said, nodding in pretended speculation. "That explains why you defied danger that night in the meadow and again on the wrecked steamboat."

Angelene took note of his dry sarcasm, but she ignored it to pose another question. "What kind of past dealing did you have with Kimball and Porter?"

"They killed my brother and cast me into the sea. They stole what was to have been my inheritance," he told her as he stared at the air over her head. "And now all that they have belongs to me and my men."

Wide green eyes focused on Sin's disciplined expression. "And my father?" she whispered apprehensively.

He met her gaze then, staring down into that stunningly enchanting face. A rare smile pursed Sin's lips as he traced the luscious curve of her mouth. "To repay your father for sparing my life twice, I have agreed to take you off his hands. You are well past marriage age, after all. Charles has grown tired of the flood of fortune hunters seeking audience with you. I have agreed to remedy the situation for him."

Angelene pivoted around to peer at her father and the three other men lounging on the gallery. They were all staring over her head, focused on Sin, no doubt. She whirled back around, but Sin's expression gave nothing away—as usual.

"And so you are taking me off Papa's hands for a hefty dowry."

Sin's gaze lifted once again, fixing on Charles. Neither

man spoke, but silent messages were exchanged—one of apologetic repentance and the other of forgiveness.

"Fine," Angelene muttered as she snatched up her satchel and propelled herself toward her room—prison cell seemed more like it. "Then you and my father can marry each other. I have decided to become a waspish spinster."

When her door slammed shut, Pearly snickered. "Before ya ask, Sin, I don't have a remedy to cure that brand of stubbornness. That's one malady you'll have to cure all by yerself." His expression sobered as he turned on his pegleg and started toward the door. "I think ya know what the cure is."

"Do I?" Sin questioned the crusty old mariner.

Pearly swiveled his head around to meet Sin's carefully blank stare. "Aye, ya know. Question is: Do ya have the courage to admit it. If ya can't, ya better slip yer moorin's before the weddin', because the marriage will definitely become yer greatest challenge. That girl's got as much fightin' spirit as you do, and then some."

"What the blazes are you two talking about?" Charles questioned, bemused.

Pearly nodded his fuzzy gray head toward Sin. "He knows what I mean. That's all that matters."

With that remark, Pearly hobbled back into the house to help himself to some of Agnes's mouth-watering pastries.

After Cyrus and Hiram disappeared into their rooms, Charles heaved an audible sign. "I don't deserve to be let off the hook and we both know it, Sinclair."

Sin's pensive gaze swung to Angelene's closed door.

"Life is not always fair and just, Sheridan, but all the same, you are my unspoken wedding gift to Angel."

"Why?" Charles wanted to know.

Sin stared him squarely in the eye. "Because you are *her* precious treasure. And even though neither you nor I rightfully deserve what we're getting, I intend to have her as my wife," he said before he turned and walked away.

# *Thirty-four*

Sin stared at the door that joined his suite to Angelene's. As predicted, she had refused to join him in his room tonight. She had also refused food when Agnes rapped on her door at lunch and supper. That feisty female was determined to defy him, just to prove that she would and she could, Sin decided. No doubt, Angelene also intended to starve herself to such extremes that she would faint during the wedding ceremony and avoid taking her vows.

If Sin went to Angelene, after giving her a direct order which she had flagrantly disobeyed, he would be setting a dangerous precedent. In every dealing with Angel he had maneuvered and calculated to ensure that it was *she* who came to *him*. Now Angelene was all but daring him to seek her out.

A pensive frown furrowed Sin's brow when Pearly's words echoed through his mind. Sin knew what cure Pearly had prescribed, but Sin was unfamiliar with the incantation that accompanied the magical potion, having never before chanted it to a living soul. It took courage, Pearly had said.

Sin smiled to himself. No one had ever questioned his

courage as captain of the *Siren*. But that crusty old swab was challenging Sin's fortitude now.

Silently, Sin rose from his chair and strode over to retrieve the velvet case that sat on the highboy. With a peace-offering in hand, Sin sought Angel out.

The door creaked open and Sin cursed the empty room. He had been too preoccupied with his own thoughts to predict Angelene's reactions. She had obviously decided to sneak away in the cover of darkness. The last time she had gone tearing off at night she had been abducted by cutthroats. Damnation, that woman defied danger for the mere sport of it! Sin loved and yet hated her daring impulsiveness. At the moment he was none too pleased with it.

Grumbling, Sin stuffed the velvet case in his pocket and exited through the terrace door. If he found himself too far behind Angel he would never overtake her. She was an experienced rider and she would probably swipe Turk to ensure the utmost speed when she made her escape.

With that in mind, Sin quickened his step. To his relief, he saw a shapely shadow dart toward the stables. A faint smile quirked his lips as he took the back stairs two at a time to block Angel's flight. He was waiting outside the door to grab Turk's reins when Angelene emerged from the barn.

A startled gasp erupted from her lips when the lean, powerful silhouette materialized before her. When she tried to bound into the saddle, a sinewy arm snaked around her waist, holding her in place.

"Let me go!" she hissed furiously.

The feel of her body against Sin's was stimulating.

Even when Angel ground her bootheels in his toes, Sin refused to release her. With one arm around his wiggling bundle, Sin tethered Turk to the hitching post and strode across the meadow.

"I mean it, Sin, I don t care what you and my father arranged, there will be no marriage!"

"There will definitely be a marriage," Sin calmly contradicted.

Exasperated, Angelene gave up trying to worm free. She hadn't fully recovered her strength, and refusing to eat hadn't helped. Physical battles with Sin were wastes of energy.

"Fine, there will be a wedding, but there will be no wedding nights," she stipulated. "I insist on separate rooms and separate lives. In fact, I demand separate homes. I vowed never to come back here and I'm sticking to that promise hereafter."

Sin set Angelene on her feet and kept a restraining hand on her elbow. "There are times, Angel, when promises must be broken." How well Sin knew that! "We will have a proper marriage and that is that."

"You are hardly proper," she scoffed at him. "You're a devil and you can deny it until hell freezes over, but it changes nothing. You have turned out to be like every other man on this planet. A fortune seeker, a man obsessed with acquisitions to elevate your social status. Well, I will not be a rung on any man's ladder to success and respectability! Never that!"

"Calm down, Angel. You're getting your wings bent out of shape."

"Calm down? You are coercing me into a marriage for material acquisitions and you expect me to calm down?

Not too long ago you shouted me out of your home after I opened my heart to you. Do you expect me to forget all those humiliating insults?" Green eyes blazed in the darkness. "Well, I can't ever forget that, Sin. And furthermore, you're making me crazy!

"You really should learn to control your temper," he advised. "You are entirely too dramatic."

"And you are not dramatic enough," she shot back. "You keep your emotions locked in cold storage, making it impossible to tell when you're bored or murderingly furious."

"There are times when not giving away one's emotions is an advantage." Sin placed the velvet case in her hand. "I have brought you a token of my affection."

Angelene stared at him in disbelief. "Affection? Don't make me laugh. I know exactly what you feel for me. I'm a body to ease your needs, one of many who would suffice. There is nothing about me that appeals to men, except my father's fortune. I have learned that lesson all too well, thanks to you."

Sin inwardly grimaced when she threw his cruel words back at him. "I'm finding that we all make crucial mistakes from time to time, ones we come to regret." He opened the velvet case since she refused to do it. "Pearly strung these for a wedding gift. They are rare Polynesian black pearls—to match your mood."

Angel stared at the luminous jewels that glistened in moonlight. Priceless though the perfectly matched strand was, the pearls were only what Sin said they were—a token, a substitute for the only thing she really wanted from him and could never have.

"I refuse to have these draped around my neck like a

slave's collar attached to your leash," she hurled at him. "They would be as cold against my skin as your heart."

"Nonetheless, you will wear them at our wedding because I insist." He scooped up the precious gems and brushed them against her cheek.

Angelene jerked away from his caressing touch and the cool whisper of pearls. He had stretched her temper as far as it would stretch with his bland commands.

"Damn you, Sin," she muttered, shoving him away. "I don't want bouquets of flowers delivered to my door in meaningless gestures and I don't want pearls."

"You don't?"

"No, I do not!" she raged while he stood there in complete and utter control. The man's lack of emotion was infuriating her. "I refuse to let you destroy me, and you will, if I agree to this ridiculous marriage."

"Destroy you? In what way?" he questioned, calm as ever.

He had the sensitivity of a rock, Angelene decided. Why in the world had she allowed herself to fall in love with him? Because the heartless devil had cast an evil spell with some kind of mystical voodoo he had picked up during his extensive travels.

Angelene had been helplessly lured to him when she saw occasional cracks in his cast-iron veneer. Like a fool, she had longed to touch the emotions he kept sealed inside him, to make a difference to him. But nothing she had ever done seemed to matter to Sin, even confessing her love. She would be a worse kind of fool if she let him wield the power he held over her. She loved him too much and he loved her not at all.

Frustrated tears slid down her cheeks as she glanced—

from the strand of black pearls that were draped over his fingertips—to his indiscernible expression. "Do you think those precious gems will buy my devotion to you!"

Sin stared at the gift. He had risked life and limb to steal these treasures from tropical seas, not to mention a nasty encounter with a shark that wanted to have him for lunch.

"Apparently not," he murmured.

"Well, at least you got one thing right." Angelene sniffed and wiped away the tears. "There is only one thing you can give me that I want and need, something more valuable to me than your black pearls."

"And what is more valuable than this perfectly matched string that men would kill for? This necklace is a fortune in itself."

Angelene drew herself up to full stature. Her chin lifted determinedly. She was going to back this cold-hearted man into a corner for a change and see how he liked it.

"Very well then, Sin, if you wish me to marry you and become an agreeable wife, then toss those precious pearls as far as you can throw them. They are worthless to me, because all I want is your love. Make up your mind if you want me or your pearls."

There, she thought with hollow satisfaction. Sin was forced into a decision. To keep the pearls he had to retract the marriage offer. To have her at his beck and call he had to profess to love her—empty though she knew the words would be. And in the end, Sin would realize that his priceless gems meant more to him than she did.

Sin brushed his thumb over the lustrous gems and met

the daring challenge in her cloudy eyes. "Angels certainly drive difficult bargains, don't they!"

"When dealing with Sin, there are no easy bargains," she countered. "I will not be bought with trinkets and tokens, no matter what their value. It's all your love or nothing at all. Make your choice, here and now. You cannot have me and the pearls both."

Her heart turned over in her chest when Sin pivoted around. Tears spilled down her cheeks when she realized she had lost him. She had demanded all or nothing, and nothing was what she would have. She wasn't woman enough to . . .

A startled gasp escaped her lips when Sin cocked his arm and sent the string of pearls arcing through the air, falling amid knee-high grass. Her jaw dropped open, and for the life of her she couldn't find her tongue—a rare moment, to be sure.

Even the shadows didn't conceal the twinkle in Sin's eyes when he slowly turned toward her. "It seems to me that only the devil himself or a witless fool would defy the divine ultimatum delivered by an Angel. And as I have recently discovered, there is no treasure on this earth or under the sea that compares to an Angel's love."

Sin met her intense gaze and struggled with the words he had never spoken to a woman. But when he looked at Angel, it was as if he were seeing the personification of that central focus needed for his survival.

"You are all I want," Sin whispered softly, sincerely. "Because loving you the way I do, I can't bear to let you go."

For the first time since Angelene could remember, vivid emotion showed on every craggy feature of his face, glistened in the depths of black diamond eyes. Sin was standing there, loving her as deeply and devotedly as she had come to love him. All vestige of cool detachment and self-containment was gone. There was no calm restraint in his voice, no nonchalant stance. Every muscle in his powerful body was taut, as if waiting for her to offer back the words she had once spoken to him and vowed never to utter again.

"I'm sorry, Angel, more sorry than you know," Sin murmured as he touched her exquisite features. "I hurt you badly, but I swear I will never do it again. Forgive me, please. I thought I knew all the tortures hell could devise . . . until I realized that you had not admitted your love for me, just to protect your father from me. I threatened to destroy Charles because I wanted you so desperately and I knew you would never come willingly to me."

And that was the honest truth, Sin acknowledged to her and to himself. He had threatened to ruin Charles, not so much as a way of getting even but because Sin was obsessed with this fiery beauty who gave his life new meaning.

"I knew the first night I saw you in the meadow that you possessed something I desperately needed in my life. You were so vital and alive that I found you irresistible. You were the wellspring of emotion I had lost touch with so many years ago.

"You taught me how to smile again, to laugh. I had forgotten how good it felt. And most especially—" He brushed his forefinger over her lips, craving a taste of her.

"And most especially!" she prompted, her heart in her eyes.

A disarming smile quirked his lips. "You taught me to live again, Angel. For that I love you most of all. You're my touch with heaven. And because living without you would be a torture worse than death, I need you, I want you to be my wife—"

Sin staggered back when Angelene leaped into his arms, showering him with adoring kisses. Her forward momentum knocked him off balance and took them both to the ground. Her supple body moved over his in a seductive caress, making the kind of silent promises that were meant to last long past forever. Sin burned in each place she touched and he savored every unleashed emotion, every incredible sensation she summoned from him.

He resented the garments that separated them, ached to feel the satiny texture of her skin beneath his exploring hands, his lips. He wanted to saturate his senses with her, until she was his every breath, his every touch, his every taste.

Hands trembling, Sin drew the shirt from her shoulders and plied every inch of skin he exposed with reverent kisses. His fingertips drifted to the fastening of her breeches and he eased her from the hindering garment one caress at a time, until she lay warm and yielding on a pallet of discarded clothes.

Each muffled sigh of pleasure he called from her challenged him to draw another and another. His moist lips trailed down the ivory column of her throat to the thrusting crests of her breasts, cherishing her, worshiping as his priceless treasure.

Ever so gently he teased the rigid peaks until she arched up like a wave breaking on the sea. His hand moved down her belly on the most intimate and tenderest of journeys, reveling in her eager responses, glorying in his own answering pleasure. His fingertips drifted over the silky flesh of her inner thighs, feeling the warmth of her uninhibited response, longing to burn alive in that secret fire that set his every emotion ablaze.

"I want you in every intimate way," he whispered as his lips trailed over her ribs and skimmed her belly. "All of you, Angel, until the taste of you is my only reality, until loving you is my eternity . . ."

"Sin?" She trembled beneath his fingertips, his lips. "What are you—?"

Her voice fractured as he teased her, savored her, seduced her. He delicately brushed his mouth over her, feeling her shimmering responses echo through her body, into his and back again. His tongue penetrated her softness as gently as a bee gathering nectar from a blossom. Angelene's muffled moan of pleasure was followed by another, and yet another.

Sin was so obsessed with arousing and satisfying Angelene's every need that nothing seemed as essential as creating a dozen different ways to ease the hurt he had caused her, to express his loving devotion.

Her soft pleas brought him back to her and he voiced not one objection when she whispered her need to touch him, to return the pleasure he had given her. Sin allowed her to undress him, relishing in her loving touch. Her hand folded around his throbbing length, stroking him until he could no longer restrain the wild, ungovernable need she ignited.

He came to her in a breathless explosion of ecstasy. Passion blazed between them with the heat of a thousand suns. Sin let go with his heart, mind and body, cherishing each immeasurable sensation that rippled through him.

And in that wild, mindless dimension that defied time Sin was reminded why Angelene held such phenomenal power over him, why she had come to matter so much. She was the key that unlocked his long-buried emotion. She was the spark that had brought him back to life. She was every beat of his heart and the whisper of his soul. Because of her Sin had learned to live rather than subsist in a world bound only by his vengeful mission. Angel had become Sin's most coveted prize . . .

Indefinable pleasure burgeoned inside him as he and Angelene moved together as one living, breathing entity, clinging to each other in infinitesimal splendor. Sin felt her body contracting around him, heard the panted words that linked his name to love everlasting. He knew he had discovered life's sweetest secret . . .

A deluge of mind-boggling and bone-melting sensations swamped Sin. He clung to Angelene as desperately as he had when he found her in the depths of the swamp. He knew beyond all doubt that losing her would have been his greatest tragedy and that regaining her love was his sublime reward.

A long time later, when Sin could breathe again, he gazed down into Angelene's utterly impish smile. He cocked an inquisitive brow when her index finger traced the grin that curved his mouth upward to wide, unfamiliar angles.

"Mmm . . . I like you best of all when all you're wearing is a smile," she said in a voice thick with the after-effects of passion.

"And I like you best when you're wearing nothing but me," he assured her huskily.

"Sin?"

"Hum?" Distracted, he pressed a kiss to the column of her throat, inhaling the fragrant scent that was so much a part of her, now such a vital part of him.

"You said you loved me enough to cast your costly pearls aside."

"I do, and I did," he assured her in all sincerity.

"I find that isn't quite enough."

He appraised the mischievous glint in her green eyes, quite certain he had made a tactical error by chasing after her. Now that this lively little elf held his heart in her hands, she would be rattling off a string of requests, insisting that he prove his deep abiding affection for her, again and again.

Oddly enough, the possibility didn't disturb Sin all that much. Loving Angel as he did, Sin discovered that he wanted to do everything in his power to please her, because having her love him back pleased him immensely.

And God knew, he had made more sacrifices for her than he would ever let on. There were some things Angelene would never know, for her own peace of mind. Sin had made a pact of silence with Pearly, Hiram, Cyrus and Charles. The past would remain where it belonged, for Angel's sake, for the sake of Sin's future happiness.

"What do you want me to do for you now, Angel?"

"I would like to have those lovely pearls you threw away. I have decided I want to wear them to our wedding."

"What changed your mind?" he questioned, mesmerized by the kittenish smile that played on her elegant features.

"It seems to me that having the cool texture of pearls against my skin, through our long years of marriage, will prevent me from burning alive with love for you."

A loud crack of laughter hovered over Raven's Hill. It was a rich, vibrating sound that spoke of pleasure beyond measure, of loving amusement.

"Do you know, elf, that I am going to enjoy loving you for all the rest of my days?"

"Are you?" she queried saucily. "Despite my refusal to become the epitome of genteel propriety?"

"Truthfully?" Sin questioned.

"Truthfully," Angel insisted.

He stared down into her face, surrounded by a cloud of curly red-gold hair. "I wouldn't change a single thing about you. I love you just the way you are."

"I'm ever so glad to hear that," she assured him as she reached for her discarded clothes. She tossed him a provocative glance, along with his breeches. "Fact is, I simply cannot resist Sinning. When it comes to you, I yield to temptation with Sinful ease."

Another deep skirl of laughter resounded in the night. Sin let every guard down when he dropped a kiss to Angel's responsive lips. His heart swelled with so much happiness he swore it would burst. For the first time in eighteen years, Sin felt as if he were truly alive and he welcomed the love and laughter this vibrant elf provided. Becoming *Angel's Sin* was a joyous new beginning and the end of his self-contained restraint.

Angel's love had set Sin free for all eternity . . .

* * *

Hiram glanced up from the cribbage game he was playing with Cyrus, Pearly and Charles. "What do you suppose that sound was?"

The unidentified sound drifted through the open window a second time, bringing all four men to their feet.

Cyrus squinted into the darkness. "Don't know what that noise is, mate?"

Pearly pulled open his spyglass to take a look.

"See anything?" Charles questioned.

"Interestin' " Pearly murmured, a wry smile playing on his lips.

"What is it?" Cyrus wanted to know.

"Sin and Angel are crawllin' around on their hands and knees in the grass, as if they're searchin' for somethin'—"

Pearly watched Angelene clasp something in her hand as she rose up on her knees and flung her arms around Sin's neck. The two silhouettes, framed by silvery moonlight, rolled across the ground in a tangle that ended up in a most suggestive position . . .

Pearly snapped the spyglass shut and stuffed it in his pocket. He was positively certain the bitter, grieving boy he had pulled from the sea and then watched grow into a man who isolated himself from the world and from his own emotions, had found a new lease on life—with the help of an Angel. Sin had finally come into his own, Pearly thought in satisfaction. The house on Raven's Hill would ring with laughter, excitement and happiness from this day forward.

Sin belonged to Angel, and Angel to Sin—body, heart and soul. All was right with the world, Pearly decided.

Hiram surveyed the broad grin that settled in the old mariner's ruddy features. "Well? Did Angel and Sin find whatever it was they were looking for?"

"I do believe they did," Pearly murmured as he turned back to the table. "I do believe they did . . ."

Dear Readers,

I hope you enjoyed Sin's story. In February you will meet Nolan Ryder—the most daring and mysterious hero yet.

The American colonies are up in arms over the latest regulations and taxes England has heaped on them to pay the debts of the French and Indian Wars. The Stamp Act, Navigation Acts and Quartering Acts are wreaking havoc with colonial economy. Nolan Ryder is spear-heading the resistance to British tyranny and urges independence.

By day, Nolan poses as a British sympathizer to glean information for the Sons of Liberty. By night, he becomes the masked vigilante who defies the Crown's army of occupation and inspires patriot spirit.

The Midnight Rider has become the symbol of American freedom in Boston, leaving the torch of liberty as his signature. Because of the high price the King's men have put on his head, Nolan must be cautious of the company he keeps. After a near brush with disaster Nolan suspects a Tory spy has infiltrated the secretive rebel network. Before his duel identity is discovered, Nolan sets out to catch the culprit.

Although Nolan needs no further complications in his life, Laura Chandler proves to be that and more. She keeps popping up in unexpected places, dressed in unusual attire, arousing Nolan's worst suspicions. He needs to know whose side this crafty lady is on, and he's pretty sure he isn't going to like what he learns.

*Midnight's Lady* is a tale of deception, intrigue and fast-paced adventure, set amid the turmoil of America's political and social unrest. It is the story of a man caught between his unswerving devotion to his cause and his unconquerable attraction to a woman who could easily betray him. Although Nolan's reckless heart urges him to take the risk—just once in his life—his instincts warn him that love is only a dangerous illusion, one that could become his greatest defeat . . .

Until February,

*Debra Falcon*

# ROMANCES ABOUT AFRICAN-AMERICANS!
## YOU'LL FALL IN LOVE
## WITH ARABESQUE BOOKS FROM PINNACLE

**SERENADE**                                 (0024, $4.99)
by Sandra Kitt
Alexandra Morrow was too young and naive when she first fell in love with musician, Parker Harrison—and vowed never to be so vulnerable again. Now Parker is back and although she tries to resist him, he strolls back into her life as smoothly as the jazz rhapsodies for which he is known. Though not the dreamy innocent she was before, Alexandra finds her defenses quickly crumbling and her mind, body and soul slowly opening up to her one and only love, who shows her that dreams do come true.

**FOREVER YOURS**                          (0025, $4.99)
by Francis Ray
Victoria Chandler must find a husband quickly or her grandparents will call in the loans that support her chain of lingerie boutiques. She arranges a mock marriage to tall, dark and handsome ranch owner Kane Taggart. The marriage will only last one year, and her business will be secure, and Kane will be able to walk away with no strings attached. The only problem is that Kane has other plans for Victoria. He'll cast a spell that will make her his forever after.

**A SWEET REFRAIN**                       (0041, $4.99)
by Margie Walker
Fifteen years before, jazz musician Nathaniel Padell walked out on Jenine to seek fame and fortune in New York City. But now the handsome widower is back with a baby girl in tow. Jenine is still irresistibly attracted to Nat and enchanted by his daughter. Yet even as love is rekindled, an unexpected danger threatens Nat's child. Now, Jenine must fight for Nat before someone stops the music forever!

*Available wherever paperbacks are sold, or order direct from the Publisher. Send cover price plus 50¢ per copy for mailing and handling to Penguin USA, P.O. Box 999, c/o Dept. 17109, Bergenfield, NJ 07621. Residents of New York and Tennessee must include sales tax. DO NOT SEND CASH.*

# SIN'S PASSION

Angelene's eyes narrowed disapprovingly. "Do I detect mocking amusement beneath that implacable expression you wear so well?"

"Perhaps. I have been told that I have a rather peculiar sense of humor."

"Then you have obviously been lied to," she sniffed. "You have no sense of humor at all. You are simply amusing yourself at my expense. Men have an annoying tendency toward patronization. I strongly resent it."

Sin watched her assess him. The young lady's astute gaze missed nothing, not the darkness of his eyes and hair, nor the smooth white scar that cut across his cheek and disappeared under his jaw.

Angelene eyed Sin warily after taking inventory of his swarthy physique, black cape and red sash. "Are you by chance a misplaced pirate?"

Sin knew the instant she arrived at the notion that she had traded one dangerous situation for another. He could feel her body tense, ready to leap off his lap if he posed the slightest threat.

"I asked you to sit still."

When his voice dropped to a quiet pitch, Angelene recoiled, misinterpreting his intent. She fought in frantic desperation, despite his attempt to hold her in place without alarming her further.

"Hold still," he demanded more brusquely than he intended.

"Go to hell and meet the devil!" she sneered.

"I've already met the devil, witch," Sin assured her. "He sends his regards."

*Pinnacle Books is proud to present this second book in a series of exciting romances where the hero takes center stage. Experience love through his eyes and rapture in his arms. Discover romance as you never have before . . . with the hero of your dreams. Let Sin steal you away on a mission of revenge where a cold heart is no match for a passionate woman's fiery love . . .*

# IF ROMANCE BE THE FRUIT OF LIFE—
# READ ON—
# BREATH-QUICKENING HISTORICALS FROM PINNACLE

### WILDCAT                                    (772, $4.99)
by Rochelle Wayne

No man alive could break Diana Preston's fiery spirit . . . until seductive Vince Gannon galloped onto Diana's sprawling family ranch. Vince, a man with dark secrets, would sweep her into his world of danger and desire. And Diana couldn't deny the powerful yearnings that branded her as his own, for all time!

### THE HIGHWAY MAN                            (765, $4.50)
by Nadine Crenshaw

When a trumped-up murder charge forced beautiful Jane Fitzpatrick to flee her home, she was found and sheltered by the highwayman—a man as dark and dangerous as the secrets that haunted him. As their hiding place became a place of shared dreams—and soaring desires—Jane knew she'd found the love she'd been yearning for!

### SILKEN SPURS                               (756, $4.99)
by Jane Archer

Beautiful Harmony Harper, leader of a notorious outlaw gang, rode the desert plains of New Mexico in search of justice and vengeance. Now she has captured powerful and privileged Thor Clarke-Jargon, who is everything Harmony has ever hated—and all she will ever want. And after Harmony has taken the handsome adventurer hostage, she herself has become a captive—of her own desires!

### WYOMING ECSTASY                            (740, $4.50)
by Gina Robins

Feisty criminal investigator, July MacKenzie, solicits the partnership of the legendary half-breed gunslinger-detective Nacona Blue. After being turned down, July—never one to accept the meaning of the word no—finds a way to convince Nacona to be her partner . . . first in business—then in passion. Across the wilds of Wyoming, and always one step ahead of trouble, July surrenders to passion's searing demands!

*Available wherever paperbacks are sold, or order direct from the Publisher. Send cover price plus 50¢ per copy for mailing and handling to Penguin USA, P.O. Box 999, c/o Dept. 17109, Bergenfield, NJ 07621. Residents of New York and Tennessee must include sales tax. DO NOT SEND CASH.*